THE R

Classic
Novels

ROUGH
GUIDES

www.roughguides.com

Credits

The Rough Guide to Classic Novels

Film reviews: Joe Staines
Editing: Joe Staines
Layout: Andrew Clare
Proofreading: Karen Parker
Production: Vicky Baldwin

Rough Guides Reference

Editors: Peter Buckley,
Tracy Hopkins, Sean Mahoney,
Matt Milton, Joe Staines, Ruth Tidball
Director: Andrew Lockett

Publishing Information

This first edition published May 2008 by
Rough Guides Ltd, 80 Strand, London WC2R 0RL
345 Hudson St, 4th Floor, New York 10014, USA
Email: mail@roughguides.com

Distributed by the Penguin Group:
Penguin Books Ltd, 80 Strand, London WC2R 0RL
Penguin Putnam, Inc., 375 Hudson Street, NY 10014, USA
Penguin Group (Australia), 250 Camberwell Road, Camberwell, Victoria 3124, Australia
Penguin Books Canada Ltd, 10 Alcorn Avenue, Toronto, Ontario, Canada M4P 2Y3
Penguin Group (New Zealand), 67 Apollo Drive, Mairangi Bay, Auckland 1310, New Zealand

Printed in Italy by LegoPrint S.p.A

Typeset in Baskerville, Gill Sans and Copperplate

384 pages; includes index

A catalogue record for this book is available from the British Library

ISBN: 978-1-84353-516-4

1 3 5 7 9 8 6 4 2

THE ROUGH GUIDE to

Classic Novels

by
Simon Mason

www.roughguides.com

Contents

Themed boxes

Preface

Classic novels are, by definition, first class. They have stood the test of time – or show the qualities that make them likely to do so. Speaking for us, and to us, they tell the best stories and contain the greatest characters. Above all, they entertain.

In *The Rough Guide to Classic Novels* the emphasis is on precisely this quality. There are no novels chosen here simply for their worthiness or their prominence in literary history. All merit their inclusion by being, first and foremost, great pleasure-givers.

In making the selection, I have also tried to be sensitive to two sorts of variety. Firstly, the variety of classic novels – the extraordinary richness of fiction produced all over the world from the time of *Don Quixote* to the present day. Here Jane Austen rubs shoulders with Milan Kundera, Dostoevsky with Raymond Chandler, Voltaire with Kenzaburo Ōe. Classic heavyweights from Tsarist Russia sit alongside Modernist masterpieces from the deep American South, solid triple-deckers from Victorian London mix with mind-bending fables from Brazil and Turkey. Secondly, I have borne in mind the variety of readers, whose tastes range from the traditional to the avant-garde, across every conceivable type, style and genre. Whether your preference is for page-turning plots or unforgettable characters, short, challenging novels or long, spell-binding ones, there is something here for you to try.

The result is a selection of 229 novels (or sequences of novels such as trilogies, etc.) by novelists from 36 different countries, published between 1604 and 2002. Titles are grouped alphabetically by author in a number of thematic chapters – "Comedy and satire", "Horror and mystery", "Crime and punishment", "Rites of passage", "Love, romance and sex" and so on – to make them easier to locate. Each main entry ends with a suggestion for further reading, usually, but not always, by the same author, and for each work originally written in a foreign language, a recommended English translation is provided. Short reviews are also provided for any outstanding film or television adaptations of the novels discussed, and there are boxes throughout the book on a range of topics, such as the historical novel and Magic Realism.

As its title suggests, the guide is limited to novels. Authors whose main achievement is in short stories – Chekhov, Maupassant and William Trevor are obvious examples – appear only in the suggestions for further reading, alongside other great exponents of the genre, such as Hemingway and Nabokov, who are also included as novelists.

Inevitably the selection is a personal one, and not likely to be precisely the same as anyone else's. Some novels choose themselves: who could exclude *War and Peace* or *In Search of Lost Time* or *Moby Dick*? But other choices are less obvious, perhaps more controversial. Together, they form a representative selection intended to stimulate readers' curiosity about some of the world's greatest novels. Enjoy!

Simon Mason

April 2008

Acknowledgements

I would like to thank Jamie Attlee, Philip Atkins, Jerry Boyd, Amit Chaudhuri, Craig Clunas, Lucas Dietrich, Ben Goodger, Dewi Harries, Eluned Harries, Michael Holyoke, Allan Hunter, Cecilia Kenworthy, Eddie Lambert, Andrew Lockett, Gwilym Mason, Richard Milbank, Suzy Oakes, Stephen O'Rahilly, Neil Palfreyman, Andrew Peerless, Tony Sloggett, Joe Staines, Will Sulkin and Martha Whitt.

About the author

Simon Mason is a publisher and author. His novels for adults are: *The Great English Nude* (1990), *Death of a Fantasist* (1994) and *Lives of the Dog-Stranglers* (1998). He has also written a series of novels for younger readers: *The Quigleys* (2002), *The Quigleys at Large* (2003), *The Quigleys Not For Sale* (2004) and *The Quigleys in a Spin* (2005).

Love, romance and sex

1

F rom the first inklings of attraction to the last formalities of faded affection, from innocent flirtation to erotic passion, from the ecstatic union of kindred spirits to star-crossed tragedy, love and romance have inspired some of the greatest splendours of fiction.

Here are the most moving of love affairs, none more so than the grand entanglement of the unhappily married Anna Karenina and the dashing Count Vronsky. Here are the most fascinating lovers: Young Werther, the quintessential sufferer in love; Manon Lescaut, the ravishing but maddeningly inconstant heroine; and Squire B, the archetypal sexual predator. And here are the most affecting experiences: Turgenev's *First Love*, capturing love's first and deepest impression, or *Doctor Zhivago* – love's classic weepy.

If male novelists have given us some great romantic heroines, female novelists have been equally generous in creating compelling leading men – Charlotte Brontë's brooding Mr Rochester, for instance, or Jane Austen's haughty Mr Darcy. Many of the most daring and intimate fictions of love have been written by women. One of the earliest, *The Princesse de Clèves*, gives a brilliant insight into women as both victims and manipulators of love; three hundred years later, Marguerite Duras' *The Lover* is an utterly convincing dramatization of love's derangement.

Derangements, machinations, eroticism, tenderness – all the tricks and triumphs of love are here. And if we want to know what it all means, we couldn't do better than read *The Unbearable Lightness of Being* by Milan Kundera – the most entertaining and provocative philosopher-poet of sex.

Emma

1816, JANE AUSTEN, ENGLISH

Austen's novels belong in a special category of entertainment, their witty, paradoxical surfaces brilliantly capturing the manners of her characters, yet hinting at rich emotional complexities below; and *Emma* is at once her sharpest and most sympathetic.

The story is swift, dramatic and, in the manner of fairy tales, unexpected yet inevitable. Like *Pride and Prejudice*, it is set among a number of interconnected families in and around a country village (Highbury), and concerns the fancies, tricks, deceits and – finally – revelations of love.

Emma Woodhouse, handsome, clever and rich, with a comfortable home and happy disposition, seemed to unite some of the best blessings of existence.

Emma is a heroine both genuinely irresistible and exasperating. Her meddlesome cleverness in setting up her naïve friend Harriet Smith with a succession of less-than-eligible bachelors is balanced by her irrepressible charm, and, more important in the end, her winning willingness to own her mistakes. Nothing escapes Austen's sharpness or sympathy: she is the

A Fine Romance, part 1

In the minds of most people, the words "romance" and "romantic" conjure up thoughts of love – often with the connotation of something dramatic or passionate. But how do these two words relate to the art of storytelling or literary fiction? The answer, rather unexpectedly, lies with the Romans. Having conquered most of Europe, one of the major legacies the Romans left was language. Romance languages – the most widely spoken of which are French, Italian, Spanish and Portuguese – were those languages which derive from the everyday Latin spoken by ordinary citizens across the Roman Empire. Thus the *romances* of the early Middle Ages were stories, written – usually in verse – in the vernacular tongue. Subject matter was often taken from the heroic exploits of Alexander the Great, King Arthur and his Knights, or King Charlemagne and his Paladins. In France, the medieval *romance* was frequently as concerned with love – albeit an idealized courtly love – as it was with adventure. This tradition of heroic, and often fanciful, tales of chivalric derring-do continued into the Renaissance, and was gently ridiculed by Cervantes in his influential work *Don Quixote* (see p.166) which introduced a more realistic element into fiction.

great novelist of change, and Emma's development from a confident organizer of other people's lives to a reflective contemplator of her own is unforced and deeply moving.

Few short novels boast such variety of characters or range of scenes, and Austen's achievement is not only to bring them into harmony but to give each a depth of light and shade. Silly Miss Bates, the old maid who cannot stop talking is at once hilarious and heartbreaking; a picnic at Box Hill seems to be a perfectly drawn social anticlimax until a moment of thoughtlessness from Emma concentrates all the inconsequential chit-chat into a moment of irretrievable cruelty. More than any other of her novels, *Emma* justifies Austen's famous claim that three or four families in a country village were "the very thing to work on".

Where to go next
Persuasion, 1818, Jane Austen

Austen's last novel once again deals with the perils of the marriage market, as the unmarried Anne Elliot finally learns to trust her own judgement in affairs of the heart.

Pride and Prejudice

1813, JANE AUSTEN, ENGLISH

Penguin

At the age of twenty-one, a country parson's daughter, recently jilted in love, sat down and wrote one of the most sparkling love stories in English fiction. *Pride and Prejudice* is one of the great pleasure-giving novels in the language.

It is also, as Lady Byron commented on the book's first appearance, "one of the most *probable* books I have ever read", the result not so much of a finely evoked Hertfordshire as of the vividly believable characters, all animated with wilful individuality, colliding with each other in bursts of prickly, witty dialogue. In the Bennets, Austen created one of the most memorable of all fictional families, and the efforts of the very flappable Mrs Bennet to find husbands for her five daughters unleash a fast-moving, suspenseful plot, at the heart of which the prejudiced Elizabeth Bennet and the proud Mr Darcy lock horns.

It is at once a novel of small, careful detail – a late-night sisterly conversation about men, an exchange of glances at a ball – and show-stopping set pieces, such as Mr Collins's ludicrous proposal of marriage or Elizabeth's duel of wits with the catastrophically snobbish Catherine de Bourgh. Throughout, Austen's style – arch, pert, ironic, delicious – miraculously encompasses serious points about appearance and reality and the nature of love, and unfolds a narrative of enormous drama.

'Mr Bennet, how can you abuse your own children in such a way? You have no compassion on my poor nerves.' 'You mistake me, my dear. I have a high respect for your nerves. They are my old friends.'

Where to go next
Sense and Sensibility, 1811, Jane Austen
The contrasting love affairs of the two older Dashwood sisters, Elinor and Marianne, are at the heart of Austen's first published – and most dramatically emotional – novel.

Screen adaptation
Pride and Prejudice, 1995, dir. Simon Langton
The BBC mini-series, adapted by writer Andrew Davies, is notorious for Mr Darcy (Colin Firth) taking a dip in the lake and being confronted by a slightly flustered Elizabeth (Jennifer Ehle). There's more to it than that, and this version is by some way the most satisfying and intelligent *Pride and Prejudice* on film, subtly revealing much that is implicit in Austen's text.

Jane Eyre
1847, CHARLOTTE BRONTË, ENGLISH

All the violent passions – love, anger, envy and the fierceness of the put-upon spirit – are here encapsulated in the unlikely figure of a frail, plain young woman without means: the orphan Jane Eyre. Famous for her romance with Rochester – a great bruising adventure of the heart – the novel is also the story of her struggle towards self-expression in a society bent on breaking her will.

Women are supposed to be very calm generally: but women feel just as men feel; they need exercise for their faculties.

A Fine Romance, part 2

From the eighteenth century the word romance took on a range of different literary meanings, but generally it was applied to stories that had an element of fantasy or exaggeration to them, as opposed to stories that were more grounded in everyday reality which were termed novels (from the Italian *novellas* meaning story or piece of news). This sense of romance can be extended to the works of Sir Walter Scott in the nineteenth century and Conrad and Tolkien in the twentieth, all of whom were masters of adventure stories with an element of the improbable to them. But the eighteenth century also saw the rise of novels that took love and romance (in the modern sense) as their main subject – often from the female point of view. Samuel Richardson's *Pamela* (1741) was an early popular example, Goethe's *The Sorrows of Young Werther* (1774), which has a male narrator, a later one. Each of these books invited the reader to feel the plight of their protagonists and both had a strong erotic dimension.

With the appearance of the Gothic novel at the end of the century – especially the wildly extravagant works of Mrs Radcliffe (see p.294) – the two senses of romance were combined. The emphasis on emotional identification was nicely sent up by Jane Austen in her parody of the Gothic, *Northanger Abbey*, and in *Sense and Sensibility*, where common sense is contrasted with an overwrought sensibility. Ironically, Jane Austen's often sardonic view of the relationship between the sexes has come to epitomize "romantic" fiction, with Mr Darcy representing the archetype of the brooding, handsome, desirable male (with the Brontë sisters' Mr Rochester and Heathcliff providing stiff competition). This is the origin of the modern "romance novel": entertaining, escapist fantasies of courtship and love produced in vast quantities by such twentieth-century authors as Georgette Heyer, Barbara Cartland, Nora Roberts and Sophie Kinsella, and by UK publishers Mills and Boon, and US publishers Harlequin. Largely sniffed at by critics, the genre is hugely popular with its (mostly female) readership, and in the US constitutes almost half of all paperback fiction sales.

Bullied as a child at the home of her vindictive Aunt Reed, brutalized at Mr Brocklehurst's poor school and scorned as a governess at

Thornfield Hall, Jane remains remarkable not only for her defiance, but also for her sensitivity. Above all, she has the courage to challenge others (and herself) on the big issues of wrongdoing and injustice. For such a serious book, it is also unfailingly exciting. Even the long, questioning arguments (and there are more arguments in *Jane Eyre* than most other novels) are gripping contests of opposing wills, spinning with increasing intensity towards deeper revelations: shameful confessions and unpalatable truths.

Penguin

The plot, a series of appalling secrets and jaw-dropping disclosures, revolves around basic questions of identity. What sort of a man is Rochester, so strangely changeable and peremptory? Who howls in the attic and appears at night in the corridors of Thornfield Hall? And who, really, is Jane Eyre? A liar, as her aunt insists; an elf, as she appears to Rochester; a pious worker suited to a missionary's wife; or a woman capable of giving and receiving passionate love?

Where to go next
Villette, 1853, Charlotte Brontë
Based on Brontë's own teaching experiences in Belgium, this is another study of a seemingly timid female protagonist, Lucy Snowe, who, in the face of isolation and misfortune, begins to reveal hidden depths of character.

Screen adaptation
Jane Eyre, 1944, dir. Robert Stevenson
Despite several subsequent attempts, this remains the strongest film adaptation of *Jane Eyre*. Joan Fontaine reprises the put-upon and washed-out routine that served her so well in *Rebecca*, while Orson Welles is an effectively brooding and saturnine presence as Rochester. George Barnes's camerawork and a great Bernard Herrmann score reinforce the novel's Gothic credentials.

Wuthering Heights

1847, EMILY BRONTË, ENGLISH

Wuthering Heights is a love story unlike any other, unrelentingly intense, unsparingly brutal and almost wholly joyless. Barren moorland and bad weather form an appropriate backdrop to violence, illness and – for most of the characters – death. The gypsyish Heathcliff and headstrong Cathy have been immortalized by movie-makers as icons of romantic passion, yet the novel is darker and weirder than this suggests.

It begins with an act of violence, the amiable Mr Lockwood set upon by dogs at Heathcliff's farm, "Wuthering Heights", and violence is a constant feature of the story that Nelly Dean, former housekeeper at the farm, tells the curious Lockwood when he returns home. She describes the orphan Heathcliff's brutalized childhood in the Earnshaw household; his preternaturally close relationship with Cathy Earnshaw; Cathy's marriage to Edgar Linton; and Heathcliff's terrible revenge on her and all her husband's family.

> 'He shall never know how I love him; and that, not because he's handsome, Nelly, but because he's more myself than I am.'

The radical originality of the novel lies in Brontë's refusal to make concessions to literary taste or conventional morality. Heathcliff and Cathy's extraordinary passion (they feel they are the same person) seems a part of the wildness of nature, like the moor or the storms, neither good nor bad but intensely a matter of fact, and the highly dramatic pattern of the novel is provided not by variety or commentary, but tension, force balanced against force. Everything exists on the same imaginative level: the goblins and ghosts of the Yorkshire Moors no less vividly than the bustling but imprisoning domesticity of "Wuthering Heights" and "Thrushcross Grange". There are no contradictions: Cathy makes her first appearance in the story as a disconcertingly corpo-real ghost bleeding at Lockwood's window. *Wuthering Heights* is the nightmare of love from which there is no awakening.

Where to go next
The Tenant of Wildfell Hall, 1848, Anne Brontë
A dark and sometimes morbid novel by the youngest of the Brontë sis-ters, which centres on the marriage of Helen Graham (the tenant) and her estranged husband, a violent drunkard, in part a portrait of Anne's alcoholic brother, Branwell.

Screen adaptation
Wuthering Heights, 1939, dir. William Wyler
A much-filmed novel (most recently with Juliet Binoche and Ralph Fiennes), this classic Hollywood version still packs the greatest emotional punch. True to the spirit rather than the letter of the book, it is dominated by Laurence Olivier's seething, passionate Heathcliff, while Gregg Toland's moody cinema-tography makes the most of the studio-bound Yorkshire Moors.

Memoirs of a Woman of Pleasure *or* Fanny Hill

1748–49, JOHN CLELAND, ENGLISH

Midway through her autobiography, Fanny Hill complains how diffi-cult it is to give variety to "JOYS, ARDOURS, TRANSPORTS, ECSTASIES" when they are described, as here, with such unremitting frequency. Later, she concludes that the only prose style for sex is fancy – and what she gives the reader is an extended series of foreplay, copula-tions and bizarre practices described with a kind of supercharged poetry of euphemism, sometimes alarming, sometimes ridiculous, and more often than not simply astonishing.

An orphan from Liverpool, the fifteen-year-old Frances Hill makes her way to London, where she falls in with a kindly brothel keeper, who introduces her to the pleasure and profitability of sex among the sophisticated libertines of the metropolis. After three years of enthusiastic practice, now an heiress, Fanny retires, marries her first lover and discovers how love brings not just the body but also the heart "deliciously into play".

The whole thing is, of course, a male fantasy, intended to arouse and console. The plot is perfunctory, the characterization weak – though Fanny is an engagingly joyous character untroubled by her conscience. From time to time, Cleland makes efforts to debate the "natural philosophy" of pleasure, and

> *I guided officiously with my hand this furious battering ram, whose ruby head, presenting nearest the resemblance of a heart, I applied to its proper mark.*

occasionally throws out the odd piece of homely wisdom, such as sex being a good foundation for a relationship. Perhaps readers will also enjoy the built-in paradox that Fanny both uses, and is used by, sex, and, in the end, proves the winner. But sex remains the book's main feature, a carnal drama enthusiastically enacted in a welter of petticoats, garters, plump thighs, mossy mounts and "maypoles of enormous standard".

Where to go next
Love in Excess, 1720, Eliza Haywood
One of the most popular English novels of the eighteenth century is striking for its frank acknowledgement of female desire, even though it is expressed in a rather more decorous mode than in *Fanny Hill*.

Chéri
1920, COLETTE, FRENCH

A clever, poised book about chic, exquisite people, *Chéri* is tougher than it looks at first glance, a clear-eyed novel about growing old and the end of love.

At forty-nine, Léa de Lonval, a wealthy Parisian courtesan, has reached the far limit of her beauty, and sees the first lines appear on her lovely throat. Her twenty-five-year-old lover "Chéri", gorgeous and spoilt, has agreed to marry a young heiress chosen by his mother, and makes arrangements to leave Léa's house, where he has lived for the last six years, her novice in the arts of love. It seems the right time for them go their separate ways. Neither expects to suffer. Both are calamitously wrong.

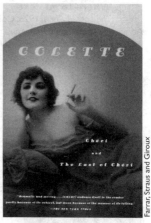

Farrar, Straus and Giroux

Colette's light, rococo style perfectly suits the disconnected, epigrammatic conversations of the *demi-monde* as they idly pass the time in their drawing rooms and conservatories. Each scene seems to shimmer in its own languid atmosphere of faintly bored pleasure. But Colette's real interest is elsewhere, in the commoner emotions of anxiety and envy below the surface. Her obvious themes are sex and power, the way lovers use each other, but the novel is less about morality than experience, less about desire than ageing. Beginning by creating a wonderful glow of eternal youth, *Chéri* finishes by pulling off the much more impressive trick of saying something painful but intelligent about the struggle to come to terms with one's own mistimed emotions.

> 'It's a strange thought that the two of us – you by losing your worn old mistress, and I by losing my scandalous young lover – have each been deprived of the most honourable possession we had upon this earth.'

Recommended translation
1951, Roger Senhouse, Vintage Classics (UK), Farrar, Straus and Giroux (US)

📖 **Where to go next**
The Last of Chéri, 1926, Colette

An equally short and penetrating novel about Chéri and Léa in later life. Now separated, both are beset by *ennui*, loneliness and depression – with ultimately tragic consequences.

Adolphe

1816, BENJAMIN CONSTANT, FRENCH

Oxford World's Classics

Shorter than many short stories, and with the same narrow focus, *Adolphe* ought to seem partial or insubstantial. Instead, it possesses the force of a comprehensive summing-up, a rapid but minutely detailed analysis of passion and all its dramas. The usual circumstantial huff and puff of secondary plots, minor characters, and local colour are entirely absent from a novel which briskly strips its subject down to essentials, and lays bare the intense, inconstant and often ridiculous behaviour of a man and a woman in love.

The plot is simple, fast-moving and violently changeable. Adolphe, a bored and cynical young man on his travels decides to seduce his host's mistress, the averagely interesting Ellénore, in order to gratify his self-esteem. Meeting resistance, he becomes desperately passionate, and, redoubling his efforts, is completely successful. Now passionately loved in his turn, he at once feels uncomfortable, but, in trying to withdraw,

It is a terrible misfortune not to be loved when you are in love; but it is a far greater misfortune to be loved passionately when you no longer love.

finds himself the helpless captive of powerful, contradictory emotions which threaten to overwhelm both he and Ellénore.

The remarkable swiftness of Constant's style never seems, as might be expected, superficial. On the contrary, in wasting no time on frills, Constant gives the impression of a deep and careful handling of his themes. He is one of the earliest psychological novelists, but seems much more modern. His uncompromising paradoxes and abrupt epigrams resonate as uncomfortably in the empty spaces of his book as the bleak quips of a Kafka or a Beckett.

Recommended translation
2001, Margaret Mauldon, Oxford World's Classics

Where to go next
Carmen and Other Stories, Prosper Mérimée
Mérimée's stories are largely concerned with the clash of cultures, viewed from an almost anthropological perspective. "Carmen" (1845) is the most famous but "Colomba" (1840) is even better, a tale of aristocratic honour and revenge set against the wild landscape of Corsica.

The Lover

1984, MARGUERITE DURAS, FRENCH

From the first page, *The Lover* gives a sense of a different sort of intelligence, a knowingness going swiftly to the heart of unexpected things. A short novel made of tiny, piercing fragments, written with a severely restricted vocabulary, it is focused less on events than on their meanings, less on characters' thoughts than on the gaps between them – the perfect style to capture all the derangement of an exotic love affair.

An elderly French writer looks back to her childhood in 1930s Saigon. She pieces together her memories: of her mother, a widowed schoolteacher "desperate with despair", and her timid younger brother and her brutal older one; of the sounds and smells of Saigon;

of herself, aged fifteen and a half, crossing the Mekong River on a native bus dressed in a man's flat-brimmed hat and a pair of gold lamé shoes; and of the man who meets her there one day, the son of a Chinese millionaire. Above all, often thinking in the third person, she remembers their intense, doomed affair: "She says: I'd rather you didn't love me. But if you do I'd like you to do as you usually do with women. He looks at her in horror."

> *I wrote about our love for our mother but I don't know if I wrote about how we hated her too, or about our love for one another, and that terrible hatred too, in that common family history of ruin and death.*

The Lover confronts – inspects, even – the illicit aspects of desire, the intimacies of hatred and fear, and the corrosive struggle for power between people. More disturbing still, it is an extraordinary portrait of a woman whose troubling, exhilarating intelligence has made her strange to herself.

Recommended translation
1985, Barbara Bray, HarperCollins (UK), Pantheon (US)

Where to go next
Moderato Cantabile, 1958, Marguerite Duras
A short, elliptical account of the relationship between a working-class man and a middle-class woman who meet regularly in a café, after she drops off her son nearby for his piano lesson. Highly structured but also enigmatic, it's a model of linguistic precision and economy.

Screen adaptation
The Lover, 1992, dir. Jean-Jacques Annaud
The husky, lived-in tones of Jeanne Moreau provide the authorial voice-over in this largely successful adaptation of Duras's masterpiece. There are moments – the lovemaking scenes in particular – that come perilously close to soft porn, but overall, the sense of burgeoning sexuality, familial estrangement and cultural irreconcilability, are all powerfully conveyed.

Adam Bede

1859, GEORGE ELIOT, ENGLISH

George Eliot is the best Victorian novelist of communal life, a patient, subtle reader of the tensions and congruences between people, and *Adam Bede* is perhaps the greatest pastoral classic in English, a deeply felt study of life in a Warwickshire village, whose peace is suddenly broken by a crisis involving teenage pregnancy and child murder.

All the stock types of rural fiction are here, from honest artisan to irascible old squire, but Eliot's handling of them is anything but stereotypical. Admittedly, she avoids sex, and her notion of love is one-dimensional, but dilemmas – moral and emotional – are her great speciality, and give the book terrific dramatic tension. Hetty Sorel is a pretty, vain farm girl loved by the upright (if quick-tempered) carpenter Adam Bede. But her head is turned by the idle attentions of Bede's friend, Arthur Donnithorne,

> Yes! thank God; human feeling is like the mighty rivers that bless the earth: it does not wait for beauty – it flows with resistless force and brings beauty with it.

the young heir to the estate, and a desperate love triangle is formed. At the same time, Adam's brother Seth is unsuccessfully courting the otherworldly Methodist preacher Dinah Morris, whose ambiguous interest lies with Hetty – and Adam.

Slow at first, the story doesn't progress so much as deepen, establishing the rhythm of life in farmyards, carpenter workshops, village schoolrooms and labourers' cottages. Particularly good is the dialogue, much of it in dialect, rough, flexible and, in the outbursts of characters such as the bitterly misogynist schoolteacher Bartle Massey and the fabulously stroppy farmer's wife, Mrs Poyser, explosively furious. Quiet by contrast ("there'd be no drawing a word from her with cart-ropes"), Hetty Sorel is perhaps the most moving seventeen-year-old airhead in fiction, vain, vague and vulnerable. Marginal to begin with, she becomes the focus of a desperate – and nail-biting – sequence of events when, halfway through the novel, the plot suddenly accelerates with a bang.

Where to go next
The Mill on the Floss, 1860, George Eliot
Eliot's melodrama tells the story of the clever, spirited Maggie Tulliver and her attempts to escape her restricted life as a miller's daughter. Descriptions of her childhood, and her relationship with her narrow-minded brother Tom, are justly celebrated for their intensity.

The Blue Flower

1995, PENELOPE FITZGERALD, ENGLISH

The Fitzgerald style is one of the most bracing in contemporary English fiction. Wild economy, swift scene-changing, delicious humour, abruptly heightened emotion and impromptu leaps into the unexpected, make all her novels vibrantly enjoyable. Perhaps she is at her best when her crisply English imagination works with exotic material – and *The Blue Flower*, which recounts the early maturity of the German Romantic poet and philosopher, Novalis, is a historical novel seemingly written from the inside, its flavour both reassuringly strange and shockingly familiar.

'Politics are the last thing we need. The state should be one family, bound by love.'
'That does not sound much like Prussia,' said the Kreisamtmann.

Before he became "Novalis", Fritz von Hardenberg was the eldest son in a family of eccentrics, improbably intended by his father to be an inspector of salt mines. But, in the years following the French Revolution, new ideas are in vogue. Romantic love is one of them. On a business trip, the twenty-two-year-old Hardenberg meets Sophie von Kühn, the twelve-year-old daughter of a tax collector, and instantly recognizes her as his "guardian spirit", his true "Philosophy". But, as he attempts to persuade her that they are destined for each other, she falls ill.

Each of the fifty-five brief chapters of the novel is a short, stabbing scene, a sort of historical reportage. Though Fitzgerald is sharp, she is not straightforward. Her characters – the atrociously precocious child, the Bernhard; the amiable, disappointed Karoline Just; the "Big Cross", the Father's godless older brother – are like people encountered in real life: brilliantly immediate but full of unknowable gaps. The vivid thinginess of domestic chaos – children under tables, laundry hanging from windows, a pile of bread rolls, slop pails – jostle against the conversations, shouted across courtyards and muttered in parlours, of philosophy, politics, religion and poetry.

Where to go next
The Gate of Angels, 1990, Penelope Fitzgerald
A deft and subtle love story set in Cambridge just before World War I, involving a young science lecturer whose ordered – exclusively male – universe is disrupted when he is thrown together with a young woman following a cycling accident.

Madame Bovary

1857, GUSTAVE FLAUBERT, FRENCH

Few novels match *Madame Bovary* for sheer accomplishment. Its story, as Flaubert said himself, is banal; but his artistry gives it unique power. Always beautifully modulated and phrased, it is also fast, compelling and shocking: a fairy story with a bitterly unhappy ending.

Among the gossipy bourgeois townsfolk of provincial France, Emma Bovary, the doctor's wilful young wife, dreams of grand passion. Constrained by her circumstances, bored rigid by pro-

vincial life, she risks her reputation, her family and ultimately her life, for a ruinously all-encompassing love of the sort she has read about in popular romances.

The artistry of the novel is evident everywhere. A rigorous stylist, Flaubert is also a writer who pays attention to the world and recreates it with sensuous exactitude. He has a marvellous ear for dialogue too; the novel is full of pungently idiosyncratic conversations that crisscross the main theme in a variety of discordant keys. Indeed, the liveliness and range of the novel's minor characters – the toadying chemist Homais, the two-faced moneylender Lheureux, the lovesick teenager Justin and many others – are among the novel's additional pleasures. The central drama, however, remains the main focus. Flaubert's artful – and ironic – juxtaposition of scenes creates a shifting balance of moods, as Emma plunges in and out of her affairs. Paradoxically, his

But who was it that made her so unhappy? Where was the extraordinary catastrophe that overwhelmed her?

carefully measured style is brilliantly successful in presenting an increasingly volatile character, and the scenes of Emma's absurd final attempts to take control of her life are among the most vividly desperate in fiction.

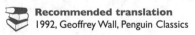
Recommended translation
1992, Geoffrey Wall, Penguin Classics

📖 **Where to go next**
Three Tales, 1877, Gustave Flaubert
Three perfectly-crafted stories set in different times: "A Simple Heart" tells
the story of an uneducated servant woman, Félicité; "The Legend of Saint Julian
Hospitator" is an account of the life of a medieval saint; "Herodias" retells the
biblical story of Salome and John the Baptist.

🎬 **Screen adaptation**
Madame Bovary, 1949, dir. Vincente Minnelli
A novel that has eluded the best attempts of several fine directors, including
Renoir (1934) and Chabrol (1991), surprisingly gets its most sensitive treatment from melodrama maestro Minnelli. Sandwiching the story between
extracts from the trial of the novel for obscenity, Minnelli suggests that Emma's
ennui is fuelled as much by self-delusion as it is by frustration.

Effi Briest

1894, THEODOR FONTANE, GERMAN

Effi Briest is a quiet book of lingering echoes, a grown-up novel about
adultery and murder which scrupulously avoids melodramatic incidents, to show instead the devastating ordinariness of tragedy.

A short book with a big scope, it evokes a whole society in the
provincial towns of late nineteenth-century Prussia, stiff, hierar-
chical places where governors,
majors and doctors call on each
other in gloomy, over-furnished
reception rooms, according to
the established sense of propriety. For radiant and child-
like teenager Effi Briest, newly married to fifty-year-old Geert von
Innstetten, governor of a Baltic province, it is a difficult world to live
in. Her impulsive sweetness receives little encouragement from the
buttoned-up Innstetten; her occasional selfishness is sternly censured
by the governor and his social circle. Downcast and homesick, she
struggles to make the marriage work, but her efforts are not helped

> 'And I shall have this guilt on
> my soul,' she repeated. 'Yes, I do
> have it. But is it really weighing
> on my soul? No. And that's why
> I am appalled at myself.'

by the arrival of the middle-aged, ginger-moustached womanizer, Major Crampas.

In a novel containing a mismatched wedding, an adulterous affair and a duel, Fontane is strikingly uninterested in such events *per se*. Both the wedding and affair occur off-stage; the duel (perhaps the fastest in fiction) takes place in two sentences. What interests Fontane much more are the calamitous effects of the events – the ways in which reasonable and sensitive people are locked into socially pre-scribed behaviour: murderous revenge, total ostracism, quietist fatal-ism. In the Prussian world of honour and dishonour, owning and disowning, collective punishment is implacable. However, the novel never strains after dramatic effects. For Effi, ordinary daily life goes on, shot through with sudden, violent insights about her husband and lover, her child and herself.

Recommended translation
1995, Hugh Rorrison and Emily Chambers, Penguin Classics

Where to go next
Cousin Basilio, 1878, Eça de Quierós
Written between *Madame Bovary* and *Effi Briest*, this Portuguese classic is a startling variant on the "fallen woman" novel, largely because the woman in question gets so much enjoyment from sex and is only brought down by the sheer malevolence of a servant.

Screen adaptation
Effi Briest, 1974, dir. Rainer Werner Fassbinder
Stunningly filmed in crisp black and white, Fassbinder's approach to Fontane's novel of adultery, is slow-moving and stylized, avoiding histrionics in favour of a cool analysis of the restraints – both social and emotional – that determine the behaviour of apparent intimates. Though a little too old, the beautiful Hanna Schygulla brings a tragic grandeur to the title role.

The Good Soldier

1915, FORD MADOX FORD, ENGLISH

The subtitle may be *A Tale of Passion*, but the opening sentence is "This is the saddest story I have ever heard", and the passion in *The Good Soldier* is frankly disquieting, alternately reckless, agonizing and bleak.

Set mainly in 1904, at Nauheim, an elegant watering hole for affluent invalids, the scene is cast with a pre-war Edwardian glow. Captain Edward Ashburnham, a good-looking but vacuous Englishman with a heart complaint, is staying at the Englischer Hof with his forceful wife Leonora. There he encounters the narrator, American millionaire John Dowell and his pretty young wife, Florence, who also suffers from a weak heart. The two couples become friendly, and, over the course of the years, intimate, with no secrets between them. So it is a shock to Dowell to learn, after Florence's death, that she had been Captain Ashburnham's lover.

'My wife and I knew Captain and Mrs Ashburnham as well as it was possible to know anybody, and yet, in another sense, we knew nothing at all about them.'

On the face of it, the story is banal – but the banality of passion is Ford's special expertise. Dowell's halting, digressive narration, vividly impressionistic, rapidly passes over the story's big moments (dropped into the narrative as heart-stopping revelations) in order to worry away at the little details, the oddities of behaviour and habits of mind. Gradually, he builds up a picture of a womanizer, sentimentally, even heroically, devoted to women, and a wife who loves her husband so much she will hatefully arrange his mistresses for him: two entirely incompatible people bound together on a wheel of fire. Brilliantly, or hideously, attuned to the trivia of obsessive desire, *The Good Soldier* is, as Ford claimed, an almost unbearably sad story of the desperate intransigence and messiness of love.

Where to go next
Parade's End, 1924–28, Ford Madox Ford
A masterly tetralogy, comprising *Some Do Not* (1924), *No More Parades* (1925), *A Man Could Stand Up* (1926) and *The Last Post* (1928), chronicling the devastating effects of World War I on English society via the life of senior civil servant Christopher Tietjens.

The French Lieutenant's Woman

1969, JOHN FOWLES, ENGLISH

A strange blend of pastiche, critique and fictional self-analysis, *The French Lieutenant's Woman* ought not to work, let alone charm and intrigue, but John Fowles's best-loved book remains mesmerizingly satisfying. Its "postmodern" technique – the famous multiple endings, the appearance of the author in his own narrative – is no longer so shocking, and its ruminations on the Victorian age seem more and more a product of the 1960s. But the pastiche is vivid and assured, and, together, the different elements combine to create a powerful, provoking story of love and loss.

> It was not a pretty face, like Ernestina's. It was certainly not a beautiful face, by any period's standard or taste. But it was an unforgettable face, and a tragic face.

It is 1867, a watershed year in an England of self-conscious piety and tradition. In Parliament, the second Reform Bill is being debated. Marx and Darwin have published their radical new theories. Women are dreaming of emancipation. And in Lyme Regis, Charles Smithson, a well-to-do if vague young man is walking along the Cobb with his fiancée, Ernestina Freeman, heiress of a successful haberdashery business, when he sees a black-coated woman standing staring out across the sea towards France.

The novel has a plenitude equal to a Victorian triple-decker's, a driving plot which rhythmically combines dramatic encounters, comic interludes and suspenseful mysteries, and a sensitivity to small, telling details. It is a sign of its essential sympathies that a novel which stresses the intellectual so much should show such an amazingly sure touch when it comes to critical emotional moments.

Where to go next
The Crimson Petal and the White, 2002, Michel Faber
A hard-hitting blockbuster of London in the 1870s, that plays off the conventions of the classic Victorian novel to devastating effect. Sugar is a nineteen-year-old prostitute whose life is transformed – not necessarily for the better – when a rich man takes her up.

Screen adaptation
The French Lieutenant's Woman, 1981, dir. Karel Reisz
Fowles's distancing device of introducing critical and historical asides into his tale is replaced, by scriptwriter Harold Pinter, with a film-within-a-film about the actors playing the two lead roles. It's a little contrived, whereas the novel's Victorian romance comes across with great power, not least through Meryl Streep's ability to express both passion and mystery in the title role.

Elective Affinities

1809, JOHANN WOLFGANG VON GOETHE, GERMAN

Elective Affinities is a novel of harmonious classical grace about the problem of disharmony. Nimbly intellectual and as artfully plotted as a Bach fugue, it maintains a formal elegance while playing variations on increasingly disturbing themes of desire and remorse.

Eduard and Charlotte spend their days contentedly planning

improvements to their country estate. But when Eduard invites his old friend, the Captain, to share the work with them, and Charlotte takes her niece Ottilie out of school to give her the benefit of her guidance, their harmony is broken. Like chemicals, they react to each other in different ways, spontaneously forming new affinities. As their improving projects continue, their conflicting passions begin to tear them apart.

The oddity and power of the novel lie in the terrible disconnection between articulation and feeling – the four characters (all thoughtful, considerate people) chatting with courtly formality about standards of human conduct while drifting steadily, almost imperturbably, into emotional chaos. The plot works like clockwork, each scene locking cinematically into a narrative sequence that progresses remorselessly to its conclusion. Goethe's poised style, stagy dialogue and heraldic descriptive detail (the gardens in bloom, the picturesque lake, the elegant summer house) only heighten the tension of impending disaster; his deft observations and sure sense of psychology animate everything. Intellectually powerful without being overpowering, *Elective Affinities* is a marvellously alert inquiry into the paradoxes of human behaviour.

> *Everything seemed to be following its usual course, as is the way in monstrously strange circumstances when everything is at stake: we go on with our lives as though nothing were the matter.*

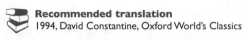

Recommended translation
1994, David Constantine, Oxford World's Classics

Where to go next
The Marquise of O, 1808, Heinrich von Kleist
The tale of a virtuous young woman who suddenly, and inexplicably, becomes pregnant to the dismay of her highly respectable family. A disturbing novella, by one of the masters of the form.

The Sorrows of Young Werther

1774, JOHANN WOLFGANG VON GOETHE, GERMAN

Perhaps no one has written better about the sheer distress of sexual passion than Goethe, who based his brief, intense novel on an unrequited and abruptly ended love affair of his own. Written in a delirious four-week burst of creativity, and published to instant success, it instigated a European vogue for agonizing love affairs, bitter disappointments and occasional suicides.

Werther, a gregarious young man of promise, escapes an unwanted love affair by travelling to a small German village, where "solitude is a precious balm" to his heart. But almost immediately, after a few days of calm, he meets a young woman, Lotte, by whom he is instantly transfixed, heart

How the thrill of it shoots through me if my finger happens to touch hers or our feet meet beneath the table!

and soul. In a series of impressionistic lyrical descriptions, Werther celebrates their instant empathy – though he already knows that she is betrothed to another man. Fearing to compromise her, he tries to avoid her company, but now "nothing is more dangerous than solitude". Far from lessening his passion, his solitary wanderings intensify it, in new, self-destructive ways.

The form of the book – brilliantly effective – is a one-sided correspondence of short, disconnected letters: a series of outbursts to which there are no balancing replies. From the first, Werther is alone with his obsession. An intellectual, he constantly searches for – and often believes he has found in the brilliant flights of his imagination – a relief for his anguish, in business, travel, philosophy or nature. But it is the particularly cruel nature of his obsession to be self-aware.

Recommended translation
1989, Michael Hulse, Penguin Classics

Where to go next
Lotte in Weimar: The Beloved Returns, 1939, Thomas Mann
Lotte in *The Sorrows of Young Werther* was inspired by a real person, Charlotte Kerstner. In this insightful look at the nature of genius and celebrity, Mann imagines her meeting up with Goethe (now a great man) forty years on from their youthful acquaintance.

Loving

1945, HENRY GREEN, ENGLISH

Henry Green was a strange and refreshing original, a technical innovator with a sharp eye for overlooked detail and an extraordinary ear for the self-revealing eccentricities of casual speech. His novels are like no others in bringing to life the anarchic privacy of people's imaginations. *Loving*, a masterful novel from his mid-period, is a subtle comedy of life below stairs in a grand house in

'All right then I'll learn you something,' Edith said and she panted and panted. 'I love Charley Raunce I love 'im I love 'im so there. I could open the veins of my right arm for that man,' she said.

Ireland during World War II. Vivid with the servants' gossip and argument, but true to the shifting undercurrents of their worry, gaiety and love, it dramatizes a season of loss and change as war threatens them from abroad.

As if happy to leave the story to its own devices, Green devotes his attention to the common incidents of daily life. Charley Raunce, newly promoted to the position of butler, takes gleeful possession of the precious notebooks which record the past tips of all visitors to the castle. The two undermaids, Kate and Edith, begin romances. Captain Davenport is discovered in Mrs Jack's bed one morning. The cook's nephew strangles one of the ornamental peacocks. And the "story" – as dramatically life-changing as you could wish – emerges magically from all these secretive and confused events, a narrative rich in sudden odd images (a cobweb in a sleeping man's hair, a live mouse caught in the weather vane's clockwork) and, above all, in the conversations, pungent, oblique, rambling and colourful. Unlike most novelists, Green not only captures the drift and garble of real speech, but – in a sort of literary conjuring trick – simultaneously shows us the train of thought behind the spoken words.

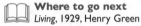 **Where to go next**
Living, 1929, Henry Green
Once you get over the linguistic tics (missing articles for instance), Green's experimental novel of factory life in Birmingham is remarkable for its authentic dialogue and unpatronizing approach to ordinary working lives.

Fiesta: the Sun Also Rises

1927, ERNEST HEMINGWAY, AMERICAN

Pacy and sexy, hard-edged and a little skewed, *Fiesta: the Sun Also Rises* is a tale of doomed love among the American and English expats hanging out in Paris and Spain in the 1920s. Hemingway, master of the casual and vapid, brilliantly captures their hedonist lifestyle, the slap and dash of their tipsy conversations late at night in the Napolitain and Café Select, and their half-serious, too-serious love affairs.

The Hemingway magic is here, in the way the reader is suddenly, abruptly, dropped into the middle of the action; in the style of the narration, flat and full of gaps; and in the laconic description, cap-

She wore a slipover jersey sweater and a tweed skirt, and her hair was brushed back like a boy's. She was built with curves like the hull of a racing yacht.

turing not just the appearance of scenes, but the feeling of them too.

The narrator, Jake Barnes, is an American journalist, trying to cope with an injury suffered in World War I. Robert Cohn is a college middleweight boxing champion turned novelist. Mike is an English bankrupt. Romero is a teenage bull-fighting sensation. All are in love with Lady Brett Ashley, an English aristocrat with a drink problem and an out-of-control temperament. At first, their tangled affairs are set among Parisian bars and cafés; later, when the scene shifts to Spain, where they visit a fiesta, their shifting passions contrast ambiguously with the balletic violence of the bull-fighting.

Where to go next
The Complete Short Stories, Ernest Hemingway
Hemingway's direct, pared-down style is perfectly suited to the short story form, where every word must count. This contains nearly all of them, from the early Nick Adams stories to later masterpieces such as "The Snows of Kilimanjaro" and "Hills Like White Elephants".

The Unbearable Lightness of Being
1984, MILAN KUNDERA, CZECH

Written in exile and banned in the author's native Czechoslovakia, Kundera's most famous novel is an intellectually nimble response to the Cold War, full of wit, paradox and scorn; but it is also – perhaps more enduringly – a beautiful, sad book about the understandings and misunderstandings of love.

Two love affairs underpin the brilliantly unstraightforward narrative. Teresa loves the womanizing surgeon Tomas, and the painter Sabina (one of Tomas's lovers) is having an affair with Franz, a fashionable academic. Their affairs are full of difficulties, due partly to the Communist clampdown after the Prague Spring of 1968, which drives Tomas, Teresa and Sabina into exile, and partly because love itself is a problem which requires the most inventive of solutions. *The Unbearable Lightness of Being* is, above all, a novel of problems, vividly posed, ingeniously analysed. What is the basis

MILAN KUNDERA

The Unbearable Lightness of Being

Translated from the Czech by Michael Henry Heim

HarperCollins

of "being"? Is "lightness" positive or negative? What does it mean to make love with your eyes closed (or open)? Never clever for the sake of it, Kundera – the philosopher-poet of sexual practices – is satisfyingly provoking in the role of novelist as witty intellectual. He is also

a constantly surprising inventor of tableau-like scenes: erotic (a woman wearing only her underwear and a bowler hat

> *Tomas thought: attaching love to sex is one of the most bizarre ideas the Creator ever had.*

looking at herself in a mirror), or troubling (a crow buried alive in the earth) or hauntingly surreal (hundreds of red, yellow and blue park benches floating down the Vltava River). As he says, "Metaphors are not to be trifled with. A single metaphor can give birth to love."

 Recommended translation
1984, Michael Henry Heim, Faber & Faber (UK), Harper Perennial (US)

 Where to go next
Immortality, 1990, Milan Kundera
A playful and profound examination of death, immortality and literary achievement that is triggered by the chance gesture of an elderly woman at a swimming pool.

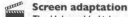

Screen adaptation
The Unbearable Lightness of Being, 1987, dir. Philip Kaufman
A highly sympathetic adaptation of Kundera's novel that underplays the philosophical aspects and stresses the erotic in a touching and tender fashion. It's helped by a shimmering performance from Juliet Binoche, who effortlessly communicates both Teresa's allure and her vulnerability – the perfect foil to Daniel Day-Lewis's controlling but confused Tomas.

Les Liaisons Dangereuses

1782, CHODERLOS DE LACLOS, FRENCH

Laclos's only book caused a scandal when it appeared, followed, naturally enough, by a vogue for sleazy novels with "Danger" or "Liaison" in the title. Ever since, it has been a byword for Sex in Literature. It is indeed focused from first to last on sex. But be warned: it isn't in the least erotic. Rather, it is, by turns, chilling, ironic, contemptuous, vicious and despairing.

Two ex-lovers, the Vicomte de Valmont and the Marquise de Merteuil, plot together to deprave Cécile Volanges, a fifteen-year-old girl fresh from a convent, and ruin Madame de Tourvel, a married young woman noted for her piety. For Valmont, it offers the chance of two dazzling triumphs to boast about with his fellow high-society rakes; for the Marquise, it holds the promise of revenge over her first lover, Mademoiselle Volanges' fiancé. But the stakes are higher than that, for the Vicomte and the Marquise are bound to each other in a sexual and psychological game of rising stakes, which even they, with all their skills of manipulation, can't guarantee to control.

'My plan is to make her understand the full price she's got to pay, the gravity of each sacrifice she'll be making ... to bring her virtue to a protracted, agonizing death.'

Les Liaisons Dangereuses is an epistolary novel (constructed entirely of letters), and one of the most celebrated. The eighteenth-century letter, with its formal flourishes and innuendo, is the perfect form for the battle of wits between the Vicomte and the Marquise, and Laclos gives all the other letter-writers their own distinctive literary style to match their characters. Particularly effective are the letters of the eagerly ungrammatical Cécile and the increasingly desperate Madame de Tourvel. But the dominant voices belong to the Vicomte and the Marquise, his smug and arrogant, hers steely and vengeful. She is, she says herself, "a self-made woman" among "dishonourable", "feeble" men, and, on one level, the letters between her and the Vicomte are exchanges in an all-out sex war, the enigmatic results of which readers must judge for themselves.

 Recommended translation
1995, Douglas Parmée, Oxford World's Classics

 Where to go next
Crimes of Love, Marquis de Sade
In this Oxford World's Classics collection of his shorter fiction, de Sade pushes the sexual frankness of Richardson and Laclos to its logical conclusion. Seven stories of vice, seduction and murder, all rather more palatable than his longer novels.

 Screen adaptation
Dangerous Liaisons, 1988, dir. Stephen Frears
Based on Christopher Hampton's highly successful stage adaptation, the film version oozes depravity and elegance in equal measure. John Malkovich as Valmont and Glenn Close's Marquise, in particular, play their hollow games of love and chance with a cynical assurance that is both fascinating and repellent.

The Princesse de Clèves

1678, Madame de Lafayette, French

A small, busy novel with perfect poise, *The Princesse de Clèves* is full of courtly chatter about the etiquette and paradoxes of love. It reads equally well as a novel of politics, philosophy or espionage, its characters engaging in theoretical discussions while adopting disguises to hide their true intentions and intriguing against each other. And it is both precise and moving about the roles of women – now manipulators, now victims – at the sixteenth-century French court.

At the heart of the novel is the Princess of Clèves's intense struggle for self-control amidst conflicting emotions: on the one hand

Ambition and love affairs were the life-blood of the court, absorbing the attention of men and women alike.

her deep-seated sense of duty to her admirable husband, M. de Chartres, and on the other, her awakening passion for the handsomest man in France, "Nature's masterpiece" M. de Nemours. The suspenseful will-she or won't-she plot is artfully set in a ceremonious royal court bristling as much with the accidents and tragedies of love as with political machinations, diplomatic initiatives and war. Though short, the novel is alive, almost noisy, with competing conversations, as the principal characters inventively argue their cases: the whole book echoes with the refined art of gossip. Slight details – a few chance words, an inconsequential thought, exchanged glances – carry tremendous importance: the Princess first sees M. de Nemours "stepping over a chair", as if the intensity of her emotion fixes the moment absolutely. As you might expect of a book made up of gossip, however refined, it is often very funny (there's a marvellously garbled French view of the scandal of Henry VIII and his wives). But in the end it is a witty and profound account of the paradoxical and agonizing effects of love.

 Recommended translation
1992, Terence Cave, Oxford World's Classics

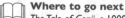 **Where to go next**
The Tale of Genji, c.1000, Murusaki Shikibu
One of the earliest – and longest – of novels is another detailed look at court life, this time in medieval Japan. Telling the story of the Emperor's second son,

the alluring Prince Genji, and his romantic and political adventures, it is well worth investigating – especially in Edward G. Seidensticker's lively translation.

The Golden Notebook

1962, DORIS LESSING, ZIMBABWEAN

The Golden Notebook is the great novel of the age of Feminism, full of terrible men and bolshie women locked together in knock-down-drag-out arguments about gender, class, race, politics and sex. It contains a very large number of love affairs (sometimes anguished, sometimes casual, always illuminating), but the giddy variety of its story-lines and its intellectual buoyancy prevent it from ever seeming heavy. A novel to stimulate and shock, it inspired a generation of women in their fight to sweep away the traditional world of male dominance.

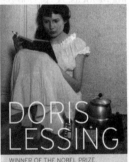

WINNER OF THE NOBEL PRIZE FOR LITERATURE 2007

DORIS LESSING

THE GOLDEN NOTEBOOK

HarperCollins

Anna Wulf, single mother, Communist Party member, novelist with writer's block, decides to record her experiences and thoughts in four separate notebooks, each dedicated to a facet of her life: a black notebook for anecdotes of her life as a professional writer; red for her political activities; yellow for her attempts to write fiction; and blue for her diary. Interleaved with these is what Lessing called a "conventional short novel", provocatively titled *Free Women*, which tells the story of Anna, her outspoken friend Molly,

> 'What about us? Free, we say, yet the truth is they get erections when they're with a woman they don't give a damn about, but we don't have an orgasm unless we love him. What's free about that?'

Molly's ex-husband Richard, a chauvinistic financier, and her disaffected teenage son Tommy.

Less a novel than lots of vivid scraps of novels jammed together – including at one point plot outlines of a further nineteen unwritten stories – *The Golden Notebook* makes disharmony its unifying theme. Nothing constrains its electrifying energy or interrupts its outpouring of ideas. A "period piece" in the best sense of the phrase, conjuring up an era of urgent debate, it remains fresh (and, indeed, raw) in its descriptions of Anna's fraught attempts with many unsatisfactory men to break through emotional complications into a simpler dimension of fulfilment and happiness.

Where to go next
The Grass is Singing, 1950, Doris Lessing
Set in her native Rhodesia (now Zimbabwe), Lessing's striking debut novel explores issues of colonialism and sexual politics by looking at the events leading to the death of Mary Turner, an unhappily married white farmer's wife.

The Sea, the Sea

1978, IRIS MURDOCH, ENGLISH

A formidably clever novelist with an interest in philosophy, myth and religion, Iris Murdoch was also a sharp-eyed, sympathetic observer of human muddle, and an audacious plotter with a wicked sense of farce. Emotional chaos and moral confusion, two of her favourite themes, come together in perhaps the best novel of her "late" period, the bracingly turbulent *The Sea, the Sea*.

> I sit here and wonder at myself. Have I abjured that magic, drowned my book? Forgiven my enemies? The surrender of power, the final change of magic into spirit? Time will show.

Like Prospero, the charismatic Shakespearean director Charles Arrowby has abandoned his magic and retired alone to Shruff End, a lonely sea-battered house on the northern coast. He wants – he says – only solitude and peace. Within days, however, he is beset with old flames and theatre friends. Worse is to follow. To his bewilderment, he recognizes a plain, elderly woman in the local village as the childhood sweetheart who ran away from him forty years earlier, and he instinctively conjures up all his old powers of charisma to enchant her again.

The novel – like the sea which forms both background and central motif – changes mood and momentum with fine unpredictability. The story is held together by Arrowby himself, whose passionate yearnings, sudden tantrums and eccentric eating habits ("cold sugared bacon and poached egg on nettles") are by turns enlivening and infuriating, but never dull. The half-idyllic, half-sinister atmosphere of Shruff End is one of the marvels of the novel; another is the brilliantly observed scenery of sky and sea and rocks. At the same time, below the surface, Murdoch has her eye on different sorts of magic – the transformations of the ego, spiritual fulfilment – and, characteristically, she offers enlightenment as well as entertainment.

Where to go next
The Bell, 1958, Iris Murdoch
The struggle between good and evil is here played out in the setting of Imber Court, where – in a lay community led by a troubled homosexual – a group of assorted misfits try to sort out their lives. Enlivened by a mischievous humour, this is an engrossing mix of the philosophical, the mythic and the bizarre.

Lolita

1955, Vladimir Nabokov, Russian

First published by the notorious Olympia Press in Paris, *Lolita* instantly became a *succès de scandale*, a byword for titillation. Nothing could be further from the truth. It is a gorgeously written story of cruelty, a tale of the agonizing abuse of a twelve-year-old girl lyri-

Sex, censorship and the novel

When it comes to writing about sex, many novelists have fallen victim to the arbiters of public morality. Works have been regularly banned, and on occasions, writers, publishers and even printers have found themselves in court on charges of obscenity. The 1960s saw hard-fought challenges to the censorship laws in both Britain and the US, but even today certain titles can still be difficult to obtain in some places. Below are three of the novels included in this chapter that have ended up on the wrong side of the law.

Lolita (see p.35)

With paedophilia as its subject matter, Nabokov's masterpiece was always going to be controversial, and only the Paris-based Olympia Press – purveyors of erotica and the avant-garde – would touch it. Published in 1955, it was prevented from entering the UK by H.M. Customs and Excise, and, following pressure from the British government, the French Interior ministry banned *Lolita* in English while allowing its publication in French. Though controversial in the US, the book escaped prosecution when Putnam published it in 1958. The following year the British firm of Weidenfeld and Nicholson followed suit (shifting 200,000 hardback copies) and the French lifted the ban when Maurice Girodias – chief editor of Olympia Press – threatened to sue.

Penguin

Vladimir Nabokov
Lolita

cally recorded by her thirty-seven-year-old abuser. It is also a half-loving, half-horrified evocation of motel America with its "clapboard Kabins" and "raid-the-ice-box midnight snacks", a suspenseful murder novel without (until the final few pages) a victim, and a comic cultural collision between old Europe and young America.

Following the fortuitous death of Charlotte Haze, the nympholeptic European émigré Humbert Humbert finds himself guardian of her young daughter,

Madame Bovary (see p.17)
Madame Bovary was dedicated to Jules Sénard, the lawyer who represented Flaubert after the writer was prosecuted following the novel's serialization in the magazine *La Revue de Paris* in the autumn of 1856. In the ensuing trial the prosecutor claimed that the novel was immoral and a threat to family values because it contained "…not a single character who can make her [Emma Bovary] bow her head." Sénard successfully argued that the novel was a warning against the sensualizing of religion, and that Charles Bovary remained a dutiful husband throughout. Author, publisher and printer were duly acquitted.

Memoirs of a Woman of Pleasure or *Fanny Hill* (see p.9)
John Cleland wrote the only work for which he is remembered as a way of paying off a large debt that had led to his imprisonment. Several months passed before author and publisher were arrested and charged in 1749, and – with Cleland expressing remorse – the book was banned. Illicitly printed copies continued circulating during the next two centuries until in 1963 the US publisher Putnam reprinted it. A further attempt at suppression was rejected by the New York Supreme Court, and since then the book has appeared in several editions, including scholarly ones.

the gum-chewing, sassy Dolores ("four feet ten in one sock"). A saturnine man addictively drawn to girls between the ages of nine and fourteen, he has long schemed to possess her. On an extended trip across the States (fabulously described), they become lovers, Lolita proving more sexually adroit than expected. But as time goes by

In the possession and thraldom of a nymphet the enchanted traveller stands, as it were, beyond happiness. For there is no other bliss on earth comparable to that of fondling a nymphet.

Lolita grows restive, Humbert suspicious. Two years later she suddenly disappears, and Humbert packs his gun and begins the long, obsessive search to find her.

The novel masquerades as a memoir addressed by Humbert to the "ladies and gentlemen of the jury" shortly before his trial, and the style in which it is written – dandyish, witty, rapt – is at the heart of the story's extraordinary tension. Humbert pulls no punches: his story celebrates Lolita's catastrophic vulnerability and his own brutishness as much as her witchy sexuality. A novel about both enchantment and the abuse of responsibility, *Lolita* charms and horrifies in equal measure.

Where to go next
Collected Stories, Vladimir Nabokov
Nabokov was the consummate literary stylist and his short stories are some of the most quirky, scintillating and original of the twentieth century, full of unexpected twists and odd flights of fancy.

Screen adaptation
Lolita, 1962, dir. Stanley Kubrick
Censorship meant that Kubrick couldn't make the novel's eroticism quite as apparent as he would have liked, it also dictated the upping of Lolita's age from twelve to fourteen (actress Sue Lyon looks more like sixteen). This – and the overly "comic" turns from Peter Sellers as Quilty – undermines the challenging perversity of the novel. It still works, however, and is less earnest than the 1997 remake.

Doctor Zhivago
1958, BORIS PASTERNAK, RUSSIAN

Doctor Zhivago is a great wilful original, a novel of political upheaval which largely ignores politics, and a tragic romance which, with plain-speaking simplicity, movingly dramatizes the complications of love.

It is also – excitingly – a novel of conflict, beginning with the 1905 revolution and ending with World War II, a desperate extended period in Russia of slaughter and confusion. In the first days of the Bolshevik uprising of 1917, the doctor and poet Yuri

Zhivago flees with his wife Tonya to Siberia, only to find himself in the thick of the fighting between the Reds and Whites. There, without ceasing to love Tonya, he falls in love with Lara, his soul mate. Soon he is separated from both women by the chaos of war – but the greater chaos is in his heart.

BORIS PASTERNAK

Doctor Zhivago

Introduction by JOHN BAYLEY

Pantheon Books

Fragmented at the beginning and with a short anthology of Zhivago's poems tacked onto the end, the narrative is notoriously uneven. But episodes such as Zhivago's epic train journey, his service at the front as a conscripted doctor, his escape from the Red Army and his first meeting with Lara, are powerfully dramatic. The frequent coincidences, which would be absurd in a plot-driven novel, here give chaos a human pattern. Unsentimental and unsensational, but rich in both joy and heartbreak, the love triangle of Yury, Tonya and Lara is justly famous. The whole novel, in fact, is lit up by Pasternak's extraordinary pow-

They loved each other because everything around them willed it, the trees and the clouds and the sky over their heads and the earth under their feet.

ers of observation. He is, in particular, the best Russian novelist of the natural world since Turgenev, and *Zhivago* is full of enlivening details – the warm smell of earth at dusk, the noise of shifting ice and a thousand varieties and moods of snow.

Recommended translation
1958, Max Hayward and Manya Harari, Everyman's Library

Where to go next
Suite Française, 2004, Irène Némirovsky
A year before she was killed at Auschwitz, the author drafted two novels about life in France after the Nazi invasion. *Storm in June* covers the escape of a group of families from Paris, *Dolce* describes how a village comes to terms with occupation. Both reveal the thin layer that separates barbarism from civilization.

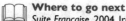 **Screen adaptation**
Doctor Zhivago, 1965, dir. David Lean
Lean was a consummate director of epics and it's the big moments and vast spaces that impinge most on the memory. The poignant central love story, between Lara (Julie Christie) and Zhivago (Omar Sharif), is less convincing, and the characterization is generally two-dimensional, apart from a barnstorming turn from Rod Steiger as sleazy lawyer Viktor Komarovsky.

Manon Lescaut

1731, ABBÉ PRÉVOST, FRENCH

Radically free of ornamentation, *Manon Lescaut* is an early triumph of fast-action storytelling, a calmly narrated tale of absolutely uncontrollable passion.

From the beginning, the plot moves with decisive swiftness. Within minutes of encountering Manon at an inn, the seventeen-year-old Chevalier des Grieux has arranged to elope with her, abandoning his family, his career and his principles. She is even younger than him, and a commoner, but bewitchingly beautiful. What the Chevalier doesn't guess is that she is also wholeheartedly immoral. To avoid poverty, she will do anything, happily taking a rich lover to pay their bills. The desperate des Grieux is forced into a life of crime, and the story that follows encompasses shady dealings, imprisonment, murder and, eventually, flight to the New World. Throughout the turmoil, despite his attempts

> 'I swear to you, my dear Chevalier, that you are the idol of my heart ... But can you not see, my poor dear soul, that, in the state to which we are reduced, fidelity is a foolish virtue?'

to break his infatuation, des Grieux's passion never falters. The same cannot be said for Manon's.

ANTOINE FRANÇOIS PREVOST
Manon Lescaut
Foreword by Germaine Greer

Hesperus Press

The contradictory Manon, unprincipled but tender, is an intriguingly elusive figure in the Chevalier's memoir, half-glimpsed, half-understood. His main preoccupation is with his own feelings, the sexual obsession which he is powerless to resist, despite his breeding and good taste. The brilliantly managed discrepancy between the Chevalier's elegantly rational narration and the concentrated anarchy of his story amplifies the contrast in the narrative itself between his intelligence and helplessness. Such unresolvable contradictions power the plot's destructive cycle of calamity, escape and fresh calamity which culminates, with mounting horror, in tragedy.

Recommended translation
2004, Andrew Brown, Hesperus Press

Where to go next
The Lady of the Camellias, 1848, Alexandre Dumas fils
The inspiration for the opera *La Traviata* and the film *Camille* is the tragic story of a high-class Parisian courtesan who sacrifices her one chance of real happiness to save the social position of her young, infatuated lover.

Pamela

1740–41, SAMUEL RICHARDSON, ENGLISH

Pamela was revolutionary: Europe's first great novel to make emotion the focal point of the narrative. It made Richardson's original readers emotional too: they wept with pity – and horrified excitement

– at the appalling trials made of the gorgeous Pamela's chastity.

The story is simple but devastating. Pamela Andrews is a fifteen-year-old serving girl in the employ of wicked young Squire B of Bedfordshire. In a series of increasingly distressed letters home to her rustic parents, she describes Squire B's persistent attempts to seduce her, aided and abetted by his villainous housekeeper, the grotesque Mrs Jewkes. Pamela persistently refuses him, while modestly preserving the social decorum which forbids her from criticizing her betters, and even (bizarrely) finding emotional room in which to develop an affection for her master.

> *I found myself in his arms, quite void of strength; and he kissed me two or three times, with frightful eagerness. At last I burst from him; but he held me back, and shut the door.*

From a twenty-first-century perspective Pamela's sentiments can be hard to take, and Richardson's oozy moralizing, fussy traditionalism and sexual teasing only make things worse. Nevertheless, she is – triumphantly – the first major working-class heroine in fiction (barring criminals): a poor young woman whose purity surprisingly turns out to be her most effective defence.

The novel remains a hugely emotive read. Pamela's letters, chronicling daily incidents in fine detail, exert the crude fascination of reality TV, the narrative racing through the domestic minutiae of conversations, meals and chores towards the next outburst of Squire B's misbehaviour. If the novel seems ropey on sexual psychology, it is undeniably assured in its gripping depiction of a society which allows vulnerable women to be trapped by a Kafkaesque logic of social etiquette.

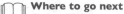

📖 **Where to go next**
Clarissa, 1749, Samuel Richardson
Richardson's later epistolary novel is like *Pamela* but on a much larger scale (originally in eight volumes). Presenting himself as her protector, the charismatic rake Lovelace rescues the chaste Clarissa Harlowe from an engagement to a man she despises, only to install her in an up-market brothel in London.

Anna Karenina

1877, LEO TOLSTOY, RUSSIAN

The special Tolstoyan drama is emotional, the intimate relationships of men and women, and of all fictional love affairs Anna Karenina's is the most passionately dramatized.

At the Petersburg railway station in Moscow, Anna, the elegant wife of a top government official, encounters Count Vronsky, a good-natured, handsome young nobleman dutifully waiting to greet his mother. Four years later, still in love – and loved in return – their affair will end in disaster. The story's trajectory is clear and strong, uncomplicated by traditional plot devices of twists and turns and sudden reversals. What Tolstoy magnificently gives the reader instead are emotional dilemmas and conflicting passions – the shock and power and mystery of the human mind and heart.

Tolstoy's skill works outwards too. He imbues individual experiences with a powerful glow: great set pieces – births, marriage proposals, arguments, forbidden meetings – are ordinary but somehow vast. Even minor characters, vividly individual, bring to life the overlapping social scenes of Moscow, St Petersburg and rural Russia.

Centre-stage, Anna and Vronsky's affair – set among opera-going high society – is entwined with the ongoing attempts of the idealistic but confused landowner Levin to win Kitty, Anna's younger sister-in-law. This drama of the countryside, allows Tolstoy to engage with the major issues of the day: agriculture and social reform. The contrast is expertly handled, aristocratic balls following harvest-gathering following political meetings. Always, Tolstoy sees the small, piercing details that shed sudden light on the whole – the great panorama of Russian life in a smile, a glance or an aching memory.

> *'I listen to you and think about him. I love him, I am his mistress, I cannot stand you, I'm afraid of you, I hate you … Do what you like with me.'*

 Recommended translation
2000, Richard Pevear and Larissa Volokhonsky, Penguin Classics

 Where to go next
The Kreutzer Sonata and Other Stories, Leo Tolstoy
Tolstoy was no less effective at short works than at long. "The Kreutzer Sonata" (1889), a viciously puritanical response to adultery, and "The Death of Ivan Illyich" (1886), a profound meditation on death, are two of his best.

 Screen adaptation
Anna Karenina, 1935, dir. Clarence Brown
Many have tried and nearly all have failed. This vehicle for Greta Garbo is the honourable exception, achieving genuine pathos through her fragile beauty. Basil Rathbone makes a perfectly loathsome Karenin, Fredric March a rather less convincing Vronsky. Director Brown shoehorns the action into ninety-five minutes by all but omitting Levin and Kitty's side of the story.

First Love

1860, IVAN TURGENEV, RUSSIAN

Turgenev is one of the best writers about love. There is no one so varied, incisive or sympathetic. Intense and swift-moving, *First Love* is the classic account of falling in love for the first time: a brief, lyrical evocation of a summer romance with a shocking twist at the end.

The events recalled by the middle-aged narrator, Vladimir Petrovich, take place in the countryside, where he spent a holiday with his parents when he was sixteen. The only child of a mismatched couple, he is used to playing on his own. But one evening he is captivated by the sight of a girl next door laughingly mocking a group of obviously infatuated young men. Her name is Zinaida – a tall, slender

IVAN TURGENEV
First Love

girl with a "clever" face and knowing grey eyes: twenty-one years old and a coquette.

From the moment Vladimir first sees her, he is flung into a confusion of new emotions, sometimes ecstatic, sometimes humiliating, sometimes simply inexplicable. Does Zinaida like him, or is she only using him in her games with her other admirers? She is all contradiction, "a peculiarly fascinating mixture of cunning and insouciance, artifice and simplicity, gentleness and gaiety". And Vladimir is caught, "like a beetle tied by the leg".

> My heart leaped within me. I felt very ashamed and unusually gay. I was extraordinarily excited.

The pace of the story is electric, the mood shifting wildly, then deepening. Suddenly Zinaida is no longer the smiling coquette, she is distraught – and Vladimir realizes that she too has fallen in love. But with whom? The answer, when he discovers it, will overturn everything he has learned about love, and childish adoration will be left behind as he witnesses the violent intensity of adult passion.

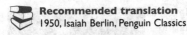

Recommended translation
1950, Isaiah Berlin, Penguin Classics

Where to go next
The Lady with the Little Dog and Other Stories, Anton Chekhov
A great collection of Chekhov's masterly late stories, this volume includes four clear masterpieces: "Peasants", "In the Ravine", "The Bishop" and the title story, in which a casual adulterous affair completely changes the people involved.

Families

2

For novelists of all cultures, and all periods, family life has provided a continuously rich source of stories. Here are the elemental relationships between parents and children, the slowly unfolding dramas of dynastic sagas, the suffering of families in adversity – their comic quirks, furies, frivolities and enduring loyalties. In writing about family life, writers have often drawn on their own experiences, producing their most deeply felt and vividly detailed book. D.H. Lawrence's *Sons and Lovers* is an extraordinary account of a mother-son relationship and also an unforgettable evocation of family life in the mining communities of the English Midlands. Other novelists, like the Colombian Gabriel García Márquez or the Irish Maria Edgeworth, have made a single family stand for the history of a whole culture.

Family relationships between the generations can be particularly intense, but they are notably varied too, from the knockdown, drag-out fights in James Baldwin's *Go Tell It on the Mountain* to the almost imperceptible currents of shifting feelings in Virginia Woolf's *To the Lighthouse*. Families themselves are just as varied: here, among others, is a genteel family from eighteenth-century England (*The Vicar of Wakefield*), a slave family from post-Civil War America (*Beloved*) and a family of dissidents from apartheid South Africa (*Burger's Daughter*), not to mention several spectacularly malfunctioning families from Tsarist Russia. The stress is not always on misery, however. Márquez's exuberant Buendías, Bruno Schulz's tenderly evoked Polish family or Louisa May Alcott's quietly virtuous March clan all show the varied joys and energies of family life in classic fiction.

Little Women

1868, LOUISA MAY ALCOTT, AMERICAN

Penguin

No longer admired as a practical guide to home economy or moral primer for girls, *Little Women* retains a compulsive power as a simple tale of domestic life, as genteel but impoverished Mrs March ("Marmee") and her four daughters, Meg, Jo, Beth and Amy, struggle to make ends meet and keep cheerful while Mr March is serving as an army chaplain during the American Civil War. How will they manage Christmas with no presents or dinner? How will they overcome their jealousy of others, their pride, their longing to live a more comfortable life? The answer, Alcott radically insists, is by being good.

There are few narratives plainer or more unaffected, its tragedies and anecdotal comedies are the stuff of common experience. Trivial adventures – skating on a pond or burning the dinner – are presented with absolute clarity; trials and triumphs, such as Jo's efforts to control her temper or Amy's to overcome her vanity, are recognizably our own; and the big dramas, such as Beth's scarlet fever, are frankly emotional. The "little women" of the first part of the novel grow into the "good wives" of the second part, building their outer lives, like Defoe's Crusoe, out of the near-to-hand

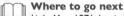

'I do think that families are the most beautiful things in all the world!' burst out Jo, who was in an unusually uplifted frame of mind, just then.

(re-darned socks, borrowed books), and their inner lives, under Marmee's influence, out of imperfect but movingly determined attempts to practise the virtues of friendship, self-sacrifice, generosity and trust.

Where to go next
Little Men, 1871, Louisa May Alcott
The next book in the series is set in the school which Jo now runs with her husband Professor Bhaer, told from the point of view of one of its pupils, Nat Blake.

Screen adaptation
Little Women, 1994, dir. Gillian Armstrong
The two "classic" Hollywood versions, of 1933 and 1949, both have their strengths, but this is the least winsome adaptation and closest in spirit to the novel. Winona Ryder makes a convincing Jo (although she's too pretty), but this is essentially an ensemble effort, effectively conveying not just a sense of family but also of the wider Massachusetts community.

Go Tell It on the Mountain

1954, JAMES BALDWIN, AMERICAN

Baldwin's furious first novel is a clashing drama of conflicts – between God and the Devil, man and woman, white and black, and father and son – and the pain is autobiographical. As Baldwin himself said: "I had to deal with what hurt me most. I had to deal with my father."

The novel's great central scene is the "tarry service" at the Temple of the Fire Baptised in Harlem, where a group of characters gather together to testify to the power of the Lord, giving ecstatic witness and speaking in tongues. But, as they pray, each of them is tormented by memories of their earlier lives: the unbending preacher Gabriel by the sins of his youth; his sister Florence by the bitter disappointments of her marriage; and Gabriel's wife Elizabeth by her lost first love. Only Elizabeth's bastard son, John, looks forward – and he is confused and uncertain in everything except his hatred of his stepfather.

Men spoke of how the heart broke up, but never spoke of how the soul hung speechless in the pause, the void, the terror between the living and the dead.

It is no casual matter that Baldwin took his title from a gospel song. Like a Negro spiritual, enlarged and complicated, but true to the essence of suffering, the novel gives voice to the conflicts of characters whose whole lives are battlegrounds: black people struggling against racism in white America, imperfect people agonizingly aware of "Sin", and, above all, ordinary, passionate people who pit their wills against each other, sometimes to death. It is a novel everywhere animated by the Word, in the thumping Old Testament style, and especially – a marvellous achievement – in the rippling, cascading arguments of the characters, vibrantly rough and true.

Where to go next
Giovanni's Room, 1956, James Baldwin
In his second novel, Baldwin explored another autobiographical theme: homosexuality. Set in Paris, where Baldwin was then living, his story focuses on a man torn between homosexual love and his love for a woman.

Manservant and Maidservant

1947, Ivy Compton-Burnett, English

By imagining what it would be like if everyone spoke plainly – acidly – what is in their hearts, Ivy Compton-Burnett created an utterly original fictional form. Twenty viciously funny novels resulted, each constructed almost entirely of unadorned dialogue. No wonder one of her characters can say, in response to a letter, "Thank you. It has broken my heart, but that is the natural result of the use of words."

NYRB Classics

Set in 1892, *Manservant and Maidservant* presents three overlapping stories: Horace Lamb's tyranny over his five children; his wife's plans to elope with her poor relation, Mortimer; and the servants' attempts to maintain decorum downstairs. The plot incorporates the usual devices of Victorian fiction (a wife's fortune misused, a letter mislaid), its jerky artificiality heightened by the strictly codified behaviour governing relations between father and child, master and servant, butler and serving boy.

'I wonder who began this treating of people as fellow creatures,' said Charlotte. 'It is never a success.'

But the novel's electrifying weirdness comes from the contrast this forms with the decided, frequently bizarre and sometimes murderous, opinions expressed so sharply by all the characters – like skewed captions applied to a silent film. The children's tutor says it would be a relief to meet someone with no self-respect; a fat serving girl longs out loud for a "serious illness" to transform her. From such intensely personal and bleakly comic juxtapositions the novel's essential tragedy proceeds.

> **Where to go next**
> *A House and its Head*, 1935, Ivy Compton-Burnett
> A masterpiece of sharp analysis, examining the tensions between the members
> of another classic Compton-Burnett family, the Edgworths.

The Brothers Karamazov

1880, FYODOR DOSTOEVSKY, RUSSIAN

Dostoevsky's last novel is not for the faint-hearted. Tangled murder mystery, delirious fantasy, hilarious panorama of Russian life and coruscating drama of sin and redemption, it is a big, passionate novel which fights the reader every inch of the way.

The three Karamazov brothers are: Aloysha, "devout and humble"; Ivan, the revolutionary nihilist; and Mitya, the noble but corrupted representative of "natural Russia" – who stands accused of murdering his father. As in many crime novels, both the murder and the mystery surrounding it are violent and ambiguous, but Dostoevsky's

'The world rests upon preposterous things, and indeed it's possible that without them absolutely nothing would ever have come into existence. We know that which we know!'

handling of his material is utterly unlike other novels in the genre. Clues and false trails abound, but they lead not to the neatly satisfying disclosure of facts, but to the greater ambiguities and violence of Russian life in general.

The story is complicated, but the novel is driven less by its plot than its characters, each living an intense, combative inner life, passionately inspired by ideals, all too often sabotaged by despair. Failing to lift themselves, they sink. Sinking, they give way to hysterical outbursts, their competing life stories filling the novel with extraordinary, often lurid, colour. More importantly for the novel's overarching ambition, they combine to form a picture of Russia at the end of the nineteenth century. Around the common Russian theme of generational conflict Dostoevsky produces a tempestuous state-of-the-nation drama which captures the furious arguments between Europhiles and Slavophiles. There are long (admittedly sometimes wearying) sections devoted to theological debate, and minute analysis of the state of the Russian soul. But the novel is filled with tremendous energy, and there are many comic passages, not least a wonderful appearance by a dandified, if slightly threadbare, philosophizing Devil.

Recommended translation
1993, David McDuff, Penguin Classics

Where to go next
The Idiot, 1868, Fyodor Dostoevsky
The idiot in question is the epileptic Prince Myshkin, whose goodness and purity is used by Dostoevsky to mirror the darkness of Russian society, as personified by the prince's friend and then rival, Rogozhin.

Castle Rackrent

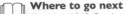

1800, MARIA EDGEWORTH, IRISH

Imagine an old man in an Irish bar. At first, his accent makes him a little hard to follow, but you soon get used to it, and in fact his way of telling a story – his turn of phrase, sly humour and odd digressions – contribute immeasurably to its power and interest. In just this way, Maria Edgeworth's tale of the Rackrents, an old Irish landowning family on the wane, gains from the remarkable speaking voice of its teller, "Honest Thady", their faithful steward. Honest Thady has seen successive generations of Rackrents squan-

MARIA EDGEWORTH
Castle Rackrent and Ennui

Penguin

der their inheritance, from the old days of the heroically dissipated Sir Patrick to the recent follies of the amiably hopeless Sir Condy. His apparently meandering account of their exploits, by turns comic and desolate, sympathetic and heartless, anatomizes their characters with brilliant exactitude.

Subtitled "An Hibernian tale, taken from facts and from the manner of the Irish squires before the year 1782", the novel is an unusually exact evocation of Ireland and the Irish way of life, from breakfast manners to agricultural customs.

> *Quickness, simplicity, cunning, carelessness, dissipation, disinterestedness, shrewdness and blunder.*

Critics have called it the first regional novel in English, and Walter Scott, one of Edgeworth's earliest admirers, immediately saw it as the route to the historical novel. The wealth of detail sets it absolutely in a specific time and place, and gives it a richness not always found in novels four or five times its length.

Where to go next
The Absentee, 1812, Maria Edgeworth
Written mainly in dialogue, Edgeworth's swift and lively story examines Lord Clonbrony's absentee life in fashionable London and the appalling effect it has on his Irish estates.

The Sound and the Fury

1929, WILLIAM FAULKNER, AMERICAN

There's no getting away from it: *The Sound and the Fury* is a "difficult" book. The fairly straightforward story – the tragic collapse of an old Southern family – must be teased out of bewilderingly disarranged snippets of action, which take place more often than not in the minds of different characters, including the mentally disabled Benjy, the "idiot" implied by the novel's title (taken from Shakespeare's *Macbeth*), whose tale is full of "sound and fury". But don't be put off. The rewards of the novel are far, far greater than its demands.

Each of the novel's four sections focuses on one of the characters: Benjy, as he endures his thirty-third birthday, looked after by his Negro servant Luster; Quentin, his eldest brother, as he suffers a mental crisis at Harvard; Jason, the last of the brothers, bossing his hysteric mother in the family home; and Dilsey, the oldest Negro servant,

Ben wailed again, hopeless and prolonged. It was nothing. Just sound. It might have been all time and injustice and sorrow become vocal for an instant by a conjunction of planets.

leaving the fractious house one Sunday to go to church. The central character of the novel, however, is none of these, but Caddy, the boys' sister, whose generous spirit and tragic misadventures preoccupy each of them in different ways.

Though the overall picture is obscure, the details are marvellously sharp. The dialogue in particular, often inarticulate and broken up, is real and fierce: the novel is full of raised voices: bickering children, arguing parents, plaintive Negroes and the wordless angst of Benjy. The big themes of the book – lovelessness, loss, redemption – arise from precisely clear images: Caddy on a swing with a boy or Uncle Maury's black eye. *The Sound and the Fury* is, in fact, a powerfully realistic novel, from which the usual element of explanation has been carefully removed to produce something very like life as it is experienced.

Where to go next
As I Lay Dying, 1935, William Faulkner
Employing an ambitious stream-of-consciousness technique, Faulkner tells the story of Addie Bundren's life and death through the varied voices of her surviving family as they cart her coffin to Jefferson to be buried.

The Vicar of Wakefield

1766, OLIVER GOLDSMITH, IRISH

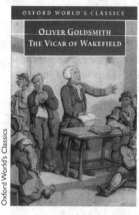

At the beginning of this, his only novel, Goldsmith placed an advertisement politely warning off potential readers. Announcing his hero to be an honest, harmless and simple person, he asked, "In this age of opulence and refinement whom can such a character please?"

In fact, the vogue for "sentimental" novels (tear-jerking tales of the suffering of the virtuous), made it a smash hit throughout Europe – Goethe's *The Sorrows of Young Werther* (see p.25) is only one of many later novels indebted to it. Opportunities for tears are certainly plentiful. Goldsmith's mild-mannered vicar's sufferings pile up like Job's: his eldest daughter is seduced and tormented to death, his younger daughter abducted, his son arrested for attempted murder, his house burned down and he himself flung into prison for non-payment of debts. Yet throughout it all, he remains secure in his sense of the inviolability of family, insisting, with beatific stoicism, that he "would not for a thousand worlds exchange situations".

I was ever of opinion, that the honest man who married and brought up a large family, did more service than he who continued single, and only talked of population.

Frankly, this is a little weird. And what, the reader may ask, are these interpolated essay-like sections in praise of the British monarchy or English liberty, which periodically interrupt the narrative? Be wary, however, in taking the novel at face value as a self-satisfied celebration of the English domestic virtues of temperance and equanimity. Its tone is marvellously ambiguous, and it is well to remember that Goldsmith himself was Irish, and saw Englishness from the outside. His tongue is often in his cheek, and his humour is a peculiar but infectious mix of ridicule and good-naturedness. The henpecked vicar with his love of trivialities and ineffective homilies is both infuriating and endearing: a precisely detailed but cheekily unstable portrait of the Englishman at home.

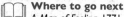 **Where to go next**
A Man of Feeling, 1771, Henry Mackenzie
Another celebrated novel of sentiment that raises the question of whether it is possible to be good in a bad world. The man of feeling is Harley, a person whose inability to flatter and deceive gets him into trouble.

Burger's Daughter

1979, NADINE GORDIMER, SOUTH AFRICAN

Nadine Gordimer belongs to that group of specially creative "political" novelists (with Turgenev and E.L. Doctorow) who devise absorbing human situations to dramatize the spirit of their times. *Burger's Daughter*, a highly detailed record of anti-apartheid politics in South Africa during the 1970s, is also a highly charged account of a thoughtful young woman, more vulnerable than she thinks, coming to terms with herself. Her

To become free is to become almost a stranger to oneself.

father, Lionel, is a heroic white radical who has just died in prison. But his death leaves her to make the painful attempt to fit the personal to the political, to discover her own meanings of commitment, betrayal and freedom.

Avoiding big set pieces (no mass rallies or police baton charges here), the novel is alive with the small domesticated details of politics – chattering arguments about Marx and Mandela at dinner parties, clandestine gatherings in front rooms, prison visits – all filtered through Rosa's consciousness, interwoven with her sudden insights, private musings, childhood memories, adult desires. In Pretoria she avoids her father's activist friends. In Nice she begins an affair with a married man. In London she unexpectedly encounters her black childhood companion, "Baasie", after years apart. Everywhere she seeks to both affirm her father and escape him.

Sometimes sharply poetic, often raggedly sensual, always true to the rhythms of ordinary thought, *Burger's Daughter* is an intensely personal history of South African politics – both close-up and oblique – and a wonderfully acute portrait of a young woman in crisis.

Where to go next
The Conservationist, 1974, Nadine Gordimer
Winner of the Booker Prize, Gordimer's first great novel is the tale of Mehring, a rich and complacent white South African landowner, whose insensitivity so alienates the people close to him that he finishes up losing everything.

Sons and Lovers

1913, D.H. LAWRENCE, ENGLISH

In later novels Lawrence can be preachy, even mystical, but his earlier novels and stories, especially those set in the Midlands mining villages where he grew up, are vibrantly down-to-earth. *Sons and Lovers*, in particular, has the rich, careless detail of personal experience, the whole culture of colliery life known and felt – not just the miners in their sweat-heavy flannel singlets traipsing home in the evening, but their wives too, baking every Friday night and struggling to manage the household budget,

'I shall never meet the right women while you live,' he said. She was very quiet. Now she began to feel again tired, as if she were done. 'We'll see, my son,' she answered.

and the children playing cobblers in the ash-pit alley behind the kitchens.

OXFORD WORLD'S CLASSICS

D. H. LAWRENCE
SONS AND LOVERS

Oxford World's Classics

Lawrence's special expertise, however, is the drama of relationships. Disappointed in her marriage to a crude and feckless miner, Mrs Morel transfers her love and ambitions onto her son Paul, a sensitive boy with artistic inclinations. As an adult, Paul struggles to find love with two women, the possessive Miriam, who shares his interest in the arts, and the sensual Clara Dawes, recently separated from her husband. Their tangled, heated emotional explorations of each other is at the centre of the novel.

Sex is here in a variety of forms – the choked clandestine meetings with Miriam, a liberating erotic scene with Clara, and the mother's sexualized adoration of her son – but it never monopolizes the narrative. There are other arenas of emotional intensity, arguments for instance, superbly naturalistic, especially those between an icy Mrs Morel and her raging, bewildered husband. As always, Lawrence is making a point, but the best scenes are strong and true, lit up with incidental detail – the miners' mouths showing red in their black faces as they speak, a shivering Yorkshire terrier looking "like a wet rag that would never dry", or Paul lapsing unselfconsciously into his father's dialect after sex with Clara. Free-flowing, if occasionally slack (especially in the middle section), the story accelerates powerfully towards the end.

Where to go next
Women in Love, 1921, D.H. Lawrence
Lawrence's favourite novel of his own, which dramatizes the love affairs and clashing opinions of two sisters in a Midlands colliery town, says everything he had to say about passion and belief.

Screen adaptation
Sons and Lovers, 1960, dir. Jack Cardiff
The teaming of Jack Cardiff and Freddie Francis (two of the UK's greatest cinematographers) results in a visual feast of black-and-white photography. But the whole film never quite coheres – despite the rock-solid performances from Trevor Howard and Wendy Hiller as Mr and Mrs Morel – and it remains, in the final analysis, an honourable failure.

One Hundred Years of Solitude

1967, GABRIEL GARCÍA MÁRQUEZ, COLOMBIAN

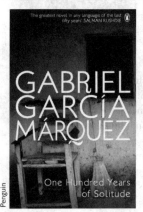

To call it a soap opera would be to underestimate its startling originality, to call it a family saga underplays its springy, incident-packed momentum. It is more like the Creation myth of a family in which everything – including the world at large – is marvellously new. Famous as the first best-selling example of Magic Realism – a literary style that combines realism with surreal imaginative flights – Márquez has always claimed that he was simply telling stories the way his grandmother did.

The novel documents the lives of six generations of the remarkable Buendías in the remote swamp-bound town of Macondo, at a time when "the world was so recent that many things lacked names and in order to indicate them it was necessary to point".

The men, almost always called José Arcadio or Aureliano, are given to soldiering or invention, both largely useless. The women are strong, implacable, loving and vengeful. Focusing on the highly charged relations between them, *One Hundred Years of Solitude* is a hugely entertaining and emotive novel about the corruption of power, the wizardries of love and the desolation of despair.

The first José Arcadio Buendía, a literal-minded man who believes implicitly in the magic of the world, sets the tone of wonderment. After that, the domestic is always fantastic and family members are wilful to the point of other-worldliness (such as Remedios the Beauty who possesses the powers of death and ascends to heaven one day while hanging out the washing). Against a

> *Many years later, as he faced the firing squad, Colonel Aureliano Buendía was to remember that distant afternoon when his father took him to discover ice.*

background of South American revolutions, gringo exploitation and terrible weather, they pursue their quixotic obsessions with style and energy. The novel contains scenes of tender love, bitter feuds and an appalling massacre. And the bursting joy and crushing horror of the last pages are as powerful as anything in literature.

 Recommended translation
1970, Gregory Rabassa, Penguin (UK), Harper (US)

Where to go next
Love in the Time of Cholera, 1985, Gabriel García Márquez
Florentino Ariza falls for the teenage Fermina Daza but his courting is unsuccessful and she marries an older man. This story of devoted, obsessive love is a triumph of a more conventionally realistic style – and Márquez's second masterpiece.

Beloved

1987, TONI MORRISON, AMERICAN

Some stories require new ways of telling, and, in *Beloved*, Toni Morrison found a form in which to shape the catastrophic story of Negro slavery: a broken-up, lyrical narrative of great intensity and pain with an unshakeable core of love.

Magic Realism

Originally used to describe German art between the wars, Magic Realism has more recently been applied to fiction in which the fantastic or miraculous is presented naturalistically as part of ordinary life. Magic Realism has been a prominent and hugely popular feature of twentieth-century Latin American fiction, especially in the works of the Argentine Jorge Luis Borges (1899–1986), the Cuban Alejo Carpentier (1904–1980) and the Colombian Gabriel García Márquez (b. 1928). Such a style, in which the impossible is commonplace, captured the political unreality of certain South American regimes in a shocking but highly entertaining way. The same might be said for the works of some East European writers of the Cold War period, such as the Czech Milan Kundera (b. 1929). More generally, Magic Realism has been a part of "postmodern" attempts to make sense of rapid, often bewildering changes in European culture since the end of World War II. Günter Grass's *The Tin Drum* (1959), Italo Calvino's *Our Ancestors* trilogy (1951–59), Salman Rushdie's *Midnight's Children* (1981) and Angela Carter's *Nights at the Circus* (1984) – all exuberantly inventive fictions which infuse recognizable reality with elements of folk myth and fairy tales – are outstanding examples of the style.

In the days after the Civil War, the runaway slave Sethe and her daughter Denver live in the free state of Ohio in a haunted house. Sethe's mother-in-law, Baby Suggs, died embittered in bed upstairs, and Howard and Buglar, Sethe's young sons, ran away in terror of their mother, but the ghost is of Sethe's daughter Beloved, brutally killed in the woodshed. Balancing these absences are two new presences: Paul D, who slaved with Sethe years earlier, and an odd, intuitive vagrant girl, who eerily calls herself "Beloved". Their unexpected arrivals prompt the story of Sethe's past, a slave woman brutalized to hardness who loves her children so tenderly she would do anything to them rather than allow them to fall into the hands of the slavers.

The story is unapologetically painful: all the suffering of the slaves is here made horrifyingly intimate in the personal stories of Baby Suggs, used like an animal for breeding, or Paul D imprisoned with an iron bit in his mouth, or Sixo put down like a dog after a failed escape. But a story which could have been only about inhumanity also evokes the beauty of human nature. *Beloved* is, among other things, an intensely felt celebration of a woman's experience,

Freeing yourself was one thing; claiming ownership of that freed self was another.

the rhythms of her body, her needs, her vulnerability and toughness, and the absorbing struggles of the mother-daughter relationship. Though Morrison reveals the unredeemable loss of normality imposed by slavery, she also shows the essential, deep togetherness won by slaves against stupendous odds.

 Where to go next
Jazz, 1992, Toni Morrison
Set against the pulsating backdrop of 1920s Harlem, *Jazz* tells the violent tale of Joe Trace and the women who love him in a jazz-inspired poetic prose.

Screen adaptation
Beloved, 1998, dir. Jonathan Demme
On one level *Beloved* is a ghost story showing how the institutionalized cruelties of slavery reverberate through time. Director Demme remains true to the novel's complex plotting and its violence, and the result is a harrowing – occasionally confusing – experience lasting nearly three hours, but definitely worth the effort.

A Personal Matter

1964, KENZABURŌ ŌE, JAPANESE

Compared to the delicate surface and inscrutable suggestiveness of much Japanese fiction, this raw, unflinching study of trauma comes as a rude shock. "Bird" is the most awkward and maladjusted of fictional heroes. Although his wife is about to give birth to their first

"Very close to a perfect contemporary novel." —The New York Times

Kenzaburō Ōe

A Personal Matter

Translated from the Japanese by John Nathan

Winner of the 1994 Nobel Prize for Literature

Grove Press

child, he can't imagine settling down. Ill at ease with himself, he clings to his adolescent dreams of running away to Africa. When he receives the shocking news that his son has been born brain-damaged, he is totally disorientated, and takes flight in a series of desperate escapist adventures in an alternative Japan of dropouts and activists, gay bars and backstreet abortionists, trying, paradoxically, to discover the truth about himself.

Fittingly for a novel about clashing painful realities, Ōe's style is spikily over-vivid, lurid adjectives and metaphors creating a sentence-by-sentence assault on the senses. Partly, the stress is on the physicality of misery: the novel contains one of the most appalling hangover scenes

He lifted the receiver and a man's voice asked his name without a word of greeting and said, 'Please come to the hospital right away. The baby is abnormal; the doctor will explain.'

in fiction, and a string of graphically described sordid sex scenes. But the book's greatest force lies in its dramatization of the emotional squalor into which Bird descends: the confusion of his shame, the perversity of his self-deception, the pain of his abandonment. Near the beginning of the book, Bird's old girlfriend, Himiko, outlines her theory of parallel universes, to comfort him with the thought that in one of them his son is still alive. Bird's task is to realize that the universe she means is this one.

Recommended translation
1969, John Nathan, Grove Press

Where to go next
A Silent Cry, 1967, Kenzaburō Ōe

The 1994 Nobel Committee singled out this story of two brothers who
return to the village of their childhood to sell the family home for its troubled
but deep understanding of the human predicament.

The Radetzky March

1932, JOSEPH ROTH, AUSTRIAN

With Kafka, Broch, Mann and Musil, Roth is one of the great
German-language writers of the early to mid-twentieth century, a
famous journalist of dash and penetration, and the author of more
than a dozen magically brisk but sensuous novels, of which the best
is *The Radetzky March*, the tale of three generations of the Trotta family in the last days of the Austro-Hungarian Empire.

After saving the life of the young Emperor Franz Joseph at the
Battle of Solferino, the Slovene peasant Joseph Trotta is abruptly ennobled as Baron Trotta of
Sipolje, an act which causes lasting confusion for him and his
descendants. Disillusioned with
the military, he decrees that his
son, Franz, will enter the civil service. In turn, Franz decrees that his
son, Carl Joseph, will return to the military, as befits the grandson of
the "hero of Solferino". Each plays a role circumscribed by history
and each is devastated by personal disappointment.

> 'The Fatherland no longer
> exists.' 'I'm afraid I don't
> understand!' said Herr von
> Trotta. 'I thought you mightn't
> understand,' said Chojnicki.
> 'The fact is we're all dead!'

It takes a writer with a light touch and scrupulously unsentimental
tone like Roth to bring out such a story's full drama, and to link it,
in quietly unobtrusive ways, to the impending catastrophe of the
Empire. His novel is an elegy not just of the Hapsburgs, but of a
vanishing code of conduct at once civilized, antiquated, tolerant and
ridiculous. The mesmerizing descriptions of the small details of the
Trottas' lives – the clothes they wear, the food they eat – all seem like

preparations for the impending disaster. The big, dramatic scenes – and there are plenty, including a horribly meaningless duel and a hilariously awful regimental party – are all sadly disjointed. The book ends during the war which would break up Central Europe, and make possible new states like Nazi Germany, from which, a few years after writing this book, Roth would be driven into exile to die.

Recommended translation
2002, Michael Hofmann, Granta Books

Where to go next
The Legend of the Holy Drinker, 1939, Joseph Roth
Set among the destitute of Paris, *The Legend of the Holy Drinker* is a jaunty, unsentimental novella about terminal alcoholism – a condition from which Roth himself was to die.

American Pastoral

1997, PHILIP ROTH, AMERICAN

Vintage

American Pastoral is America's "Paradise Lost" for the end of the twentieth century. What does it mean to be blessed and then cursed? How does the perfect family destroy itself? How did the hard-working, over-achieving 1950s turn into the crime-ridden, drug-fuelled 1990s? A howl of rage, a cry of pain, Roth's late masterpiece is a sinew-straining attempt to solve the terrible puzzle of failure.

College sports star Seymour Levov – known within his Jewish community as the "Swede" on account of his Nordic good looks – had the perfect life. Having married Miss New Jersey 1949 and inherited his father's successful glove-making business, he settled with his wife and beloved daughter Merry in a dream home in the country. Modest, dutiful, decent, he deserved it all. But twenty years later, despite apparently never putting a foot wrong, his family is destroyed. How? Roth's alter ego, novelist Nathan Zuckerman, who hero-worshipped the Swede at high school, determines to find out.

For an American tragedy, an American voice – muscular and articulate and button-holing. The novel's free-wheeling narrative, taking in

> He was a very nice, simple, stoical guy. Not a humorous guy. Not a passionate guy. Just a sweetheart whose fate it was to get himself fucked-over by some real crazies.

the booming post-war years, Vietnam and the student riots, and the affluent but fractured 1990s, is grounded in hard-edged specifics – the techniques of traditional glove-making, the daily routines of the American middle classes and the dogma of activists' arguments in the late 1960s. But what begins in clarity ends in confusion; the narrative, driven at first by curiosity, is consumed finally by rage as Nathan struggles to understand how ignorance comes out of knowledge, violence out of tranquillity, and evil out of goodness, in the terrible conflagration of the American dream.

 **Where to go next**
Sabbath's Theater, 1995, Philip Roth
Roth's other great masterpiece of his late years is a scabrous, sexually fixated *tour de force*, featuring the lecherous, self-indulgent puppeteer Mickey Sabbath and his rages against the dying of the light.

The Golovlevs

1875–80, M.E. SALTYKOV-SHCHEDRIN, RUSSIAN

According to one critic, *The Golovlevs* is "the gloomiest novel in Russian literature". We may be forgiven for thinking this an understatement, for no other novel presents so compelling and devastating a picture of family misery. The Golovlev estate is remote and isolated in that special Russian sort of isolation – a vastness of mud-soaked fields and frozen copses of birch trees. There, three generations of the family destroy themselves with feuds and treachery. They have no joys, no consolations. Their spiteful victories rebound with terrifying consequences, and their fates are violent and comfortless. In each generation the same weaknesses and obsessions appear in a merciless cycle, and deaths by drink are varied only with deaths by suicide and self-destruction arising out of sheer despair.

Adversity or vice will suddenly, like an infestation of lice, seize on a family and consume it. It spreads through the whole organism, worms itself to the very core, and goes on gnawing away generation after generation.

Though grim, the novel is never tedious. The setting is brilliantly observed, the psychological details are always acute, and the great set-piece scenes of family arguments are brought to life with sharply nuanced dialogue. It is a mark of Saltykov's genius that the unvarying lives of his characters exert an unflagging fascination. Two of them, in particular, are imaginative creations of enduring power. Arina Petrovna is a classic example of the tyrannical matriarch, in her prime harsh to the point of malice, and in her dotage hollow and alone. Her son Porfiry – "Judas" or "the Bloodsucker" – is a different but no less deadly type, a hypocritical humbug spouting pieties while scheming his way to his inheritance. He drives one of his sons to suicide, one to crime, and sends a third to a foundling hospital, commenting with chilling insouciance that the child is nothing to do with him. His endless prattling is no harmless quirk: his peasants say that it can "fester the soul". In the end, it is his own soul he festers.

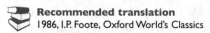 **Recommended translation**
1986, I.P. Foote, Oxford World's Classics

📖 **Where to go next**
Lady Macbeth of Mtsensk and Other Stories, Nikolai Leskov
Writing in the mid-nineteenth century, Leskov was a marvellous writer of pungent tales of ordinary Russians. His masterpiece is "Lady Macbeth", a powerful and ironic study of sexual obsession and murder.

The Street of Crocodiles

1934, BRUNO SCHULZ, POLISH

On 19 November 1942, in the streets of Drohobycz in Poland, a Gestapo officer shot dead a local art teacher, who was carrying home a loaf of bread. That art teacher was Bruno Schulz, a lonely, perhaps difficult, man, who left behind two impassioned, freakish books about his family: *The Street of Crocodiles* and *Sanatorium Under the Sign of the Hourglass*.

Penguin

The Street of Crocodiles is divided into thirteen separate stories, all featuring the same family eccentrics, and animated by the same charged atmosphere, a heightened, almost delirious, sensitivity. Like no other book, it captures the intense emotional strangeness of family life.

Though eccentric, even grotesque, Schulz's characters are never improbable. If they seem larger than life, it is because they are lit up by the adventures of the own personalities. Like Chagall, Schulz can pin down a character with a few lyrical touches (Touya, the halfwit girl living on the dump whose face "works like the bellows of an accordion") or elaborate them in a sequence of surreal situations. He treats the city, the weather and objects in the same intense way. The days are loose: waves of passion gust through them. Like the rhythmical seasons (it seems always either very cold or very hot), the emotional pressure of the characters fluctuates wildly, as they are suddenly filled with furious energy and dwindle again to lethargy. At the heart of the book is the Father, "that fencing master of the imagination", whose obsessions and, eventually, lunacy, form the central bizarre domestic tragicomedy. One moment pontificating on the Demiurge and the next silenced into childish fear by the sight of the stockinged foot of Adela, the blue-eyed servant girl, he is at once the saviour and destroyer of family life.

In July my father went to take the waters and left me, with my mother and elder brother, a prey to the blinding white heat of the summer days.

 Recommended translation
1963, Celina Wieniewska, Penguin Books

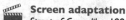 **Where to go next**
Sanatorium Under the Sign of the Hourglass, 1937, Bruno Schulz
More surreal and fantastical stories recalling the author's own family life in Drohobycz. Words are beautifully complemented by Schulz's vivid and quirky drawings.

Screen adaptation
Street of Crocodiles, 1986, dir. Timothy and Stephen Quay
This twenty-minute film is a very free and highly imaginative response to Schulz's book. Employing sinister puppets and stop-frame animation, the directors conjure up a strange nether world of mysterious machinery, nightmare encounters and a pervading mood of sexual tension.

The Makioka Sisters

1943–48, JUN'ICHIRŌ TANIZAKI, JAPANESE

In some ways, Tanizaki seems the most Western of the great modern Japanese writers, his novels are psychologically acute and imaginatively daring, jumping back to the exotic past of the ninth century or exploring contemporary sexual perversity. But he was also deeply interested in traditional Japanese culture, and *The Makioka Sisters* is his elaborate and moving recreation of a vanished world.

It is a world of formal poise and circumscribing social customs already outdated by the 1930s. The Makiokas, a distinguished mercantile family of old Osaka, have been in decline for some time, and now they must face the tortuous difficulties of arranging marriages for the two younger sisters, first Yukiko, then Taeko. Taeko, a natural rebel, impatiently waits for the older Yukiko to accept an offer. Yukiko, withdrawn yet stubborn, delays.

Not lacking in big effects, which include a nail-bitingly tense, documentary-style account of the Tokyo flood and an unblinking description of death by gangrene, the novel is more impressive still as a record of family life in the Imperial period. Hundreds of domestic incidents are chronicled with complete assurance: a visit to see the flowering cherries in Kyoto, a house

> The fact was that Yukiko could never really be at home in the modern world... He had therefore come to believe that a match would make neither of them happy.

move, a bout of jaundice, a dance recital, a miscarriage – and, most important of all, a series of *miai* (chaperoned meetings between prospective brides and grooms) reluctantly undertaken by Yukiko and described by Tanizaki in minute – and excruciating – detail. Tanizaki is, in fact, one of the great male writers about women, subtle and unafraid. His closely observed details accumulate without sentimentality to express the larger meanings of the Makioka sisters' lives, their dilemmas, humiliations and endurance.

 Recommended translation
1957, Edward G. Seidensticker, Vintage

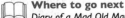 **Where to go next**
Diary of a Mad Old Man, 1961–62, Jun'ichirō Tanizaki
The fascinating but disturbing story of Utsugi, an elderly man who records the details of both his deteriorating health and his continuing sexual obsession with his beautiful Westernized daughter-in-law, Satsuko.

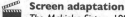 **Screen adaptation**
The Makioka Sisters, 1983, dir. Kon Ichikawa
Capturing all the traditional beauty of Japan, this film is also largely faithful
to Tanizaki's novel despite cutting some key moments. The pace is slow and
stately and there's more talk than action, but the cumulative sense of an old-
fashioned family buckling under the strain of the modern world is subtly and
sensitively achieved.

Fathers and Sons

1862, IVAN TURGENEV, RUSSIAN

Penguin

A lucid, moving dramatization of the
clash between the old and new generations, Turgenev's most celebrated novel
is also alarmingly perceptive about the
unpredictable outcomes of both ideology and passion. At its heart is Bazarov
the nihilist, a cynical student doctor, who
opposes the sentiment and memories of
the older generation, propounds a creed
of scientific materialism, and, above all,
despises love.

The novel is remarkable for the range
and nuance of its characters. Even the
minor ones, like Bazarov's fawning dis-
ciple Sitnikov and the emancipated young heiress Eudoxie, possess vivid particularity. In the older generation, Nikolai Petrovich
(the dreamy, impractical father of Bazarov's friend, Arkady) and
Arkady's exquisite French-speaking uncle Pavel, are richly complex
characters who reveal unexpected qualities throughout the novel.
But Bazarov stands at the centre of the action, almost as if to direct
it, infuriatingly opinionated, outspoken and indifferent to conventions and manners alike – until he meets the "sumptuous" aristo-

cratic beauty, Anna Odintsova, and finds himself less than fully in
control of his emotions.

As always, Turgenev was responding to social and political
issues – and *Fathers and Sons* remains the classic account of the
clash between revolutionary youth and reactionary old age. But he
was also an original and varied writer
of love. Nearly all his novels take up
some aspect of the theme. Here, he
writes with stinging realism about the
pain of falling in love against your will,
about the uxorious love of old age, the

> *In my opinion it's better
> to break stones working
> on a road than to let a
> woman control so much
> as the tip of your finger.*

quieter affections of mutual dependency, and, finally, despite the
bitterness between fathers and sons, about the adoring love of parents for their children, even when they can no longer understand
them.

Recommended translation
1965, Rosemary Edmonds, Penguin Classics

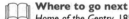

Where to go next
Home of the Gentry, 1859, Ivan Turgenev
A heartbreaking story of disillusionment as Lavretsky, a minor Russian landowner, returns to his homeland after a disastrous period of married life
abroad.

Of the Farm

1965, JOHN UPDIKE, AMERICAN

Updike is the poet-historian of late twentieth-century America,
and his "Rabbit" tetralogy (*Rabbit, Run*; *Rabbit Redux*; *Rabbit is Rich*
and *Rabbit at Rest*), which covers four decades from the becalmed
fifties to the affluent eighties, is the most attuned and alive fictional
record of the period. By comparison, *Of the Farm* is a miniature – a
brief, intense, lyrical description of a single weekend: two days of

emotional warfare between a middle-aged man, his new wife and his elderly mother.

From the moment of his arrival at the farm where he grew up, Joey dreads the meeting between the two women. His mother, ill and given to harsh opinions, openly disapproves of his remarriage.

I turned on to the gray whirring surface of the township road, and then down our dirt road, and saw Peggy, and laughed, for she was on the garden ridge, hoeing in her bikini.

His good-looking but unsophisticated wife, Peggy, accuses the older woman of driving Joey's father to an early death. Joey, the classic cosseted only child, capable of betraying both, wavers between them. Unspoken anger turns the weekend routines – clearing up the dinner things, shopping at the supermarket, mowing a meadow, attending Sunday morning service – into unmanageable ordeals, and the lucid narrative rapidly discloses a murky family history of unresolved resentments.

Updike's sensuous appreciation of the world gives the novel its brilliant light and shade: a bat "like a speck of pain" jerking in the twilight, a dog's tongue "spotted black like a pansy". In such simple material things he records the fraught alterations of confusion and love. As a dramatization of family tensions, *Of the Farm* is unbeatably sharp, taut and rich.

Where to go next
Rabbit, Run, 1960, John Updike
Faced with the reality of his hopeless life, Harry "Rabbit" Angstrom decides to take drastic steps to remedy things. The first novel of a tetralogy which provides the best portrayal of life in America in the second half of the twentieth century.

To the Lighthouse

1927, VIRGINIA WOOLF, ENGLISH

Woolf's great subjects are the dramas of everyday moods and the adventures of ordinary thoughts, and *To the Lighthouse* is a beautifully moving celebration of the unsuspected inner lives which exist, hidden but gorgeously rich, in everyone.

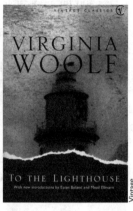

Vintage

Woolf's style is highly patterned, full of echoes and associations: like a piece of music, the story is formally divided into three movements, in which the themes vary and develop. In the extended first movement, set on a single day during a tranquil summer shortly before World War I, the Ramsays entertain friends at their holiday home in Scotland. Mrs Ramsay, maternal and elegant, gently organizes her guests, tries to soften the moods of her husband, a famous intellectual, and frets over her eight children, while her youngest, James, thinks only of a promised trip to the lighthouse. Abruptly changing mood, the brief, meditative second movement describes the house left empty during wartime, ten years of loss and tragedy. And in the final, ambivalent section a few surviving visitors, much older now, return to the decaying house, and the trip to the lighthouse is finally achieved.

> One wanted, she thought, to be on a level with ordinary experience, to feel simply that's a chair, that's a table, and yet at the same time, it's a miracle, it's an ecstasy.

The story is slight, the incidents mundane. The real action – dramatic and absorbing – lies in the interplay of the characters' transient emotions. An ordinary dinner conversation is a blaze of moods and thoughts, the characters flickering in and out of sympathy with each other. Throughout, Woolf is attuned to the transience of happiness and the impossible desire to hold onto it, a theme delicately presented in the motifs of light and shade running through the novel, conjuring up lives filled with both beauty and pain.

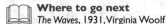

Where to go next
The Waves, 1931, Virginia Woolf
Woolf's most radical novel is also her most characteristic: a sustained exploration of the inner lives of six friends as they pass from childhood to old age.

Screen adaptation
To the Lighthouse, 1983, dir. Colin Gregg
With its minimal plot and an emphasis as much on thoughts as actions, *To the Lighthouse* seems unlikely film material. Shot in Cornwall (rather than the Scotland of the original), this TV adaptation largely succeeds by maintaining the novel's melancholy tone and highlighting those seemingly insignificant moments that have such poetic resonance for the characters' inner lives.

Rites of
passage

3

Those two great rites of passage – of a child into adulthood, of an adult through old age towards death – have inspired some of the most moving of all novels – fiction that goes to the heart of who we are.

Every adolescence is unique, but the particular experiences of a few fictional characters have become universal – like Huck Finn spinning down the Mississippi on his raft and learning adult life the hard way, or Augustin Meaulnes, unable to find his way out of the fairy tale of adolescence, or Holden Caulfield, as comic as he is tragic in his rebellions against the "phoney" world of grown-ups.

The experiences of a girl growing into a woman have been the subject of no less vivid novels. Fanny Burney's *Evelina*, set in Georgian England, and Buchi Emecheta's *The Bride Price*, set in twentieth-century Nigeria, are equally powerful accounts of a young woman's first encounters with a male-dominated adult world.

Dealing with the other end of the human span, novelists have sometimes been – understandably – elegiac. In Yourcenar's beautifully unsentimental *Memoirs of Hadrian*, the dying emperor struggles to make sense of his apparently shapeless life. Artemio Cruz, on the other hand, rages against the dying of the light. While for Geiser, the hero of Max Frisch's *Man in the Holocene*, the dying is in the mind as he slips into senility.

All these novels record the effects of time. In Proust's breathtaking masterpiece, *In Search of Lost Time*, time itself is the elusive subject, and the past – all the vividness of human experience – is its hiding place, where it waits to be rediscovered.

Le Grand Meaulnes

1913, ALAIN-FOURNIER, FRENCH

HENRI ALAIN-FOURNIER
The Lost Estate (Le Grand Meaulnes)

Dreamy, anguished and a little weird, *Le Grand Meaulnes* is the classic doomed fairy tale of adolescence, written by a man whose own adolescence was not long over when he was killed in action in World War I. At once childish and sophisticated, it perfectly embodies the odd, aching yearning of a boy grown up beyond his years but still trusting to the instincts of childhood: Augustin Meaulnes.

Unexpectedly turning up at a small boarding school in a remote French village, the seventeen-year-old Meaulnes is, from the first, a remarkably self-possessed but mysterious young man, alternately idolized and victimized by the local boys. One afternoon, attempting an adventure in the surrounding countryside, he becomes hopelessly lost. Two days of wandering brings him to a run-down chateau populated almost entirely by children, where he briefly encounters a beautiful young woman. Forced to flee when the fete abruptly breaks up, he realizes too late that he has no idea where the chateau is, just as the obsession to find it again takes hold of him.

A variation on the theme of the quest of the prince for his lost princess, *Le Grand Meaulnes* unerringly tunes into the extremism of adolescence.

> *When I discovered the Estate Without a Name, I reached a height, a degree of perfection and purity that I shall never achieve again. In death alone, as I once wrote to you, I may perhaps recapture the beauty of that time.*

True to its fairy-tale mode, it creates a floating mood of expectancy and fear punctuated by offbeat images: a distraught Pierrot running through the night with a body in his arms, a sudden cry in a deserted wood. For long periods, time seems to expand endlessly, then, at moments of heightened awareness, the prose freezes into the present tense. Descriptions of the French countryside are rudimentary and haunting, as in myth. The story proceeds by secrets, learned by chance, misunderstood, kept for the wrong reasons, and finally, devastatingly, revealed. No other novel captures adolescence so well.

Recommended translation
2007, Robin Buss, Penguin Modern Classics

Where to go next
The Devil in the Flesh, 1923, Raymond Radiguet
Completed before the author's nineteenth birthday, Radiguet's astonishing tale of a teenage boy's affair with a married woman while her husband is away fighting in World War I is sensual, poetic and frequently disturbing.

Screen adaptation
Le Grand Meaulnes, 1967, dir. Jean-Gabriel Albicocco
A dreamy, languid, very 1960s take on Alain-Fournier's novel, complete with Vaseline on the lens, indulgently subjective camerawork, lush landscapes and a soupy score from Jean-Pierre Bourtayre. Something of a cult, partly due to its virtual disappearance, its young actors are certainly easy on the eye, but the suffocating sentimentalism will appal as many as it pleases.

School books

The time spent at school – supposedly the happiest days of our life – has proven fertile ground for novelists, and spawned its own separate genre of school stories. Thomas Hughes is credited with its creation, with his nostalgic, fictional memoir *Tom Brown's Schooldays* (1857). But – beginning with Dickens's grim depiction of Dotheboy's Hall in *Nicholas Nickleby* (1839) – other writers have taken a rather more jaundiced view of school life. Here are five of the very best novels with a school setting:

Tom Brown's Schooldays, 1857, Thomas Hughes
The archetypal English public school tale, embodying the strongly held belief of the Victorian middle classes, that hard work and fair play will triumph over sloth and immorality. Based on the author's own schooling at Rugby, the adventures of Tom and his friends – particularly their besting of the bully Flashman – still makes compelling reading.

Botchan, 1906, Natsume Sōseki
Largely autobiographical, *Botchan* is the eponymous tale of a feckless and somewhat spoilt young man from Tokyo whose first teaching job takes him to the distant provincial town of Matsuyama. Arrogant and plain-speaking, Botchan's clashes with both pupils and fellow-teachers are highly entertaining and often very funny.

The Death of the Heart

1938, ELIZABETH BOWEN, ENGLISH

Bowen is a tremendously expert novelist, her novels highly controlled but highly charged. *The Death of the Heart* is her masterpiece, precisely, almost remorselessly, imagined: a slow-burning story of the destruction of a girl's innocent notion of love.

Orphaned at sixteen, Portia Quayne is brought to London to live with her older half-brother Thomas and his wife Anna in their elegant town house in Windsor Terrace, overlooking Regent's Park.

Frost in May, 1933, Antonia White
A fascinating insight into the strict, hermetic world of a Catholic girls' boarding school, as related from the perspective of one of its pupils, Nanda Grey. As the daughter of a recent convert, Nanda never entirely fits in – despite her best efforts – and her independent spirit finally leads to her downfall in the book's poignant last pages.

The Prime of Miss Jean Brodie, 1961, Muriel Spark
Spark's most famous novel is a tale of domination and subversion set in an Edinburgh girls' school of the 1930s. The charismatic and unorthodox Miss Brodie moulds the characters of her favourite girls to her own liking, but her decision to confide her feelings to one of them proves to be her undoing.

Old School, 2003, Tobias Wolff
Set in the hothouse atmosphere of a top American boys' school in the 1960s, where every term a writing contest is held, with the winner being judged by – and then meeting – a distinguished visiting author. When the author turns out to be Hemingway, the competition becomes especially intense and friendships start to buckle.

There she encounters the highly strung, amoral Eddie, and falls in love. Mounting tension between Portia and her relations throws her affair into dramatic relief, and leads eventually to a crisis which implicates everyone's hidden feelings – an absolute emotional explosion in the Quayne household.

'After all, Eddie, anything that happens has never happened before. What I mean is, you and I are the first people who have ever been us.'

Bowen's style is refined, arch, occasionally catty. Her powers of observation are extraordinarily acute – descriptions of inanimate objects are wonderfully expressive – and she pins the physical world from drawing rooms to facial expressions with sharp, enlivening brilliance. She sees into things too. Like Henry James, she unravels the psychological complexities of her characters, layer by layer, to their astonishing origins. Her characters are in fact, straightforwardly, magnificently realized – the housekeeper Matchett, with her "helmet of stern hair"; Anna, irritably self-aware; Eddic fecklessly striking a farouche pose; trusting but puzzled Portia; and a handful of absorbing minor characters. It is such psychological solidity that makes the final crisis, when it comes, so devastating.

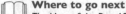

Where to go next
The Heat of the Day, 1949, Elizabeth Bowen
Much of Bowen's best work is about the war, which here is the setting of a love affair between Stella Rodney and Robert Kelway, a relationship which changes for ever when he is revealed to be a spy.

The Death of Virgil
1946, HERMANN BROCH, GERMAN

'One of the most extraordinary and profound experiments ever to have been undertaken with the flexible medium of the novel.' – Thomas Mann

Vintage

Broch is one of those "difficult" European giants of fiction regarded with awe and suspicion in the anglophone world, and *The Death of Virgil* is that awful thing: an uncompromising work of genius. The tone is intellectual; there is no plot, only one character; and page-long sentences are the order of the day. But it spectacularly breaks into ground untrodden by other novels, and engages some of the big, elusive issues of life and death with grim tenacity.

It is 19 BC, and the great Roman poet Virgil is dying in the small Italian town of Brundisium. In his room, he is attended by a slave and a boy called Lysanias. He suffers fevers through the night, and becomes convinced that he must destroy his unfinished masterpiece *The Aeneid*. In the morning a doctor examines him. His friends Plotius and Varius call, and then the Emperor Augustus visits. As the day draws to a close, he dies. None of these incidental occurrences matter. What matters are the poet's questing, discursive, digressive thoughts as he dies – his attempts, as he hovers between life and death, to see through material things to deeper patterns, to the immutable truths of existence.

In a sense, the novel is about the strangeness of dying. Situated entirely

> 'You are Virgil.' 'I was once, perhaps I shall be again.'

in the mental borderlands between life and death, reality and unreality, it attempts to express the state of mind as it collapses and dies (and it seems no coincidence that it was written during the destruction of World War II, which forced Broch, a Jew, into exile). As Virgil trembles on the brink of sanity, sometimes slipping into a dreamlike trance of delirium, paradoxically he sees with greater clarity the possibilities of eternal life. Slowly, the tone shifts. What first appeared as the stark inscrutability of the pagan gods takes on a distinctly Christian tone, as Virgil comes to believe in the redemption of love.

The book, always elemental, is divided into four sections: Water, Fire, Earth and Air. Stay with it through the fever-induced ramblings of Fire, and you will be rewarded with the absolutely unique fantasy-vision of the moment of death in Air.

 Recommended translation
1945, Jean Starr Untermeyer, Vintage Classics (UK), Vintage International (US)

Where to go next
The Notebooks of Malte Laurids Brigge, 1910, Rainer Maria Rilke
The great German poet's only novel is an experimental, semi-autobiographical account of a young man who comes to Paris in order to write. Sinking into illness, the author finds himself meditating on death – the deaths of his family and friends, of figures from history, and of himself.

Evelina

1778, Fanny Burney, English

It is a pity that Fanny Burney is so overshadowed by her greater contemporary Jane Austen, because, in *Evelina*, at least, Burney proved herself a marvellously acute writer on the quintessential Austenesque theme of a girl's problematic maturity into womanhood.

Evelina, mysteriously disinherited by her father, has been brought up in rural seclusion by her guardian, a village rector. But when she is seventeen, and already a startling beauty, he reluctantly allows her to visit family friends in London, precipitating her suddenly into the unfamiliar world at large. There, totally unprepared, she encounters the bewildering pleasures of eighteenth-century entertainment at the theatres, Vauxhall Gardens and Sadler's Wells, in the company of even more bewildering characters: the cheerfully xenophobic Captain Mirvan, foppish Sir Clement Willoughby, stately Lord Orville, her robustly vulgar cousins the Branghtons, and almost every unattached male who catches sight of her.

> *Every other moment, I was spoken to by some bold unfeeling man, to whom my distress, which I think must be very apparent, only furnished a pretence for impertinent witticisms or free gallantry.*

The pace of the narrative is slower than in *Pride and Prejudice*, the tone less varied than in *Emma*; the epistolary style lacks the sophistication of *Les Liaisons Dangereuses*, published only four years later. And it is true that Evelina's constant state of flustered helplessness in the face of repeated harassment can be exasperating. But Burney is unerringly accurate in striking at the two great targets of her satire: the smug licentiousness of men and the social constraints of women. Moreover, her style is instinctively dramatic. With her amazingly sure sense of group dynamic, her unsurpassed ear for dialogue and, above all, her fierce, slightly catty wit, she excels in scenes of multiple confrontation, each character speaking past the others, and is equally good at anatomizing toffs, with their acid airs and graces, and the prickly posturing of the *hoi polloi*.

📖 **Where to go next**
Mary and *The Wrongs of Women*, 1788 and 1798, Mary Wollstonecraft
The feminist author of *A Vindication of the Rights of Women* wrote two short fictions in which young single women strive to determine their own fates. Less accomplished than *Evelina*, they nevertheless bring a sharp, intellectual focus to bear on the situation of women in late eighteenth-century England.

The Bride Price

1976, BUCHI EMECHETA, NIGERIAN

Buchi Emecheta's third novel is a beauti-fully observant and compassionate account of a young girl's struggle to defy and sur-vive tribal customs, and an upsettingly tense drama of a forbidden love affair.

It opens in 1950s Lagos, Nigeria, where thirteen-year-old Aku-nna lives with her family. A shy girl, hoping to do well at school, she doesn't anticipate misfortune. But within a few weeks she will be living precariously with a new family in the tribal town of Ibuza, where Ibo tradi-tions dictate an early marriage to the first suitor to pay the "bride price". And three

George Braziller Inc.

years later, after a shocking sequence of events, the novel will end with Aku-nna a fugitive – and a mother.

The novel is a marvel of balance. In the early scenes, described with a quiet, precise emphasis, Ibo customs (cooking the evening meal in a communal kitchen or dancing all night at a wake) give common events force and dignity. Later, they will utterly deform Aku-nna's life. The pace of the narrative is brilliantly handled too: hesitant at first, quickening in the middle section, and exploding in a monstrous rush towards the end. Best of all is the developing drama of Aku-nna's teenage maturity as she grows from a child to a woman, turning intuition into understanding, experiencing her first periods, falling in love and attempting to assert her will in a male-dominated society.

She was trapped in the intricate web of Ibuza tradition. She must either obey or bring shame and destruction on her people.

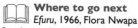 **Where to go next**
Efuru, 1966, Flora Nwapa
Set during the Nigerian civil war in the 1960s, Nwapa's beautifully engaging novel tells the story of a young Igbo woman's efforts to balance the demands of duty, children and work, while experiencing a growing sense of her own individuality.

My Brilliant Career

1901, MILES FRANKLIN, AUSTRALIAN

Miles Franklin forbade the re-publication of *My Brilliant Career* during her lifetime, and it wasn't until 1966 that readers had a chance to discover that her novel, dashed off in a few weeks when she was sixteen, is one of the world's great stories of adolescence, a fresh and uninhibited comedy of love and ambition set among the pioneer farmers of the Australian bush, where Franklin grew up.

Her heroine Sybylla Melvin is also a young teenager of the bush, high-spirited, clever and unpredictable. When her family is ruined by her father's profligacy, she finds herself drudging on a poor dairy farm in drought-stricken Possum Gully, longing for a brilliant career of art and music. An extended stay with her well-to-do grandmother at Caddagat in the Australian alps of New South Wales unexpectedly provides an entry to a new world of refinement. But she has lost none of her old feistiness. A flirtation with an extremely eligible neighbour – a hilarious series of misadventures including one of the most calamitous marriage proposals in fiction – shows all Sybylla's tomboyish perversity and wilful determination to be true to herself.

Few novels have the freshness or directness of *My Brilliant Career*. The charmingly egotistical Sybylla is a highly impressionable narrator, and her story is full of vivid descriptions of the Australian bush and the (very masculine) life of its station managers, squatters and swagmen (including, in a

> I thought of Gertie, so pretty, so girlish, so understandable, so full of innocent winning coquetry … Could anyone help preferring her to me, who was strange, weird and perverse?

troubled middle section, an account of Australian philistinism as brilliant as Chekhov's descriptions of Russian peasants). But the story's greatest triumph is its passionate evocation of a girl's contradictory, powerful emotions as she becomes a woman.

Where to go next
The Getting of Wisdom, 1910, Henry Handel Richardson
The Getting of Wisdom, which draws on Richardson's own childhood experiences, is an eye-opening coming-of-age novel about the jealousies, fights, power-struggles, friendships, hatreds and sexuality of teenage girls being educated in an exclusive school in Melbourne at the beginning of the twentieth century.

Screen adaptation
My Brilliant Career, 1979, dir. Gillian Armstrong
The rediscovery of the novel coincided with the feminism of the 1960s and 70s, and the film version reinforces this aspect. Judy Davis, in her first major film role, is not just suitably spirited as Sybylla but also effectively conveys the character's complex inner life in her struggles to pursue her own path. Sam Neill plays Harry Beecham, the attractive suitor to whom she almost succumbs.

Man in the Holocene

1979, MAX FRISCH, SWISS

Both playwright and novelist, Max Frisch was one of the most distinguished modern writers in the German-speaking world. *Man*

in the Holocene, published in Frisch's sixty-eighth year, is an unsparing but moving story of encroaching senility.

One winter, Geiser, an elderly widower from Basel, now living alone in the Ticino mountains, begins to lose his memory. The weather is terrible: thunderstorms, fogs and floods. The power is cut off, the highway is closed, and Geiser fears that a landslide will bury the village. But the real landslide is going on in his own head.

He has forgotten the names of his grandchildren. He finds himself standing in his front room with his hat on, unsure if he was just about to go out or has just come back in. A whole world of knowledge is slipping away from him, and with muted but increasing desperation he attempts to hold onto it, pasting cuttings from encyclopedias onto his walls, facts from the deep past: the natural history of the Ticino, the lives of the dinosaurs, the evolution of man, and the geological eras, of which the present one (the Holocene, the age of man) is the one which has witnessed, he says, the phenomenon of metamorphosis – the "changing of human beings into animals, trees, stone, etc." Geiser too seems to be merging with nature. And in this precarious mood, he leaves his house early one morning, with a knapsack and an umbrella, and makes for the pass.

> *Obviously brain cells are ceasing to function. More serious than the collapse of a dry-stone wall would be a crack across the grounds, narrow at first, no broader than a hand, but a crack.*

Brief and piercing, elegant and exhausted, made of dislocated fragments of writing and pictures, *Man in the Holocene* is an unforgettable novel about forgetting.

 Recommended translation
1980, Geoffrey Skelton, Dalkey Archive Press (UK), Harvest Books (US)

 **Where to go next**
Homo Faber, 1957, Max Frisch
Swiss rationality collides with Latin American exoticism in this story of ultra-careful UNESCO engineer Walter Faber, whose life is changed by wildly unpredictable events after his flight crash-lands in the Mexican desert.

The Death of Artemio Cruz

1962, CARLOS FUENTES, MEXICAN

One of the great novels of the Latin American "boom", *The Death of Artemio Cruz* is both a dizzying technical *tour de force* and a distressingly violent tale of ambition and brutality. Finding a whole national history in the chaotic memories of a dying man, it charts a course through the dark soul of modern Mexico – "a thousand countries with a single name".

The prose is raw and angry, the story bewilderingly disarranged. Scenes of the media tycoon Artemio Cruz's agonized death, made shockingly vivid by close-up details of his physical deterioration and stream-of-consciousness thoughts, alternate with sudden plunging memories of his earlier life.

You will live seventy one years without realizing it. You will not stop to think about the fact that your blood circulates, your heart beats, your gallbladder empties itself of serous liquids ... Until today.

His life doesn't so much pass before him as pile up unbearably. It begins with the brooding memory of meeting his wife for the first time, the sister of a man whose death he caused during the Revolution, the daughter of a man he will shamefully exploit for his land, and it ends with a sharp impression of his own birth, the half-caste offspring born into orphaned poverty. In between, he will think about his luxurious old age as a wealthy despot with his mansions and mistresses; about his crooked business deals; about the death of his son in the Spanish Civil War; about his terror and harshness during the Revolution (including a particularly vivid scene of capture). Throughout, he returns to the memory of Regina, the girl he loved and found hanged in one of the towns he captured from the *federales*. Unafraid of big effects, *The Death of Artemio Cruz* attempts no less than a history of modern Mexico in its aspects "of love and solitude, of hatred and effort, of violence and tenderness, of friendship and disillusion, of time and oblivion, of innocence and surprise".

 Recommended translation
1991, Alfred Mac Adam, Atlantic Books (UK), Farrar, Straus and Giroux (US)

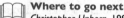 **Where to go next**
Christopher Unborn, 1989, Carlos Fuentes
By turns funny and savagely satirical, *Christopher Unborn* gets to grips with the Mexican near future, an apocalyptic period of economic collapse, environmental meltdown and military invasion. How his parents attempt to survive the national disaster is narrated by Christopher, an unborn foetus.

The Master of Go

1954, YASUNARI KAWABATA, JAPANESE

In the West Kawabata is considered the most "Japanese" of Japanese novelists, celebrated for the delicate inscrutability of *Snow Country* and *Thousand Cranes*. *The Master of Go* is different – solider, plainer, but just as haunting, and focused on a very Japanese subject: Go, a chess-like game of territorial possession and capture. The novel began as reportage: a series of newspaper articles covering a famous tournament in 1938 between the "invincible" Master, Honnimbō Shūsai, and his challenger, Otaké of the Seventh Rank. In a single match lasting six months, the failing Master – austere and inward practitioner of the old style – combated the ferocious attacking play of his younger opponent. For Kawabata, it symbolized the pivotal moment between tradition and modernity, the loss of a spiritual art, and the dawn of a more facile age.

It is not necessary to know the rules of Go to feel the excitement of the intensely combative match with its contrasting styles of play, changing fortunes and, eventually, fatal error of judgement. More compelling still is the human drama contained in the gaps between sessions, Shūsai and Otaké's desultory exchanges about the weather or their ailments, Otaké's nervous irritability and Shūsai's obsessive game-playing. Finally, as the Master grows weak, absently seeking relief

The Master would seem, in a variety of meanings, to have stood at the boundary between the old and the new. He went into his last match as the last survivor among idols of old.

among the plum blossoms and *yatsudé* flowers of the hotel gardens, he seems to outgrow the contest altogether, becoming a genuinely tragic figure filled with "the still sadness of another world".

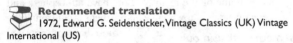

Recommended translation
1972, Edward G. Seidensticker, Vintage Classics (UK) Vintage International (US)

Where to go next
Snow Country, 1935–47, Yasunari Kawabata
As allusive and understated as a haiku, Kawabata's celebrated classic tells the story of a brief love affair at a mountain hot spring between a wealthy sophisticate and a geisha.

To Kill a Mockingbird
1960, HARPER LEE, AMERICAN

Hovering beautifully between a children's book and an adult one, *To Kill a Mockingbird* is a one-off. Quite literally, because it is Harper Lee's only book. But also because its unique magic casts a spell like no other novel, conjuring up a translucent but mysterious world of childhood fancy and adult folly, which its narrator, nine-year-old "Scout" Finch, will never see the same way again.

It contains one of the most famous court scenes in fiction, in which Scout's father, Atticus, defends a black man accused of raping a white woman, a brilliantly tense and emotionally involving piece of theatre, all the more effective for being delivered in so quiet a tone. But the novel is far more than a legal drama. It is a delicately knowing description of small-town life in the American South of the 1930s, a tender, comic evocation of childhood and, above all, a simple but enormously resonant celebration of courage and dignity in the face of furious racism.

The scenes of the half-scared, half-swaggering childhood pranks on the Radley House, home of the reclusive Boo, have atmosphere and charm. The scene outside the town jail where Atticus is confronted by a lynch mob has concentrated tension. Throughout, the novel's poised tone never compromises either the dramatic variety or the compulsive momentum of the narrative. Is Atticus – patient, honourable, saintly – a little too good to believe? Is the lesson that to kill a mockingbird is a sin a little too simplistic? Under the spell of the novel, such quibbles dissolve.

She did something that in our society is unspeakable: she kissed a black man. No code mattered to her before she broke it, but it came crashing down on her afterwards.

Where to go next
Other Voices, Other Rooms, 1948, Truman Capote
The first novel by Harper Lee's childhood friend (and model for one of the children in *To Kill a Mockingbird*) is a haunting story of a half-orphaned boy sent to live with his unknown father in the Deep South.

Screen adaptation
To Kill a Mockingbird, 1962, dir. Robert Mulligan
All clean-cut, unassailable integrity, Gregory Peck is perfectly cast as Atticus,

and if the courtroom scenes don't quite generate the requisite tension it's the director's rather than the actor's fault. More compelling are the moments seen through the eyes of Scout (whose adult voice narrates much of the film), and her anxious fascination with the Radley House and its oddball inhabitant.

Weep Not, Child

1964, NGUGI WA THIONG'O, KENYAN

A short, stark novel, both political and emotional, *Weep Not, Child* is a frighteningly intimate account of growing up during the Mau Mau struggle against the British colonialists in post-war Kenya.

The novel begins with innocent hope: Njoroge's hardly dared-for wish to go to school and receive an education. His brothers' and father's hope for the return of the Kenyans' lands after a war fighting for the British is more apprehensive still. Both hopes seem doomed to founder. The young boy's education places him in new, troubling relations to other villagers. The adults' protests result in intimidation and injustice. And finally, both the village and the country erupt with violence.

Though stark (it contains powerfully plain descriptions of appalling physical and mental suffering), *Weep Not, Child* is sensitive to the troubling ambiguities

> Every day there have been some new arrests and some houses burnt down by Mau Mau. Fear in the Air. Not a fear of death – it's a fear of living.

of the situation. The characters fail to divide along simple racial lines. The Kenyan Jacobo helps enforce white supremacy; Njoroge's brothers are uncompromisingly opposed to the British, but his father, Ngotho, is hesitant about the protests. For Njoroge, growing in awareness but still a child, this breakdown in family relations will be the most calamitous outcome of the uprising.

Depicting both crude power and fragile emotions, shot through with images of darkness and light, Ngugi's first and most famous novel is an important fictional statement about an episode at once historical and personal.

📖 **Where to go next**
A Grain of Wheat, 1967, Ngugi Wa Thiong'o
Also set during the Kenyan war of independence, this later but equally celebrated novel focuses on the loner Mugo. Though he is a hero of the resistance
against the British, he hides a shameful secret.

In Search of Lost Time

1913–27, MARCEL PROUST, FRANCE

The reputation of this book is in direct proportion to its alarming
physical dimensions (six volumes, 3,600 pages). The famous scene
with the madeleine cake dipped in tea, which produces a "Proustian"
reverie of memory in the narrator, goes intimidatingly before it.

None of this prepares the reader for its absorbing brilliance.
Demanding? Yes. Exhausting? Often. But for those who brave its
first few pages, this may just be one of the great reading experiences
of their lives.

When from a long-distant past noth-
ing subsists, after the people are dead,
after the things are broken and scat-
tered, taste and smell alone, more
fragile but more enduring, more imma-
terial, more persistent, more faithful,
remain poised a long time, like souls.

The plot focuses on
groups of characters ris-
ing and falling in high-
society France in the
early twentieth century.
Great scenes of soirées,
balls and supper parties,
described by Proust with a sort of savage tenderness (and in huge
detail), form a mighty strand of the narrative. But plot is not the
point. Proust's main interest is psychological, and his novel contains
hundreds of characters, the most fleeting of which are described
more richly (and more unsparingly) than main characters in many
other novels. The lives of the debonair Swann, the elusive *cocotte*
Odette, the relentlessly ambitious Madame Verdurin and the out-

rageous aristocratic pederast M. de Charlus, as they intrigue, love, clash, make up and grow old, intertwine like passages in a great symphony. Swann's intense and controversial love for Odette in the first volume and, in *The Captive* and *The Fugitive*, the narrator's woundingly suspicious obsession with Albertine, a girl he meets on a beach, are perhaps two of the most extraordinary love affairs in literature. But the most gripping psychological adventure in the book lies in the narrator's search for a way to regain passing time as it slips from him. His attempts to find layers of deeper meaning in every-thing around him give rise to the novel's characteristic scrutinizing descriptions of the world. Perhaps in the end this is Proust's uniquely generous gift to his readers. In no other novel will you find twenty pages describing a goodnight kiss. More than this, you won't find another novel which gives the reader such a generous habit-forming impulse to see more deeply and intensely into his own world.

Recommended translation
1922–31, C.K. Scott-Moncrieff, (revised by Terence Kilmartin and D.J. Enright), Vintage (UK), Modern Library Classics (US)

Where to go next
The Immoralist, 1902, André Gide
Like Proust, Gide was homosexual, and his greatest novel, set partly in Tunisia, explores the hidden longings of a young married man, Michel, for boys.

Screen adaptation
Swann in Love, 1983, dir. Volker Schlondorff
Pinter's screenplay, written for Visconti, was never filmed, leaving Schlondorff to make the first serious attempt at a slice of *Lost Time*. Despite the two lead actors (Jeremy Irons and Ornella Muti) being dubbed into French, this day-in-the-life-of Swann works well, with strong performances (Alain Delon especially convincing as Charlus) and a stunning period look created by cinematographer Sven Nykvist.

Screen adaptation
Time Regained, 1999, dir. Raoul Ruiz
Avant-garde director Ruiz adopted a more adventurous style than Schlondorff when he filmed volume four of Proust's great work. The combination of sump-

Novel sequences

While many writers have found it perfectly possible to plot the trajectory of an individual's life within the confines of a single novel, others have felt the need to extend the process through more than one volume and, in a few cases, through several.

Such novel sequences can concentrate on one person's life, as in Cooper's five Leatherstocking stories (1823–41, see p.169); focus on a family as Zola does in his Rougon-Macquart series (1871–93); or attempt to anatomize a whole society, for instance Balzac's hugely ambitious *Comédie humaine* novels and novellas (1827–47, see p.135).

In *A la recherche du temps perdu*, Proust attempted to do all three while, at the same time, exploring the inner life of the narrator and the very nature of memory and time. The French term for a novel sequence is *roman fleuve*: *roman* meaning novel and *fleuve* meaning river, thus suggesting a narrative flow made up of different currents but which makes up a single unified whole. Individual novels within a sequence can nearly always be read separately. A genre fiction series, for instance Simenon's Maigret stories (see p.329), in which the same character appears from book to book, is not regarded as a novel sequence.

Celebrated sequences in English include the two six-novel series by Anthony Trollope (see p.262), and the following twentieth-century examples:

tuous production values with some tricksy, occasionally bizarre, camerawork, suggests the way that memory works against the idea of narrative continuity. The sadistic Charlus once again elicits a mesmerizing performance – this time from John Malkovich.

The Catcher in the Rye
1951, J.D. SALINGER, AMERICAN

No less disquieting for being extremely funny, *The Catcher in the Rye* is the great tragi-comedy of troubled adolescence, and Holden Caulfield – highly strung, fabulously unpredictable and more than

The Forsyte Saga, 1906–21, John Galsworthy (5 books)
Three novels and two novellas tracking the vicissitudes in the lives of a middle-class, *nouveau riche* family – notably their rivalries and failed love affairs – across three generations.

Pilgrimage, 1915–38, Dorothy Richardson (13 books)
A reviewer invented the term "stream of consciousness" to describe Richardson's method for conveying the thought processes of her protagonist, Miriam Henderson, an independent and free-thinking woman at the start of the century.

A Dance to the Music of Time, 1951–75, Anthony Powell (12 books)
Beginning with a group of friends at a boys' boarding school in the 1920s, the sequence explores the interlocking lives of a group of friends and acquaintances, in particular Nick Jenkins and the ambitious and widely loathed Widmerpool. The volumes touching on the war years are among the strongest.

Children of Violence, 1952–69, Doris Lessing (5 books)
Set mostly in Africa, the books follows the personal development of Martha Quest, from her adolescent existence on an African farm, through an unsatisfactory marriage, to her increasing radicalization and eventual arrival in London.

a little fragile – is one of the most mesmerizing young characters in modern fiction.

Talking a blue streak, the seventeen-year-old Caulfield relates all the "madman stuff" that happened to him after he ran away from his expensive school the previous year and holed up in New York

'Look, sir. Don't worry about me,' I said. 'I mean it. I'll be all right. I'm just going through a phase right now. Everybody goes through phases and all, don't they?'

with the last of his grandmother's birthday money. Increasingly bizarre encounters with several suspicious cab drivers, a menacing hotel elevator guy, some "whory-looking blondes", a depressingly

First Back Bay

real prostitute, some old school friends and assorted "tiny kids", link together to form an accelerating drama of emotional chaos, which ends with him planning to go out West as a deaf-mute.

The hypnotic Caulfield voice – an off-beat adolescent ramble full of jokes, out-bursts of innocence and incessant com-plaints about "phony" adults – carries the story brilliantly. The facts don't emerge so much as swing embarrassingly into view at odd angles, and veer away again, like Caulfield himself, impetuously trying him-self out in different situations, though his tragedy is to feel comfort-able nowhere, not with the whory-looking blondes or the tiny kids or even – most heartbreakingly of all – with his beloved older brother, DB, and kid sister, Phoebe. Sharply of its time, *The Catcher in the Rye* is an enduring classic of adolescent not-belonging.

Where to go next
Nine Stories/For Esmé with Love and Squalor, 1953, J.D. Salinger
Wry, funny, strange, tragic and shot through with mysticism, Salinger's stories are all high-impact fiction of the first order. This collection includes the famous "A Perfect Day for Bananafish", "Uncle Wiggly in Connecticut" and "For Esmé with Love and Squalor".

Memento Mori

1959, MURIEL SPARK, SCOTTISH

Of all Muriel Spark's briskly luminous books, *Memento Mori* is the brightest, a metaphysical enquiry disguised as a crime novel, com-pulsively readable, wickedly funny and highly serious.

Spark liked to work with self-contained groups, like the nuns in *The Abbess of Crewe* or the schoolgirls in *The Prime of Miss Jean Brodie* (see p.81); here, she turned her penetrating gaze on the world of geriatrics. Seventy-nine-year-old Dame Lettie Colston has been receiving nuisance calls from a man who always gives her the same message: "Remember you must die". The baffled police cannot trace the calls. Only retired Chief Inspector Henry Mortimer (just turned seventy) can hazard a logical, if highly unusual, theory: Death himself is the culprit.

Penguin

All the Sparkian hallmarks are here: word-perfect comic timing, a golden sense of the absurd, fierce intelligence and a precise realism which proves to be uncompromisingly otherworldly on closer inspection. No one has been so irreverently acute about old people, their obsessions (Lettie searching the house from top to bottom every night before going to bed) and quirks (Godfrey paying his housekeeper to see her stocking tops), their grumpiness, fears and childish glee. Her style is fast but never simple: matter-of-fact sentences contain unsettling hints

> Being over seventy is like being engaged in a war. All our friends are going or gone and we survive among the dead and the dying as on a battlefield.

and allusions, and the bustling action swells the main theme: the role of death in life, and the virtues – modesty, charity, cheerfulness and generosity – which will enable us to complete our lives with dignity.

📖 Where to go next
Loitering With Intent, 1981, Muriel Spark

All of Spark's quirky, unpredictable humour is brought to bear in this playful exploration of the relationship of fiction to reality. Fleur Talbot is a would-be novelist who goes to work for the eccentric Sir Oliver Reynolds and discovers that his group, the Autobiographical Association, is even more peculiar than it seems.

🎬 **Screen adaptation**
Memento Mori, 1992, dir. Jack Clayton
The very last film of veteran British director Jack Clayton proved to be a darkly witty but touching swansong. With a cast of highly distinguished, elderly thesps (including Michael Hordern, Maurice Denham, Stephanie Cole and Thora Hird), the show is almost stolen by Maggie Smith as sinister professional companion Mrs Pettigrew. Made for the BBC, it has never been released as a video or a DVD.

The Adventures of Huckleberry Finn

1884, MARK TWAIN, AMERICAN

Time has turned *Huckleberry Finn* into an icon – the novel in which American literature first found its voice – but it is best approached in Huck's own style, with flat-out disregard for fine reputations, to be enjoyed as one of the breeziest, truest stories of growing up an outcast.

At the end of *The Adventures of Tom Sawyer*, Twain's cheery tale of boyhood in the American South, the homeless waif Huck Finn is taken in by the Widow Douglas, who intends to "sivilize" him with her "dismal regular"

> *If I had a yaller dog that didn't know no more than a person's conscience does I would pison him. It takes up more room than all the rest of a person's insides, and yet ain't no good, nohow.*

ways. Worse, however, is the ill-treatment he suffers at the hands of his drunken vagrant father. Faking his own death, and escaping in a canoe down the Mississippi, Huck meets up with Jim, a runaway slave trying to make it to the free states, and together they spin downriver on their raft, from one breathless adventure to another.

One of the glories of the novel is Huck's voice: a backwoods drawl expressively raw. Another is its evocation of the Mississippi, a colourful, often surprising sweep of detail exactly pitched: a thunderstorm or a fog, a surly fisherman setting a trot-line in a skiff, or a two storey frame house floating down the river. Equally vivid are the descriptions of local town life: con men working the temperance meetings, feuding aristocrats, small-time farmers with their few hogs and a slave or two. But Huck's journey is also mental, a gradual, bravely intuitive understanding of the world he lives in, and his own place in it. Everywhere he goes, he encounters principles: poor folk's superstitions, Tom Sawyer's picture-book notions of adventure, feuding fami-lies' codes of honour. Conventional moral-ity tells him that a Negro is another man's property, and to help him get his freedom is a crime punishable in hell. Although he still believes in the punishment, his journey gives him the courage to acknowledge the natural truth that Jim is his friend; to say to the so-called civilized world, "All right then, I'll *go* to hell."

Where to go next
The Adventures of Tom Sawyer, 1876, Mark Twain
This prequel to *Huckleberry Finn* is aimed at a younger audience, but the adventures of Huck's friend have charm, warmth and real excitement. Like the later book, *Tom Sawyer* is also a wonderfully intimate portrait of the American South.

Memoirs of Hadrian

1951, MARGUERITE YOURCENAR, FRENCH

Dying of a dropsical heart, the great reforming emperor looks back on his life, appalled to find it such a "shapeless mass". Resigned to his failings but proud of his achievements, he tries to find the secret meanings of his empire and the deeper patterns of his own life. The result is a historical novel which recreates the Roman Empire in minute but living detail, and a thrillingly intimate portrait of an unusually self-scrutinizing man of power.

Yourcenar's scholarship is evident but not obtrusive. A funeral in Egypt, a military campaign in Palestina, political jockeying in Rome (and a dozen other varied scenes in Britannia, Syria, Hispania and Hadrian's beloved Greece) convey the distinct flavours of an enormously diverse empire. But Hadrian's search for a form of private truth beyond official history leads him to reflect more on the common humanity of the peoples

Little by little this letter, begun in order to tell you of the progress of my illness, has become the written meditation of a sick man who holds audience with his memories.

under his government. Here, the novel is persuasively personal, the free drift of a dying man in whom the extremism of youth has given way to the disillusionment of age. Pungent opinions on Christian dogmatists and Jewish zealots mingle with observations on the uses of power, the rigours of self-discipline and the joys of friendship. Finally, in Hadrian's still-raw recollections of a devastating love tragedy of his middle age, the novel finds its most moving theme.

Recommended translation
1955, Grace Frick, Penguin (UK), Farrar, Straus and Giroux (US)

Where to go next
I, Claudius and *Claudius the God*, 1934 and 1935, Robert Graves
The poet and scholar Robert Graves produced a number of entertaining historical novels, of which these two are the best. Racy, sensual and gripping, they plot the crimes and conspiracies of the Roman aristocracy between the assassination of Julius Caesar and the death – and deification – of the narrator, the Emperor Claudius.

Heroes and anti-heroes

S ome novels feature not simply a lead character, but a hero – the novel's true focal point and *raison d'être*. Like a hero of antiquity, he or she stands for humanity, engaged on our behalf in the big, dangerous adventures of life. This is not to say that a hero of classic novels dutifully fulfils the heroic stereotype of classical tradition. Far from it. Heroism comes in all shapes and sizes. And one person's hero is another's anti-hero.

So it is no surprise to find so many outcasts and dropouts ranked among the heroes of classic fiction. Here are the gleeful rejecters of hateful conformity, like Knut Hamsun's splendidly rude Johan Nagel, who terrorizes the bourgeoisie of a quiet Norwegian town. Here too are the misfits rejected by a conforming society, like Djuna Barnes's tormented homosexuals in 1920s Paris, or wronged by hypocritical morality, like Hardy's Tess Durbeyfield. Most recogniz-able of all are those who would fit in if they could, but find them-selves out of tune with the majority, like the great tragic-comic figure

Oblomov, who would be perfectly happy to conform if only he could get out of bed.

Other heroes are completely representative. Lermontov's "hero of our time" is the Romantic hero *par excellence*, and the down-and-outs of Beckett's trilogy represent humanity at its most nakedly helpless. There are clown-heroes, like Endo's "wonderful fool", tormented-genius heroes, like Ondaatje's jazzman Buddy Bolden, and compromised heroes, like Nostromo. There are even inverted heroes – take Jonathan Wild, a vicious criminal whose "greatness", Fielding implies, turns the whole notion of heroism on its head.

Nightwood

1936, DJUNA BARNES, AMERICAN

New Directions

Written in a mode of tragic grandeur, its prose gorgeous and twisted, its milieu depraved, *Nightwood* is a fairy story of doomed lesbian love set in the hedonistic Paris of the 1920s. Giving voice to a theatrical cast of noblemen, circus performers and the idle rich, it swells operatically (with, as T.S. Eliot noted, "a quality of horror and doom very nearly related to that of Elizabethan tragedy") to a grand and furious lament for forsaken lovers and misfits of every sort.

Robin Vote, a woman with the body of a boy, whose life is "a continual accident", is loved by Baron Felix Volkbein, by Nora Flood, and by Jenny Petherbridge. But Robin, drifting alone through Parisian debaucheries, is lost even to herself. In despair, Nora goes at 3.00 in the morning to seek the truth about love from the Irish-American doctor Matthew O'Connor, "the greatest liar this side of the moon", whom she finds in bed heavily rouged and wearing a curly blonde wig. As you see, he says, "you can ask me anything".

Throughout the novel, comedy is very close to agony. The immense allusiveness and poetic insights of the doctor's philosophizing, brilliant and ranting by turns, give colour and music to a great, sad, bitter, wild-hearted hymn to homosexual love.

'For the lover, it is the night into which his beloved goes,' he said, *'that destroys his heart; he wakes her suddenly, only to look the hyena in the face that is her smile...'*

Where to go next
Ryder, 1928, Djuna Barnes
A family saga that attacks patriarchal values, as represented by the grotesquely machismo figure of Wendell Ryder, served up in Barnes's characteristically overwrought "Jacobethan" prose style.

The Beckett Trilogy
Molloy | Malone Dies | The Unnamable
1955–59, SAMUEL BECKETT, IRISH

Beckett is the great comedian of despair, funny, intellectual and foul-mouthed. With his gallows humour and radical hopelessness, he defines the European decade after the end of World War II.

His post-trauma characters are reduced to grim essentials: Molloy labouring on his crutches across a desolate landscape to find his way back to his mother; the bedridden Malone telling himself stories as he tries to find the right way to die; the unnamed narrator of the third book, incapable of any certain statement, at last discovering life's horrible continuity. Beginning perkily and ending in exhaustion, the trilogy captures the querulous, outraged, bleakly hilarious tone of a common humanity.

Through the three novels there is a vertiginous decline. *Molloy* is a showcase of Beckett's dramatic scene-setting – in Molloy's convoluted attempts to ride a bicycle, his crawl through the forest, or his remembered life with his deaf mother when he communicated with her by rapping on her skull. In *Malone Dies*, with the protagonist now inert, the comedy is intellectual, a rant of opinion, argument and wild speculation. Finally, beyond all tomfoolery of narrative, a character who doesn't even know whether he is clothed or not focuses on the impossibility of any meaningful thought or action. From jaunty tramp to the voice in the skull, *The Beckett Trilogy* is the most persuasive account in fiction of human reduction.

> Now that we know where we're going, let's go there. It's so nice to know where you're going, in the early stages. It almost rids you of the wish to go there.

Where to go next
Mercier and Camier, 1970, Samuel Beckett
Written in French just after World War II (but unpublished for over two decades), this comic, existential tale of two tramps is close in tone to the author's play *Waiting for Godot*, and is full of extraordinarily funny and obscene dialogue. Beckett made his own translation in 1974.

Herzog

1964, SAUL BELLOW, AMERICAN

The Jewish novel, the novel of ideas and the confessional novel all collide in *Herzog*, a brainy, vigorous book that seems to take on the whole of Western civilization in its bruising exploration of one American man's sexual humiliation and mental collapse.

Bellow's man of sorrows is Moses Herzog, a middle-aged historian of Romanticism thrown into a spin by the betrayal of his wife, "that bitch". Holed up in a crumbling house in the middle of New England, he begins to write letters, "to the newspapers, to people in public life, to friends and relatives, and at last to the dead, his own obscure dead, and finally the famous dead". Ransacking history, interrogating his own memories, Herzog seeks consolation, entertains revenge, and above all tries to make sense of his torment.

The plot, with its overtones of sex and despair, swirls between past and present, in and out of Bellow's favourite cities (nobody describes them so well): New York, Montreal and Chicago. Often criticized for his portrayal of women (the female leads here are apparently a bitch and a seductress), Bellow excels with Jewish mothers, eccentric aunts and trusting daughters. The whole novel, in fact, is tensely balanced between public and private.

> *If I am out of my mind, it's all right with me, thought Moses Herzog. Some people thought he was cracked and for a time he himself had doubted that he was all there.*

His letters to famous figures – dashed-off scraps, impromptu outbursts – fuel Herzog's quarrels with the president, Heidegger, Nietzsche, God and others, on thorny issues of history, morality and the law. His letters to members of his family prompt torrential memories of his Jewish upbringing, releasing the distinctive Bellovian raw, big-hearted poetry. Better than anyone, Bellow captures the half-marvellous, half-farcical energy and uncertainty of post-war America.

📖 Where to go next
The Adventures of Augie March, 1953, Saul Bellow
Bellow's breakthrough novel is a classic American picaresque. Augie is a young Jewish boy from Chicago trying to make his way in the world while rejecting the thrusting materialism of his older brother, Simon.

The Outsider
1942, ALBERT CAMUS, FRENCH

The classic existentialist novel, short but eerily spacious, is a tale of murder told by the murderer – but it is also a philosophical novel which grips as much by its disquieting ideas as by its brutal action.

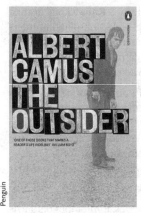

Penguin

Meursault, a young man living in Algiers, has an upsetting habit of saying what he thinks. When his boss asks him if he wants a glamorous overseas promotion, he thinks about it, and says that he doesn't really mind one way or the other. His girlfriend asks him if he loves her: "I told her that I didn't think so." At his mother's funeral, he doesn't cry because he doesn't feel sad. And when he kills a man, he doesn't feel regret so much as "a kind of annoyance".

Meursault's spare mental outlook is matched by Camus's pared-down style: stripped of all stylistic contrivances and social conventions, the book floats free in its own almost empty space. Like a movie with the soundtrack turned off, its visual effects are magnified, and the slightest details – a tiny steamer on the horizon of the sea, the "peculiar" sound of a man crying through a partition wall – echo loudly in the silence. In the first part of the novel, Meursault's thoughts are almost entirely absent, as if he is deliberately trying to empty his mind. Later, during his imprisonment, he will think about his life with sudden, wrenching passion – but even then he will refuse to embrace the extenuating consolations of guilt, contrition or terror. *The Outsider* can be read as a murder novel or a deadpan absurdist comedy, or, in the words of Camus himself, as a novel about a man who, "without any heroic pretensions, agrees to die for the truth".

> *My whole being went tense and I tightened my grip on the gun. The trigger gave, I felt the underside of the polished butt, and it was there, in that sharp but deafening noise, that it all started.*

Outsiders

Marginalized, outcast and alienated characters have always featured in classic fiction, but in the twentieth century, the outsider became representative of humanity in general.

It was a novelist – Turgenev – who was the first to popularize the term "nihilist" – a person (like his character Bazarov in *Fathers and Sons*) who believes in nothing, rejecting the values of society, politics and religion and putting himself beyond their bounds. Knut Hamsun (1859–1952) was another who specialized in characters who aggressively attacked prevailing orthodoxies. By the 1920s, the Austrian Robert Musil (1880–1942) could draw on an intellectual tradition in creating a character so out of tune with "actual reality" that he wishes to abolish it. In the 1940s and 1950s, with the devastation of the war, writers such as Jean-Paul Sartre (1905–1980), Simone de Beauvoir (1908–1986) and Albert Camus (1913–1960) extended the theme, and a new character appeared: existential man, a man in a world utterly without meaning, who has to create meaning for, and out of, himself. Though Camus rejected the "existentialist" label, his character Meursault remains the classic example of the outsider. The tramps of Samuel Beckett (1906–1989), in particular the heroes of his trilogy, Malloy, Malone and the "unnameable", lack not only belief but any verifiable objective truth. And in the work of Austrian novelist Elfriede Jelinek (b. 1946), herself an agoraphobic, we see the anxiety of alienation taken to mental and physical extremes.

Recommended translation
1982, Joseph Laredo, Penguin Modern Classics

Where to go next
The Plague, 1947, Albert Camus
Camus's first masterpiece, a harrowing account of an outbreak of bubonic plague in the city of Oran, Algeria, is also a metaphorical exploration of the wartime occupation of France.

Nostromo

1904, JOSEPH CONRAD, POLISH-BRITISH

Conrad is one of the most thoughtful and surprising writers of adventure. His male world of tough action is intriguingly troubled by moral ambiguities. Here, a full-blown melodramatic tale of dictatorship, revolution, and stolen treasure is given strange new life with his radically sophisticated telling. And at the heart of the action stands one of Conrad's favourite paradoxical figures, the fallible hero: Nostromo, man of the people.

In the country of Costaguana, a fictional dictatorship on the Latin American seaboard – superbly imagined down to the last details of its exotic topography, leading personalities and geopolitical profile – a revolutionary army advances on the coastal town of Sulaco, location of the legendary San Tomé silver mine, controlled for generations by the English Goulds. In desperate need of someone courageous – and honest – enough to smuggle the silver to safety before the army arrives, Charles

> 'Listen to reason, Padrona,' he said. 'I am needed to save the silver of the mine. It is true. I am resolved to make this the most desperate affair I was ever engaged on in my whole life.'

Gould turns to the foreman of the men who work at the local wharves, Nostromo, an Italian immigrant renowned for his selfless feats of heroism. This feat, however, will test not only his physical bravery but also his psychological sureness and moral strength.

In *Nostromo*, Conrad shows himself master of all his gifts. His descriptions of South American politics have the authenticity of historical report. His widely varied characters, even minor ones like the coolly gracious Emily Gould (one of Conrad's relatively few great female characters) or the sweaty opportunist Sotillo, leader of a rebel army, are as fascinatingly hard to pin down as people in real life. His scenes of action – a riot at the quayside, a night-time escape across the silent harbour – are fraught with tension. Above all, his storytelling, with the shifting viewpoints of different characters and dazzling time-changes, dramatizes what seems to be a straightforward narrative in totally unexpected ways.

📖 Where to go next
Lord Jim, 1900, Joseph Conrad
One of the great narratives of life at sea, the novel doubles as another tale of flawed heroism, in which the idealistic Jim, disgraced by an act of cowardice, attempts to redeem himself.

🎬 Screen adaptation
Nostromo, 1996, dir. Alistair Reid
This BBCTV mini-series, made in collaboration with other European companies, boasts authentic locations, several strong performances (including Albert Finney as Dr Monyghan), and a marvellous Morricone score. It still fails to do real justice to the novel, largely because scriptwriter John Hale fails to juggle the many disparate characters into a dynamic and convincing whole.

Hopscotch

1963, JULIO CORTÁZAR, ARGENTINE

Cortázar is one of the great showmen of experimental fiction, and *Hopscotch* – one of the first novels of the Latin American literary "boom" – is an unashamedly avant-garde spectacle: a freewheeling tale of bohemian life in 1950s Paris. Unremittingly intellectual in emphasis, it focuses on a group of dropout artists and thinkers who meet in cafés and run-down apartments to engage in offbeat metaphysical speculations – but at its heart is an ordinary tragedy of love involving a fragile young woman and her disabled child.

Pantheon Books

The fame of the novel rests partly on its experimental structure: it can be read at least two different ways. Fifty-six chapters, "read in a normal fashion", form the rapid, dense and sometimes disorientating narrative of Horacio Oliveira's relationship with his enigmatic mistress, La Maga, and her child Rocamadour. But a further ninety-nine chapters – some filling in gaps, some amplifying themes, some supplying observations of a philosophical nature – can be shuffled into the main story to create a new and very different version of his novel.

What good can we get from the truth that pacifies an honest property owner? Our possible truth must be an invention.

The novel is certainly one of the most vivid evocations of Paris café-life with its jazz and *mate*-drinking, and, above all, supercharged brandy-and-coffee-dregs conversations about art and life. Cortázar's winding, nudging sentences packed with puns and word games capture the competitive blag of intellectuals at play, and his multi-directional arrangement of chapters is an exactly apt vehicle for the search for reality beyond convention. Admittedly, the whole thing would only be of specialist interest if Cortázar didn't possess a sense of humour, and know how to communicate love, passion and tragedy. But he does.

Recommended translation
1966, Gregory Rabassa, Pantheon Books

Where to go next
Blow-Up and Other Stories, 1967, Julio Cortázar
Cortázar was also a master of short stories (often both experimental and fantastic), and this selection from his first two volumes, showcases his finest, including the title story, famously filmed by Michelangelo Antonioni.

Wonderful Fool

1959, SHUSAKU ENDO, JAPANESE

Wonderful Fool is an indignant and poignant satire masquerading as a light, comic tale, and its mockery is all the more effective for its air of quiet humour. Like many of Endo's novels, it has an obvious Christian theme, but it also presents a clear-sighted picture of 1950s Japan, rich in material things but poor in spirit, lacking, above all, in common trust.

It is a Japan in need of a saviour, and in Endo's novel he duly arrives in the form of Gaston Bonaparte, a Frenchman so ugly, ungainly and simple-minded that his hosts, Takamori and his sister Tomoe, almost laugh out loud when they meet him. Their opinion of him does not improve when, dining in a restaurant, he tries to please them by wearing what he insists is a traditional Japanese napkin, a gift to him from a Japanese sailor. He is sadly mistaken; the napkin is in fact a traditional Japanese loincloth, and he maximizes Takamori and Tomoe's embarrassment by sitting throughout the entire meal with someone else's underpants tied proudly round his neck.

> To be a saint or a man of too good a nature in today's pragmatic world, with everyone out to get the other fellow, was equivalent to being a fool, wasn't it?

His wonderfully good nature, as much as his simplicity, gets Gaston into trouble. His misadventures continue, grow desperate, become dangerous, and finally prove to be deadly. Striking out on his own, he is thrown into the company, first, of crooks and prostitutes, and then of the assassin, Endo. Throughout, he remains a mystery not just to them, but also to himself: he can't understand why he should feel so compelled to give these people his affection and trust. Only the bogus diviner, Chotei, understands at once that Gaston has come to Japan with "some great enterprise in mind". Funny, touching and troubling, Gaston's escapades take on the appearance of a spiritual mission.

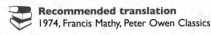

Recommended translation
1974, Francis Mathy, Peter Owen Classics

Where to go next
Silence, 1966, Shusaku Endo
Often described as Endo's masterpiece, *Silence* describes the persecution of Christians in seventeenth-century Japan. Awarded the Tanizaki Prize, it prompted an outcry over its graphic portrayal of the tortures perpetrated by the Japanese authorities on Japanese Christians.

Jonathan Wild

1743, HENRY FIELDING, ENGLISH

The History of the Life of the Late Mr Jonathan Wild the Great, a ferocious satire on success for its own sake, seems as sharply relevant today, in the era of media stardom, as when it was first written, in an age of lawlessness.

Wild, a real historical figure, was hanged in London in 1725 after a short but hectic life of grand-scale, high-profile thieving. His ruthless rise to pre-eminence in his chosen career was legendary, and Fielding's comic masterstroke was to logically treat him as truly great, the equal of Caesar or Alexander, men who imposed their wills with a similar disregard of common morality. In this sense, goodness is not to be confused with greatness; they are, in fact, incompatible. From this simple premise, Fielding's whole novel proceeds.

> *While greatness consists in power, pride, insolence and doing mischief to mankind, so long shall Wild stand unrivalled on the pinnacle of Greatness.*

The effect is hilarious and sickening, and although Fielding pursues his theme with an absolutely unwavering purpose (even the chapter headings continue the joke), he is far too witty a writer ever to be wearying. Changes of pace and tone continually offer dramatic variation as Fielding narrates Wild's early beginnings as a pickpocket, his heyday as a brutal kingpin of organized crime, and his downfall as he overreaches himself in attempting to rob the innocent jeweller Heartfree of both his fortune and his wife. Riotous scenes, such as Wild's stormy address to his gang of thieves when they attempt to rebel against his authority, and intimate scenes, like his courtship of the "chaste Laetitia Snap" (a trollop), emphasize strikingly different aspects of greatness. Wild is even given a remarkable soliloquy on the loneliness of the great after he has been cast adrift at sea in an open boat. Never has irony been more deftly handled or devastatingly effective.

Where to go next
Captain Singleton, 1720, Daniel Defoe
An intriguing, virtually forgotten, novel about a child abducted and raised by gypsies, whose later adventures involve travelling in Africa and becoming a pirate.

Oblomov

1859, IVAN GONCHAROV, RUSSIAN

Oblomov is surely the greatest novel about laziness ever written. Sensitive to all varieties of apathy – stupefying tedium, barely contained restlessness, idealistic daydreams and suicidal depressions – it is funny, sad, chilling and, in the end, heartbreaking.

Ilya Ilyich Oblomov, a minor landowner, is constitutionally unable to stir himself. To the despair of his German friend, the energetic Stolz, he would rather live idly in St Petersburg than make the simplest of efforts to collect the full revenues of his country estate, spending his days lounging at home in his filthy, old dressing gown, bickering with his equally lazy servant, Zakhar. One by one, his old friends lose touch with him and his life contracts.

> He was a man of about thirty-two or -three, of medium height and pleasant appearance, with dark grey eyes, but with a total absence of any definite idea, any concentration, in his features.

IVAN GONCHAROV
Oblomov

Penguin

Such remorseless diminishment would be intolerable, but the delicate tragedy of the novel springs from Oblomov's genuine honesty and faithfulness, and the temporary bursts of hopefulness in his life, as Stolz attempts to rouse his friend to action, or in Oblomov's unexpectedly tender (hesitant, clumsy and funny) love affair with the much younger Olga Sergeyevna. In fact, love between the main characters forms a varied and optimistic counterpoint to the main theme, as does the sharply observed energy of the minor characters, especially their Beckettian dialogue of rapid-fire insults and off-the-point rants. But laziness remains the dominant note, a pathological indolence which, Goncharov intimates, is latent in us all.

Recommended edition
1954, David Magarshack, Penguin Classics

Where to go next
Eugene Onegin, 1833, Alexander Pushkin
Pushkin's cynical verse novel, which tells the story of the heartless dandy Onegin and his cavalier treatment of the spirited Tatyana, stands behind many Russian classics, including *Oblomov*. James E. Falen's brilliant translation is the one to go for.

Screen adaptation
Oblomov, 1979, dir. Nikita Mikhailkov
Star Russian actor Oleg Tabakov really looks and acts the part of the lethargic Oblomov in an almost faithful adaptation of Goncharov's "unfilmable" portrait of inertia. The film's overall impact is, in its own way, stunning: like an anaesthetic, the film's surface beauty hides tragedy and soothes pain before the viewer is forced to confront both – and the sheer blankness of it all.

Mysteries

1892, KNUT HAMSUN, NORWEGIAN

In the English-language world, Hamsun is in danger of becoming a one-book novelist known only for *Hunger* (1890), but the second of his great novels, *Mysteries*, is as raw and uncomfortable as his masterpiece, and more coherent.

One day a stranger arrives in a small Norwegian coastal town, dressed in a bright yellow suit and carrying a fur coat and a violin case full of soiled linen. His name is Johan Nagel, and in the course of the next few weeks he will bewilder the local population with his bizarre behaviour, befriending the local grotesque known as The Midget, confronting the magistrate's deputy, insulting the doctor and his wife, falling in love with one woman and proposing to another. No one can work him out. He is by turns bluntly *I think I've fulfilled a function. I've created one scandal after another in your dreary conformist lives.* intrusive and painfully withdrawn. He makes himself out to be worse than he is. He belittles the townsfolk's liberal principles, and mesmerizes them by recounting his nightmares. And finally he disappears as suddenly as he arrived.

In English fiction of the late nineteenth century there is nothing remotely like Hamsun, with his direct, bruising style and wounding insistence on the hidden chaos of human experience. He is closer to the visual artists of the period, Symbolists like his compatriot Edvard Munch or the early Expressionists, also outsiders, who ridiculed European civilization with their skewed perspectives and discordant colours. Like them, Hamsun championed the primitive, and, like their paintings, his novels provide the electric shock of the new.

Recommended translation
1971, Gerry Bothmer, Picador (UK), Farrar, Straus and Giroux (US)

Where to go next
Hunger, 1890, Knut Hamsun
An avant-garde work recording in dislocated prose a writer's descent into alienation and madness as a result of poverty, *Hunger* remains Hamsun's main claim to fame.

Tess of the d'Urbervilles

1891, THOMAS HARDY, ENGLISH

All Hardy's essential qualities – his narrative genius, his ingrained knowledge of country life and, above all, his passion – come together in *Tess*, an absolutely furious novel, which affronted many of its original readers who perceived it (correctly) to be a bitter attack on conventional morality. It is also one of the great tragic romances, and has lasted because of its remarkable and unforgiving storytelling: the narrative of a young woman in love, and her destruction by the men who say they love her.

'O my love, my love, why do I love you so?' she whispered there alone; 'for she you love is not my real self, but one in my image; the one I might have been.'

Discovering that he is descended from the aristocratic d'Urbervilles, the village haggler Jack Durbeyfield sends his sixteen-year-old daughter Tess ("a mere vessel of emotion untinctured by experience") to their mansion to claim kinship and employment. What follows is an appallingly moving story of both experience and emotion as Tess becomes entangled with two men, Alec d'Urberville, libertine, and Angel Clare, the idealistic son of a clergyman.

It is a novel of many journeys, wonderfully described, as Tess crisscrosses South Wessex, following or fleeing her fortune: the early-morning ride in a van to Trantridge, or the late-afternoon walk down the Egdon slopes into the "oozing fatness" of the Vale of the Var, or the hunted night-time tramp to barren Flintcombe Ash. Nobody knows the Dorset countryside like Hardy, from the sound a river heron makes ("a great bold noise as of opening doors and shutters") to the coarse, springy dialect of the villagers. But Tess's travels are also journeys into new emotional territory – of hope and desolation, fear and regret – and here Hardy's passion comes powerfully into play. His anger is obvious in the big scenes of betrayal (Tess's wedding night, for instance, a frozen nightmare), but he is a startlingly vivid writer of the freshness of new love, and Tess's tragedy would not be so anguished if it were not balanced by the

Penguin

tender scenes at Talbothays dairy. It is both tragedy and romance, an unashamedly emotional blockbuster.

Where to go next
Jude the Obscure, 1895, Thomas Hardy
So hostile was the reception of this novel, an overwhelmingly bleak account of a young working-man's thwarted ambition and failed relationships, that Hardy wrote no more fiction.

Screen adaptation
Tess, 1979, dir. Roman Polanski
Northern France stands in for Dorset in Polanski's lush and over-sentimental take on Hardy's novel. It all looks very beautiful (largely due to the luminous cinematography) and Nastassja Kinski proves a radiantly sensuous screen presence despite the wonky accent. But she is too much the victim figure and this undermines rather than reinforces the tragedy.

Against Nature

1884, J-K HUYSMANS, FRENCH

For Des Esseintes, the hypersensitive hero of Huysmans' most famous novel, decadence is a form of self-assertion. In seclusion from stultifying Parisian society, he cultivates extreme tastes in a solitary attempt to break free of a "loathsome age of shameful duplicity".

Decorating the rooms of his house in "morbid" orange and indigo blue enamel, perfuming them with scents to match his moods, and filling them with monstrously exotic flowers, Des Esseintes champions artificiality against nature. He even encrusts the shell of his pet tortoise with jewels so it will complement the glowing colours of his rare Ottoman carpets (it dies). But although the imagination is powerful, nature can be distressingly assertive. Somewhat to his surprise, Des Esseintes begins to suffer nightmares and stomach cramps, and, as his health fails, he contemplates a return to the hated metropolis.

> *The imagination can easily compensate for the vulgar reality of actual experience.*

One of the great antisocial novels, vividly creating an immediately recognizable interior world of dissatisfaction and alienation, *Against Nature* is perhaps ideally read in adolescence. In a sense, it describes a state of psychological revolution. Revolutionary also in literary terms, it has no plot, and only one character, and each chapter functions as an essay on a favourite topic: perfume, colours, flowers, the decadent Latin writers of late antiquity, Symbolist art. Don't read it for the thrill of the story. But do read it for an authentically, even exhilaratingly, claustrophobic account of moodiness and defiance.

Recommended translation
1998, Margaret Mauldon, Oxford World's Classics

Where to go next
The Damned, 1891, J-K. Huysmans
Decadence meets Satanism in Huysmans' *La-bas* (also translated as *Down There*), in which a scholar working on a biographer of Gilles de Rais is gradually sucked into a world of black magic and debauchery.

The Piano Teacher

1983, ELFRIEDE JELINEK, AUSTRIAN

Jelinek likes to shock, and her uncompromising masterpiece, *The Piano Teacher*, is an absolute jaw-dropper: a horrifying comedy of sex and violence played out by three perfectly respectable Viennese people: an old lady, her pianist daughter, and her daughter's pupil.

Serpent's Tail

The old lady is a hysterical tyrant. Her daughter, Erika, an instructor at the Vienna Conservatory, secretly tours porn shows after work, and harms herself with razor blades and pins. Her youthful and supremely self-confident pupil, Walter Klemmer, dreams only of a romantic entanglement. Together, they perform a macabre dance of love and hatred.

Be warned, Jelinek's themes of violent dependency and control are deliberately disturbing. But they are always developed with a fine provocative intelligence: pornography has rarely been discussed so vividly or seriously in fiction. Her style is expressionistic, jarring metaphors turning the characters into animals or things; her tone is sardonic, a harsh lighting which gives the novel's great set-piece power struggles – between mother and daughter, teacher and pupil, man and woman – their clashing boldness. For all Jelinek's focus on psychology (particularly in her memorably merciless examination of a dysfunctional mother-daughter relationship), the narrative action is precisely staged and powerfully visual. A bloody cat-fight between Erika

Pain itself is merely a consequence of the desire for pleasure, the desire to destroy, to annihilate; in its supreme form, pain is a variety of pleasure.

and her mother, a horribly tense episode of night-time voyeurism at a funfair, and a breathtakingly bizarre sex scene in a school toilet are dramatic *tours de force*, grotesquely combining horror and hilarity.

Recommended translation
1998, Joachim Neugroschel, Serpent's Tail (UK), Grove Press (US)

Where to go next
Wonderful, Wonderful Times, 1980, Elfriede Jelinek
Every bit as grim as *The Piano Teacher*, Jelinek's second novel is about four teenagers whose violence and alienation function as a metaphor for post-war Austria's inability to face up to the horrors of its recent history.

Screen adaptation
The Piano Teacher, 2001, dir. Michael Haneke
Less unrelenting than the novel, the film version is deeply disturbing none-theless. Though dealing with emotional dependency and sexual fantasy in an explicit way, there is no sense of titillation thanks to Haneke's direct and unflashy direction and a performance from Isabelle Huppert (in the title role) that is astonishing for its raw honesty and depth.

Independent People

1934–35, HALLDOR LAXNESS, ICELANDIC

As elemental as any folk tale of trolls and magicians, *Independent People* is the story of a heroic – and pig-headed – struggle in the harsh Icelandic wilderness, when crofters of the early twentieth century still lived in turf hovels with their sheep. A bleak novel for a bleak landscape, it is also a harrowing and moving study of one man's obsession with his independence.

The uplands basalt valley where Bjartur of Summerhouses builds his cottage is remote and inhospitable. Worse, it is haunted by the fiend Kolumkilli from Icelandic legends of old. Bjartur is an independent man, immune to superstition, impervious to the frequent blizzards and free of any obligation, but from the death of his first wife Rosa, who dies giving birth to another man's child, his resilience will be tested.

Laxness raises the question: is Bjartur a legendary hero – or a fiend himself? His feats of endurance are marvellous: in one astonishing episode he wrestles a bull reindeer in the freezing water of Glacier River, then walks through a storm for twenty hours to reach the nearest shelter. But there is coldness in his heart. Caring for his sheep more than his family, he works his children for sixteen hours a day in the fields and drives away his daughter when she succumbs to the love of an itinerant teacher.

> 'What the devil do you think you know about any bloody world? This is the world, the world is here, Summerhouses, my land, my farm is the world.'

Like a tale meant to be recited round a fire at night, the saga-like narrative has a slow, powerful rhythm. Cunning time-shifts provide dramatic breaks – the opening section of Part Two, which jumps several years and begins with the fresh and curious perspective of Bjartur's young son Nonni is especially good – and a comic chorus of old rustics, all creaking joints and blue cheeks, provides periodic relief. Evocations of the northern Icelandic crags and marshlands, with their unruly skies and icy torrents, are wonderful throughout. It is one of the great novels of slow devastation.

 Recommended translation
1945, J.A. Thompson, Harvill Press (UK), Vintage International (US)

Where to go next
The Fish Can Sing, 1957, Halldor Laxness
Laxness's later story of an orphan brought up by an old fisherman is lighter, funnier (and shorter) than *Independent People*.

A Hero of Our Time

1840, MIKHAIL LERMONTOV, RUSSIAN

A book to read in a single sitting, *A Hero of Our Time* is a superior adventure story set during the Russian campaigns against the Muslim peoples of the Caucasus mountains. The writing is bold, the action

Penguin

MIKHAIL LERMONTOV
A Hero of Our Time

terrific, with abductions of princesses, encounters with smugglers and fatal duels following each other in rapid succession – but what gives it special excitement is Lermontov's expert handling of the submerged "human joys and sorrows" of the characters, in particular the young Russian officer Pechorin, a Byronic hero disenchanted with warfare, society and women, even with himself, whose extraordinary actions are at the heart of the narrative.

Lermontov, who served in the Caucasian campaigns himself (as did Tolstoy, see p.220), is completely convincing in his depiction of military life, whether it involves double-dealing with dubious allies, gallantry on leave or boredom in the barracks. It is a male life, unsentimental and gruff, and the manner of his narration is in the tradition of tales told over evening cigars in the mess, a recycling of hearsay and new gossip concerning Pechorin's exploits, all of which is given a shocking twist when Pechorin's journals are discovered, detailing an unexpected love intrigue and a literally cliff-hanging duel. Each episode in Pechorin's short, eventful life, exciting in itself, deepens the enigma. A genuine page-turner, Lermontov's novel is also a sophisticated exploration of deeper currents of a particularly male sort of bitterness.

> *The first time we suffer, we see the pleasure to be had from torturing others.*

Recommended translation
1966, Paul Foote, Penguin Classics

Where to go next
The Queen of Spades and other Stories, Alexander Pushkin
This collection (translated by Rosemary Edmonds) contains four of the best stories, full of vivid local colour, by Lermontov's great literary hero.

The Hour of the Star

1977, CLARICE LISPECTOR, BRAZILIAN

Few novels manage to be both provocatively "postmodern" and thoroughly enjoyable, but *The Hour of the Star* is a rarity: a genuinely entertaining (and revealing) novel about writing a novel.

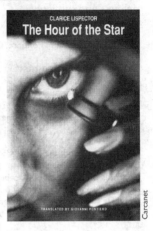

Rodrigo has invented a character called Macabéa, a dull girl living in a Rio de Janeiro slum, whose infuriating simplicity makes her, paradoxically, an enigma. For how can Rodrigo understand her? How can he elaborate a story out of her emptiness? Slowly, obliquely, she swims into focus, revealing herself to be a (very poor) typist, developing (touchingly banal) habits and inclinations, and acquiring, quite abruptly, a (thuggish) boyfriend. By the end of the novel, she stands on the shining brink of self-awareness. But her destiny, arriving out of the blue, takes both her and Rodrigo utterly by surprise.

Allowing us to eavesdrop on the novelist's imagination generously doubles the narrative: the story of the story-making, with its false starts, wrong turns and sudden breakthroughs, is boldly interlinked with the story of Macabéa's life in Rio, as she falls in love and discovers herself. Both stories begin vaguely, questioning and problematic, gradually become clear, and suddenly resolve themselves together in a storming ending. A running thread of comedy unites it all, and two crazily entertaining encounters (with a cyni-

The girl blew her nose on the hem of her petticoat. She lacked that elusive quality known as charm. I am the only person who finds her charming. As the author, I alone love her.

cal doctor and flamboyant fortune-teller) conclude a book about the difficulty of narrative with a terrific narrative flourish, transforming Macabéa, once a dull and empty proto-character, into a figure of richness and subtlety.

 Recommended translation
1986, Giovanni Pontiero, Carcanet (UK), New Directions (US)

 Where to go next
Three Trapped Tigers, 1967, G. Cabrera Infante
Infante's postmodernist epic, which chronicles the night-time activities of a group of artists and writers in pre-revolutionary Cuba, is one of the funniest novels to come out of Latin America.

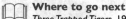 **Screen adaptation**
The Hour of the Star, 1985, dir. Suzana Amaral
Director Amaral dispenses with the character of the writer and simply concentrates on the story of Macabéa. Having moved to the big city, her dreams of the future are hampered by her poverty, her ignorance and lack of self-worth. It should be relentlessly grim but its refusal to glamorize at any point makes it a simultaneously powerful and moving experience.

Max Havelaar

1860, MULTATULI, DUTCH

Considered in the Netherlands to be the book that destroyed colonialism, *Max Havelaar* is a novel of documentary directness and force. With no use for finesse or subtlety, Multatuli mixed history, reportage, fable and caricature to create a powerful exposé of Dutch colonial rule in Java. It caused an outcry, and within ten years of its publication, the system was completely reformed – but Multatuli (a pseudonym meaning "I have suffered much") remained an outcast until his death.

Though the novel makes much use of factual evidence, it is a multi-layered fiction. The hypocritical and bigoted Amsterdam coffee broker Droogstoppel allows the idealistic son of a business partner to prepare a report on Javanese coffee plantations for him, utilizing some of the papers brought over by a shadowy figure known as "Scarfman". But these papers gradually take up the story of a Dutch colonial administrator, Max Havelaar, an eccentric who has ruined himself trying to stamp out corruption in the service.

> The more loudly my book is condemned the better I shall be pleased, for so much the greater will be my chance of being heard. And that is what I want!

Like the pictures of Van Gogh, Multatuli's arrangements are strikingly awkward, his colours thick, his message blunt, the whole ensemble calculatedly shocking. But the crudeness of his artistry is itself artfully constructed: conversations echo each other in discordant keys, meticulous analyses of administrative accounting sit next to Javanese folk tales. In the end Multatuli rudely interrupts his characters to speak direct to the reader ("the book is chaotic … disjointed … striving for effect … the style is bad"), but the voice is of a piece with the whole. *Max Havelaar* is a book that will not shut up.

Recommended translation
1967, Roy Edwards, Penguin Classics

Where to go next
Noli Me Tangere, 1887, José Rizal
An angry denunciation of Spanish colonialism in the Philippines forms the background for this melodramatic but compelling love story.

Screen adaptation
Max Havelaar, 1976, dir. Fons Rademakers
The epic backdrop of the Indonesian landscape, strikingly filmed in muted colours, lends this adaptation the quality of a myth. If, at nearly three hours, it is an occasionally heavy-going experience, its burning sense of indignation and a compelling central performance from Peter Faber make it well worth the effort.

The Man Without Qualities

1930–42, ROBERT MUSIL, AUSTRIAN

Commonly grouped with *Ulysses* and *In Search of Lost Time* in the trinity of Modernist masterpieces, *The Man Without Qualities* is part novel, part brilliant discussion – an acute, dandyish and unexpectedly jaunty analysis of European life on the eve of World War I.

With his "relentless lucidity", Ulrich (a charismatic mathematician who has lost his way) prefers ideas to life. Possible realities interest him, but actual reality is something he would frankly like to abolish. He is therefore the very worst person to be appointed secretary to the Austrian "Parallel Campaign" whose grandiose purpose is to propose a great idea to underpin the celebration of the seventieth jubilee of the Emperor.

> For high-flown thoughts a kind of poultry farm has been set up called philosophy, theology or literature, where they proliferate in their own way beyond anyone's ability to keep track of them.

Massively long, but divided into 131 very short chapters, the plot is sometimes glacially slow and sometimes niftily quick. Rapid seductions and sudden deaths (and occasional meetings with the jailed sex murderer Moosbrugger) alternate with the interminable (and hilariously inconclusive) meetings of the Parallel Campaign committee, while Ulrich keeps himself amused by pondering a hundred disconnected subjects from money and sports to theology and love. Never less than intellectually high-powered, Musil is also witty and irreverent, and he is, furthermore, one of the great writers about sex, sensible, refreshing, with an unblinking eye for telling details. Ulrich's affair with Bonadea (a "nymphomaniac"), his quasi-sexual relationship with his sister Agathe, his ambiguously poised relations with his exalted cousin Diotima, and Diotima's quiveringly high-minded relations with Arnheim, a Prussian armaments manufacturer, are all shockingly intense and infectiously amusing. Technically unfinished (Musil died of a sudden stroke, with – according to his widow – a look of ironic amusement on his face), the novel culminates, as Europe descends into war, with the Parallel Campaign's absurdly inappropriate choice of goodness as the great idea to celebrate.

 Recommended translation
1995, Sophie Wilkins and Burton Pike, Picador (UK), Vintage (US)

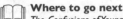 **Where to go next**
The Confusions of Young Törless, 1906, Robert Musil
Set in a military boarding school in the Austro-Hungarian Empire, this short novel follows the increasingly perverse relationship between four pupils. Disturbingly prescient in the way it seems to anticipate twentieth-century fascism.

Coming Through Slaughter

1979, MICHAEL ONDAATJE, SRI LANKAN-CANADIAN

Like Ondaatje's remarkable later pair of novels, *In the Skin of a Lion* and *The English Patient*, *Coming Through Slaughter* is a narrative full of intense moments – troubled bursts of conversation and oblique silences – but the earlier work, a fictionalized life of the pioneering jazzman Buddy Bolden, is harsher, riskier and even more exhilarating. Mixing documentary fragments of evidence (interviews, playlists, newspaper reports) with abrupt scenes from Bolden's life, Ondaatje creates a jumpy, noisy story of genius and disorder in the slums and

brothels of New Orleans at the turn of the twentieth century.

Mainly, the novel chronicles a crisis in Bolden's out-of-control life, when he temporarily abandons both his family and his music. Though the story has a beginning, middle and end, the writing works more like jazz, its riffs, syncopated rhythms and key refrains picked up and played in different registers – the emotional "squawks" and "whistles" of Bolden's life which hit the nerves like unexpected notes. The evocation of backstreet New Orleans, with its promiscuity and violence, is raw; its characters are off-the-wall and fiercely loyal, and Bolden is a man mesmerizingly on the edge, his mind going straight to the hidden meanings of things. There are numerous novels about shattered genius, but few with such heat and electricity.

> *He was the first to play the hard jazz and blues for dancing… When he bought a cornet, he'd shine it up and make it glisten like a woman's leg.*

Where to go next
In the Skin of a Lion, 1987, Michael Ondaatje
Tells the extraordinary story of the immigrants who built Toronto, and incidentally introduces one of Ondaatje's most famous characters, Caravaggio the thief.

Lolley Willowes

1926, SYLVIA TOWNSEND WARNER, ENGLISH

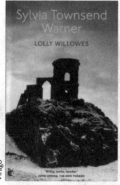

Virago

After her father's death, Laura Willowes (Aunt Lolley) leaves Somerset, and goes to live with her brother's family in London. There, she uneasily accommodates herself to the routines of a spinster's life, every Tuesday changing the library books, every Saturday taking her nieces to their dancing class, and on Sunday attending two church services, followed by cold supper, with "extra trivialities such as sardines and celery". Her growing horror at her life, a vague but powerful urge to connect with some untapped part of herself, is kept hidden from her family, until at teatime one day she abruptly announces that she is leaving them to go and live alone in the Chilterns village of Great Mop, which she knows only from a map bought a few days before, where she will fulfil her destiny by becoming a witch.

Warner writes a beautiful formal prose, slyly – and rebelliously – tending to quirkiness and fantasy, though her effects are never straightforward or loud. Her char-

> 'I can't take warlocks so seriously, not as a class. It is we witches who count. Women have such vivid imaginations, and lead such dull lives.'

acteristic mode is a quiet, unsettling ambiguity. At its most formal and precise, her prose contains echoes of hidden ferocity; when she writes of the supernatural she is punctiliously decorous, not above recording that Lolley's first Witches' Sabbath in the woods around Great Mop is a sad failure on account of the general lack of manners. But when Lolley later meets the Devil, appearing as a gardener complete with basket and shears, she is delighted to find him so thoughtful, explaining to her that one doesn't become a witch to fly around on a broomstick, but to "have a life of one's own, not an existence doled out to you by others". In a social world which forces women into the sanctity of marriage or imprisons them in respectable spinsterhood, only Satan offers them the dignity of independence.

Where to go next
Mr Fortune's Maggot, 1927, Sylvia Townsend Warner
Another characteristically ambiguous novel tells the story of a missionary who loses his faith in the process of trying to convert South Sea islanders to Christianity.

The Quest for Christa T

1968, CHRISTA WOLF, GERMAN

When Christa T dies, leaving behind a folder of notes, letters and diaries, her grieving friend begins the difficult task of preventing her from disappearing into "the oblivion which people call memory". The result is a subtle quest of the imagination, a delicate but piercing attempt to recreate an elusive young woman, whose very individuality was anomalous in Communist East Germany.

She was – eccentric. She never managed to recognize the limits which, after all, everyone does have. She lost herself in everything… She was after something else.

Who was the paradoxical Christa T? Outwardly conformist – a spell at college, a few years as a schoolteacher, marriage, a love affair, children – she quietly gave the sense of being capable of anything, bewildering her friends, giving offence to others. But the narrator comes to believe that Christa's demurely dangerous nonconformity holds the key to a true understanding of ourselves. "She doesn't need us," she says. "We need her."

Made up of haunting moments (Christa as a teenager fleeing the Soviet troops, Christa dancing with her future husband, Christa turning to look at her children one last time as she is driven to the hospital), and full of beautiful, troubling imagery of the natural world, the novel's focus is less on actions than meanings. Though it contains scenes of incongruous comedy (including a brilliantly disorientating trip to "the West", during which her husband's cousin offers to smuggle her out a bra), the tone of the novel wavers between grief and affirmation. At its heart is a strange doubleness (East Germany/West Germany, Christa Wolf/Christa T), in which the narrator's quest for Christa is a stunningly acute way of thinking about herself.

Recommended translation
1971, Christopher Middleton, Virago Modern Classics (UK), Farrar, Straus and Giroux (US)

Where to go next
King David's Report, 1972, Stefan Heym
Wolf's compatriot Heym found a way to write about the East German state in this account of a fictional biblical hero, Ethan the Scribe, commissioned by Solomon to write the official – laudatory – history of his father.

Making it

K afka said, "In the struggle between you and the world, back the world." But it is human nature to do exactly the opposite, to struggle against the odds, to defy circumstances, to pit ourselves against our rivals, to risk everything to get to the top – or die trying. The great novelists have long celebrated, and lamented this trait in its different forms, for "making it" covers many possibilities, from brute survival to get-rich-quick.

Two hundred years separate *Robinson Crusoe* (1719) from the Soviet writer Platonov's *Soul* (1935), but both provide extraordinary accounts of staying alive in an unforgiving natural world. The human world can be unforgiving too, particularly for women, such as the unmarried working-class mother Esther Waters in George Moore's novel of the same name, or Lily Bart, the independent-minded heroine of Edith Wharton's *The House of Mirth*. Sometimes characters struggle against their own demons: there are few more dramatic accounts of the battle with the self than that of Michael Henchard, the Mayor of Casterbridge.

Great novelists have also run the rule over that other inextinguishable human trait: burning ambition. The fierce need to make it to the top (and the attendant risk of crashing to earth) is a particular speciality of the two great French writers, Stendhal (*The Red and the Black*) and Balzac (*Lost Illusions*). Less well known, but equally acute, is John Galt's *The Provost*, set in small-town Scotland at the end of the eighteenth century. And for a super-sophisticated analysis of underhand scheming, Henry James's *The Wings of a Dove* is hard to beat.

Cousin Bette

1846, HONORÉ DE BALZAC, FRENCH

Oxford World's Classics

All the power and speed of Balzac combine in this, one of his last great novels, a tragi-comic story of compulsive philandering and grim jealousy. When Hector Hulot, ennobled by Napoleon and elevated to a senior post in the civil service, takes mistresses, his wife, the "sublime" Adeline, determines on a course of dignified stoicism. The outcome is disaster for both. As Balzac says, "Noble feelings carried to extremes produce results similar to those of the greatest vices."

Cousin Bette is a novel of martyrs and harlots. In Balzac's brilliantly described Parisian society of the 1840s, profligate lechers rub shoulders with self-sacrificial old soldiers, rapacious courtesans join with avaricious financiers. And at the heart of the plot stands a peasant woman from Lorraine, Cousin Bette, Hulot's poor relation, who wreaks an implacable revenge on her relations after her protégé, the Polish artist Wenceslas

La Comédie humaine

One thing Balzac was not short of was ambition. His enormous series of novels and stories known as *La Comédie humaine* (1827–47) was intended, he said, "to portray all aspects of society, so that not a single situation of life, not a face, not the character of any man or woman, not a way of life, not a profession, not a social group, will be missing". Containing 91 works (70 of them novels) and over 2,000 characters (some of them, like Vautrin, the master criminal, reappearing several times), it is a colossal achievement, a great fictional portrait of Paris, the world's first great modern city, and an acute psychological study of modern men and women.

Emphasizing the comprehensiveness of his plan, Balzac divided the series into three discrete sections: *Études de mœurs au XIXe siècle* (Studies of manners in the nineteenth century), *Études philosophiques* (Philosophical studies) and *Études analytiques* (Analytical studies). The following nine are the most outstanding novels in the scheme, all are from the *Études de mœurs* apart from *The Wild-Ass's Skin* which is from the *Études philosophiques*.

- *Les Chouans* (1829)
- *The Wild-Ass's Skin* (1831)
- *Colonel Chabert* (1832)
- *Eugénie Grandet* (1833)
- *Old Goriot* (1835)
- *Lost Illusions* (1837–43)
- *Cousin Bette* (1846)
- *Cousin Pons* (1847)
- *A Harlot High and Low* (1838–47)

Steinbock, spurns her in favour of Hortense, Hulot's daughter.

Balzac's tone, sometimes casually satirical, sometimes sentimental and preachy, buttonholes the reader from the first page. The pace of the novel is terrific, like speeded-up Dickens, set piece tumbling after set piece, the scene changing from backstreet slum to ministerial chambers and back again. At times, the reader may want to slow down, to dwell on pivotal moments, but that's not Balzac's style;

You must look on people in society as tools you make use of, that you pick up or lay down according to their usefulness.

he races on. In any case, the power of the book comes from Balzac's sharp eye for detail and merciless understanding of human appetites. No other novel shows quite so dramatically how the virtuous and the vicious die together.

 Recommended translation
1992, Sylvia Raphael, Oxford World's Classics

 Where to go next
Cousin Pons, 1847, Honoré de Balzac
The companion piece to *Cousin Bette* (the two are sometimes published together as *Poor Relations*), which tells the story of a male poor relation, Sylvain Pons, swindled by his family when they learn that his collection of art is worth a fortune.

Lost Illusions

1837–43, HONORÉ DE BALZAC, FRENCH

Nowhere is Balzac's energy and attention to detail so evident as in this, his grand, sustained study of disillusionment. An unstoppable juggernaut of a novel, its implacable momentum follows the classic trajectory of personal downfall, but its satirical range takes in the whole of 1820s France.

From the provincial town of Angoulême, with its narrow-minded minor aristocrats and swindling tradesmen, to the metropolis of Paris, where amoral journalists destroy the reputations of noblemen and actresses alike, the story charts the rise and fall of Lucien Chardin, a "childish creature", good-looking enough to turn heads, talented enough to write passable verse and unhesitatingly capable of ruining his dearest friends to bolster his vain illusions of fame and fortune.

Lucien is superbly drawn, with just enough sympathy to make his faults uncomfortably familiar, but the novel finds room for dozens of other characters, each with his own overflowing individuality: illiterate printers, childlike actresses, unscrupulous newspaper proprietors, infatuated millionaires; there is even a disguised appearance of Balzac's famous master-criminal, Vautrin. The rhythm of the novel is similarly varied, grippingly concentrated in the great scenes (a hectic post-theatre party thrown by journalists drunk on their own importance, a destitute Lucien sitting next to the laid-out corpse of his lover, writing drinking songs for twenty francs apiece) and slowly expansive during Balzac's knowing descriptions of paper-making processes, the running of a newspaper (he had briefly and disastrously owned one) or the laws of moneylending. A great mass of drama and information, which sometimes threatens to sink under its own weight, *Lost Illusions* is kept triumphantly buoyant by Balzac's tremendous confidence and expertise.

> *It's hard to keep one's illusions about anything in Paris. Everything is taxed, everything is sold, everything is manufactured, even success.*

Recommended translation
1971, Herbert J. Hunt, Penguin Classics

Where to go next
Old Goriot, 1834, Honoré de Balzac
Aided by the sinister Vautrin, the idealistic law student Eugène de Rastignac hatches a plot to win a position in high society involving the well-to-do daughters of an impoverished vermicelli manufacturer, Père Goriot.

Robinson Crusoe

1719, DANIEL DEFOE, ENGLISH

So much a part of our common culture, Virginia Woolf noted, *Robinson Crusoe* seems less "the effect of a single mind" than "one of

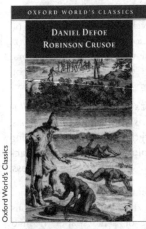

Oxford World's Classics

the anonymous productions of the race itself". The impression is reinforced by the lack of literary authorial voice. What we seem to hear instead is the flat, awkward voice of Crusoe himself – an ordinary man bluntly recounting the most astonishing adventures.

The story, of a shipwrecked sailor living alone on an uninhabited island for twenty-eight years, is one of the best known in all literature: scenes such as the storm which wrecks Crusoe, his discovery of Man Friday's footprint in the sand and the fight with the cannibals are all justly celebrated. But more to the point and equally gripping are Crusoe's painstaking efforts to survive on an island which, at first, fills him with dread.

Superficially resembling Shakespeare's *The Tempest* and Aphra Behn's *Oronooko* (see p.189), *Robinson Crusoe* is far more down-to-earth. Humble endeavours, modestly, even pedantically described, prove as adventurous as cannibal-killing. Defoe is the great poet of mistakes, difficulties and setbacks. Crusoe spends five months building a boat with nothing but a chisel and mallet, only to find he has built it too far up the beach to get it into the water; more months are spent on a number of umbrellas made of goatskin, none of which works. As always – and how true to life – his progress is slow and painful.

I began to look round me to see what kind of Place I was in, and what was next to be done, and I soon found my Comforts abate, and that in a word I had a dreadful Deliverance.

Equally slow and painful – but just as crucially important – are Crusoe's mental struggles, which he records with the stark exactitude of a clerk. Stubbornly fighting despair, he carefully writes out a list of the pros and cons of his situation in a ledger. Coming to see that situation in terms of sin and redemption, he debates with himself the spiritual meaning of his life on the island (a typically brilliant passage rehearses his very rational arguments for and against the footprint in the sand having been left by the Devil). His deepening relationship with Friday is all the more moving for being so plainly described. In fact, it is precisely because there are no flights of fancy, no deliberate colour, no high-flown drama, that Defoe's novel has come to belong to everyone.

Where to go next
A Journal of the Plague Year, 1722, Daniel Defoe
Defoe's classic reconstruction of the Great Plague of 1665 has the vivid immediacy of an eyewitness documentary, recounted by a fictional resident of London.

Screen adaptation
The Adventures of Robinson Crusoe, 1952, dir. Luis Buñuel
While the novel lends itself to Buñuel's customary irony, the great master of the surreal adopts a relatively straightforward approach – apart from a typically imaginative dream sequence in which Crusoe (Dan O'Herlihy) is cursed by his father. The island scenery is suitably lush and the appearance of Friday (Jaime Fernández) provides the opportunity for some sharp observations about class.

Great Expectations

1860–61, CHARLES DICKENS, ENGLISH

The best novel of Dickens's late period is fresh and clever, but genial and warm too, and marvellously generous in its entertainments. The occasional Dickensian vices of theatricality, sentimentality and bagginess are absent: *Great Expectations* is fast-paced, tightly constructed and wise, and its first-person narration gives it an attractively intimate, contemplative air.

At once a mystery, a romance, a fairy story and a *bildungsroman*, the novel begins with a tremendous shock, when Pip, a young orphan being brought up "by hand" by his older sister, encounters an

Bildungsroman

Literally "formation-novel", *bildungsroman* is the name given to a novel which describes the gradual maturity of an individual from childhood to adulthood, in effect a quest for one's "proper" identity through a process of trial and error. The name reflects the fact that many key works in the genre are German, beginning with *Agathon* (1765–66) by Christoph Wieland and popularized by Goethe's *Wilhelm Meister's Apprenticeship* (1795–96). Dickens wrote a number of *bildungsromans*, including *David Copperfield* (1849–50) and *Great Expectations* (1860–61).

escaped convict one evening on the Kent Marshes near his home, an incident both terrifying and anarchically comic. But Pip's life is even more drastically destabilized soon afterwards by the embittered recluse, Miss Havisham, who imperiously requests him to visit her at Satis House, her decaying home, where he meets the young and haughty Estella, and is taught,

> *What would it signify to me, being coarse and common, if nobody had told me so?*

despite himself, the meaning of dissatisfaction. When he receives a third shock – the news that he has come into a handsome property and will be brought up as a gentleman – he begins to entertain great expectations of his future prospects; but, curiously, his sense of dissatisfaction only increases. Previously, he yearned only to be a gentleman; now he is forced to ask himself what a gentleman truly is.

The narrative has deep energy: a story written with journalistic dash and packed with shocking incident, and a great array of characters so vividly individual as to exist in their own brilliantly coloured auras. Minor figures, like Wemmick the clerk living with his aged father in a miniature castle, burst with the same vitality as the main characters, such as Magwitch the convict or the superbly vindictive Miss Havisham, still wearing her bridal dress years after being stood up at the altar. The emotional range of the novel is similarly capacious, encompassing love, jealousy, rage, tenderness and joy. The hectic variety of it all would destroy an ordinary novel, but here, in the figure of Pip, with his slow, baffled struggle to break the spell and see things as they really are, the conflicting energies are miraculously balanced.

Where to go next
David Copperfield, 1850, Charles Dickens

Partly autobiographical, Dickens's own favourite of his novels tells the story of David Copperfield, who, put out to work in his stepfather's warehouse, escapes and falls in with his old servant Clara Peggoty and a host of colourful characters, including the charming spendthrift Mr Micawber.

Screen adaptation
Great Expectations, 1946, dir. David Lean

This is, arguably, the greatest of all Dickens film adaptations largely because Lean and his cinematographer Guy Green create such a powerful sense of darkness and menace. Pip's childhood scenes – not least the meeting with the convict on the marshes, and the visits to Estella at Miss Havisham's ghostly house – are particularly disturbing.

Sister Carrie

1900, THEODORE DREISER, AMERICAN

Sister Carrie is an unnerving original. Downbeat, drab and clumsily written, it is also the best-ever fictional portrayal of sink-or-swim life in capitalist America.

Boom-town Chicago and flat-broke New York of the 1890s provide much more than setting. Described by Dreiser in minute detail – their stores and shows, their millionaires and bums, the constant circulation of news and rumour – they dictate the destinies of his characters: Drouet, the eager travelling salesman with an eye for the good things on offer; Hurstwood, the comfortably established manager of a Chicago nightspot, who longs for a different life; and the teenage Carrie, arriving from the country with only the vaguest of

plans and little to recommend her except some native wit and a pretty face.

The classic conflict of vice and virtue would be the obvious narrative to pursue, but Dreiser isn't interested; shockingly – and it still seems shocking – he ignores the moral question completely: to become a man's mistress or bigamous wife in return for essential comforts in a hostile city is normal. Dreiser shows little more interest in the rags-to-riches possibilities of his story; on the contrary, many of the most dramatic incidents (a theft, a headlong escape to Canada, a new love affair) prove dead ends. The most powerful part of the book is Hurstwood's extended crack-up, a downward spiral of worsening fortunes, which takes him from Fitzgerald and Moy's elegant saloon in Chicago's theatre district to the Bowery flophouses in New York. Here, Dreiser's awkward prose is acutely appropriate: a heartless, painful unfolding of a peculiarly American tragedy.

> When a girl leaves her home at eighteen, she does one of two things. Either she falls into saving hands and becomes better, or she rapidly assumes the cosmopolitan standard of virtue and becomes worse.

Where to go next
An American Tragedy, 1925, Theodore Dreiser
Based on a real murder case, the novel recounts the disastrous attempts of Clyde Griffiths to insinuate himself into high society. Having fallen in love with a society belle, he decides to take drastic action when he learns that his working-class girlfriend is pregnant with his child.

Screen adaptation
Carrie, 1952, dir. William Wyler

Laurence Olivier gives one of his most restrained and effective film perform-ances as George Hurstwood, meticulously – and movingly – chronicling his disastrous love for the much younger Carrie Meeber (Jennifer Jones). Wyler's slow, but never ponderous, direction succeeds admirably in getting to the emo-tional heart of Dreiser's novel.

The Great Gatsby

1925, F. SCOTT FITZGERALD, AMERICAN

Fitzgerald's masterpiece is the great American novel of the Jazz Age, a crystal-clear portrait of the fast set of flappers and sports jocks, and a deeply ambiguous exploration of the self-determinism – and unattainable ideals – of the American dream.

Even among Long Island's mil-lionaires, Jay Gatsby's extravagance is conspicuous. At the same time, he is a puzzlingly absent figure, hesitant in meeting his neighbours and nowhere to be found at his own lavish parties. Sometimes he claims to have inherited his money, at others that he made it in

MODERN CLASSICS

F. Scott Fitzgerald
The Great Gatsby

Penguin

the drugstore business. And what are his new acquaintances to make of his frankly implausible stories of heroic service during World War I? For the narrator, Nick Carraway, his neighbour at West Egg, Gatsby is an intriguing mystery to be solved. For Nick's friend Tom Buchanan, an ex-college football hero disappointed by life, he is an irritation. But for Tom's sad and lonely wife Daisy, Gatsby turns out to be a strangely reinvented figure from her past.

Fitzgerald is one of those effortlessly economical stylists whose characters, settings, moods and situations seem to drop into place, fully formed, with a few brilliantly chosen remarks. The writing is simple but resonant, the drama of his story clear and swift, full of unexpected and explosive narrative surprises. Though short, it is

If personality is an unbroken series of successful gestures, then there was something gorgeous about him, some heightened sensitivity to the promises of life.

a book of many moods, as Fitzgerald's young millionaires move from breezy cynicism to restless discontentment to pointless violence. There are some very funny scenes, and some very sad scenes, but no false ones, and, as the story develops (Gatsby revealing more of himself and his mysterious romantic purpose slowly becoming clear), the tone deepens and darkens, and the troubling note that had been faintly present from the beginning dominates. The book's final section, in which Fitzgerald proposes Gatsby's "greatness", is superbly poignant.

Where to go next
This Side of Paradise, 1920, F. Scott Fitzgerald
The novel which first caught the tone of the Jazz Age retains its exhilarating freshness and bounce as it follows the pampered Amory Blaine in his quest for inner peace through a series of unfulfilling love affairs.

The Provost

1822, JOHN GALT, SCOTTISH

The Provost is a quiet masterpiece of irony and observation, with a sharp, particular flavour. In it, James Pawkie (Scots for "sly") recounts his long public life as a councillor of Gudetown. Pawkie by name, pawkie by nature: he is a brilliant political manipulator. When, in 1760, he is first elected to the Council, he owns a single modest haberdashery shop. Fifty years later, retiring from his third term as Provost, he is one of Gudetown's principal owners of property. Like a "caterpillar", he has eaten up the town. His account of his career, intended as pious testament to years of devoted public duty, is in reality the unwitting self-portrait of a small-town politician on the make.

Much of the novel's distinctive flavour derives from its details. The jaunty Scots dialect enlivens the dialogue ("'Gang your ways home,' quo I very coolly, 'for I hae a notion that a' this hobbleshaw's but the fume of a gill in your friend Robin's head.'"), and brings the characters to life with an astonishing rapidity of description ("he was a queer and quistical man, of a small stature of body, with an outshot breast").

> To rule without being felt ... is the great mystery of policy.

The narrative too attends to the details of small-town realities. Each of the forty-seven brief chapters contains an incident from public life (many taken directly from the public records of Galt's own town of Irvine), humdrum events jostling with the sensational: the quelling of a riot with the repair of the kirk, the subscription for street lamps with the execution of a woman who has murdered her baby. Combining brilliantly with the Provost's own tale of ambition and power, such scenes succeed in little more than 150 pages in communicating a powerful sense of the violent sweep of small-town politics.

Where to go next
The Annals of the Parish, 1821, John Galt
Another brilliantly observant chronicle of small-town life in eighteenth-century Scotland, narrated by the Reverend Michael Balwhidder, whose descriptions of social and economic activity provided the source for the philosopher J.S. Mill's concept of "utilitarianism".

The Mayor of Casterbridge

1886, THOMAS HARDY, ENGLISH

One of the great page-turning classics, with a plot that sucks you in, *The Major of Casterbridge* is also a richly detailed description of small-town society, a gritty picture of the agricultural world, and, above all, an unflinching account of one man's angry self-destruction.

One Fair Day, an out-of-work hay-trusser, Michael Henchard, gets drunk and sells his wife and infant daughter to the highest bidder, a

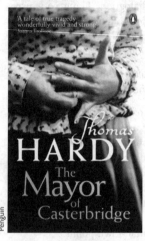

passing sailor. Filled with remorse for what he has done, but unable to trace his family, he takes a vow not to drink for twenty-one years. Nineteen years later, supposing her sailor "husband" drowned, Susan Henchard returns to Casterbridge with her daughter, to find that Michael Henchard is now the most powerful corn merchant in the town, a teetotaller, and Mayor.

The novel's dramatic opening is typical of the whole. Hardy works in two ways: close-up and long-range, turning out intensely realized set pieces (charged encounters, shocking revelations, unexpected outbursts) artfully arranged within the long-term trajectory of the plot – the relentless decline of Henchard's fortunes. Not just Henchard, but all the characters struggle to escape their past – the talented, popular Donald Farfrae, who first serves then supplants Henchard; Elizabeth-Jane, who blossoms into a woman despite Henchard's paternal ill-treatment; flighty Lucetta Templeman, Henchard's lover, who comes to Casterbridge to claim him then changes her mind. Their characters might be their fates (as Hardy claims), but their dilemmas are finely balanced and their collisions constantly spin them in new directions. Such whirling action could easily unbalance the story, but Hardy's narrative is solidly grounded in his fictional Wessex, a region of the

> '*I don't drink*,' he said in a low, halting, apologetic voice. '*You hear, Susan? I don't drink now. I haven't since that night.*'

imagination tangibly real in its landscape and seasons, topography and trades, social customs, domestic lives and individual passions.

📖 Where to go next
Far From the Madding Crowd, 1874, Thomas Hardy
Also set in Wessex, this early novel is a thumping melodrama of love involving the selfless shepherd Gabriel Oak, his spirited employer Bathsheba Everdene and the dashing Sergeant Troy.

🎬 Screen adaptation
The Mayor of Casterbridge, 2003, dir. David Thacker
The 1978 BBC mini-series (starring Alan Bates) may be more celebrated, but this recent two-part TV version is the one to go for. It is dominated by a performance of granite-like authority from Ciaran Hinds as the flawed protagonist. The psychological impact of his fluctuating fortunes is brilliantly portrayed and makes the final tragic denouement all the more powerful.

Their Eyes Were Watching God

1937, ZORA NEALE HURSTON, AMERICAN

Zora Neale Hurston's novel gave American literature what it had been missing: the first masterpiece of the African-American experience. Simpler than Toni Morrison's *Beloved*, it is perhaps stronger, a story of romance and melodrama full of plain pictures glowing with life and – an equally great achievement – the rich fluidity of everyday talk. Like an old recording, it conjures out of the air a crowd of electrifying individual voices and instantly evokes a vanished past.

Naïve but spirited, Janie Starks is disillusioned by her first marriage to the unimaginative farmer Logan Killicks, and constricted in her second to the go-getting Mayor of Eatonville, Jody Starks. But is the fun-loving Tea Cake, twelve years her junior, a man who will finally allow her to express herself in an equal partnership of love and respect – or is he only after her money?

Though simple, *Their Eyes Were Watching God* is not simplistic. Though melodramatic – featuring a hurricane, flood and a face-off with guns

– it is never crudely plot-driven. Largely bypassing racial issues (there are very few white characters) and, despite its title, uninterested in religion, the novel primarily explores the relationships between black people in their own social world, between neighbours, friends, rivals and, most of all, between men and women. The marvellously distinct minor characters who cluster round Jody, Janie and Tea Cake form a gossipy chorus of town life with its civic rituals and trivial power struggles (enlivened at one point by the hilarious extempory funeral of a mule). The main characters – including Janie's ex-slave grandmother – have all the complicated ordinary richness of real people.

> *Us talks about de white man keepin' us down! Shucks! He don't have tuh. Us keeps our own selves down!*

Where to go next
Invisible Man 1952, Ralph Ellison
The impassioned and eloquent story of a nameless narrator who escapes from the bigoted South to find only disillusionment in New York. On the eve of the Civil Rights Movement, it laid bare and made unignorable the African-American experience.

The Wings of the Dove
1902, HENRY JAMES, AMERICAN

Late Henry James is not to everyone's taste. His plots are lingeringly slow and his characters bafflingly complex; his very sentences are curiously elaborate. But there is no subtler novelist of relationships, no more exacting dramatist of moral dilemmas, and, far from being overblown or turgid, his "difficult" late novels – *The Wings of the Dove*, *The Ambassadors* and *The Golden Bowl* – are grippingly tense stories of sensuality, corruption and betrayal.

The Wings of the Dove is a conspiracy novel, full of murky concealments and dangerous revelations. Kate Croy (passionate and manipulative) is the penniless ward of her wealthy aunt, who insists on her making a brilliant match. Secretly, however, Kate is engaged to Merton Densher, a journalist. Their prospects look bleak until they meet Milly Theale (the "dove"), a loveable, fatally ill American heiress, who is also attracted to Densher. The plot Kate formulates is brilliantly attuned to all their desires, but morally dubious and fraught with risks.

The plot is literally a matter of life or death, but James is focused less on the action than on the psychology of the characters caught up in it. His circuitous style perfectly suits their ambiguous acts, ambivalent feelings and evasive conversations in which unspoken understandings (and misunderstandings) create a mood of almost continuous suspense. Though rarefied in its general tenor, the novel features marvellously concrete evocations of two cities – James the travel writer at his best – wealthy London simultaneously ostentatious

HENRY JAMES
THE WINGS OF THE DOVE
EVERYMAN JAMES
Everyman/Orion

'We're of no use to you – it's decent to tell you. You'd be of use to us, but that's a different matter. My honest advice to you would be to drop us while you can.'

and discrete and the gorgeous polyglot confusion of Venice, where, during days of autumn downpour, the plot reaches its finale.

Where to go next
The Portrait of a Lady, 1881, Henry James
One of the most straightforwardly engaging of James's novels, his early masterpiece tells the story of the penniless but lovable American Isabel Archer, who travels to England and there has to make a choice from the different men who offer her marriage.

Screen adaptation
The Wings of a Dove, 1997, dir. Ian Softley

While the verbal intricacy of Henry James is not obviously cinematic, the deft psychological interplay of his self-absorbed characters is – as this masterly adaptation reveals. Ian Softley adds a dollop of sex, builds up the tension (especially in the sumptuously filmed Venice scenes) and gets beautifully nuanced performances from Helena Bonham-Carter as Kate and Alison Elliott as Milly.

Esther Waters

1894, GEORGE MOORE, IRISH

Though written by an Irishman, in a "French" style (Moore, with his cool focus on social detail, was an enthusiast of the naturalism of Zola), *Esther Waters* seems purely English, a novel which understands the limpid Englishness of racehorses cantering across the South Downs as intimately as the squalid Englishness of drunkenness in the soiled brick slums of Wandsworth. It begins and ends with the same quiet, intense

We don't choose our lives, we just makes the best of them.

scene: Esther Waters arriving alone at a country house to take up a "situation" as a servant. In the first she is a young girl, in the last a middle-aged woman. The desperate years in between are the subject of the novel.

The quiet narrative tone, matching the illiterate Esther's working-class stoicism, throws her story into stark relief. Seduced and abandoned by both the father of her child and her family, she is dismissed from her post as kitchen-maid, and left utterly alone and without money in a hellishly inhospitable London to fend for herself as an unmarried mother. The story could have been sensational, but there are no false theatricalities here. It could have been sentimental, but it is not, because Esther is not. Ignorant but tough, religiously minded but sulky, sometimes outspoken and always fiercely protective of her child, she is one of the great survivors of fiction, and a genuinely moving heroine.

If *Esther Waters* is a classic weepy, it is also a classic page-turner. The changing scenes – servants' quarters, backstreet baby-farmers, the bustling new London suburbs, Derby Day, the public houses – are all brilliantly observed, and the passage of time – and with it growth and loss, births and deaths, the spinning seasons, the cycles of good and bad luck – is beautifully handled. Unlike many Victorian novelists, Moore is an invisible presence, and *Esther Waters* is a book without moralizing, balancing long periods of suffering against moments of shared joy, unexpected bliss, however brief, and the tenderness between a mother and her son.

Where to go next
New Grub Street 1891, George Gissing
Poverty and hardship are the key themes in Gissing's narrative about the unscrupulous writer of reviews Jasper Milvain, who seeks his fortune in the literary world of hack journalists, poor scholars and failed novelists.

A House for Mr Biswas

1961, V.S. NAIPAUL, TRINIDADIAN

Naipaul's reputation as a fierce, sometimes haughty, writer is confounded by his great early novel, *Biswas*, a comic but tender story of a Trinidadian man's struggle to assert his dignity.

Born with six fingers and an "unlucky sneeze", Mr Biswas is marked at once for a life of trouble. Prickly and sarcastic, given to outbursts of infantile anger, he has few talents and fewer opportunities. As it turns out, his professional failures – as a religious "pundit", shopkeeper, sign-painter and overseer – prove less traumatic than his ill-considered marriage to Sharma Tulsi, whose terrifying and populous family threatens to overwhelm him. With no natural resources but his defiance, Biswas opposes the forces of custom and ritual, and haphazardly works towards the fulfilment of his dream: to possess his own home.

The extended family is one of Naipaul's most savagely funny themes. Scenes of discord in the teeming Tulsi household – the bitter but irrepressible Biswas usually being outmanoeuvred by his

> 'That is the whole blasted trouble,' he said. 'I don't look like anything at all. Shopkeeper, lawyer, doctor, labourer, overseer – I don't look like any of them.'

savvy in-laws – are excruciating but hilarious, brilliantly coloured by the expressive Trinidadian patois. The whole novel, in fact, is hypersensitive to all aspects of domestic misery: bravado and cowardice, arguments and insults, beatings, sullen silences and compromised reconciliations. There is sympathy in the detail, however. Biswas's childlike rapture as a sign-painter (what can compare with the "swing and rhythm" of the letter S, he asks) or the "happy, hopeful" period of his life, when, discovering a large, unused tin of paint, he paints everything in the house yellow, "even the typewriter", are moments of genuine uplift. *Biswas* is a marvellously entertaining and passionately felt testament to a life of many humiliations and infrequent triumphs.

Where to go next
The Enigma of Arrival, 1987, V.S. Naipaul
Considered by many to be Naipaul's masterpiece, the novel describes the journey of a writer from Trinidad to a small village near Salisbury in England, where he must learn to see – and understand – his new home.

The Violent Bear it Away
1960, FLANNERY O'CONNOR, AMERICAN

Flannery O'Connor is famous for her fiercely dramatic short stories set among the poor whites of the American South, but her second novel is equally memorable: a grotesque comedy about religious vocation in an age of materialism.

Tennessee in the late fifties: the world burns with corruption.

Octogenarian Mason Tarwater, a prophet, wants to make it burn with the Word of the Lord, beginning by baptizing the idiot son of the schoolteacher Rayber. When the old man dies at breakfast one morning, he bequeaths his mission to his pyromaniac fourteen-year-old nephew, whom he has raised himself in the backwoods of Tennessee. A voice in young Tarwater's head counsels him to resist, but the woods are full of strange signs, and he finds himself hitching a ride to the city where Rayber lives.

Farrar, Straus and Giroux

The classic O'Connor style – half Old Testament, half dirty realism – full of concrete details and dangerous metaphors, makes Tarwater's world both real and strange: hiking along the highway, he feels "as if he were walking on the back of a giant beast which might at any moment stretch a muscle". Outbreaks of violence are O'Connor's great subject, not least the purifying violence of belief with its constant images of fire, which destroys and purges, and water, which baptizes and drowns. Old Tarwater's life, which we see in flashbacks, features kidnap, insanity and a shooting; young Tarwater's quest ends in murder.

Francis Marion Tarwater's uncle had been dead for only half a day when the boy got too drunk to finish digging his grave and a negro named Buford Munson, who had come to get a jug filled, had to finish it.

And here is a problem: O'Connor, a devout Catholic, claimed the Tarwaters spoke for her, not the rationalist schoolteacher Rayber. Dark, contradictory, oddly hilarious, the novel ends with a new beginning, young Tarwater repeating his journey from the backwoods to the city in obedience to the command "GO WARN THE CHILDREN OF GOD OF THE TERRIBLE SPEED OF MERCY."

📖 **Where to go next**
Everything That Rises Must Converge, 1965, Flannery O'Connor
In her last collection of short stories, which includes "Revelation", "Judgement Day" and "Parker's Back", O'Connor's themes of religion and generational conflict find their fullest expression.

Hester

1883, MARGARET OLIPHANT, SCOTTISH

Most of the output of the hyper-productive Mrs Oliphant (Queen Victoria's favourite novelist) has not lasted. But *Hester*, a forthright tale of money and sex in an age of snobbery and piety, remains an enduringly entertaining novel of strong women and vile, bewildered men.

At its heart is the headstrong teenager Hester, who hates living off the charity of her Aunt Catherine, the splendidly authoritarian retired owner of Vernon's provincial bank – who, unknown to Hester, was jilted years before by the girl's father. Catherine keeps a beady eye on her younger cousins, stolid Harry and calculating Edward, who now run the bank, and when she sees their growing interest in Hester she is quick to voice her disapproval. Irregularities at the bank, however, are more puzzling and less easy to control.

> 'The moment has come that I have so long foreseen ... Meet me at dusk under the holly at the Grange gate. The most dangerous place is the safest.'

More slapdash than Trollope, less intellectual than George Eliot, Oliphant is nevertheless an acute psychologist, specializing in the unspoken interplay between characters – glances, silences, tones of voice – and the novel is full of ordinary domestic scenes seething with unexpressed emotion. It contains a tortured clandestine affair – "a curious duel of mingled love and dislike" – and two toe-curling marriage proposals, one as awkward as anything in Austen, the other perhaps the fastest in all fiction. Slow-moving at first, the plot surges into melodrama in the final third, but the novel's power remains invested in the characters' psychology – dramatized in the trials placed upon the headstrong Hester, and the temptations laid before Edward, one of Victorian literature's great hysterics.

📖 **Where to go next**
Robert Elsmere, 1888, Mrs Humphrey Ward
This nineteenth-century best seller deals not with money or sex but the Victorians' other great obsession, religion. Driven by a sense of duty, the eponymous clergyman resigns his orders to devote himself to social work in the East End of London – to the consternation of his wife.

Soul

1935, ANDREY PLATONOV, RUSSIAN

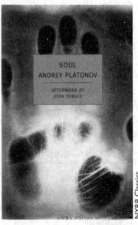

NYRB Classics

Long subject to official opprobrium (Stalin is said to have written "scum" in the margin of one of his stories), Platonov is now regarded as one of the greatest Soviet novelists, a stylist to rank alongside Modernist masters such as Musil and Beckett – though his utterly disconcerting blend of idealism and brutality makes him unique. *Soul*, the story of an outcast nation's struggle to survive in the Kara Kum Desert of Turkmenistan, is a socialist epic of ambiguous progress shot through with mysticism and cast as tragedy. No wonder Stalin hated it.

Trained as an economist in Moscow, and filled with revolutionary zeal, Nazar Chagataev returns to the desert on a mission to lead his scattered, destitute people (called the Dzhan – "soul" – because they have nothing else left) to their ancestral lands, a journey of extreme harshness. More dead than alive, they are reduced to eating wet sand and drinking the blood of wild sheep "straight from the veins of their throats".

The humanist tradition in the West places the emphasis on the psychological, but Platonov's interests are social and metaphysical.

Wild animals were silently following the nation all the time, keeping at an invisible distance and eating those who fell.

His human dramas are starkly theatrical matters of life and death – the butchering of a camel, a desperate defence against giant eagles – and his revolutionary aesthetic, all rapid departures and abrupt juxtapositions, constantly transforming the particular into the universal, is a genuinely new language in fiction.

Recommended translation
2003, Robert and Elizabeth Chandler, Harvill Secker (UK) and NYRB Classics (US)

Where to go next
The Foundation Pit, 1973, Andrey Platonov
A group of workers alternate between building a new apartment block and the enforced collectivization of a nearby village. Both activities seem futile and destructive and the novel – published some forty years after it was written – is even more despairing than *Soul*.

Midnight's Children
1981, SALMAN RUSHDIE, INDIAN

Rushdie is one of the great conjurers of fiction, a natural master of outrageous plots, colourful embellishments and inexhaustible digressions. In *Midnight's Children*, his flourishes of magic are genuine eye-openers, offering on the one hand a blazingly satirical myth of post-Independence India, and, on the other, a troubled exploration of personal experiences.

Saleem Singh, whose story this is, is one of 1,001 children born at the stroke of midnight on 15 August 1947 – the moment of

India's independence – and endowed with magical powers. Saleem, an unlucky, unhandsome boy, is granted the problematic ability to see into the hearts and minds of men. Over the next thirty years, swept up in the political events of the subcontinent (the Indian conflict with China, the India-Pakistan War, Bangladeshi liberation and "the Emergency", among others) he will act as a mirror to his country, but also embark on a thwarted personal quest for the meaning of his life.

> *The children of midnight were also the children of the time: fathered, you understand, by history. It can happen. Especially in a country which is itself a sort of dream.*

His confident voice and springy, exuberant prose mark a distinctive originality, but, like Márquez and Grass, Rushdie also possesses the raconteur's traditional gifts, an "old-time fabulism" perfect for capturing a country of ancient myths busy re-inventing itself. A humorous and generous writer with a love of contradiction and paradox, he is implacable in his denunciations (he hates Mrs Gandhi deeply) and unafraid to spell out the horrors of war and corruption. For all its literary charm, the novel has, as Saleem says, "the taste of truth". For all its violence (and some of the episodes are very violent), it celebrates "acts of love". Both tenderness and rage are magically brought together.

Where to go next
Shame, 1983, Salman Rushdie
Rushdie followed his examination of Indian independence with this controversial take on Pakistan, its leaders and its history of violence. Some critics think it every bit as good as *Midnight's Children*.

The Grapes of Wrath
1939, JOHN STEINBECK, AMERICAN

The Grapes of Wrath is the big novel of the American Depression, a sustained lamentation of pity and anger, and a minutely detailed

Penguin

record of the unbearable hardships of the sharecroppers whose lives were blighted by the dust storms that hit the Midwest in the 1930s. It is the fictional counterpart to the celebrated documentary photographs of the period, capable both of wide-angle panning across ruined landscapes and highly detailed close-ups of single figures. The effect is hugely emotional.

When Tom Joad is released from Oklahoma State Penitentiary, he makes for the old farm, only to find it abandoned, his family forced out, like thousands of other tenant farmers, by the land's barrenness and unsympathetic landlords. Catching up with them, Tom shares their desperate journey to California, where they have been promised work as fruit-pickers – only to find that life in the west is even worse than the life they have left behind.

'They was the time when we was on the lan'. Ol' folks died off an' little fellas come an' we was always one thing – we was the fambly – kinda whole and clear. An' now we ain't clear no more.'

For a big subject, a big-hearted style. From the beginning, the novel is a tear-jerker, not subtle but bold – sometimes laid on a bit thick, but marvellously controlled. Documentary sections – journalistic pieces on migrant camps or the repossession of homes – are interspersed with the narrative action, emphasizing the wider scope of the story. A furious denunciation of capitalism in general, it remains, however, a richly detailed story of particular suffering. Mesmerizing half-articulate conversations (the thinking-aloud of desperate men) give the book its bass notes, and it contains an impressively high quota of memorable scenes, including an electrifyingly tense birth in a storm, and one of the most haunting final images in fiction.

📖 **Where to go next**
Of Mice and Men, 1937, John Steinbeck
The friendship between two itinerant farm labourers – George Milton and the feeble-minded Lennie Small – is the subject of Steinbeck's short but intense novella.

🎬 **Screen adaptation**
The Grapes of Wrath, 1940, dir. John Ford
Ford's film has become as much a classic as the novel on which it is based, and it remains remarkably faithful to it. Gregg Toland's austere black-and-white photography creates a documentary feel that highlights the Joad family's gradual descent into bewildered desperation as their Californian dream turns into a nightmare.

The Charterhouse of Parma

1839, STENDHAL, FRENCH

Dictated at high speed (apparently in only 52 days) *The Charterhouse of Parma* is almost wilfully scrappy, but its energy and resourcefulness make it one of the most acute explorations of the vagaries of the human heart, and a eye-opening exposé of political machinations. A tidy narrative is the least of Stendhal's concerns: he is much more interested in people than stories. He trains his telescope abruptly here and there, fixing his brief, intense gaze on the behaviour and moods of his characters, and the result is an analytical romance of political and erotic intrigue in his beloved Italy, a country where "happiness consists of leaving things to the inspiration of the moment".

The principal objects of Stendhal's attention are: Fabrizio del Dongo, the impetuous younger son of a reactionary Italian aristocrat; Count Mosca, the scheming but humane Prime Minister of Parma; and the Duchessa Sanseverina, Fabrizio's charismatic and beautiful aunt.

Mosca loves the Duchessa, the Duchessa loves Fabrizio, and Fabrizio – an appealingly spontaneous, naïve young man – loves no one. Their entanglement is less a story than a disjointed series of fiercely observed dramatic moments – the Battle of Waterloo (a bewildering scene which leaves Fabrizio wondering if he has taken part in the battle at all), Fabrizio's imprisonment in and escape from the citadel at Parma, a murder and countless intrigues, in which the Duchessa (the most vibrant of the characters) struggles to control the contradictions and complications of her emotions.

> '*A woman of forty is no longer anything save to the men who have loved her in her youth!*'

Vigorous and to the point, mostly Realist though sometimes operatically Romantic, *The Charterhouse of Parma* constantly seeks to weigh Machiavellian calculation against erotic spontaneity, while remaining fascinated by both.

Recommended translation
1999, Richard Howard, Picador (UK) and Modern Library (US)

Where to go next
A Sentimental Education, 1869, Gustave Flaubert
Love and politics are also at the heart of Flaubert's novel set in France during the Revolution of 1848. The young provincial Frédéric Moreau, becoming obsessed with Madame Arnoux, follows her to Paris and cultivates a friendship with her husband in order to be near her.

The Red and the Black

1830, Stendhal, French

No one has written better than Stendhal about the ecstasies and miseries of ambition. His most celebrated novel, *The Red and the Black*, provides an acute analysis of the strange blend of ruthlessness, timidity, prickliness, awkwardness and overpowering will in a young man on the make.

Julien Sorel is a poor carpenter's boy determined to escape his brutal peasant upbringing. By the age of seventeen, having memorized the entire New Testament in Latin to prove his mental prowess, he is chosen to be tutor to the local mayor's children, a remarkable advancement. But his sense of destiny remains unsatisfied. Over the next few years, imposing his will on those around him, he will ultimately rise to the position of confidential adviser to one of the greatest noblemen in France with unexpected and catastrophic results.

Oxford World's Classics

A soldier and diplomat, Stendhal was a knowing writer with a fierce interest in worldly life: longish, highly detailed sections of his novel satirize bourgeois small-town society, the religious establishment and the *haut monde* of the Faubourg Saint-Germain; he knew both workhouse managers and hereditary peers inside-out. Though his fictional world is predominantly male, the artless Madame de Rênal and the wilful Mademoiselle de la Mole are two convincingly forceful women. For them, and for Julien himself, love is a vicious and unstable power struggle. Stendhal was not a tidy writer, but a brilliant one, attuned to the vicissitudes of the mind under stress, and *The Red and the Black* is an absorbing psychological drama of a man determinedly but erratically pursuing success.

> Who could have guessed that this face, as pale and gentle as a girl's, hid the unshakeable determination to risk a thousand deaths rather than fail to make his fortune!

 Recommended translation
1991, Catherine Slater, Oxford World's Classics.

 Where to go next
Selected Short Stories, Guy de Maupassant
No one has written so incisively about the ambitions, passions, hopes and fears

of French men and women as Maupassant, whose stories, written towards the end of the nineteenth century, range brilliantly from comedy to tragedy.

Vanity Fair

1848, WILLIAM MAKEPEACE THACKERAY, ENGLISH

Don't be deceived by its bulk. Ample it may be, but *Vanity Fair* is also wonderfully nimble and − a racy panorama of early nineteenth-century England awash with money from the colonies and bustling with bankers and officers, lords and paupers, gambling men and dowagers.

The story follows the diverging fortunes of two girls as they leave Miss Pinkerton's Academy for Young Ladies: the amiable Miss Amelia Sedley, commended by all for her industriousness and obedience, and Becky Sharp, the original artful little minx, with her "famous frontal development" and a feisty look in her eye. If, as Thackeray claims, his novel has no hero, it can at least boast an ambiguously captivating heroine in Becky, whose wit and ambition

My kind reader will please to remember that this history has 'Vanity Fair' for a title, and that Vanity Fair is a very vain, wicked, foolish place, full of all sorts of humbugs and falsenesses and pretensions.

propel her boldly into society, with alarming consequences. For Amelia, doting on the vain and careless Captain George Osborne, and loved in turn by George's faithful friend, the homely Dobbin, the future looks less glamorous but equally risky.

The novel's capaciousness is matched by the pertness of its detail. Scene and mood vary dramatically as the story shifts from the collapsed rural grandeur of Queen's Crawley in Hampshire, the house where Becky first finds employment, to a frantically disarrayed Brussels on the eve of the Battle of Waterloo, and from a poor-genteel mews in Fulham, where Amelia cares for her bankrupt father, to Curzon Street, Mayfair, where Becky and her husband live in grand style on nothing a year.

Such generous variety also marks the huge cast of characters, which includes, in addition to those already mentioned, star performers such as Jos Sedley, the lazy and peevish tax collector of Boggley Wollah, and the lascivious tyrant Lord Steyne. Thackeray appears as himself, a genially self-mocking narrator, who opens proceedings by introducing one of the world's great books as a bustling performance of "dreadful combats", "light comic business" and "love-making for the sentimental", "the whole accompanied by appropriate scenery and brilliantly illuminated with the Author's own candles."

Where to go next
The History of Pendennis, 1848–50, William Makepeace Thackeray
A classic *bildungsroman* that recounts the lifelike adventures of the good-humoured Arthur Pendennis, a young man with high aspirations who finds himself embroiled in a succession of troubling love affairs.

The House of Mirth
1905, EDITH WHARTON, AMERICAN

The House of Mirth is a perfectly formed story of disappointment among the perfectly arranged house parties and gala dinners of Old New York high society – a tale of gilded lives, good manners and quiet desperation.

Lily Bart, beautiful and intelligent, but inconveniently poor should be looking for a husband with money

> 'Everyone knows you're a thousand times handsomer and cleverer than Bertha; but then you're not nasty. And for always getting what she wants in the long run, commend me to a nasty woman.'

and position. At twenty-nine, after a decade gracefully accepting the luxurious hospitality of the super-rich, she can delay no longer; but – to everyone's incredulity – she instinctively recoils from both her suitors, the infantile millionaire Percy Glyde and the vulgar *nouveau riche* property tycoon Simon Rosedale. Instead, buying herself time,

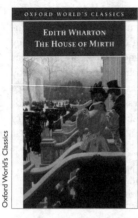

Oxford World's Classics

she naively becomes involved in her friends' domestic dramas – and soon finds herself exposed to scandal.

The biblical reference of the title ("the heart of the wise is in the house of mourning but the heart of fools is in the house of mirth") sounds the authentic note of tragedy, though at first the novel is all lightness and glitter, written in a style as poised and cutting as the New York millionaires and their catty wives. No one is more uncomplimentary about women than Edith Wharton, but few have her searching and expressive intelligence. The cleverly changing perspectives and varied scenes entertain as the tone deepens and grows murky. In a world where social graces involve moral transactions, gossip is, literally, deadly: *The House of Mirth* is a terrifying indictment of Old New York society by one of its own. But the novel's compelling central drama is Lily's own determined course of action, at once a defiant gesture of independence and a catastrophic betrayal of her own heart.

Where to go next
The Age of Innocence, 1920, Edith Wharton
The primly respectable Newland Archer is torn between his sweet young fiancée and the beautiful, enigmatic Countess Olenska. The ensuing clash between passion and social convention exposes the hypocrisy and intolerance of his strictly codified milieu.

Screen adaptation
The House of Mirth, 2000, dir. Terence Davies
Gillian Anderson's radiant and authoritative performance is the centrepiece of Terence Davies's hard-hitting adaptation of Wharton's novel. The lavish costumes and rich interiors intensify the hothouse atmosphere, making Wharton's attack on the petty snobbery and cruelty of New York's upper crust all the more devastating.

Adventure

6

A dventure covers a multitude of excitements, but all great adventure novels have one thing in common: a racing plot. They take the reader on a switchback narrative ride, involving fast-moving action, desperate dilemmas and epic endeavours. In classic adventure novels, heroes – and heroines – pit themselves against the odds to fulfil their destinies.

Some classic adventures take historical events as their starting point, like Hugo's big and bustling *The Hunchback of Notre Dame*, set during a period of civic turbulence in late medieval Paris. Others are bang up to the minute, like *The Riddle of the Sands*, a racy spy story written on the eve of the World War I to warn England of the imminent danger of invasion. With so much at stake, passions tend to run high – as they do in the greatest novel of revenge, *The Count of Monte Cristo*: over 1,000 pages of sustained suspense and tension.

A different sort of obsession is involved in adventures of epic endurance, such as *Voss*, which tells the story of the first attempt to cross Australia on foot, and *Moby Dick*, the justly celebrated story of Captain Ahab's quest to kill the White Whale. Not that classic adventures lack humour. *Don Quixote*, the European novel's original ancestor, is a wild picaresque (see p.198) which begins as a hilarious send-up of tales of chivalry. Nor are all adventures physical. Haruki Murakami's glorious and unsettling *The Wind-up Bird Chronicle* is a dazzling adventure of the mind.

Don Quixote

1604 & 1614, MIGUEL DE CERVANTES, SPANISH

Both hero and anti-hero, Don Quixote is one of the most famous and endearing characters in fiction, and Cervantes' eponymous story stands astride the beginning of European novel-making like a colossus.

For all that, to be frank, the book starts badly: crude, derivative and sadistic. The premise is simple: an elderly gentleman whose brains have been addled by a lifetime's devotion to old tales of chivalry, takes a peasant – Sancho Panza – as his "squire", and sets out to reproduce medieval knightly quests. Alongside the iconic scenes, justly celebrated, in which the Don tilts at windmills and scatters flocks of sheep which he mistakes for armies, are crude episodes of knockabout comedy, primitive jokes of the vomiting and shitting variety, and – worst of all – long digressive tales of lovelorn shepherds, a fashion of the day.

> *This aforementioned gentleman spent his times of leisure ...*
> *reading books of chivalry with so much devotion and enthusiasm that he forgot almost completely about the hunt and even about the administration of his estate.*

But in the second part something magical occurs. The relationship between the idealistic Don and down-to-earth Sancho deepens, and they harmonize strangely. They are, in fact, much more alike than it seemed: Sancho Panza has as many unrealistic dreams as his master; Don Quixote employs as many earthy proverbs as his servant. Enchantment, which in the first part produced farce, becomes in the second part the emotional tie that binds the two together. And when, in the end, Don Quixote comes to his senses on his deathbed, saying that his madness has lifted, Sancho bursts into tears and implores his master to rouse himself for one last mad adventure – and the reader cheers him on.

Don Quixote is undoubtedly one of the most influential novels ever written. The original, however, retains a special quality of unsentimental affection, humour and fantasy unsurpassed by later writers.

 Recommended translation
2003, Edith Grossman, Vintage (UK), Perennial (US)

 Where to go next
Exemplary Stories, 1613, Miguel de Cervantes
This collection of novellas, which range from the the comic to the serious, virtually created the idea of moral ambiguity in fiction. Of the six regularly translated stories, "The Dog's Colloquy" is the most entertaining – a philosophical conversation between two dogs, overheard by a man in hospital with the pox.

 Screen adaptation
Don Quixote, 1957, dir. Grigori Kozintsev
In the absence of Pabst's mutilated 1932 version and Orson Welles's uncompleted, alleged masterpiece, this Russian version is the best *Don Quixote* film around. The double act of Nikolai Cherkassov's dignified Don and Yuri Tolubeyev's spherical Sancho suggests a real relationship, and the bleak Crimean locations – shot in cinemascope – make a convincing substitute for La Mancha.

The Riddle of the Sands

1903, ERSKINE CHILDERS, IRISH

"THE FIRST AND BEST OF SPY STORIES" *THE TIMES*

Penguin

The tremendous realism of Erskine Childer's spy adventure, with its minutely mapped background of German coast and authentic whiff of danger – is no accident. A passionate yachtsman with intimate knowledge of the North Sea, Childers fought for the Republicans in the Irish Civil War (during which he was court-martialled and shot by firing squad). He knew both sailing and danger, and his novel is powerfully evocative of each.

When Carruthers, a bored young landlubber in the Foreign Office, receives an invitation to join a half-forgotten college chum yachting in the North Sea, he thinks it might be a pleasant diversion – though he is slightly disconcerted by the peremptory request to bring with him a pair of rigging screws, a No. 3 Rippingille stove and a prismatic compass. On arrival at Flensburg, he encounters the full horror of a primitive boat, bad weather and ceaseless hard work. Even more irritating is his friend's determination to avoid the usual ports. And why are the Germans so icily keen for them to return to England? The mysterious shifting sands of the coast, it turns out, hold an appalling secret.

I heard a sound outside, a splashing footstep as of a man stepping into a puddle. I was wide awake in an instant, but never thought of shouting 'Is that you, Davies?' for I knew in a flash that it was not he.

The plot may not be the constantly cliff-hanging tease of later spy thrillers (though the cat-and-mouse pursuits along the eerie coast have terrific dash and atmosphere). Instead, we have the Kiplingesque, boyish thrill of anticipated conflict mixed with a patriotic rage at English unpreparedness for war. But best of all is the detailed evocation of the sometimes bracing, sometimes baffling world of boats: the unpredictable moods of sea and weather, the lore of tides and bars, the fogbound coast with its treacherous sands and the constant nautical action – the kedging off and paying out the warp and the jib flying to blazes.

Where to go next
The Compete Richard Hannay, John Buchan
If Childers invented the spy thriller then Buchan largely defined it with the creation of his stiff-upper-lipped Scottish action hero Richard Hannay, who made his first appearance in the World War I adventure "The Thirty-Nine Steps" (1915). It, and a further four stories, form this Penguin collection.

The Last of the Mohicans
1826, JAMES FENIMORE COOPER, AMERICAN

Don't be put off by Cooper's weirdly inappropriate prose, with its coldly formal flourishes, or his historical-tour-guide tone, complete with a-word-in-your-ear footnotes: *The Last of the Mohicans* is superbly exciting from first to last, a master-class in adventure narrative by a brilliant manipulator of suspense, shocks and sudden reversals.

Set in the wilderness of eastern America during the French and Indian Wars of the mid-eighteenth century, the story follows the efforts of the scout Natty Bumppo (known as Hawk-eye) and his Mohican companions Chingachgook and Uncas to safeguard the daughters of the British General Munro from the marauding Hurons, allies of the French. Stomach-churning massacres, desperate escapes, vengeful pursuits, violent ambushes and impetuous rescues form a narrative cycle of constant excitement against the superb backdrop of the forested mountains of upstate New York.

The Last of the Mohicans shaped European views of America for generations. Perspectives may have changed, but the book remains remarkable for its deeply imaginative – and troubled – engagement with Native American culture at the moment when European soldiers and settlers were obliterating it. Central to the novel is an unpredictable dance of destruction between characters who have the most to lose: Hawk-eye, also known as Leatherstocking,

> *The whole band sprang upon their feet, as one man, and giving utterance to their rage in the most frantic cries, they rushed upon their prisoners in a body, with drawn knives and uplifted tomahawks.*

the white man who lives like a native; the broodingly malevolent Huron chief, Magua, a magnificently convincing villain; and Chingachgook and his son Uncas, the last of the Mohicans, stoical and doomed. Few adventure stories match the novel's headlong action, and hardly any achieve a poignancy which, by the novel's catastrophic ending, sounds a lament for the destruction of an entire people.

 Where to go next
The Pioneers, 1823, James Fenimore Cooper
Cooper wrote four other Leatherstocking tales (*The Pioneers, The Prairie, The Pathfinder* and *The Deerslayer*). Set in upstate New York in the 1790s, *The Pioneers* (the first in the series) tells of the threat posed to the solitary Hawk-eye, and the wilderness which he inhabits, by settlers in a nearby town.

 Screen adaptation
The Last of the Mohicans, 1992, dir. Michael Mann
Cooper's classic has been regularly filmed by Hollywood, with a fine silent movie of 1920 and a solid, if predictable, 1936 version. Mann's attempt brings a genuinely epic sweep to the proceedings, with some stunning landscape shots, but the introduction of some love interest for the indomitable Hawk-eye (a long-haired Daniel Day-Lewis) is an unnecessary deviation from the original.

The Count of Monte Cristo

1844–46, Alexandre Dumas père, French

A magnificently elaborate story of injustice and revenge, *The Count of Monte Cristo* is a blockbuster of a novel, dramatic, exotic and grand.

PENGUIN ❶ CLASSICS

ALEXANDRE DUMAS
The Count of Monte Cristo

Penguin

On 28 February 1815, as he celebrates his betrothal to his childhood sweetheart, the fisherman Edmond Dantès is arrested on false charges and left to rot in the notorious prison of the Château d'If. Fourteen years later, succeeding at last in escaping, he makes his way to the Isle of Monte Cristo, an uninhabited rock in the Mediterranean, and disappears. Coincidentally, in the best society of Rome and Paris, where Dantès' enriched and ennobled enemies now move, a mysterious stranger makes an appearance: the singular, bewitching Count of Monte Cristo.

Unlike Hugo, Dumas has no gift for setting; unlike Balzac, he shows little interest in psychology. Such literary elements are ruthlessly stripped out to make room for the vast parade of narrative – a gorgeously inventive plot bursting with action, suspense and special effects. Big scenes abound: the impossible prison breakout, kidnap by bandits, a duel, midnight poisoning. All the stock-in-trade character parts are here too: the Mafioso assassin, the innocent heroine, the corrupt financier, the

> '...for fourteen years I suffered, fourteen years I wept and cursed. Now, I say to you, Mercédès, I must have my revenge.'

royal slave-girl, the wicked lawyer, and, above all, the icily polite, multilingual, fabulously wealthy Count, crack shot, expert swordsman and self-styled Agent of Divine Providence. Inevitably, in such a long book there are moments of slackness, but the tension always tightens again, and the hair-raising finale, perhaps the longest in fiction, is sustained over 250 gripping pages.

Recommended translation
1996, Robin Buss, Penguin Classics

Where to go next
The Three Musketeers, 1844, Alexandre Dumas *père*
The first of three rip-roaring stories involving D'Artagnan, a young nobleman, whose attempts to join the Musketeers are assisted by three (already serving) members. Their ensuing adventures earn them the enmity of the scheming Cardinal Richelieu and the duplicitous Milady.

Screen adaptation
The Count of Monte Cristo, 1998, dir. Josée Dayan
A slightly too old (but otherwise convincing) Gérard Dépardieu heads the cast as Edmond Dantès in this lavish French TV version of Dumas' revenge melo-drama. At around 400 minutes, it's best viewed in bite-sized chunks but it's well worth the time, despite a little softening of the original's implacable edginess, including a rather more positive ending than the one Dumas wrote.

Tom Jones

1749, HENRY FIELDING, ENGLISH

Tom Jones is English fiction's great ancestor. Combining a riotously energetic plot, passionate descriptions of the English countryside, rugged championship of common sense, and, above all, a frank and unfailing comic touch, it is the first expression of the English novel as entertainment, superior and unflagging.

Like all genuine page-turners, it doesn't feel like a long book: over two hundred short, snappy chapters give it pace and crackle. But it is also wonderfully coherent: Coleridge said that it contained one of "the three most perfect plots ever planned", (the other two are *Oedipus Tyrannus* and Ben Jonson's *The Alchemist*), which revolves – with compulsive bounce and dash – around mistaken identities, love affairs and lost inheritances, gravitating from the roads and inns of Somerset to the metropolis. Fielding himself appears in the narrative, a witty guide to developments in the plot and a teasingly ironic pontificator on all manners of subjects, from Honesty and Charity to Love and Englishness.

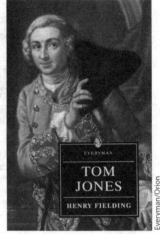

Everyman/Orion

Its central characters, drawn from standard types but brilliantly observed and vigorously modelled, include: the orphan Tom Jones, whose good nature, good looks and headstrong spirit cause much of the trouble; his benefactor, the benevolent Squire Allworthy; Tom's step-brother, the odious Blifil; the beautiful and spirited Sophia and her sensationally vulgar father, Squire Western; and

> *Reader, I think it proper, before we proceed any farther together, to acquaint thee, that I intend to digress, through this whole history, as often as I see occasion.*

the flirtatious woman of fashion, Lady Bellaston. But such an abbreviated cast-list excludes a whole range of minor characters – including a host of innkeepers and their redoubtable wives – whose frank emotions and quick tempers (there must be more bloody noses here than in any other classic novel) give the book its sheer richness of humanity.

Fielding's experience as a playwright is evident in the book's continuous diversions; his duties as a Magistrate (he drew up the plans for London's first police force) inform his deep interest in models of acceptable social behaviour. *Tom Jones* is that rare thing: a novel which debates, informs and even instructs as it entertains.

📖 Where to go next
Amelia, 1752, Henry Fielding
Fielding's favourite of his own novels, *Amelia* has been preferred by some for its greater psychological complexity. The story concerns the marriage of Amelia and Captain Billy Booth, jeopardized when the innocent Captain is thrown into Newgate because he lacks the funds to bribe the officials.

🎬 Screen adaptation
Tom Jones, 1963, dir. Tony Richardson
Fielding's picaresque tale is here filtered through the new-found permissiveness of the 1960s and the result is an enjoyably rambunctious romp. A fresh-faced Albert Finney exudes a gleeful energy as Tom, no more so than in the, now notorious, scene in which he and Mrs Waters (Joyce Redman) slurp their way – with mounting sexual excitement – through a meal at an inn.

The Hunchback of Notre Dame
1831, VICTOR HUGO, FRENCH

Brutal but shot through with wild humour, *The Hunchback of Notre Dame* is a *tour de force* of storytelling. With no interest in suggestive halftones or tints, Hugo works on a vast and crowded canvas filled with colour, creating a picture of medieval Paris teeming with drunken criminals, lascivious soldiers and corrupt clerics. These are the supporting actors to a cast of equally theatrical principals: Archdeacon Frollo, all evil; gypsy waif Esmeralda, all innocence; the bitter King Louis XI and crazed recluse Gudule; and – brooding magnificently over them all – Quasimodo, the deaf and deformed bell-ringer at the cathedral, doomed in love.

The plot is instantly guessable, but Hugo deals less in the suspenseful than the spectacular: he can always be relied on to pull out all the stops. In particular he excels in crowd scenes, such as the Feast of Fools, in which Quasimodo is elected mock King and paraded through the torchlit streets, or the night-time storming of Notre Dame by the criminal fraternity, both great show-stoppers. In general, the novel naturally tends to mass effects, detail piling up on detail in surging passages of description. The fates of individuals, bewildered, cheated and abused, are caught up in vaster and

> 'God's Cross! Holy Saint Peter! You are the ugliest creature I have ever seen. You deserve to be Pope of Rome as well as of Paris.'

darker forces – of the history of the cathedral, Paris, and, ultimately, France itself. Under such circumstances, as the narrative charges headlong to its conclusion, the only question is whether Hugo will lose his nerve and produce a happy ending. But Hugo never loses his nerve.

Recommended translation
1965, Walter J. Cobb, Penguin Classics

Where to go next
Les Misérables, 1862, Victor Hugo
Hugo's sprawling epic of France in the early nineteenth century is an intimidatingly long but thrillingly dramatic read, full of glorious set pieces including an account of the July Revolution. At its heart is the story of the persecuted ex-prisoner Jean Valjean and his attempts to turn his life around.

Screen adaptation

The Hunchback of Notre Dame, 1939, dir. William Dieterle
Lon Chaney was admirable in the 1923 silent version but the best Quasimodo is, indisputably, Charles Laughton, whose astonishing performance turns a well-crafted period extravaganza into a masterpiece. Beneath the disfiguring make-up, the actor conveys a subtle range of conflicting emotions and his final line – "I wish I was stone like you" – spoken to a gargoyle has real tragic poignancy.

Kim

1901, RUDYARD KIPLING, ENGLISH

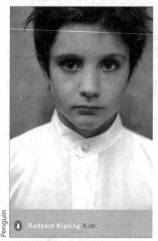

Penguin

Rudyard Kipling Kim

Kipling was one of those shockingly direct writers who follow their instincts, wherever they lead. His Boy-Scoutish enthusiasm for the British Empire sits oddly with his best short stories, plain tales containing disturbing depths of sorrow and anger. His best novel is yet another surprise, a heart-warming masterpiece of sheer good nature, an inventive, ringing tale of common humanity.

In the heyday of the British Raj, two unlikely companions fall in together: a holy lama from Tibet and a Hindu-speaking white street urchin called Kim. The lama is searching for the River of the Arrow of Buddhist legend, which will wash all sins clean. Kim, taking up his role as the lama's *chela* (disciple), is happy just to see the sights along the teeming Grand Trunk Road, but he too is on a quest: to solve the mystery of his own birth.

This is the great world, and I am only Kim. Who is Kim? One insignificant person in all this roaring whirl of India, going southward to he knew not what fate.

Their quests take them across northern India, a breathtakingly diverse and colourful country, which Kipling knew from the inside (his first language was Hindustani), not only its sights and smells, but also its proverbs, customs and habits. He knew its politics too: *Kim* is, among other things, a racy spy story, set against the background of the "Great Game", the struggle between Britain and Russia for domination in South Asia. Kim's sharp wits soon bring him to the attention of other players – the red-bearded Afghan horse-trader Mahbub Ali, Colonel Creighton, an officer "without a regiment", Lurgan Sahib, who understands the gifts of illusion, and the glorious Hurree Babu, the perfumed master of deception.

The novel culminates in an adventurous mission in the Himalayas, but the emotional centre of the novel is the relationship between Kim and the lama, each so different, yet unswervingly devoted. Together, they represent something rare in fiction: a genuinely convincing – and powerfully moving – evocation of harmony.

> **Where to go next**
> *Selected Stories*, Rudyard Kipling
> Right from his earliest collection, *Plain Tales from the Hills* (1888), Kipling was an outstanding writer of short stories. The Penguin selection by Andrew Rutherford contains many of his best, including the harrowing tale based on Kipling's early years "Baa Baa, Black Sheep".

Moby Dick

1851, HERMAN MELVILLE, AMERICAN

What are we to make of a novel which incorporates dozens of mini essays on out-of-the-way topics such as the meaning of clam chowder or the colour white? How can we cope with a narrative in which the main character doesn't make an appearance for the first a hundred or so pages, and the creature which gives its name to the book's title is entirely absent until thirty pages from the end? This is the tremendous, exhilarating originality of *Moby Dick*, a sort of smash collision between an epic

Drink, ye harpooners! Drink and swear, ye men that man the deathful whaleboat's bow – Death to Moby Dick! God hunt us all if we do not hunt Moby Dick to his death!

Vintage

adventure story and an encyclopedia, a gorgeously sweeping sailor's yarn containing multitudes.

Melville's distinctively American voice, declamatory and direct ("Call me Ishmael!"), buttonholes the reader immediately: there's no escaping a narrator who begins by telling you how he once shared a bed in a boarding house with a tattooed cannibal called Queequeg. Worldly-wise, yet full of wonder, Ishmael enlists with Queequeg on the whaling ship, the *Pequod*, only to find that its captain, the one-legged Ahab, is obsessively pursuing his own private quest – to find and destroy the legendary white whale, Moby Dick.

The sheer variousness of the novel is thrilling, from the dramatically mixed narrative forms (tall tales, encyclopedic entries, interior monologues and footnotes) to the startling range of topics, incidents, characters and moods. Nothing is alien on a voyage which takes the *Pequod* through the world's oceans with a crew containing Americans, Africans, Polynesians, several Parsees, an Icelander, a Manxman and a Gayhead Indian.

It's typical of Melville's plurality that he should be both graphically realistic and boldly symbolic at the same time. Few novels show the same intense preoccupation with physical objects, and nowhere else will you find such vivid descriptions of whaling, including harpooner's-eye accounts of the chase and kill, and disturbingly intimate accounts of baling the tun, stripping the skin and boiling the blubber. But Melville's frequent digressions into whale-lore – whales considered from the historical, scientific, biblical, commercial and poetic perspectives – and his insistence on the deeper meanings of even tiny events give these realistic details a vibrant symbolic energy. The result is a novel as amplified and raw as myth.

📖 **Where to go next**
Billy Budd, Sailor and Selected Tales, Herman Melville
Extreme individuals and situations also feature in Melville's shorter fiction: Bartleby, the mild-mannered but stubborn clerk, and – most famously – the Christ-like seaman, Billy Budd, destroyed by the subtle persecution of the malevolent officer Claggart.

🎬 **Screen adaptation**
Moby Dick, 1998, dir. John Huston
Huston prided himself on his casting, but Gregory Peck lacks the mystery and complexity of Ahab, leaving a hole at the heart of the film. There are great moments, however, including a hell-raising cameo from Orson Welles as Father Mapple, but it's the look of the film that registers most: a sun-bleached, pallor that suggests (more than most costume dramas) another time and another place.

The Wind-up Bird Chronicle

1994, HARUKI MURAKAMI, JAPANESE

After the delicate pastels of Kawabata and the exquisite erotics of Tanizaki, Murakami's novels seem to pulse with a frankly vulgar big-city glow. No less enigmatic than his literary forebears, his style is totally different: tone casual and jazzy, characters disaffected and disoriented, plots surreal, effects postmodern. Claiming that he wanted to bring Dostoevsky and Raymond Chandler together in his books, Murakami has produced a string of novels which combine quasi-gumshoe plots with psychedelic situations and freewheeling riffs on big themes, and *The Wind-up Bird Chronicle* is his most captivating and puzzling book to date.

Like many of Murakami's heroes, Toru Okada is a humble misfit, a man quietly avoiding Japanese corporate culture. In doing so, however, he invites a sequence of strange, not to say mind-boggling, escapades involving a crowd of enigmatic characters – clairvoyant war veterans, sinister politicians, dropout weirdo teenage girls and women who manipulate his dreams – each propelling him in a new direction. In Murakami's novels, the first sign of derangement is often very ordinary – in this case, the disappearance of the family cat. After that, Toru Okada is a man struggling to preserve himself in a buffeting quest for self-discovery.

> *To tell you the truth, my sister says that this will be a longer story than it seemed at first ... this story will be about more than the disappearance of a cat.*

As much fairy tale as mystery, Okada has to break the spell that will release his wife from captivity. To do this, he must understand the symbolic meanings of the stories people tell him – including some horrific stories of Japan's notorious occupation of Manchuria. All in all, *The Wind-up Bird Chronicle* combines page-turning excitement with offbeat humour and deeply resonant psychological and historical themes.

 Recommended translation
1997, Jay Rubin, Vintage Books (UK), Harvill Press (US)

 Where to go next
Norwegian Wood, 1987, Haruki Murakami
The novel that made Murakami into a literary superstar (it sold over four million copies in Japan alone) takes its title from the Beatles song, and captures something of the hopefulness and fragility of the 1960s, as the narrator, Toru Watanabe, remembers his youthful love affairs with two very different young women.

The Heart of Midlothian

1818, SIR WALTER SCOTT, SCOTTISH

The former undisputed heavyweight champion of the European novel – and inventor of historical fiction – has long been off the reading lists, and a generation has grown up without ever encountering him. Why? A novel like *The Heart of Midlothian* shows both the worst and best of Scott, and offers arguments both for and against.

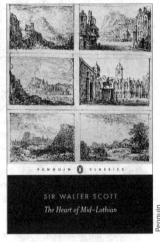

Penguin

The plot unites two historical narratives of 1736: the Edinburgh riots, in which an enraged mob stormed the city jail (called "The Heart of Midlothian") and lynched a villainous Captain of the Guard, John Porteous; and the extraordinary efforts of a young Presbyterian woman, Jeanie Deans, to secure a Royal pardon for her sister Effie, wrongly accused of child-murder, and abandoned by her strict Covenanter father, Davie.

The novel's beginning (slow and digressive) and ending (fast and absurd) may justify the critics who have condemned Scott's lack of attention to plot; the key character of scapegrace George Staunton (improbably melodramatic) is distinctly unconvincing; and the many debates about religious schisms may eventually weary the reader. But these

> 'But the life of your child, goodman – think of that – if her life could be saved,' said Middleburgh. 'Her life?' exclaimed David – 'I wadna gie ane o' my grey hairs for her life, if her gude name be gane.'

The historical novel

Writers have always been attracted to the past. Myths, histories and epic poems have glamorized, explored and exploded historical events, mingling imaginary characters with real ones, and presenting made-up stories in the context of historical developments. In the modern tradition, Madame de Lafayette's *The Princesse de Clèves* (1678), set in the heyday of Renaissance France a hundred years earlier, is an early example of the imaginative use of history. More imaginative still, the "Gothic Novel" explicitly exploited history to convey the exotic (and often sinister), as in Walpole's *The Castle of Otranto* (1765) which is set in medieval Italy. With Edgeworth's *Castle Rackrent* (1800), the historical novel applied itself to specific regions, leading to the modern boom in historical fiction with the novels of Sir Walter Scott, whose *Waverley* (1814), exploring the history of Scotland, introduced notions of nationalism. At the same time, James Fenimore Cooper found hugely dynamic stories in the history of America, beginning with *The Spy* (1821), set during the Revolutionary War.

Through the nineteenth century the historical novel developed with classics such as Hugo's *The Hunchback of Notre Dame* (1831), set in medieval Paris, Dickens's *Tale of Two Cities* (1859), set during the French Revolution and Flaubert's *Salammbô* (1862), set in ancient Carthage. The twentieth century saw the development of a popular genre of historical novels, such as Patrick O'Brien's "Master and Commander" series, set during Napoleonic naval warfare, in which the fiction uses history as a highly detailed – and hugely evocative – backdrop.

are exceptions rather than the rule. The themes of duty and conscience are movingly dramatized, and throughout the middle sections of the novel, the plot has tremendous pace and force, a sweep of action not blurred by its speed, but crystallizing everywhere in brilliant detail. Scott's handling of big crowd scenes is justly celebrated (the Edinburgh lynching is electrically atmospheric), but he is just as good at intimate encounters which catch fire from the conflicting passions of sharply drawn individual characters. He especially excels in dialogue, especially the Scots dialect spoken by his "peasants", and the voices of his characters echo vividly in the head after reading.

Where to go next
Rob Roy, 1817, Walter Scott
Set just before the Jacobite rising of 1715, *Rob Roy* tells the story of Francis Osbaldistone, banished by his father to the north of England, where he encounters the high-spirited Diana Vernon and his cousin, the scheming Rashleigh Osbaldistone. In the adventurous tangle that ensues, Francis is aided by the outlaw Rob Roy.

Voss

1957, PATRICK WHITE, AUSTRALIAN

A novel displaying all the grace and cruelty of classical tragedy, *Voss* is nevertheless distinctively Australian, attuned to the wildness of the country's bush, the smugness of its provincial cities, and, above all, to the self-punishing ambitions of a people not at home in their land. The story of an epic journey of exploration, it is just as much a drama of the tormented mind, passionate and contradictory.

In 1845, Johann Ulrich Voss leads a small band of misfits in an attempt to cross the continent for the first time. Wilful and ill at ease, he clashes with his handyman, the ex-convict Judd, belittles the party's ornithologist, Palfreyman, and goes out of his way to patronize "Jackie", the young Aborigine guide. Gradually, their food supplies dwindle; the months pass; torrential rain is succeeded by the endless aridity of the desert. But, even as his strength fails, Voss keeps up a mental dialogue with a young woman he has left behind in Sydney, Laura Trevelyan, as inscrutably passionate as Voss himself, to whom his survival is absolutely crucial.

> Miss Trevelyan bit her lip. 'Voss could have been the Devil if at the same time he had not resembled a most unfortunate human being.'

White's style is refined and cynical, sometimes tending to sarcasm, creating tension and an eerie stillness. While looking into each other's souls, each character seems alone: there is a sense that to come together would risk fatal conflict. The telepathic love affair of Voss and Laura, handled with such technical brilliance that it seems a natural part of the delirium of the journey, goes to the heart of this struggle. The expedition itself, with its desperate privations, is a masterpiece of description at once realistic and symbolic.

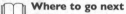 **Where to go next**
The Tree of Man, 1955, Patrick White
The premise of White's novel is straightforward: a young husband and wife, the Parkers, move into the bush where they build a home, start a family and live a fairly uneventful life. But from this raw simplicity, the author fashions a very human picture revealing the poetry beneath the surface of the most ordinary lives.

War, violence and conflict

7

War is one of literature's oldest, most universal subjects, so it comes as no surprise to find writers from so many different cultures and periods making fiction from it. Historical conflicts – from the Wars of Religion in the 1630s (*Simplicissimus*) to the Battle of Stalingrad in 1942 (*Life and Fate*) – have inspired novelists to recreate the terrible energy of combat, the chaos of the war zone and the inhumanity and heroism of men under pressure. The great novelists have the magical – if alarming – powers to make us feel something of war's appalling experiences.

Some have celebrated the fighters, such as the outlaw Mehmed in the Turkish classic *Mehmed, My Hawk*. Others, like the great Serbian novel of the Holocaust, *Garden, Ashes*, have lamented the victims. The war novel has many moods. Hemingway brilliantly captured its fatalism in *A Farewell to Arms*, Norman Mailer its psychological dramas in *The Naked and the Dead*. And in the blackly hilarious anti-war classic *The Good Soldier Švejk*, Jaroslav Hašek presents the desperate ingenuity of the little man engaged in the very natural attempt to save his own life.

Danger and violence are not limited to war, however. This section also features novels which take as their subject assassination (*Libra*), apartheid (*Waiting for the Barbarians*) and slavery (*Oroonoko*). There is room too for fictional engagements with some of the menace of everyday life: Ballard's cult classic of the erotic violence of car culture, *Crash*, for instance. Viciousness, in its many different forms, remains the inspiration for some of the most gripping works in fiction.

Things Fall Apart

1958, CHINUA ACHEBE, NIGERIAN

Probably the most widely read of all African novels, *Things Fall Apart* tells two absolutely gripping stories: one man's downfall and the subjugation of his people. The people are the Ibo of Eastern Nigeria; the man is Okonkwo, a former wrestler with an iron will, which he uses to dominate his family. After a skirmish with a rival clan, Okonkwo is made guardian of a young hostage called Ikemefuna, and a close friendship develops between him and Okonkwo's eldest son. But the "Oracle" (the final authority of local custom) calls for Ikemefuna's death, and Okonkwo knows he cannot refuse. It is the beginning of a series of misfortunes which culminates in Okonkwo's temporary banishment. And while he is away, English missionaries move into the area.

> *We were amused at his foolishness and allowed him to stay. Now he has won our brothers and our clan can no longer act like one. He has put a knife on the things that held us together, and we have fallen apart.*

The story begins at a time when the Ibo people's belief in their gods was absolute. Like Márquez, Achebe is both lyrical and plain-speaking, and with great naturalness he shows the magic in everyday life, interweaving fictional narrative, fable and history. He is psychologically acute too: Okonkwo's fate is also his character. A strong man dominated by his fear of weakness, a fear "deeper and more intimate than the fear of evil and capricious gods and of magic", he possesses a fatal flaw which drives him towards tragedy. Though historically specific, the novel seems timeless. Carefully situated in the Ibo region, and resonant with local detail, it is also an archetype in which the distinctively human episodes of violence and emotion – as in the Greek tragedies – could be played out anywhere.

Penguin

Where to go next
Anthills of the Savannah, 1987, Chinua Achebe

Politics and history are at the heart of Achebe's powerful late novel, set in the imaginary West African country of Kangan during a military dictatorship. Three friends (a governmental commissioner for information, a finance official and a newspaper editor hostile to the new regime) are pulled by events towards a tragic finale.

Crash

1973, J.G. BALLARD, ENGLISH

Cerebral and graphic, the appropriately titled *Crash* is a high-speed assault on the senses – formally arranged tableaux of twisted metal and spattered bodily fluids presented as sickeningly playful combinations of technology, violence and sex.

The plot is simple and absurd. Heavily scarred, sexed-up crash-

j. g. ballard · crash / a novel

Picador

junkie Dr Robert Vaughan dreams of destroying himself and glamour-star Elizabeth Taylor in a head-on collision. The novel opens as Ballard (playing the part of a director at the Shepperton film studios) recovers in hospital from a crash of his own. Slowly, he comes to feel a strange fascination with automobile accidents, seeing in them vivid metaphors of the promiscuous sex and emotional violence in his life. For Vaughan, Ballard has a specific use, having brought Taylor to London for a commercial shoot. A strange triangle of desire and self-destruction develops between Vaughan, Ballard and Ballard's wife, Catherine, as Vaughan plots to draw the actress into his appalling scheme.

The plot, however, is not the point. Like the close-up photographs of crashes which Vaughan obsessively takes, the novel is essentially a

Vaughan died yesterday in his last car crash. During our friendship he had rehearsed his death in many crashes, but this was his only true accident.

sequence of scenes – sordid, grotesque, shocking – which pile up, almost haphazardly, to form a nightmare picture of a world in which morality has been replaced by technology. Ballard calls the book a "cautionary tale", but he never preaches a moral. His aim is to disturb, his harshly elegant style, rich in the terminology of car parts and body parts, revealing unknown horrors of the contemporary world.

Where to go next
The Drowned World, 1962, J.G. Ballard
Ballard was ahead of the game in his invention of a world drowned when tem-

peratures soar and the polar icecaps melt, leaving the major cities of Europe and North America submerged – and the survivors strangely entranced by their new environment.

 Screen adaptation
Crash, 1996, dir. David Cronenberg
No less shocking now than when it was first released, Cronenberg's film is remarkably faithful to the dark spirit of Ballard's book: the tone is cool and detached, the look sleek, glossy and technological. While the film is, arguably, a serious look at the fetishization – and dehumanization – of sexuality in the machine age, its repetitiveness and perversity is, at times, close to pornography.

Oroonoko

1688, APHRA BEHN, ENGLISH

A highly original novel by a highly original author (Behn, the first English woman to earn her living by her pen, also served as a government spy), *Oroonoko* is a lucid, quietly impassioned tale of a noble-hearted African prince, separated from his wife, tricked into slavery and barbarically killed by English plantation owners in the New World. The prose is dignified, the action fast and the anti-slave message – years ahead of its time – totally clear.

> 'And why ... should we be slaves to an unknown people? We are bought and sold like apes and monkeys, to be the sport of women, fools, and cowards.'

Behn's professional skills as a playwright are immediately apparent: the characters – in particular Oroonoko, with his natural refinement and dazzling looks – are figures from heroic drama; and the narrative unfolds with the speed and clarity of classical tragedy. Beautifully timed big scenes, such as the clandestine night-time meeting between Oroonoko and his lover Imoinda or the slave uprising which Oroonoko leads against the English, are among the novel's most impressive features. But what really startles is the way in which Behn's literary poise is constantly enlivened by touches of genuine realism, homely asides and gossipy digressions packed with vivid details. The description of Surinam, in South America, which Behn herself visited, is as sharp-focused as a travelogue, with incidental scenes involving wild beast hunts and dinners of roast armadillo. In the end, the story seems both theatrical and real, just as Oroonoko and Imoinda's dreams of bliss co-exist agonizingly with their brutal mistreatment.

Where to go next
Rasselas, 1759, Samuel Johnson
Like Behn, Johnson employed an exotic setting in his story of a prince of Abyssinia who travels the Arab world in search of wider experience. Unlike Behn, Johnson did not provide a fast-action plot. His novel is rather a humane and beautifully written meditation on the rarity of happiness.

The Lost Honour of Katharina Blum

1974, HEINRICH BÖLL, GERMAN

"The first facts to be presented are brutal…" At a party, Katharina Blum meets and falls in love with a young man on the run. Arrested as an accomplice the following day, she becomes the subject of wildly distorted front-page stories in a best-selling German tabloid, describing her as a Communist, an atheist and a whore. Three days later, she finds the journalist responsible, shoots him dead, and gives herself up to the authorities.

KATHARINA BLUM, OUTLAW'S SWEETHEART, REFUSES INFORMATION ON MALE VISITORS

Subtitled "How Violence Develops and Where it Can Lead", Böll's brief novel is a furiously tight-lipped condemnation of police and media intrusion at a time when a newly affluent Germany had been polarized by the terrorist attacks of the Baader-Meinhof gang. Written in an obsessively orderly style, and presented as a "report" rather than a piece of imaginative fiction, it cathartically recounts the misrepresentation of facts which has stolen the honour of Katharina Blum.

Katharina Blum is an unlikely heroine, strait-laced, serious-minded and charmless. But her refusal to answer insultingly intrusive police questions, and her inability to tolerate media mistreatment, highlights the ethical issues and ultimately turns her into a martyr. In the end she controls her own story. The stories in the press are all about the wrong issues: terrorism, Communism, atheism, promiscuity; she doesn't recognize herself in any of them. Her real story is about her falling in love with a stranger at a party one evening, something no one has talked about.

Recommended translation
1975, Leila Vennewitz, Vintage Classics (UK), Penguin Classics (US)

Where to go next
The Clown, 1965, Heinrich Böll
Hans Schneir is an alcoholic professional entertainer abandoned by the woman he loves. In considering himself and his family (his anti-Semitic mother still brooding on the war, his brother who has retreated to a Catholic seminary), he draws a grim picture of post-war German society.

Screen adaptation
The Lost Honour of Katharina Blum, 1975, dir. Volker Schlondorff
Something of a specialist in respectful adaptations of serious novels, Schlondorff excels himself with this version of Böll's questioning work. He is helped by Angela Winkler's astonishingly intense but sympathetic performance as the diffident Katharina. A powerful attack on state and press morality (or lack of it), both film and novel still seem powerfully relevant.

Journey to the End of the Night

1932, LOUIS-FERDINAND CÉLINE, FRENCH

Not for the squeamish, *Journey* is a big ugly book about big ugly things, a blast against the hellishness of humanity.

Largely autobiographical, the story follows the progress of a French medical student, Bardamu, on his "journey to the end of the night". It begins in World War I, where he is traumatized by the senseless destruction. He escapes first to colonial Africa, where different horrors of squalor and exploitation await him, then to the United States, where the artificial romance of the cinema is the only relief offered by an automated society. Returning to France, he works as a doctor in a deprived district of Paris, and for a while finds an edgy calm among the lunatics of an asylum – but the night closes in again, and his journey ends in murder.

> I felt my self-respect weakening, weakening a little more, seeping away, and finally abandoning me completely, officially as it were. Say what you like, that's a beautiful moment.

Few books are so obsessed by human darkness: life stripped down to the last brutalities of poverty, violence, crime and disease. Céline has a style to match too, vulgar and loud, frequently obscene, often blackly funny and always cynical: an inspired rant which gives the book a drunk's lurching momentum and a welter of memorably stark images: a man's face in the lamplight "veiled by a curtain of insects", a war victim's bloody neck "glugging like jam in a pan". Everywhere, Céline's disgust animates the book with a violent energy. Looking back to the war brutality of *Simplicissimus*, and ahead to *Catch-22*, the Beat novels of Jack Kerouac and the crime novels of James Ellroy, *Journey* is a landmark book in the novel's ongoing horrified fascination with degradation.

 Recommended translation
1983, Ralph Manheim, John Calder (UK) and New Directions (US)

Where to go next
Death on Credit, 1936, Louis-Ferdinand Céline
Céline fans often claim *Death on Credit* – the sequel to *Journey* – to be his masterpiece: a deliberately rough-edged, indeed chaotic, account of Bardamu's experiences as a doctor in Paris.

Waiting for the Barbarians

1980, J.M. COETZEE, SOUTH AFRICAN

Few contemporary novelists match Coetzee's ability to create stories both utterly gripping and powerfully resonant. Writing in an austerely poetic, angry style, he has produced a number of major novels (*Life and Times of Michael K*, *Age of Iron* and *Disgrace* among the best of them) which not only evoke the horrors of apartheid and post-apartheid South Africa, but also say something horrifying but necessary about the human condition.

Waiting for the Barbarians, his third novel, has all the taut elegance of a fable. In an outpost of the Empire, the elderly, easy-going Magistrate is one day confronted by an important visitor, Colonel Joll of the Third Bureau, come from the capital to investigate rumours of Barbarian forces gathering on the frontier. The Magistrate's life of quiet triviality, with his antiquarian interest in Barbarian culture and his erotic interest in Barbarian women, is about to change forever. Of the two prisoners captured immediately by Joll, one dies during interrogation. More arrests and torture follow. Under the emergency powers, a new punitive regime is established in the Magistrate's town, and he has to decide whether to protest or acquiesce.

> *I did not mean to get embroiled in this. I am a country magistrate, a responsible official in the service of the Empire, serving out my days on this lazy frontier, waiting to retire.*

Coetzee has the gift of unflinching lucidity: his fictional world (the sleepy frontier town and the wilderness beyond) is utterly credible and clear, his characters painfully real, and his narrative scenes (love-making as much as torture) simple and stark. What gives the book its special power, however, is its clouded and troubled meaning, with which the Magistrate grapples. As representatives of the Empire, in what essential respect is he, compassionate but complicit, different from the clinically inhumane Joll?

Where to go next
Life and Times of Michael K, 1983, J.M. Coetzee
As South Africa disintegrates into civil unrest, a young black gardener flees with his mother. Captured and imprisoned on suspicion of collaboration with the guerrillas, he bewilders his jailers with his simplicity. Few novels portray the human spirit in extremity with such power.

Heart of Darkness

1902, JOSEPH CONRAD, POLISH-BRITISH

MODERN CLASSICS
Joseph Conrad
Heart of Darkness
Penguin

Possessing the spellbinding fascination of a ghost story and the hypnotic allure of a tale of horror, *Heart of Darkness* begins as a "yarn" and quickly becomes a nightmare. The reasonable, almost clubbable voice of the English narrator, Marlowe, strains to keep control – throwing the horror into stark relief – as he tells the story of his journey up the Congo to find Mr Kurtz, the agent of a European trading company who has gone strangely silent.

From the beginning, Marlowe's tale is one of uneasy foreboding. As he approaches the mouth of the

Congo, a man-of-war anchored offshore is bombarding the empty jungle; it sets a tone of inexplicable violence. Entering Africa is like entering a dream, an unreal place of shifting, delirious scenes: dying Africans crouching silently in the gloom of the trees, manacled prisoners shut into their own world of pain, idiotic European station managers in their starched uniforms.

> 'And this also,' said Marlowe suddenly, 'has been one of the dark places of the earth.'

On his tramp steamer, Marlowe journeys upriver into the interior. The rumours about Kurtz grow: he was a prolific trader of ivory, a special man, a "universal genius", a man with high-flown ideas of improving the natives. But it is said that he has fallen "ill". Weeks later, after battling through scrapes and ambushes, Marlowe finally arrives at Kurtz's station, a decayed building half-hidden in grass and fronted with fenceposts topped with human heads. The Englishman's meeting with Kurtz is one of the most hair-raising in fiction.

Where to go next
The Secret Agent, 1907, Joseph Conrad
Irony and horror combine in Conrad's only London-based novel, which features an anarchist bomb attack on Greenwich Observatory masterminded by the unassuming "secret agent", Verloc.

Libra

1988, DON DELILLO, AMERICAN

DeLillo is one of the toughest, coolest chroniclers of American excess, his novels on-the-spot bulletins from the zones of power and affluence. *White Noise*, a satire of consumerism, family life and the fear of death, is his funniest book. *Libra*, a fictional secret history of the assassination of J.F. Kennedy, is his deepest engagement with the processes of history, American style.

His novel, like history, consists of overlapping layers. Lee Harvey

Penguin

Don DeLillo
Libra

Oswald, bunking off school in the Bronx, failing as a marine in Japan, unable to find himself in either the Soviet Union (to which he briefly defects) or the USA, is an activist looking for a way to leave his mark on history. Coincidentally, a group of ex-CIA operatives, disaffected by America's "Bay of Pigs" fiasco, is plotting to stage a failed assassination of Kennedy, traceable to Castro, to get the invasion of Cuba back on the agenda. All they need is an assassin to manipulate.

DeLillo writes a harshly elegant prose tilting often into droll comedy and perfectly suited to his themes of conspiracy and complicity. Scenes are vivid and elliptical. A hard intelligence probes hidden histories – the unstable plots, the unexpected coincidences, the farcical errors. The characters are invariably male – DeLillo's astonishing mimicry here encompasses all sorts of mangled, inarticulate macho-speak – and the action is always tense. No other contemporary novelist gets between the great tidal movements of history and their dark, little origins so well. "A novel about a major unresolved event" (in DeLillo's own words), *Libra* operates between the macro and the micro, between global newsflashes of Kennedy's death and "the sleet of bone and blood and tissue" as the President is hit.

> 'Think of two parallel lines,' he said. 'One is the life of Lee H. Oswald. One is the conspiracy to kill the President. What bridges the space between them? What makes a connection inevitable?'

📖 **Where to go next**
White Noise, 1984, Don DeLillo
Hugely funny and brilliantly insightful, *White Noise* is the great comedy of the madness of late twentieth-century American life, focusing on Jack Gladney, Chairman of the Department of Hitler Studies at Blacksmith College.

The Tin Drum

1959, GÜNTER GRASS, GERMAN

Labelled "experimental", Grass actually possesses all the raconteur's traditional gifts, taking delight in detail – sometimes piling it up in mind-boggling heaps – at the same time as keeping an eye on the grand sweep of his story. *The Tin Drum*, his anti-history of World War II, is a swooping yarn containing laughs, shocks and hideous revelations, at the heart of which stands Oskar Matzerath, a midget, whose manic drumming expresses, by turn, his fury, gaiety, disgust and sorrow in an adult world of horrors.

Oskar is a boy-man of unusual talents: he can, through sheer force of will, stop growing at three years old, shatter glass with his voice, and,

> I clung to my drum and from my third birthday on refused to grow by so much as a finger's breadth. I remained the precocious three-year-old, towered over by grownups but superior to all grownups.

Pied-Piper-like, drum grownups into a trance. His memoirs, put together from his bed in a prison hospital, narrate his adventures as leader of a gang of hooligans, entertainer of the troops, tombstone-cutter and messianic percussionist.

Grass is one of the great contemporary conjurers of astonishing scenes and extraordinary images: a horse's head pulled from the sea seething with eels; a black mass (complete with drumming); a game of skat between a coward, a midget and a dead man; and the casual butchery of some nuns at the "Atlantic wall", which Oskar witnesses in the company of the lordly dwarf Bebra. Deaths and funerals fea-

The picaresque

Taking its name from the Spanish *pícaro* (a rogue or trickster), a picaresque novel recounts a rogue's adventures. Though classical forerunners have been claimed (such as Apuleius's *The Golden Ass*), the origins of the modern form lie in Spain with the publication of the anonymous *Lazarillo de Tormes* (1553) and Alemán's *Guzmán de Alfarache* (1599–1604), both of which feature wily servants who outwit their masters with ingenious tricks. With these novels, a narrative pattern was laid down: of low-life, devil-may-care heroes, fast, comic action and (in the classic Spanish form), final repentance. An immediate hit, the picaresque spread throughout Europe, especially after the publication of best-selling *Don Quixote* (1605), which contains picaresque elements made newly strange and rich. As the form spread, it changed. In the German *Simplicissimus* (1669), it merged with the war chronicle. In the English *Moll Flanders* (1722), it became more subtly psychological. In *Candide* (1759), it encompassed philosophy. By the nineteenth century, it had become much looser, responsive to all sorts of cultural pressures – Romanticism arguably achieves its fullest expression in Byron's great verse picaresque, *Don Juan* (1819–1824), and America first finds its national voice in the picaresque adventures of *Huckleberry Finn* (1884). With the upheavals of the twentieth century, it is hardly surprising that many great modern novels show strong affinities with the picaresque, not least Hašek's *The Good Soldier Švejk* (1921–23), which found in it an ideal comic form for the chaos of World War I and *The Tin Drum* (1959), a demented picaresque of shocks and disorientation, perfectly suited to the trauma of World War II.

ture prominently throughout, magnified by a style which veers from comedy to pathos, rising nimbly to obscenities, and sometimes – as when describing the anti-Semitic riots and destruction (known as Kristallnacht) – exploding with anger. *The Tin Drum* is a masterpiece in the German tradition, energetic, bawdy, earthy and serious, which vividly engages with evil through the beating of a toy drum.

Recommended translation
Ralph Manheim, 1961, Vintage Classics

Where to go next
The Flounder, 1977, Günter Grass

Grass's hefty epic concerns the roles of, and the struggle between, men and women. Spanning several thousand years, from the Stone Age to the present day, it features a great deal of sex, numerous arguments, colossal amounts of food, and a talking fish.

Screen adaptation
The Tin Drum, 1979, dir. Volker Schlondorff

Where Schlondorff's version of *The Lost Honour of Katharina Blum* had a gritty realist edge, his adaptation of *The Tin Drum* is a demented fantasy, a nightmare come to life. As Oskar, the eleven-year-old David Bennent proved inspired casting, convincingly suggesting a malevolent intelligence beyond his years and an objectionable brat attempting to subvert the course of history.

Simplicissimus

1668, JOHANN GRIMMELSHAUSEN, GERMAN

A jaunty comedy, a pilgrim's progress, a war novel of savage realism, *Simplicissimus* is fast, earthy, violent and pious: a Renaissance woodcut come to life in thickly inked scenes of bawdy drama and blood-curdling morality.

When soldiers destroy his hamlet and drive away its inhabitants, the young peasant Simplicius Simplicissimus is caught up in the Thirty Years War, a mainly religious conflict which engulfed Europe in the first half of the seventeenth century (and in which

> *When I went into the world after my father's death I was simple and pure, upright and honest, truthful, humble, unassuming, but I quickly became malicious, false, deceitful, arrogant, restless and, above all, completely ungodly.*

Grimmelshausen himself served). From this point on Simplicius is a victim of fortune, a wanderer in the world, buffeted this way and

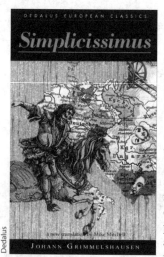

DEDALUS EUROPEAN CLASSICS

Simplicissimus

a new translation by Mike Mitchell

JOHANN GRIMMELSHAUSEN

Dedalus

that. Fighting first for one side, then for the other, now rich with booty, now robbed of everything, he lives a soldier's life of coarse pleasure and inevitable pain, always nagged by the feeling that this is not the life he should be leading.

The plot is swift, bewildering even, and full of incident, usually violent. Torture, rape and pillage are commonplace in a series of wild adventures frequently enlivened by ingenious tricks and improbable disguises. The emphasis is on the physical, and blood, innards, lice and the pox seldom go unmentioned for long. But the novel is also rich in ideas. In typically forthright Renaissance fashion, classical literature is ransacked for useful and vivid lessons about life-as-it-should-be-lived, and, even at his most ungodly, the Bible is never far from Simplicius's thoughts. Often brutally realistic, the novel also includes a hair-raising witches' dance, the Devil speaking through a possessed man and an amazing underwater trip with a curious collection of sylphs to the centre of the earth.

Recommended translation
1999, Mike Mitchell, Dedalus Books

Where to go next
Memoirs of a Cavalier, 1720, Daniel Defoe
In Defoe's usual style of reportage, *Memoirs of a Cavalier* is a lively, highly detailed novel of the Wars of Religion and the English Civil War masquerading as the autobiography of an English soldier of fortune.

Life and Fate

1980, VASILY GROSSMAN, RUSSIAN

When in 1960 Vasily Grossman submitted his masterpiece to an official literary journal, he was told there was no chance of it being published in the Soviet Union for two hundred years. No wonder. An extraordinary action drama, based in part on his own observations of the heroic Russian defence of Stalingrad in 1942, it is also a heartfelt, irrefutable condemnation of the whole Soviet system of gulags, informers and terror.

Featuring over a hundred characters, both Russian and German (not to mention, unnervingly, Hitler and Stalin) and ranging across a dozen major settings, from the bunkers of Stalingrad to the gas chambers of Auschwitz, the narrative has Tolstoyan scope and ambition. More remarkably still, it also possesses a Chekhovian intimacy, a quiet sensitivity to private moments.

> *Whatever life holds in store – hard-won glory, poverty and despair, or death in a labour camp – they will live as human beings and die as human beings; and in this alone lies man's eternal and bitter victory.*

At the heart of the story is the Shaposhnikov family: Lyudmila, whose son Tolya is missing in action; her sister Yevgenia, whose ex-husband, the commissar Krymov, finds himself in the Lubyanka prison just as her current lover, Colonel Novikov, is leading the tank corps against the Germans; and her husband, Viktor Shtrum, a Jewish nuclear physicist in an elite laboratory increasingly terrified of a Stalinist purge. Their lives – and fates – seem not their own as they struggle to survive.

The novel is huge, but the chapters are short (nearly two hundred in all), and Grossman cuts rapidly between the different plot lines to create a crackling tension. Suspenseful dramas – in the ruins of Stalingrad, where a wayward Soviet platoon is holding out in

"House 6/1", behind the lines where Novikov's tanks are massing and in two concentration camps, one Soviet, one Nazi – are all unstoppably exciting. But the novel's page-turning power derives less from driving action than from the finely balanced predicaments of the many characters. What will happen to them? Will Yevgenia choose Novikov or Krymov? Will Lyudmila find Tolya? Will Viktor's mother, herded by the Nazis into a ghetto, survive? Grossman has the generous and analytical power of creating utterly individual characters whose lives and fates matter deeply precisely because they are individuals. His fury – heartbreaking by the end of the novel – is with a system that ruthlessly denied them such distinction.

Recommended translation
1985, Robert Chandler, Vintage Classics (UK), NYRB Classics (US)

Where to go next
Forever Flowing, 1989, Vasily Grossman
After thirty years in a gulag, Ivan Grigoryevich attempts to start a new life in the Soviet Union. His first attempts are failures and a new relationship with a war widow in the provinces is promising but untenable. Only when he returns to his boyhood home on the Black Sea will he find the opportunity to come to terms with Soviet life.

The Good Soldier Švejk
1921–23, Jaroslav Hašek, Czech

The projected six-volume novel by anarchist and vagrant Jaroslav Hašek was cut short by his premature death after only four rambling but brilliantly intuitive volumes. Who knows how it would have finished. Apparently written during frequent bouts of drunkenness, it is often loose, sometimes confused. But it has the energy and hilarity of a bar-room-full of anecdotes, and, in the figure of Švejk, contains one of the great portraits of the little man caught up in the surreal world of officialdom.

An idiot ("officially certified by a special commission" he says proudly), a saint, a Lord of Misrule and, above all, an anecdotalist of startling stamina, Švejk is a survivor in times of the slaughter and madness of World War I. Nothing fazes him. His original superior, an alcoholic chaplain, loses him in a game of cards to a lieutenant in the infantry; his new superior threatens to kill him. But, falling in with the gluttonous coward Baloun and the irascible Lieutenant Dub, and encountering literally hundreds of eccentric characters on the way, Švejk maintains a

JAROSLAV HAŠEK
The Good Soldier Švejk

ludicrous but uplifting calm as he progresses, very erratically, more or less in the direction of the front. The suspicion grows that his idiocy hides a deep strategy.

Fabulously rude and unblinkingly observant of the gluttony and lechery of the troops, the novel bursts with life. It has, and needs, no form: long-windedness (never less than entertaining and often

> 'Listen, Švejk, are you really God's prize oaf?'
> 'Humbly report, sir,' Švejk answered solemnly, 'I am.'

inspirational) is the appropriate mode for a war novel which completely ignores military glory ("utter bunkum") and celebrates the calamitous vitality of people trying to avoid it.

Recommended translation
1973, Cecil Parrott, Penguin Classics (UK & US)

Where to go next
War with the Newts, 1936, Karel Čapek
This marvellously unpredictable comic satire of the future, tells the improbable

story of mankind's fight for survival against a species of giant newt. Totally different in tone and style from *Brave New World*, *Nineteen Eighty-Four* and *We*, it nevertheless deserves a place alongside them as one of the great mid-century dystopias.

Catch-22

1961, JOSEPH HELLER, AMERICAN

Heller's crazy novel is the perfect response to the craziness of war – a vision of hell played for laughs.

As World War II comes to an end, Bombardier Yossarian has long ceased to have any interest in bombing Italian towns: all his ingenuity is devoted to avoiding combat. He develops a pain in his liver which cunningly falls just short of being jaundice; he turns up to receive a medal for bravery stark naked; for a time he walks everywhere backwards. But the war's surreality is greater than his, expressed, formula-like, in the famous Catch-22: anyone can be excused combat duty if he's crazy, all he has to do is ask. But if he asks to be excused combat duty he must be sane…

He no longer gave a damn whether he missed or not. He had decided to live forever or die in the attempt, and his only mission each time he went up was to come down alive.

Scenes are jumpy but sharp-focused. In the cockpits of the strafed planes and the brothels of Rome the focus of the anarchic action is on the weirdness and anguish of men permanently on the verge of violent death. As the novel progresses, their varied petty madnesses – jokey, jealous, naïve or beatific – are slowly absorbed into the colossal madness of war, and Heller's brilliance shows best in iconic scenes which yoke together the hilarious and the horrific: Milo Minderbinder, the enterprising mess officer, bombing his own airfield for cost plus 6 percent, or ace pilot McWatt buzzing the beach for a lark and slicing Kid Sampson in two with his propellers.

Where to go next
Something Happened, 1974, Joseph Heller
Bob Slocum, successful corporate man, soliloquizes about his futile career, unhappy marriage, unfulfilling affairs and distressingly unsympathetic children. Could the problem be him?

Screen adaptation
Catch-22, 1970, dir. Mike Nichols
Screenwriter Buck Henry, who also acts in the film, discarded several story-lines and combined characters, but the result is still very close to Heller's vision in its grotesque absurdity, black humour and fragmented narrative. Though filmed in widescreen Panavision, ex-theatre director Nichols gets a real sense of ensemble from his starry cast, led by an inspired Alan Arkin as Yossarian.

A Farewell to Arms

1929, ERNEST HEMINGWAY, AMERICAN

Hemingway's radically laconic account of the Italian campaigns of World War I, in which he served, is a masterpiece of concision: cynical, fatalistic and funny. Sentences pared down to bleak essentials, troubling gaps in description, abrupt – and lyrical – juxtaposition of dissimilar elements, all wrench the reader's view into new perspectives, and show war in a harsh, flat light free of patriotism and sentiment.

> He said we were all cooked but we were all right as long as we did not know it. ... The last country to realize they were cooked would win the war. We had another drink.

The young American Frederic Henry is serving in the ambulance corps of the Italian Army in the fight against the Austrians in the mountains. He falls in love with an English nurse, Catherine Barkley, is badly wounded and despatched to a hospital, recovers and returns to the front, and deserts with his lover to Switzerland. There he discovers that, although he might bid a farewell to arms, he can't escape the killing.

There is a sense throughout the book that the narrator and his com-

Novels of the Great War

World War I retains a powerful hold on the imagination, not least because of the poems, novels and autobiographies – by participants on all sides – which memorialize the conflict. Later writers too, such as Pat Barker (*The Regeneration Trilogy*, 1991–95) and Sebastian Faulks (*Birdsong*, 1993) have produced outstanding imaginative recreations of new aspects of the war.

Under Fire, 1916, Henri Barbusse
The first of the war novels, by a French soldier, shocked readers with its graphically realistic descriptions of trench warfare. Barbusse was 41 when he enlisted, and claimed to have taken notes for the novel while under fire in battle. It remains unmatched for its rawness and immediacy.

All Quiet on the Western Front, 1929, Erich Maria Remarque
The famous novel by a German soldier was an instant international bestseller (and major film). Brilliantly told and hugely emotional, it records the horrific experiences of an eighteen-year-old boy who, enlisting under pressure from his schoolmaster, witnesses the deaths of his close friends in conflict.

rades belong to a doomed generation. War seems gloomily permanent, a way of life. Cut off from the past and denied a future, they are isolated, vulnerable, without beliefs. The immediacy of their lives makes them comic, sexy, bitter or bored, and Hemingway is wonderfully evocative of all these modes. At the heart of this war novel is a love story, a great and moving juxtaposition. In a book of banal surfaces, both love and death are experiences to which characters struggle to attach meanings.

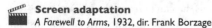

Where to go next
The Wars, 1977, Timothy Findley
The Wars investigates the traumatic impact of World War I on a young Canadian cavalry officer whose life, and mysterious death on the Western Front, is being researched by an archivist.

Screen adaptation
A Farewell to Arms, 1932, dir. Frank Borzage

The Return of the Soldier, 1918, Rebecca West
The home front was the subject of many war novels. In West's sensitive and intelligent book, written during the war itself, a young officer returns to England on leave with no memory of anything that has happened since 1901, not even of his wife, who is waiting for him.

In Parenthesis, 1937, David Jones
Many novels of the war are notable for their realism. By contrast, Jones's Modernist novel-poem is remarkable for its experimental mixture of first-hand experience, history and myth. But it brilliantly captures the dialogue and behaviour of men in the army, and is, occasionally, heartbreakingly funny.

The Regeneration Trilogy, 1991–95, Pat Barker
Barker's magnificent and moving recreation (comprising *Regeneration*, *The Eye in the Door* and *The Ghost Road*) is set in the Craiglockhart War Hospital in Scotland, where psychoanalyst Dr Rivers works with traumatized soldiers, many of them historical figures, such as Siegfried Sassoon, Wilfred Owen and Robert Graves.

Borzage was one of Hollywood's truest romantics which means that this, the first of three film versions of the novel, accentuates the love rather than the war story. It is still the best screen adaptation of Hemingway, and Gary Cooper as Frederic and Helen Hayes as his lover have a touching vulnerability, underscored by the fact that the film was made a mere fourteen years after the war's end.

Mehmed, My Hawk

1958, YASHAR KEMAL, TURKISH

The story, with its dramatic cycle of exile and revenge, belongs to folk myth. The flavour of the novel seems more primitive still – like the original stuff that myths are made from – an epic of the bleak Anatolian highlands stinking of goat and woodsmoke.

Dikenli – the "plateau of thistles" – is the personal fiefdom of the

tyrant Abdi Agha, who works the young boy Mehmed like a slave but cannot break his spirit. When Mehmed dares to elope with the Agha's nephew's betrothed, Hatché, he is driven into the mountains to become a bandit. First a member of Mad Durdu's gang, later a Robin-Hood-type legend on his own, he constantly strives to free Hatché from prison and revenge himself on Abdi Agha.

Kemal's sheer matter-of-factness not only brings out the roughness of the picturesque scenery, it also gives his characters their spiky individuality. Mad Durdu, the bandit who collects his victims' underwear, or Sergeant Rejeb, slowly and irritably dying in the marshes of Chukurova, are vividly present but in the end unfathomable.

He's not much to look at. Small, thin, with a big head and wide-set eyes. Anyone who hasn't seen him shoot or been beside him in a skirmish cannot understand his character.

The gangsterish action is strong and crude, and the narrative leaps forward unpredictably in fits and starts, whispered conversations in smoky mud huts suddenly punctuated by shoot-outs, succeeded by long vigils in mountain-top caves. Never articulated, the novel's themes – of honour, revenge and freedom – grow roughly but thickly out of the narrative, like the thistles in the poor soil of Dikenli. Scratchy and pungent, *Mehmed, My Hawk* provides a bracing antidote to the more facile adventures of contemporary best-sellers.

Recommended translation
1961, Edouard Roditi, NYRB Classics

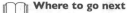

Where to go next
They Burn the Thistles, 1969, Yashar Kemal
During the long war between the poor farmers of the Anatolian mountains and the domineering Aghas, the outcast Mehmed must recover his sense of himself and his destiny before he can act to save the people he loves.

Schindler's Ark

1982, THOMAS KENEALLY, AUSTRALIAN

No arty prose trivializes its appalling subject, no narrative tricks obscure the relentless march of events. With its glossary and maps, and plain, careful style, Keneally's masterpiece about the Holocaust is fiction-as-history, an unflinching account of documented horrors – and, in the figure of Oskar Schindler, the uplifting tale of an unlikely hero.

> So the story of Oskar Schindler is begun perilously, with Gothic Nazis, with SS hedonism, with the thin and brutalised girl, and with a figure of the imagination somehow as popular as the golden-hearted whore: the good German.

Schindler came to Cracow in the wake of the Nazi armoured divisions in September 1939, seeking business opportunities. As Herr Direktor of the Deutsche Emailwaren Fabrik, which used Jewish slave labour to provide the German army with enamelware, he would be a familiar figure for the next five years: a heavy-drinking, womanizing tycoon, boon companion to the SS top brass and, unknown to them, saviour of hundreds of Jews.

At the outset of the novel, Keneally vows "to avoid all fiction"; his material is verifiable. The system of the concentration camps, with their hyper-efficient bureaucracy of slavery and murder, is documented as a matter of fact, implacable and astonishing. The characters, seen from the outside, have the unknowable solidity of figures from history. Interwoven with the chain of events that begins with Cracow's occupation by the Germans and ends with its liberation by the Russians are these characters' individual stories, among them the rise and fall of SS Hauptsturmführer Amon Goeth, who likes to begin his mornings by shooting a prisoner or two with his hunting rifle, and the precarious survival of Helen Hirsch, his savagely beaten Jewish maid. But the heart of the novel belongs to the magnificent and contradictory Schindler, a millionaire of lazy morals who risked his neck (and bankrupted himself) to save his Jewish workforce. In a world of darkness, he believed what his Jewish chief accountant told him – that "he who saves one man, saves the entire world".

 Where to go to next
This Way for the Gas, Ladies and Gentlemen, 1959, Tadeusz Borowski
Borowski was himself an inmate of the Nazi concentration camps (both Auschwitz and Dachau), and he draws on his experiences in a series of powerful short stories. Macabre but oddly comic, they show how life continues, in horribly altered forms, for the imprisoned and brutalized Jews of the camps.

Screen adaptation
Schindler's List, 1993, dir. Stephen Spielberg
The Holocaust is not an obvious subject for Hollywood, and this adaptation of the Schindler story is only partially successful. There are several powerful and deeply affecting moments, but the sheer gloss of the production and John Williams's music inevitably softens, and aestheticizes, the horrific everyday reality of the events depicted. Liam Neeson does his best to convey Schindler's complexity but is undermined by Spielberg's need to sentimentalize.

Garden, Ashes

1965, DANILO KIŠ, SERBIAN

As a novel about the strangeness of childhood, *Garden, Ashes* is thrillingly lyrical. As a novel about the Holocaust, it is shattering.

In fact, the Holocaust is hardly mentioned directly, the novel's focus is on a poor family in Serbia, whose domestic life is tenderly, half-comically recounted in anecdotes by the hypersensitive adolescent son, Andi Scham. Most of his stories concern his father, an eccentric genius forever working on the revised edition of his classic *Bus, Ship, Rail and Air Travel Guide*. At first he seems merely odd, the fact that he is often dressed in striped pyjamas just an eccentricity. Then one day, hitching a lift in Mr Rhinewine's cart, "blowing kisses like soap bubbles" to his family, he is taken away.

Seen through Andi Scham's eyes, everything is subjective and intense. Ordinary details take on new meanings. Proust aside, there are few writers who can devote a whole page to describing the nickelized glaze of an old tea-tray, and not just get away with it, but make it seem important. Andi turns the same rapt gaze on people as well as things: the

> *The last time I saw him, he was wearing a black ribbon around his sleeve. He sat, surrounded by drunkards, explaining vigorously to them that he was wearing the band in mourning for himself.*

epileptic but desirable Miss Edith, for example, or the vegetarian Mr Gavanski, his pockets overflowing with fruit. Most intensely of all, with a mixture of love and exasperation, Andi studies his father, a holy fool or "Wandering Jew", who spends his last days rambling the countryside for days on end, arousing the suspicion of local peasants and the Church, and leaving nothing behind him but scraps of the German newspaper, the *Neues Tageblatt*, on which he has blown his nose.

Recommended translation
1978, William J. Hannaher, Dalkey Archive Press

Where to go next
A Tomb for Boris Davidovich, 1976, Danilo Kiš
A series of biographical studies of fictional figures from the underworld of revolutionary Communism, this novel-cum-short-story-collection displays Kiš's talent for swift, brutal action and dark fatalism. The victims in his stories are all Jews, and their persecution links Soviet brutality to the tradition of pogroms.

The Naked and the Dead

1949, NORMAN MAILER, AMERICAN

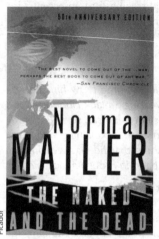

Picador

The American epic of the Pacific campaign, and a blockbuster in the best sense of the word, Mailer's first novel is a gritty all-action adventure and – better yet – an uncannily knowing dramatization of the bravado, prejudices, idiocies, hatreds and terrors of men under pressure of war.

General Cummings's task force is bogged down in its attempt to capture the island of Anopopei from the Japanese. Like everyone else, the soldiers of recon sluggishly follow orders, hauling equipment, digging latrines, enduring the filthy weather and bitching at each other until, as Army HQ demands progress, they are sent on a risky mission behind enemy lines. The arrival of the disgraced Lieutenant Hearn to command them only makes them more unstable. Alone in the jungle, the tensions in the platoon intensify.

All the deep dark urges of man, the sacrifices on the hilltop, and the churning lusts of the night and sleep, weren't all of them contained in the shattering screaming burst of a shell?

Mailer, who served as a rifleman in the Philippines, knew both the unbearable lulls and unpredictable violence of war. Passages of tedium are as brilliantly described as the sudden flaring scenes of combat – an argument between wound-up comrades can be as vicious and revealing as a night attack of mortars and grenades.

Lengthy but disciplined, the narrative switches expertly between scenes, changing pace, varying the atmosphere, always gripping. The real drama, however, is in the soldiers' heads – *The Naked and the Dead* is one of the great psychological novels of warfare. Working confidently with a huge cast of Northerners and Southerners, Jews and Catholics, Harvard graduates and vagrants, Mailer succeeded – with a sort of swagger – in creating all the dramas of cowardice, sadism, fear and guilt of fighting men.

Where to go next
The Thin Red Line, 1962, James Jones
Jones's experiences serving in the US army in the Pacific formed the basis for three novels, of which *The Thin Red Line* covers the Guadalcanal campaign. Less a literary stylist than Mailer, Jones is no less concerned with the everyday realities of soldiering – both the bloody and the banal.

Blood Meridian *or* the Evening Redness in the West

1985, CORMAC McCARTHY, AMERICAN

One of the most impressive writers of the American South, McCarthy has produced a number of harshly beautiful novels remarkable for their evocation of the locale's extreme landscape and their radical engagement with its history of struggle. The best of these, *Blood Meridian*, is a Western purged of all romance and glamour – an epic of concentrated and unremitting violence.

Aged fourteen, "the kid" runs away from his home in Tennessee and begins a life of barbarous subsistence in the squalid towns that dotted the Texas-Mexico border in the 1850s. An episode with Captain White's irregulars plundering Mexican villages ends with White's head in a glass jar, but this is merely preparation for the kid's later adventures with Glanton's troop, scalping Indians for a hundred dollars a head. So begins a confused, bloody journey across the plains and deserts of the borderlands, which is both quest and expiatory pilgrimage.

The novel has both immediacy and resonance. McCarthy's muscular style captures the physicality of the men with their lice and wounds and tight-lipped, mangled speech no less than the overwhelming landscape through which they journey, and his bib-

They saw patched argonauts from the states driving mules through the streets on their way south through the mountains to the coast. Goldseekers. Itinerant degenerates bleeding westward like some heliotropic plague.

lically rolling sentences give everything a mythic tone. The novel also features one of the most powerful representations of the Devil in fiction – a man known as "the judge", who rides with Glanton's party as its philosopher. Huge, "bald as a stone", a man of wisdom and serenity, he is lovingly devoted to butchery, killing and scalping even the children he encounters. His complicit and murderous relationship with the kid is not the least nightmarish aspect of this nightmarish novel.

Where to go next
Suttree, 1979, Cormac McCarthy
Cornelius Suttree, a high-class dropout scraping a living on a dilapidated house-boat near Knoxville has a talent for getting into trouble. McCarthy's description of the community of drifters and squatters to which Suttree belongs is extraordinarily vivid and very moving.

Snow
2002, ORHAN PAMUK, TURKISH

A clever, playful thriller, whose frankly relaxed realism incorporates farce as easily as noirish menace, *Snow* is a daring exploration of the dangerously difficult relationship between Western secularism and Islamist fervour. Pamuk's idea-juggling literary skills are to the fore: *Snow* features a character known – Kafkaesquely – as Ka, stuck in the snow (Turkish: "Kar"), in a northeastern Turkish town called Kars. But at the same time he is boldly direct in his engagement with issues of the day.

A poet and political exile "playing the intrepid reporter", Ka visits snowbound Kars to investigate the recent suicides of a number of young women (one of whom is a girl prohibited from wearing her Muslim headscarf at university). Once there, he finds himself caught up in a political coup, literally "staged" by a revolutionary actor opposed to the Islamists and supported by the dreaded "Special Operations" force, MİT. He falls in love, witnesses an assassination, meets the disaffected youth of Kars, writes poems and attempts to mediate between revolutionary forces and underground Islamist terrorists. His end is terrible but he is one of literature's most sensitive and moving heroes.

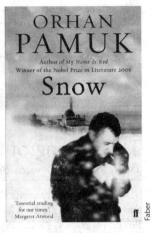

'Mr Poet, Mr Ka, you've made no secret of the fact that you were once an atheist. Maybe you still are one. So tell us, who is it who makes the snow fall from the sky? What is the snow's secret?'

The novel's narrative incidents are definitely thrillerish: murders, interrogations, sudden disappearances. More thrilling still are the volatile arguments between different characters about a range of contentious issues such as police surveillance, poetry, headscarves, Turkish-ness and European-ness, love, suicide and God. Constantly entertaining and intelligently provoking, *Snow* shows why novels matter.

Recommended translation
2004, Ralph Manheim, Faber (UK), Vintage (US)

Where to go next
The White Castle, 1985, Orhan Pamuk
A young Italian scholar is captured by the Ottomans and becomes the servant of a man eager to absorb the knowledge of the West. Pamuk's short, early novel is a brilliant exploration of two men's symbiotic relationship and, by extension, the relationship between West and East, progress and tradition.

The Crying of Lot 49

1966, THOMAS PYNCHON, AMERICAN

San Narciso, Southern California. Oedipa Maas is named executor of the estate of her late boyfriend, the real estate mogul Pierce Inverarity. As she says, "things then did not delay in turning curious".

Her quest to unravel the mysteries of Inverarity's legacy leads her into strange places – such as the "Echo Courts" motel, staffed entirely by teenage Beatles lookalikes and the headquarters of Yoyodyne, a shadowy electronics corporation. The people she meets there are even stranger: Mike Fallopian, for instance, member of the "right-wing nut" Peter Pinguid Society, and John Nefastis, champion of "Maxwell's Demon", a device for raising temperatures.

Change your name to Miles, Dean, Serge and/or Leonard, baby, she advised her reflection in the half-light of that afternoon's vanity mirror. Either way they'll call it paranoia. They.

At every point, clues of an overwhelming secret multiply. But what is it?

The unravelling of a tremendous, all-pervasive mystery plays out here as kinky striptease, arousing, alarming and very funny. Shiny details of 1960s Americana, from lapel pins to pop lyrics, are not only brilliantly themselves but also hieroglyphs of concealed meanings. Indeed, the humour, always slick and knowing, conceals a core of violence: at one point a psychiatrist called Hilarius runs amok with a rifle. In the course of Oedipa's investigations, hidden histories appear, hideous and unexpected, like the hushed-up slaughter of a platoon of US marines at Lago di Piéta in 1943. Pynchon's peculiar elongated sentences, full of fun and weirdness, add to the general sense of zany paranoia. When it first appeared, reviewers noted the novel's "strong European flavor". With the passing of time it has come to seem madly, quintessentially American.

Where to go next
Gravity's Rainbow, 1973, Thomas Pynchon
Pynchon's blockbuster of World War II features over 400 characters, and weaves together a range of esoteric themes from the sexuality of technology to the mystical meanings of mathematics. Hugely funny, often bewildering, frequently disgusting, it represents the high-water mark of postmodern fiction.

The Emigrants
1993, W.G. SEBALD, GERMAN

Like Sebald's equally impressive *Rings of Saturn* and *Austerlitz*, *The Emigrants* is a puzzle, or perhaps a dream, entrancing but naggingly unsolvable. Is it a novel? Is it a memoir? Are the photographs really taken from family albums? And how do the four stories – quasi-biographies of people distantly known to Sebald – fit together?

Dr Henry Selwyn, whom Sebald meets when renting a flat in Norfolk, was originally Hersch Seweryn from poor Lithuania. After emigrating to England he

Certain things, as I am increasingly becoming aware, have a way of returning unexpectedly, often after a lengthy absence.

became wealthy, but in old age blew his brains out with a hunting rifle. Paul Bereyter, Sebald's exemplary teacher from Germany, also committed suicide, throwing himself under a train after periods of

W. G. SEBALD
THE EMIGRANTS

'Strange, beautiful and terribly moving'
A. S. BYATT

claustrophobia from which he had suffered since the war. Sebald's émigré Great-Uncle Ambros Adelwarth was butler to the Solomons of Long Island for years before he voluntarily admitted himself into a sanatorium in Ithaca. And Max Ferber, a reclusive German artist Sebald met in Manchester in the 1960s, hardly spoke about his parents until, as he was dying, he gave Sebald his mother's journal for the war years before she was sent to a camp.

Like a tombstone, the title page of each story contains a person's name and an epitaph, emphasizing the sense that what follows are memorials. Sebald's prose is precise, almost cautious, but shimmering with implications. He writes of the little things that stick in the mind, and adhere together, slowly, hypnotically, creating a picture of catastrophic loss. Although – perhaps because – the Holocaust is never mentioned by name, a book that seems neither novel nor history nor witness statement, succeeds in articulating the private devastations of Jewish experience lingering long after the war.

Recommended translation
1996, Michael Hulse, Vintage (UK), New Directions (US)

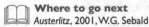

Where to go next
Austerlitz, 2001, W.G. Sebald
Jacques Austerlitz, a Jewish refugee child during the war and now an architectural historian, tries to trace the fate of his father in Prague and Paris. Like all Sebald's works, *Austerlitz* blends history, reportage, memoir and fiction (and illustrations) in a magically unsettling way.

Cancer Ward

1968, ALEXANDER SOLZHENITSYN, RUSSIAN

Solzhenitsyn is the Soviet writer who wouldn't shut up. Part-novelist, part-investigative reporter, he employed the system's officially sanctioned realist style – plain, dour, exact – against the system itself. In between his tale *One Day in the Life of Ivan Denisovich*, which first broke the news of the hell of the camps and, a decade later, his extraordinary documentary exposé *The Gulag Archipelego* (which resulted in his expulsion from the USSR), he wrote two fierce and vivid novels which combine the detail of reportage with fictional colour and thrust. *The First Circle* is one. The other, *Cancer Ward*, is an autobiographical novel set in a provincial hospital – and a bitter, sustained denunciation of the Soviet Union.

> On top of it all, the cancer wing was 'number thirteen'. Pavel Nikolayevich Rusanov had never been and could never be a superstitious person but his heart sank.

The variety of patients (including a wonderfully loathsome party informer) make the cancer ward a natural microcosm of society, but Solzhenitsyn also emphasizes other resonant themes: the chaos of the understaffed, under-resourced hospital and the enforcement of approved healing techniques (radiation) which are ambiguous at best, and sometimes fatal. Against a background of surgery, blood transfusions and radiation treatment, patients and staff talk politics and ideology, doubly helpless. But the novel wouldn't work half so well without Solzhenitsyn's psychological understanding of illness. His terrified patients change under pressure of their disease: Vadim the ambitious young geologist slipping into apathy; the illiterate thug Yefrem turning to books for consolation; the lecturer Schulubin, survivor of the university purges, tortured by guilt; and, above all, the political prisoner Oleg Kostoglotov, difficult and embittered, experiencing the paradoxical stirrings of new emotional life as his disease takes hold.

Recommended translation
1968, Nicholas Bethell and David Burg, Vintage Classics

Where to go next
One Day in the Life of Ivan Denisovich, 1962, Alexander Solzhenitsyn
The book that blew the lid off the gulag system is a brief, measured but horrifying account of one prisoner's ordinary day in a Soviet camp, based on Solzhenitsyn's own experiences.

Hadji Murat

1912, LEO TOLSTOY, RUSSIAN

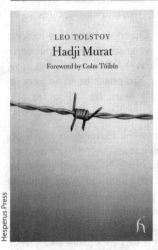

LEO TOLSTOY
Hadji Murat
Foreword by Colm Tóibín

Hesperus Press

In his last major work of fiction, a swirling tale of war, Tolstoy returned to his fifty-year-old memories of serving in the Russian army against the Muslim mountaineers of the Caucasus, where he first heard the name of the renowned Chechen general. The novel, short but broad-ranging, sensitive but filled with brutality, depicts a bitter clash of cultures centred on the enigmatic figure of Hadji Murat, who finds himself caught between the two.

After quarrelling with his imam, Shamil, Hadji Murat defects to the Russians, offering to fight for them if they will supply the troops needed to rescue his wives and son who have been taken hostage by Shamil. For several weeks, Hadji Murat waits for orders to filter down from the Tsar, until finally he can wait no longer, and, with the decisive swiftness that is his hallmark, he acts on his own, precipitating the narrative's sudden and violent end.

Hadji Murat is trapped between opposing forces. The whole novel, in fact, is built on oppositions: between Muslims and Christians, aristocrats and peasants, friends and enemies, life and death. The story progresses rapidly in a series of dramatic juxtapositions, as Tolstoy switches the setting from Shamil's court to the Tsar's Winter Palace, from Muslim village to Russian camp. From the beginning there seems no possible understanding between the gambling, drinking Russians and the Chechens, whose poorer lives find their most moving

Ahead of them all on a white-maned horse, wearing a white Circassian coat, a turban on his sheep-skinned hat and weapons decorated with gold, rode a man of impressive appearance.

expression in folk songs celebrating fallen martyrs. Their only common point of reference is Hadji Murat himself, and, fittingly, each side fails to interpret him correctly. To the end he remains mysterious, now openly friendly, now silently withdrawn, a man of action ironically become the subject of other people's idle talk.

Recommended translation
2003, Hugh Aplin, Hesperus Books

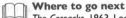

Where to go next
The Cossacks, 1863, Leo Tolstoy
Like *Hadji Murat*, *The Cossacks* is set in the Caucasus mountains, to which the Muscovite Dmitri Olenin travels in search of excitement and authenticity. His life with the Russian army provides the excitement, but his unrequited love for a local girl leads to something wholly unexpected: a spiritual awakening.

War and Peace

1865, Leo Tolstoy, Russian

Simply put, nothing matches it. An irresistible adventure story on a massive and profound scale – like a whole sequence of novels orchestrated and condensed into one unstoppable sweep of drama – it is gorgeous, powerful, varied and, above all, mesmerizingly readable.

Its much-publicized length, lazily cited as a problem, is in fact one of its great strengths. Here are hundreds of vividly real characters, a huge variety of experiences, all the frantic, jolting richness of life. Massive day-long battle scenes and fleeting intimate moments are equally hypnotic. Magically, Tolstoy *knows*. He seems to know what it is like to kill and be killed, to fall in love and suffer a spiritual crisis, to give birth and go bankrupt. His range is astonishing, his ability to capture it all uncanny.

Set during the period of Europe's Napoleonic wars, the battle scenes are justly famous: the rearguard Russian defence at Schöngrabern, a chaos of lost orders and impromptu heroism; the humiliating catastrophe of Austerlitz; and the mind-boggling slaughter of Borodino in 1812. A mastery of crowded action is matched by acutely vivid detail. The same is true of the scenes of "peace" – fashionable soirées in St Petersburg and Moscow, family rows, betrothals, betrayals and births – which balance and amplify the military episodes. It seems that all Tsarist Russia is here, suffering, confused and magnificent. But Tolstoy never loses sight of individual experience, the pressure and crisis of it, the illuminating moments which can change a person forever. The slow, surprising growth or helpless diminishment of his main characters, as they respond to the irresistible forces of love and war, form the great narrative drama which binds everything together. Pierre, haphazardly searching for spiritual fulfilment; Prince Andrey, embittered by both love and war; and Natasha, impulsively yielding to the transforming excitements of life – they are, quite simply, three of the deepest-felt, most powerfully moving characters in fiction. Both vast and intimate, grandly measured and superbly exciting, *War and Peace* trumps most other novels.

> *War is not being nice to each other, it's the vilest thing in human life, and we ought to understand that and not play at war. It's a terrible necessity, and we should be strict about it and take it seriously.*

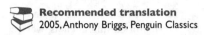

Recommended translation
2005, Anthony Briggs, Penguin Classics

Where to go next
Before The Storm, 1878, Theodor Fontane
A fascinating German counterpart to *War and Peace*, *Before the Storm* is set in the winter of 1812–13 as Napoleon's troops, retreating from Moscow, arrive in Berlin. The impact of historical forces on ordinary people – one family in particular – forms the focus of Fontane's great work.

Screen adaptation
War and Peace, 1968, dir. Sergei Bondarchuk
The Russian version is looking a little dated but it retains an edge over the excellent BBC series starring Anthony Hopkins. Bondarchuk himself plays Pierre as a surprisingly assertive character, but it is the military scenes – with hand-held cameras and 120,000 Russian army extras – that bring this version to life, highlighting the contrast between uncertain peace and the messy madness of war.

The Ogre
1970, MICHEL TOURNIER, FRENCH

Car mechanic Abel Tiffauges, hero of Tournier's menacing but oddly tender novel about World War II, believes himself to be an ogre. He has, from the start, a special ambiguous affinity with children. Of all the mythological figures who haunt his world, he identifies most with St Christopher the Child-Bearer and the Erl King, spectral child-snatcher of German folklore. But which is he?

The outbreak of war saves him from a charge of child molestation,

The Director signalled to him through his office window. He held out a sheet of cheap paper which bore a roughly stencilled text: BEWARE OF THE OGRE OF KALTENBORN! He is after your children.

and sends him as a prisoner to Germany, "the country of pure essences", where he works first as a forestry assistant at the

East Prussian hunting reserve of Hermann Göring, then as overseer of recruitment to the Hitler Youth training camp at Kaltenborn – all the time moving closer to the fulfilment of his vocation.

The tone of the novel is grave but delicately sensuous, its firm realism animated but never distorted by the myths and symbols that Tiffauges sees everywhere. It contains wonderfully vivid scenes from history (including an absolutely hilarious hunting expedition on Göring's estate and a desperate last stand made by the Hitler Youth against invading Soviet troops), and strikingly original, often highly technical observations on topics such as pigeon-fancying, phallology, antler-measurement, photography, dressage and the distribution of human body hair. Its special achievement, however, is atmospheric – it conjures up a haunting mood of despair and dignity, at once terrifying and consoling, perfectly suited to the horrors of World War II.

 Recommended translation
1972, Barbara Bray, Johns Hopkins University Press

 Where to go next
Gemini, 1975, Michel Tournier
Gemini describes the love between two identical twins Jean and Paul (known collectively as Jean-Paul). When Jean betrays his brother for a mistress, they embark on a strange quest that takes them round the world, giving Tournier the opportunity to elaborate with typical ingenuity on the themes of twinship and duality.

Germinal

1885, ÉMILE ZOLA, FRENCH

A high-impact blockbuster with a crusading message, Zola's most famous novel made such an impression on the French public that the crowd at his state funeral chanted its title. Meticulously researched and expertly arranged, *Germinal* is a big-screen, close-up drama of a miners' strike, and a furious protest against the inhuman conditions of working men and women.

Zola spent six months among miners in preparation for the novel; more impressive still is his determination to tell it as it was. There are no saints among his poor. Poverty degrades, and the miners and their families are coarse, vicious and crudely promiscuous. Drunken miners beat their wives, the women scream at their children, and the children graduate from slinging stones to cutting throats. Sex and violence are common denominators. Even Étienne, the idealistic young wanderer who inspires the strike with half-understood ideas of socialism and anarchism will kill a man in a fight over a girl.

Oxford World's Classics

> *Now the miners were waking from their slumbers in the depths of the earth and starting to germinate like seeds sown in the soil ... an army of men fighting to restore justice.*

From the beginning, when Étienne arrives in the middle of a freezing night at the killing-fields of the Montsou mines, the novel has sweep and purpose. Crowd scenes are Zola's speciality: the silently tramping workers arriving at the pitheads for the morning shift; the agitated meeting of the strikers in the woods; and, above all, in the great hundred-page central section of the novel as the rampaging mob swirls from pit to pit, wrecking and looting. Such scenes, though long, remain dynamic because Zola sees the eddies in the general current – a woman shouting insults, the idler at the edge of the crowd – and because he possesses a theatrical, at times Romantic, sense of action. A novel of ideas tumultuously debated in the miners' frequent arguments, *Germinal* is also a galloping series of adventures – underground explosions, manhunts and sabotage.

Recommended translation
1993, Peter Collier, Oxford World's Classics

Where to go next
L'Assommoir, 1887, Émile Zola

Zola's breakthrough novel is a bleak study of alcoholism set among working-class Parisians. Abandoned by her lover, the washerwoman Gervaise Macquart struggles to support her family. But her husband's drinking undermines all her efforts until, worn out, she begins to drink herself.

Screen adaptation
Germinal, 1994, dir. Claude Berri

Unfairly criticized by some as worthy "heritage" cinema, this is an an honest, unpretentious – and occasionally spectacular – version of Zola's epic, which succeeds in finding the right balance between the broad political sweep of the novel and individual personal tragedies. French singer Renaud, daringly cast as Étienne Lantier, more than holds his own against the powerful presence of Gérard Départieu.

A sense
of place

8

Locations in classic fiction – whether real or imagined – can be so much more than mere setting. They create atmosphere, shape the storyline, define the themes, and sometimes provide the principal focus. Who is the main character of *The Alexandria Quartet*? The city itself, with all its secrets, passions and labyrinthine plots.

Cities have long fascinated novelists as places of energy and change, where new ideas find strange new forms. Sometimes the change is fast, as in the 1920s Manhattan of *Manhattan Transfer*, where fortunes are made and lost overnight. Sometimes they are slow and painful, as in Naguib Mafouz's gloriously moving saga of life in Cairo over three generations.

Elsewhere tradition and continuity are powerfully enforced – in the Sicily of *The Leopard*, for instance, or Anthony Trollope's cloistered Barchester. And sometimes a place can be haunted by its past, as the narrator of Daphne du Maurier's electrifying *Rebecca* discovers.

A place can also be defined by the people who live there: their social interaction gradually building up a detailed picture of an actual location, as in George Eliot's provincial town of *Middlemarch*. The hidden lives of such places – from genteel *Cranford* to midwestern *Winesburg, Ohio* – have provided fertile territory for some of the greatest writers.

Finally, there are those locations which evoke a sense of strangeness and disorientation precisely because they are so unfamiliar – both to the characters and to the reader. Such places can be used to create a sense of alienation, reflecting the way people lose and find themselves when they travel – whether it is to a small North Yorkshire village (in *A Month in the Country*) or the beautiful and inhospitable Moroccan desert (in *A Sheltering Sky*).

Winesburg, Ohio

1919, SHERWOOD ANDERSON, AMERICAN

Properly speaking, the book that made Anderson a classic American author is a collection of interrelated short stories, but it works like a novel, each story fitting a new character into the communal life of a small midwestern town. Like one of Edward Hopper's paintings, the book conjures up the haunting image of a place saturated with the private emotions of lonely individuals.

One shudders at the thought of the meaninglessness of life while at the same instant, and if the people of the town are his people, one loves life so intensely that tears come into the eyes.

The characters of Anderson's Winesburg are ordinary people – the teacher, the farmer, the barman, the doctor, the newspaper reporter – rooted in the common rounds of daily life, but they have intense, sometimes fantastical inner lives, which they struggle to express. Anderson's gift is his ability to give voice to this outlandish interior poetry.

Winesburg, Ohio is short and simply organized, but never neat. The characters' outward lives may be nicely organized, but Anderson shows their essential disorder, the mounting pressure which spills out suddenly in dramatic action, creating havoc. The middle-aged minister obsessed with spying on the school-mistress gives himself up to lust, with unexpected results; the disappointed young shopkeeper cannot control the urge to run naked through the rain. Sometimes, these gestures are a break-through, sometimes they only intensify the loneliness: Anderson is never easy or sentimental. Nevertheless, the exploration of a place through the secret lives of its inhabitants places the emphasis on the quality of human emotions, and a major – finely balanced – theme of the book is men and women, and the shifting possibilities of love between them.

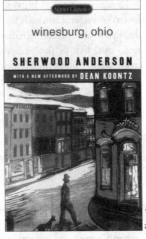

Signet

Where to go next
Time Will Darken It, 1948, William Maxwell
Maxwell's fourth novel is a beautifully observed look at the quiet tragedies of American small-town life in the early twentieth century, which combines penetrating insight with a meticulous style.

The Sheltering Sky

1949, PAUL BOWLES, AMERICAN

Hallucinatory and creepy, Paul Bowles's first novel is a disturbing story of a man and wife cast adrift – mentally and physically – in the heat and dust of North Africa. Combining a French feel for ideas and emotions with an American specificity of detail, the novel grips and haunts, as tension builds towards a shattering climax.

Escaping post-war Europe, Port and Kit Moresby journey from the towns of Algeria towards the Sahara, where – Port believes – they will finally be able to free themselves from all traces of Western civilizations and live in the present moment. But they are also estranged from each other; their responses to the characters they encounter – the smoothly stupid Tunner, the bizarre mother and son travelling on British passports – are gratingly different. And when they reach the desert, they find themselves alone with their own obsessions.

Though Bowles's writing is occasionally laboured, the slanted psychology of his characters is enormously effective – the sudden, startling vagaries of thought, which brilliantly capture Port and Kit's essential extremity. Even better is the wired atmosphere, part *ennui*, part irritability, part perversity, which seems to emanate from the increasingly inhospitable landscape through which Port and Kit travel. The meta-

'Nothing ever happens the way one imagines it is going to. One realises that most clearly here: all your philosophic systems crumble. At every turn one finds the unexpected.'

phor of sickness and health runs through the whole book, and, as Port falls ill in the novel's final stages, his fever gives him a weird lucidity, another way of thinking, and his thoughts – like abstract paintings – lose their connection with the world. In his delirium, he will wonder what will happen if he should pierce the fabric of the "sheltering sky" and discover what horror lies above.

Where to go next
The Stories of Paul Bowles, Paul Bowles
Bowles lived much of his life in Tangier, and many of his stories are from the perspective of an outsider in North Africa. The tone is cool but there is a constant air of threat that gets under the skin in a disturbingly eerie fashion.

Screen adaptation
The Sheltering Sky, 1990, dir. Bernardo Bertolucci
Bertolucci turns Bowles's novel into the travelogue from hell, counterpointing Kit and Port Moresby's disintegrating relationship, played with dissolute despair

by John Malkovich and Debra Winger, against the majestic desert landscape. Inevitably, it lacks the psychological depth of the novel, but is still a convincing portrayal of self-destructive impulses fuelled by cultural alienation.

A Month in the Country

1980, J.L. CARR, ENGLISH

Looking back fifty years to the famously hot summer of 1920, Tom Birkin recalls the month he spent in the tiny Yorkshire village of Oxgodby, uncovering a great medieval painting of the Last Judgement on the wall of the parish church. Judgement, with all that it implies of Heaven and Hell, will prove a significant theme in Birkin's life.

Both a southerner and a war victim, Birkin initially felt himself in "enemy country", but was soon drawn into village life. In his deepening relationships with the people around him – the stationmaster's daughter Kathy, fellow veteran Charles Moon and, most importantly, the vicar's radiantly pretty wife, Alice Keach – he began a process of personal restoration which mirrored his work in the church.

> 'This is what I need, I thought – a new start, and, afterwards, maybe I won't be a casualty anymore.'

The simplicity of the story and the small scale of the novel (less than a hundred pages long) belie its richness and subtlety. Carr's relaxed but supple tone of voice is capable of springing abruptly from one mood to another. Descriptions of a tranquil August in the countryside are punctuated by sudden outbursts and revelations, like summer lightning, which vanish in an instant to leave the tranquillity apparently undisturbed. Like a ghost story, the atmosphere is haunted by what lies below the surface, by what hasn't yet been uncovered, and Carr excels in capturing the life that slips between the bigger narrative moments. In a pivotal scene, Alice Keach conducts Birkin round the vicarage – a vast, neglected house as gloomy and bare as her marriage – leading him finally to the living room, empty except for an inexplicable piece of furniture taking up an entire wall. "We're not sure what it is," Mrs Keach says at last, "Actually, we think part of it's missing." *A Month in the Country* is a novel in which the mystery of things matches the mystery of people.

Where to go next
The Collected Stories, 1976, William Trevor
Considerably more prolific than Carr, William Trevor possesses the same masterly restraint. In these stories he gently amasses telling details of character and place with an insight and delicacy that is breathtaking.

My Ántonia

1918, WILLA CATHER, AMERICAN

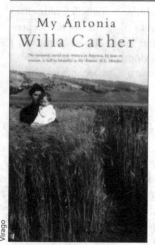

Tracing with equal assurance the small, reckless sweep of individual lives and the broad surge of history, *My Ántonia* is one of the most compellingly authentic novels of pioneer America: a fiction that works with the quiet power and casual realism of memoir.

The novel is presented as a memoir, in fact: the middle-aged Jim Burden's recollections of a girl he grew up with and has never forgotten. When we first see Ántonia Shimerda, she is the spirited twelve-year-old daughter of a poor Czech family which has arrived – with neither experience nor resources – to farm the virgin prairies of Nebraska. At the close of the book, when Jim meets her again after a gap of twenty years, she is a poor farmer's wife on the same land. Her hardships have been the common lot – poverty and hard work, failures in love and family tragedies – but her vitality has made them both unique and exemplary, a pioneer life story marked as much by generous energies as sorrows.

Cather writes an artfully relaxed prose full of easy-paced descriptions of the extraordinary Nebraskan landscape and climate. Her equally unforced descriptions of the characters perfectly match the elisions and awkwardnesses of their lives: we seem to meet them as we might in real life, in the same vivid but sporadic encounters, rapid intimacy followed by growing distance, vague first impressions developing into new understandings. Besides Ántonia herself, there are a dozen characters here whose lives are easily imaginable beyond the immediate confines of the novel. And, in Ántonia, Cather created a vividly memorable character of mingled sorrows and joys, who stands for a whole generation.

> There was nothing but land: not a country at all, but the material out of which countries are made.

 Where to go next
A Lost Lady, 1923, Willa Cather
Another tale of frontier life in Nebraska in the late nineteenth century, this time focusing on the life of a bewitchingly graceful but duplicitous Marian Forrester, whose varied fortunes seem to mirror those of the town in which she lives.

Ragtime

1975, E.L. DOCTOROW, AMERICAN

Like a flickering reel of Pathé news, showing rapidly changing sequences of people who astonish us by being at once so strange and so familiar, *Ragtime* is a fascinating and entertaining historical pastiche with serious heft.

It is America in the early 1900s, vivid and racy. Harry K. Thaw, husband of the society beauty Evelyn Nesbit, shoots her former lover, the famous architect Stanford White. Harry Houdini, heavily manacled, escapes from locked cabinets, giant footballs and sausage skins. Emma

MODERN CLASSICS

Penguin

E. L. Doctorow
Ragtime

Goldman the anarchist is arrested every time there is a civil disturbance. And at Coney Island, visiting European psychoanalysts Freud and Jung solemnly ride together through the Tunnel of Love.

Mingling with these historical figures are Doctorow's own characters: a well-to-do family living in New Rochelle, New York; an impoverished immigrant father and daughter; and a self-possessed black pianist, Coalhouse Walker Jr – a man who doesn't know he is a Negro.

The style is cod-historical reportage, packed with bizarre discontinuities and comic juxtapositions: a ragtime, intricate, clear and rousing. Never has a political novel that raised such profoundly uncomfortable questions about the injustices of race and gender been so startlingly full of vibrant and glittering detail – including perhaps the most demented sex scene in fiction, involving a stout female anarchist with massage oil, an undressed society beauty, and a withdrawn young man with blond moustaches hiding in the closet. Read it for both its gorgeous comedy and high-impact political message.

> *There seemed to be no entertainment that did not involve great swarms of people. Trains and steamers and trolleys moved them from one place to another. That was the style, that was the way people lived.*

Where to go next
Billy Bathgate, 1989, E.L. Doctorow
A fast-moving, spellbinding tale of an adventurous American boy who gets caught up in the criminal underworld of 1930s New York, and finds himself a member of the Dutch Schultz gang.

Screen adaptation
Ragtime, 1981, dir. Milos Forman
Forman's film lacks the sheer chutzpah of Doctorow's kaleidoscopic novel, but
still boasts an infectious energy. Several of the key strands of the novel are
excised, and the focus is firmly on the tale of Coalhouse Walker Jr – a strong
performance from Howard Rollins – but there remains a powerful sense of
the teeming life and potentiality of *fin-de-siècle* America.

Manhattan Transfer

1925, JOHN DOS PASSOS, AMERICAN

USA may be Dos Passos's most ambitious fiction, but *Manhattan
Transfer* was the first novel in which he found his essential style, and
it remains fabulously fresh – a hot-off-the-press prose poem to the
most hyperactive city on earth. Shop-signs, ads ("WE BUY FALSE
TEETH"), headlines ("SLAYS SELF WITH SHOTGUN"), theatre
bills, popular songs ("Everybody's Doing It") and all the Americana
of the sidewalks give a neon buzz to a sequence of snappy, disconnected scenes from the lives of chorus girls, Bowery bums, prohibi-
tion millionaires, "parlour snakes and flappers", all burning brightly
as they risk everything in a desperate bid to make it big.

Evoking a Manhattan of horse-drawn
milk-carts, gaslamps, skyscrapers and
dockyards with a lyricism ("lemoncol-
oured dawn was drenching the empty
streets") as in-your-face as any of the
novel's pushy characters, Dos Passos
recreates the city's varied moods – from

> 'Cities of orgies walks and
> joys.' 'Orgies nuttin, as we
> say at hun'an toitytoird
> street...Do you realise
> that I've lived all my life in
> this goddam town?'

the wild glee of a downtown party to the desolation of the deserted
harbourside at dawn. The characters too show the hectic variety of big
city experience: Congo Jake jumping ship to make his fortune; Ellen the
beautiful chorus girl tired of capitulation; Dutch Robertson and Francie
the "flapper bandit" taking matters into their own hands; George

Baldwin, the opportunist lawyer disillusioned with life. Their stories, told in short dramatic spasms, form a broken but colourful newsreel of ups and downs as they pursue the ubiquitous American dream.

Where to go next
USA, 1938, John Don Passos
A trilogy of novels – *The 42nd Parallel* (1930), *1919* (1932) and *The Big Money* (1936) – worked into a wide-angle panorama of the US in the first three decades of the twentieth century. Alongside the potted biographies of historical figures are Dos Passos's traders, labour leaders, heiresses, chorus girls and vagrants.

Rebecca

1938, DAPHNE DU MAURIER, ENGLISH

Virago

Some novels cast a spell from the first page: *Rebecca* is one of them. As haunting as a ghost story, as tense as a murder mystery (and it is both of these), the story grips with a dreamlike fascination and will not let go. A novel about memory, loss and, ultimately, a hideous secret, it is as alluring as myth.

When the young and gauche narrator marries the elegant widower Max de Winter, she is quickly overawed. One week she is a paid companion, the next mistress of Manderley, her husband's famous ancestral home. The house, built on the Cornish coast, is beautiful, but Mrs Danvers, the politely vicious housekeeper, is keeping alive the memory of the first Mrs de Winter, the beloved Rebecca, who drowned. Beautiful and charismatic, Rebecca was the perfect wife. Why then does Ben, the halfwit who roams the beach, say that she gave him "the feeling of a snake"?

The plot has force and suspense, sickening tension broken by spine-tingling revelations – perfect English manners exploded by sudden outbursts of emotions. But the book is lifted into a different category of power by its tone, the narrator's mesmerizing voice remembering and grieving, and – above all – the extraordinary evocation of Manderley and its grounds, the perfect, cold east wing, where the narrator has her rooms, the opulent rooms of Rebecca's

> Mrs Danvers came close to me, she put her face near to mine. 'It's no use, is it?' she said. 'You'll never get the better of her. She's still mistress here, even if she's dead.'

west wing, the misty lawns and blood-red rhododendrons, the moss and azaleas of Happy Valley, the beach hut down at the cove, the soft, complacent sound of pigeons and the smoky smell of bluebells.

Where to go next
Don't Look Now and other stories, Daphne du Maurier
Du Maurier was equally adept at the art of short story writing and this collection contains five of her best. The title piece in particular is a concentrated miniature of anguish and suspense set in a claustrophobic Venice.

Screen adaptation
Rebecca, 1940, dir. Alfred Hitchcock
In this superb adaptation, Hitchcock places the emphasis on the struggle between the diffident new wife, a fragile Joan Fontaine, and the tyrannical housekeeper Mrs Danvers – played with frightening relish by Joan Anderson. George Barnes's *noir*-style photography gives Manderley a suitably claustrophobic oppressiveness and the whole film is freighted with a pervasive mood of guilt and disillusionment.

The Alexandria Quartet

Justine | Balthazar | Mountolive | Clea

1957–60, LAWRENCE DURRELL, ENGLISH

In the 1950s literary world of kitchen-sink dramas and gritty working-class novels by angry young men, the appearance of Durrell's exotic and lyrical quartet made him, briefly, the most celebrated living English novelist. Nowadays he is more often dismissed as a self-indulgent writer of purple passages and psycho-babble. Both views seem unfair. True, Durrell's densely poetic prose sometimes clots, and the aphorisms of his philosophizing characters can be relentless; readers may wince at examples of misogyny and pretentiousness. But, like the arch-stylist Oscar Wilde before him, Durrell is deliberately, indeed angrily, provocative. His high-flown style is appropriate to his subject: "love – an absolute which takes all or forfeits all."

The politics of love, the intrigues of desire, good and evil, virtue and caprice, love and murder, moved obscurely in the dark corners of Alexandria's streets and squares, brothels and drawing-rooms...

The story describes the tangled affairs of a group of men and women living in Alexandria immediately before and during World War II – an "impossible city of love and obscenity". The first three novels recount the same basic sequence of events from different perspectives, and the fourth moves the narrative forward in time.

The shifts in perspective function like sliding panels in a kaleidoscope to reveal surprising features of familiar scenes. At the heart of it all stands Justine, the enigmatic, desirable, damaged, rapacious spirit of the city itself, and round her range those she has loved or betrayed.

It is in the set pieces that Durrell's style produces real power, and he excels in crowded scenes of dizzying tension and drama: the duck shoot in *Justine*, for instance, or the carnival in *Balthazar*, both of which culminate in murder. Above all, Durrell triumphs in his descriptions of Alexandria, teeming, passionate and contradictory, a city of the mind and memory as much as physical reality, and vibrant and unforgettable as both.

Where to go next
The Levant Trilogy, 1977–80, Olivia Manning
Manning provides a very different, but no less effective, perspective on Egypt during World War II. The trilogy continues the story of Guy and Harriet

Pringle (from the earlier *Balkan Trilogy*) who, having escaped the war in the Balkans, find themselves embroiled in the conflict once again.

Middlemarch

1871–72, GEORGE ELIOT, ENGLISH

It's not only its length that makes *Middlemarch* unusually intimidating, but also its reputation as a master-piece of moral enquiry. It *is* long (eighty-six chapters plus a Preface and Finale) and countless exam questions have been set on aspects of Eliot's moral vision – but insistence on the novel's undoubted seriousness overlooks the fact that it is a continuously compelling narrative of force and variety, in which intimate dramas are just as important as the measured sweep of the novel as a whole.

Penguin

Not that this sweep isn't justly celebrated. The provincial town of Middlemarch is an utterly convincing fictional world, a whole society of doctors, manufacturers, squires, curates and estate managers who sink or swim in the unpredictable currents of local politics and commerce. If class differences are crucially important (and pub landlady Mrs Dollop's voice is as distinctively individual as that of landowner Sir James Chettam), so too is a person's reputation or "standing". Improvement, in various forms, energizes characters as different as the narcissistic Rosamond Vincy, the dedicated young Dr Lydgate, the desiccated scholar Casaubon and the novel's "heroine", the idealistic Dorothea Brooke.

Several miraculously intertwining plots – dealing with courtship and marriage, financial corruption, genealogical discoveries and that great staple of Victorian fiction, the controversial will – draw in dozens of characters, nearly all vibrantly believable, in numerous satisfyingly varied dramas. Scenes such as Dorothea and Casaubon's honeymoon in Rome, the marital bickering of Rosamond and Lydgate, and the corrupt banker Bulstrode's silent confession to his wife are memorably piercing and exact.

> 'But my dear Mrs Casaubon,' said Mr Farebrother. 'Character is not cut in marble. It is something living and changing, and may become diseased, as our bodies do.' 'Then it may be rescued and healed,' said Dorothea.

Where to go next
Daniel Deronda, 1876, George Eliot
Like *Middlemarch*, this is another grandly sprawling saga of interlocking lives, featuring the contrasting existences of spoiled rich girl Gwendolen Harleth and the self-sacrificing Daniel Deronda. Unusual for the time in presenting Jewish life in a serious and sympathetic manner.

Screen adaptation
Middlemarch, 1994, dir. Anthony Page
Adapted by the BBC's most favoured writer, Andrew Davies, this mini-series has decidedly soapish qualities. Some will feel this is no bad thing, but lessening the intellectual aspirations of Dorothea (excellently played by Juliet Aubrey) and Lydgate's struggles to improve the world, makes both characters seem priggish and the series – especially when viewed end-to-end – sometimes drags.

Valmouth

1919, RONALD FIRBANK, ENGLISH

Everything is in the detail. Like all Firbank's novels, *Valmouth* is a tiny, glittering pile of fragments – glimpsed ambiguous incidents and overheard snippets of conversation – which we must piece together ourselves to form an intelligible mosaic. But this puzzling process is very much part of the fun, and, for all its eccentricity, the novel triumphantly captures the thrill of real life – a sharp, comic and distinctly smutty sensation.

In the picturesque town of Valmouth on the West coast of England, famous for its pure air and wealthy centenarians, a small crowd of typically Firbankian characters are gathered: Eulalia Hurstpierpoint, Betty Thoroughfare and Lady Parvula de Panzoust, three gossipy, opinionated and occasionally amorous old ladies. Over the course of a few days, they involve themselves with intrigues, go to parties, visit the flamboyant black masseuse, Mrs Yajñavalkya, for sessions of "drubbing", and round things off by attending a fantastically subversive wedding.

> 'Ah ... I shall never forget how Mr Comedy (when he lost his first wife) passed the night in the graveyard, crying and singing and howling, with a magnum of Mumm.'

The manners are arch, the behaviour is camp, and the novel's natural medium is innuendo. Much is made of Firbank's effeminacy (he was homosexual, and homosexuality is a major submerged theme in the novel) and decadence (in some sense he belongs with Oscar Wilde and other aesthetes of the "naughty nineties"), but his literary technique is tough, radically abbreviating and cropping narrative scenes to give them a cinematic mobility, something which both Hemingway and Waugh learned from. Don't be fooled by the comedy (though it is outrageously funny), below the apparently inconsequential chitchat of the stylized characters lie the big, dangerous subjects of life.

Where to go next
Concerning the Eccentricities of Cardinal Pirelli, 1926, Ronald Firbank
In the fictional Andalucian city of Clemenza, the antics of the sybaritic Cardinal Pirelli – he has baptized a dog and has inappropriate relations with both sexes – arouse the disapproval of Rome. This short, fantastical caricature of camp Catholicism is always outrageous, but also oddly moving.

A Passage to India

1924, E.M. FORSTER, ENGLISH

Penguin

Forster is the poet of little misunderstandings, an assiduous lyricist of personal disconnections. With his mild and modest style, he seems an unlikely radical. But *A Passage to India*, quietly and implacably judgemental, changed the views of an entire generation about the British Empire.

Chandrapore, an unremarkable city, boasts few natural attractions except the Marabar Caves, some twenty miles away. The British administrators, whose lives centre on the Club, never go there. But when the City Magistrate's fiancée, Miss Quested, arrives from England, determined to "see India", the Muslim Dr Aziz optimistically arranges an excursion. Returning to the city that evening, he is arrested at the railway station, charged with a gross assault on the Englishwoman. His anguish is nothing to the cold fury of the British imperium.

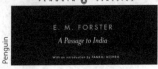

He spoke at last. 'The worst thing in my whole career has happened,' he said. 'Miss Quested has been insulted in one of the Marabar Caves.'

Forster's exemplary liberalism makes him a careful, even cautious writer. At first, the novel goes on tiptoe, quietly, and comically, exploring the mutual incomprehension of the British, Muslims and Hindus. Adela Quested with her force and lack of instinct; her future mother-in-law Mrs Moore, kindly and intuitive; Mr Fielding who loves India and the impulsive Dr Aziz – all try, and fail, to understand one another.

But with the incident at the Marabar Caves all the suppressed violence between the British and Indians breaks out. With its political, racial and psychological themes, *A Passage to India* has perhaps been more taught than read, but it remains a marvellously involving story. The narrative is spellbinding, the irony beautifully nimble and Forster is one of the best observers of the flickering, insubstantial movement of the emotions.

Where to go next
Howards End, 1910, E.M. Forster
A tale of two opposed families – the artistic Schlegels and the commercial Wilcoxs – tested by the love affair between Margaret Schlegel and Henry Wilcox, whose house (modelled on Forster's own childhood home) is Howards End.

Screen adaptation
A Passage to India, 1984, dir. David Lean
Forster's novel is, implicitly, highly critical of the British presence in India; Lean's film rather less so. Once you get over this imbalance there is a lot to enjoy, in particular the commanding landscape photography and the performances of Peggy Ashcroft as Mrs Moore and Judy Davis as Miss Quested. Alec Guinness as the Hindu Prof. Godbole, on the other hand, is definitely not the actor's finest hour.

Cranford

1851–53, ELIZABETH GASKELL, ENGLISH

If you think Victorian novels are all bulging triple-deckers, try Mrs Gaskell's much-loved miniature: a short, relaxed sequence of comic sketches describing the lives of the snobbish, tender-hearted old ladies of a small town famous for its sense of propriety. Gossipy anecdotes bristle with brilliantly observed details, and artfully half-hidden among the blameless domestic trivia of afternoon visits, changing fashions in bonnets and "elegant" household economies are the big ugly subjects of loss, grief, suppressed passion and terror.

The genteel Cranford ladies, apparently so alike, are in fact sharply dissimilar. Opinionated Miss Pole (whose "sighting" of a gang of burglars throws the town into panic), torpid Mrs Jamieson (arbiter of taste by virtue of her aristocratic connections), patri-

> *In the first place Cranford is in possession of the Amazons; all the holders of houses, above a certain rent, are women. If a married couple come to settle in the town, somehow the gentleman disappears.*

otic Mrs Forrester (known to be able to detect French spies in their midst) and sweetly deferential Miss Matty Jenkyns (still troubled by a marriage proposal she rejected thirty years earlier) struggle in very different ways to balance their instincts with their shared notions of decorum. The novel's surface detail would form an encyclopedia of Victoriana, from bread-jelly and top boots to leg o' mutton sleeves and Wombwell's travelling circus, but Gaskell also draws attention to the deeper meanings of the Cranford ladies' domestic world, and a novel so full of delightful trivialities is equally sensitive to more solemn themes: anxieties about money, trials of conscience, guilty regrets, the dictates of duty and the consolations of stoicism.

Where to go next
North and South, 1854, Elizabeth Gaskell

Classes and cultures collide in this troubled love story between sensitive southerner Margaret Hale and hard-nosed, northern industrialist John Thornton. Set against the grimy backdrop of Milton (a city inspired by Manchester), the novel is hugely critical of the degradations caused by poverty and exploitation.

Screen adaptation
Cranford, 2007, dir. Simon Curtis

The BBC's five-part adaptation combines events from *Cranford* with two minor works (*Mr Harrison's Confessions* and *My Lady Ludlow*) and adds a completely invented character. This mix-and-match approach is disconcerting if you know *Cranford*, but is largely successful. What is missing is the "elegant economy" of Mary Smith's narration, which in the original adds an extra layer of irony to every joke.

Lanark

1981, ALASDAIR GRAY, SCOTTISH

Alasdair Gray's *Lanark* is like a Hieronymus Bosch painting: minutely realistic, bizarrely grotesque and very crowded. The action is located in four extraordinary cities all, in some sense, Glasgow. There's Unthank, a corrupt metropolis lacking daylight, where people develop dragon-scales and quite often vanish altogether; the Kafkaesque "Institute", responsible for turning humans into fuel; Provan, where social control is enforced by security robots; and the real post-war Glasgow, home to an artistic child called Duncan Thaw. Though *Lanark* is a big-hitting novel which rages against politics and commerce, at its heart is a beautifully intimate description of a difficult adolescence.

Alasdair Gray/Canongate

Gray takes risks from the beginning, combining strip-cartoon sci-fi action with a downbeat realism: people living ordinary lives in Glaswegian tenements are liable to develop claws or grow mouths all over their bodies. Technically, too, Gray is audacious: the four "books" of the novel are deliberately disordered, with a prologue appearing well after the beginning,

> I believe there are cities where work is a prison and time a goad and love a burden, and this makes my freedom feel worthwhile. My one worry is the scab on my arm.

and an epilogue – in which the main character, Lanark, complains to the author about the plot – well before the "finale". Gray's hyperactive drawings and wilfully distinctive typography reinforce the novel's idiosyncrasy. And if we begin to doubt that there's a point to all this mad invention, Gray obligingly makes an appearance in his novel to impress on us that "an illusionist's main job is to exhaust his restless audience by a show of marvellously convincing squabbles until they see the simple things we really depend on".

> **Where to go next**
> *Poor Things*, 1992, Alasdair Gray
> Another self-illustrated, genre-defying, phantasmagoria from Gray, purporting to be the memoirs of a nineteenth-century Scottish doctor, Archibald McCandless. His colleague, Godwin Baxter, has brought to life a full-grown woman with the mind of an infant, and the ensuing mayhem is both challenging and highly comic.

Ulysses

1922, JAMES JOYCE, IRISH

Ulysses has become so much a part of the curriculum – the stamping-ground of theory-minded professors – that it is easy to forget how exhilarating it is, one of the great comedies of modern urban life. Often strange or puzzling, it is rich in instantly recognizable common humanity, full of banter, tenderness, regret and love.

and first I put my arms around him yes and drew him down to me so he could feel my breasts all perfume yes and his heart was going like mad and yes I said yes I will Yes.

Celebrated as experimental, it is also intensely realistic. Few novels recreate public reality so minutely: its record of a particular city, Dublin, on a particular day, 16 June 1904, is astonishingly detailed. But its great originality is that it also captures, in many different ways, *felt* reality, in particular the private world of thought – musings, recollections and reveries.

Principally, the novel is about the crisscrossing lives of three characters going about their daily business in Dublin: the kindly Jewish advertising salesman Leopold Bloom, his wife Molly as she embarks on an affair with Blazes Boylan, and the brilliant but embittered

young teacher Stephen Dedalus. The layer of mythological meaning, at which the novel's title hints, is present but muted: though each
of the eighteen chapters corresponds in some way to an episode in
Homer's adventures of Odysseus (Ulysses), this is not the main point.
Joyce's formal experimentation is more conspicuous – the parody of
literary forms, the wordplay which sometimes (as in the "Circe" scene
in Dublin's night-town) boils over into fantasy, and, above all, Molly's
famous, unpunctuated "stream-of-consciousness" soliloquy that closes
the book. But these are also means to an end, a way of getting to the
heart of human experience. *Ulysses* is a vast and detailed celebration
of those experiences – of disgust and bigotry as much as kindness and
love – and a genuine comedy, witty, uproarious and satisfying.

Where to go next
A Portrait of the Artist as a Young Man, 1915, James Joyce
Joyce's semi-autobiographical novel tells of the often agonized development of
earnest intellectual Stephen Dedalus – from priest-ridden childhood to intellectual maturity.

The Leopard

1958, GIUSEPPE DI LAMPEDUSA, SICILIAN

A shimmering, tender book of reveries and musings, *The Leopard* is
a half-infatuated, half-appalled elegy for old aristocratic Sicily as
the Risorgimento of 1860, led by Garibaldi, attempts to create a
united Italy by sweeping away the past. The gorgeous formalities of
Sicilian tradition, the rituals of courtship, family life and devotion so
sensually noted by the nostalgic but detached Prince of Salina (the
"Leopard"), begin to change and fade. Like the antique but decayed
Salina dinner service or the worn mythological statuary in the
elaborate gardens of his country estate at Donnafugata, the Prince
is representative of an already-vanished species.

Given to abstract thought, the Prince deliberates on the meanings of these changes for Sicily. In particular, he ponders the futures of those close to him: his dashing young nephew Tancredi who joins Garibaldi, the meek reactionary Father Pirrone, upstart land-owner Don Calogero and his voluptuous daughter Angelica, and his own daughters, plainer and already doomed to disappointment.

> *One of them asked me what those Italian volunteers were really coming to do in Sicily. 'They are coming to teach us good manners,' I replied. 'But they won't succeed because we are gods.'*

Lampedusa's feathery-light style is both tender and humorous. Grand scenes of balls or banquets are full of tiny, touchingly coarse human detail – embarrassments, outbursts of spite, misplaced longing. It captures not only aristocratic solemnities but also the ingrained poverty of the Sicilian peasants. Most movingly of all, it conjures up moments of joy (in particular a quietly shattering scene of half-innocent hide and seek played by Tancredi and Angelica among the endless, disused rooms at the Donnafugata palace) made heartbreakingly transient by sudden allusions to a sadder future just a few years ahead.

 Recommended translation
1961, Archibald Colquhoun, Vintage Classics (UK) and Pantheon (US)

 Where to go next
The Garden of the Finzi-Continis, 1962, Giorgio Bassani
The action of *The Garden of the Finzi-Continis* is set within the Jewish community of Ferrara at the start of World War II. Narrated by a young man, in love with the well-to-do Micol Finzi-Contini, the novel subtly offsets his personal tragedy against the rising tide of anti-Semitism.

 Screen adaptation
The Leopard, 1963, dir. Luchino Visconti
Aesthete, aristocrat and Marxist, Visconti was the ideal director to transfer *The Leopard* to the screen, delivering a long, slow-moving meditation on historical change that is both visually gorgeous and politically astute. The inspired casting of Burt Lancaster as the Prince lends the proceedings a magisterial authority, while Nino Rota's score brings an operatic quality to the unfolding events.

The Cairo Trilogy
Palace Walk | Palace of Desire | Sugar Street
1956–57, NAGUIB MAHFOUZ, EGYPTIAN

All the traditional pleasures of fiction are here in Mahfouz's gorgeous soap opera of Cairo's ancient quarter: a strong plot of highs and lows, firmly modelled characters and a beautifully atmospheric setting. Though the trilogy is long, lightness is one of its cardinal virtues; a delight in the human world with all its trivial splendours is another. On the one hand a family saga of continuous dramas, on the other a deeply engaged study of Egypt between the twentieth-century wars, it offers a superior sort of entertainment, at once serious and moving.

Everyman's Library

Al-Sayyid Ahmad Abd al-Jawad is a shopkeeper of great dignity and patriotism, revered by all for his ultra-conservative tyranny at home. Unknown to his family, however, he is also celebrated as a boon companion in the local brothels and bars.

Over the next thirty years, such contradictions of sex, religion and politics will also torment his children as they grow into adults and have children of their own. In a multi-faceted story full of agonizing births, bitter funerals and a bewildering

'Perhaps patriotism, like love,' he thought, 'is a force to which we surrender, whether or not we believe in it.'

number of improbable marriages, the characters are flung, as by a sort of centrifugal force, towards their individual destinies.

Mahfouz was one of the great novelists of feelings – the small passions of shame or regret as much as the big ones of love and fury

– and here he depicted an astonishing variety of emotional experiences, all the more dramatic for being juxtaposed against a framework of strict Islamic codes of behaviour. Throwaway conversations at the family coffee hour are as marvellously vivid as full-on wedding festivities or the aerial bombardments of World War II. Key themes, such as imprisonment and freedom or obedience and recklessness, brilliantly unite the many personal narratives, and locate them firmly within the overarching tragic history of Egypt under British rule. Best of all, *The Cairo Trilogy* fulfils the requirement of the greatest family sagas: to explore the human mysteries of passing time, hopes and fears, triumphs and losses, learning and forgetting, and growing old.

Recommended translation
1990–92, William Maynard Hutchins, Olive E. Kenny, Lorne M. Kenny and Angele Botros Samaan, Everyman's Library

Where to go next
Midaq Alley, 1947, Naguib Mahfouz
This lighter tale of Cairo street and café life bubbles up with all the customary Mahfouzian vitality. Here the urban social scene is a little more to the fore than the family dynamics of the trilogy it preceded.

The Magic Mountain

1924, THOMAS MANN, GERMAN

As Mann himself commented, *The Magic Mountain* resembles a piece of music, a linked sequence of expertly orchestrated arguments, a grand symphony of ideas. No other novel matches its intellectual density and symbolic colouring. Glacially slow-moving and with the flimsiest of plots, it is a hugely expressive meditation on the European mentality, as the continent exploded into war in 1914.

The story is so slight that Mann flatly disbelieved anyone would devote time to a book which has "little or nothing in common with a novel in the usual sense of the word". A naïve and mediocre young

German, Hans Castorp, pays a visit to his tubercular cousin at a sanatorium in the Swiss Alps, and is soon diagnosed as being tubercular himself. In isolation from the world "down there", Castorp changes. He begins to reflect on the nature of things – on love and death, freedom and justice – and is caught up in the arguments of fellow sufferers about the course of European civilization. His visit lasts seven years, ending only – dramatically – with the outbreak of war.

The Magic Mountain is massive, but never stately; it is full of thousands of surprising, often disturbing, frequently odd, details – of the mannerisms, looks, habits of speech of the sanatorium's inmates and staff – which build obsessively to form highly charged motifs that give the intellectual debates their colour. If only rarely funny (though Mann himself considered it a comedy), it is constantly, sometimes bitterly, ironic.

> *Disease was life's lascivious form. And for its part, what was life? Was it perhaps only an infectious disease of matter?*

In truth, it cannot be described as entertaining in the conventional sense. But neither is it so daunting as often made out. Though it requires stamina and effort, the rewards are substantial. Castorp remains a deliberately muted figure, but other characters are rich and full of life. In Madame Chauchat, the Russian beauty with the moist spot on her lungs – whose X-ray Castorp clasps to his breast and who frustratingly becomes the lover of the mysterious and charismatic Mynheer Peeperkorn – the novel has its embodiment of love and death. And the eccentric revolutionary man of letters, Settembrini, and his arch rival, the viciously brilliant Jesuit Naphta, who meets such an extraordinary end, are profoundly distinctive individuals: their drawn-out and heated disputes carrying the novel to its violent conclusion on a tide of elegant, hostile phrases.

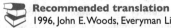

Recommended translation
1996, John E. Woods, Everyman Library Classics (UK) and Vintage (US)

Where to go next
Death in Venice, 1907, Thomas Mann
The most famous example of Mann's shorter fiction describes how a distinguished writer, in an attempt to renew his creativity, heads to Venice where he becomes enraptured by both the ideal and the tangible beauty of a young Polish boy.

The Heart is a Lonely Hunter

1940, CARSON MCCULLERS, AMERICAN

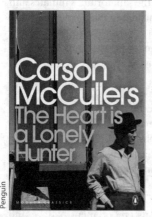

Penguin

There is something precocious about all McCullers' writing, and her first novel, *The Heart is a Lonely Hunter* – lyrically intense, full of unsettling gaps and emotional rushes, and strangely knowing – is among other things a marvellously intimate account of a girl's erratic passage into young adulthood. It is not a one-character novel, however. Equally compelling are the town's two mutes, the thoughtful John Singer and his beloved friend, the dreamy, obese Spiros Antonapoulos. Indeed, the book succeeds in evoking a whole town, its moods and rhythms, sudden bursts of violence and empty days of idleness.

The novel has the simple pragmatism of American fiction, a spare, clean, concrete style making everything instantly visible. But at the same time it is finely tuned to the characters' inner lives, catching the weirdness of their thoughts drifting through their minds. Straightforwardly dramatic incidents – an accident with a loaded rifle, a drunken fist-fight, sex – take their place alongside desultory conversations in late-night cafés and solitary vigils and musings, dramatic in less obvious ways. McCullers' stories are famous for their grotesques, and this novel has its share, with its mutes and alcoholics, religious freaks and fire-breathing radixals, but the author has the knack of making them less freakish, more deeply, or humanly, strange, as their stories develop and entwine. True to its childlike nature, the novel remains jumpy

The town was in the middle of the deep South. The summers were long and the months of winter cold were very few. Nearly always the sky was a glassy brilliant azure and the sun burned down riotously bright.

and unpredictable, and wilfully thwarts a happy ending.

📖 **Where to go next**
The Ballad of the Sad Café, 1951, Carson McCullers
Also set in a small town in the Deep South, this long story narrates the struggle of love and power between a café owner, a hunchback who claims kinship with her, and her estranged husband who unexpectedly returns.

🎬 **Screen adaptation**
The Heart is a Lonely Hunter, 1968, dir. Robert Ellis Miller
Despite the fact that Alan Arkin was nominated for an Oscar for his moving performance as the sympathetic deaf mute Singer, this film has undeservedly disappeared from view. While it simplifies the subtle web of relationships that McCullers so skilfully weaves, it succeeds in capturing the essential loneliness of the few characters it concentrates on, only occasionally sliding into sentimentality.

The Moon and the Bonfires

1950, CESARE PAVESE, ITALIAN

Pavese's last book, published four months before he killed himself, is a haunting, and haunted, novel about yearning. In the years following World War II, the unnamed narrator returns from America to the isolated Italian village of his childhood. Now middle-aged and affluent, yearning to repossess the past, he explores the once-familiar countryside with an old friend, remembering the years when, as an orphan brought up in terrible poverty by a hardscrabble farmer, he had yearned for a different future. In the end, his explorations will

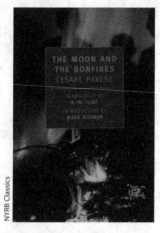

NYRB Classics

result in the shocking discovery of concealed wartime violence which makes it clear to him that the past is a foreign country to which, simply and brutally, he can never return.

The novel is haunted by the village, just as the village is haunted by the past. Both remain tantalizingly obscure. Lyrical descriptions of the countryside – dusty scrub on a hillside, a bare vineyard, a vista of scattered farms – are incomplete glances. The villagers talk and fall silent, the gaps between their words as enigmatically loaded as the symbols of the moon and the bonfires which reappear throughout the novel. The narrator's memories of the people he knew and loved swim in and out of focus.

On evenings like that, a light, a bonfire seen on a distant hill, would make me cry out and roll on the ground because I was poor, because I was a boy, because I was nothing.

The whole story, in fact, seems a series of uneasy balances threatening to tilt violently one way or the other. Until, in the end, they do – and, to his horror, the narrator discovers what really happened in the village during the war.

Recommended translation
2002, R.W. Flint, NYRB Classics

Where to go next
Two Women, 1958, Alberto Moravia
Set in World War II, *Two Women* is the disturbing story of a Rome shopkeeper and her teenage daughter who flee the city prior to the German occupation. When Allied victory comes, their return home is fraught with even greater privations and danger.

Life A User's Manual

1978, GEORGES PEREC, FRENCH

Perec was one of the great experimenters, famous for writing an entire novel (*A Void*) without using a single letter e, a fact which some of its first reviewers missed. (No self-indulgent trick, it found a thought-provoking way of addressing another unprotested disappearance: six million Jews during the Holocaust.) *Life A User's Manual*, a greater novel, similarly combines dizzying technical achievement with a narrative rich with life. Perec set out to amaze, but also to charm and move. The novel's postmodern structure, derived from a mathematical "machine" built by Perec to establish the position, order and coverage of each of the 99 chapters, is matched by a wholly traditional emphasis on storytelling. Constructed like a giant puzzle, his novel celebrates and elegizes the comic, bizarre, heart-warming or heart-breaking puzzles in people's ordinary lives.

> *The stairs, for him, were, on each floor, a memory, an emotion, something ancient and impalpable, something palpitating somewhere in the guttering flame of his memory.*

Perec's focus is both microscopic and long range. Each chapter of the novel describes with obsessive detail one of the 99 rooms in a Parisian apartment block. But the teeming life stories of the residents, spreading far beyond France, contain multitudes – a murder in the Italian lakes, a disaster in the cowrie-shell trade in Aden, revenge killings on the Mississippi, and many others. The central story involves an eccentric English multimillionaire, Bartlebooth, who has dedicated his life to a project which is discreet, logical and entirely useless – the creation, completion and dissolution of 500 jigsaw puzzles. It is a project, singular and analytical but vibrant with the hits and misses and heartaches of life, that matches *Life* itself.

 Recommended translation
David Bellos, 1987, Vintage Classics (UK) and David Godine (US)

📖 **Where to go next**
W or the Memory of Childhood, 1975, Georges Perec
Two apparently disconnected tales alternate in Perec's book: the story of an island state run according to Olympian ideals, and Perec's autobiographical account of his wartime childhood. Eventually, and chillingly, they begin to fit together.

The Maias

1888, EÇA DE QUEIRÓS, PORTUGUESE

The idle, opulent world of Lisbon high society in the late nineteenth century provides Eça de Queirós's greatest novel with its setting. Its true subject, however, is love in a variety of melancholy forms: frivolous affairs, awkward liaisons, demeaning compromises, unattainable ideals and black despair.

At the heart of the story is a tremendous secret. Carlos Eduardo, last of the aristocratic Maia dynasty, finds it hard to fulfil the expectations of his puritanical grandfather, Afonso. Wasting his time

She went pale and slipped heavily into his arms in a swoon; and her long hair, which had come unfastened, shone in the light with flashes of gold as it trailed on the ground.

with friends such as the literary dilettante João da Ega or the gourmandizing Marquis of Souzellas (and a dozen other characters, all superbly individualized), he contents himself with amusing illusions. But his life changes irrevocably when he meets Senhora Dona Maria Eduarda Gomes, recently arrived from Brazil with her millionaire husband. As she and Carlos begin an intrigue, her radiant freshness promises him love in its purest form. But the intrigue is many-layered. How can they conceal their affair? What will Carlos tell his grandfather? And – most desperate of all – who is Senhora Gomes really?

De Queirós's prose, stately and concentrated, but capable of sudden rapidity and emotion, is magnificently evocative. A great indoors novel, *The Maias* is richly furnished throughout – full of heavy drapes, antique porcelain and hissing gas jets – and bathed in the warm glow of money. When the action strays outdoors, it is to saunter to the Jockey Club or ride to a country estate. For three hundred pages, the pace of the plot is frankly sedentary as de Queirós elaborates the scene (carefully creating a pattern of resonant events and themes), before perking up with the appearance of Maria Eduarda, and positively plunging through levels of sudden discoveries towards the catastrophic denouement.

Recommended translation
1965, Patricia MacGowan Pinheiro and Ann Stevens, Carcanet Press

Where to go next
The Relic, 1887, Eça de Queirós
A dissolute young man plays lip service to religion in order to placate his devout aunt, whose fortune he may just inherit. A trip to the Holy Land to obtain a special relic for her takes a very unexpected turn, while the novel's comic ending reveals Eça at his sardonic best.

Wide Sargasso Sea

1966, JEAN RHYS, DOMINICAN

In Charlotte Brontë's *Jane Eyre* (see p.5) Mr Rochester's first wife famously makes a brief and terrible appearance. But who was she and what was her history? *Wide Sargasso Sea* supplies some possible – and intensely imaginative – answers.

Jamaica, 1830s. On the exotically lush estate of Coulibri, among the pink

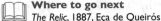
Our garden was large and beautiful as that garden in the Bible – the tree of life grew there. But it had gone wild. The paths were overgrown and a smell of dead flowers mixed with the fresh living smell.

and red hibiscus, the octopus orchids and the frangipani trees, Antoinette Cosway grows up fragile and strange. Her mother is a Martinique beauty, her stepfather a wealthy Englishman – both bit-

Penguin

terly resented by the locals. One night, these local feelings explode into violence, and Antoinette and her family are driven away. With her mother in a permanent state of shock, and her stepfather largely absent, Antoinette spends the rest of her youth in a convent school. When she leaves, she meets a young man called Rochester, in the Caribbean to find an heiress.

The first part of the novel is narrated by Antoinette, the second by Rochester, but the style is always skewed, elliptical and fraught. Like Kipling and Gogol, Rhys has the knack of mainlining directly into the emotional lives of her characters. Details of the narrative refuse to resolve themselves into comfortably encompassing meanings, they remain prickly and separate and true, clashingly colourful, like the landscape. Heavy symbolism – a place called Massacre, a character called Disastrous Thomas – adds to the rich swirl. Like the patois spoken by the Creole servant Christophine, the novel is a vibrant and brutal assertion of other realities hidden in the Victorian picture of the world. Read it immediately after *Jane Eyre* for an electrifying culture shock.

Where to go next
Quartet, 1929, Jean Rhys
In part based on her own doomed love affair with the writer Ford Madox Ford, Jean Rhys's first novel is a bittersweet tale of female emotional vulnerability set against the backdrop of expat bohemians in interwar Paris.

The Devil's Pool

1846, George Sand, French

Apparently a limpid tale of rural romance, *The Devil's Pool* was for many years considered a children's book, especially suitable for girls. But, like the mysterious pool at the centre of the story, it contains ambiguous depths. Unapologetically brief and simply told, it manages to catch unsettling emotional undercurrents below the surface of the narrative, which continue to reverberate after the straightforwardly happy ending.

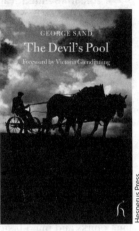

Hesperus Press

Persuaded by his father-in-law to seek a new wife, Germain the ploughman (a sensible but shy man) reluctantly makes a journey to court a wealthy widow, taking with him his infant son, Petit-Pierre, and giving a lift to a neighbouring teenage girl, "little Marie", who is going away to work. On the way they get lost and are forced to spend the night outdoors, by a lake reputed to be haunted. And it is there that Germain becomes bewitched by Marie.

It was only when they had finally found a nice straight path and reached the end of it, and Germain could look around to see where they were, that he realised he was lost.

The novel is, among other things, an empathetic account of peasant life in Sand's home province of Berry. But her fascination with country lore (displayed in a detailed coda describing peasant wedding customs) also serves to heighten the mesmerizing atmosphere of the story. For all its realism, bewitchment is its natural mode, and the central motifs – the misty lake, the woods at night, the bolting horse and the vulnerable young woman

– belong to pagan fairy tale, hinting at sex, violence and the conflicting forces of good and evil.

Recommended translation
2005, Andrew Brown, Hesperus Books

Where to go next
Indiana, 1831, George Sand
Sand's first novel is a powerful, if melodramatic, romance about a young Creole woman, Indiana, who marries a much older man, then finds herself drawn to his dashing but shallow neighbour.

The Year of the Death of Ricardo Reis

1984, José Saramago, Portuguese

Saramago's flowing style gives his novels a soothingly traditional feel. On closer inspection, though, they are full of subversive wit, startling quirks and mind-boggling paradoxes. *Ricardo Reis* describes the brief continuing existence of a writer's *nom de plume* after his death. Fernando Pessoa, the great modern Portuguese poet, wrote under a number of pseudonyms, and, in Saramago's novel, on the day after Pessoa's death in 1936, one of them – Ricardo Reis – arrives in Lisbon from Brazil, where Pessoa had imagined him living. Over the next nine months, Reis will wander the streets, sit in the parks, embark on two love affairs, and, several times, meet Pessoa (still wearing the black double-breasted suit in which he was buried) to talk about life and death.

> *Ricardo Reis asked, Tell me, how did you know that I was staying at this hotel. When you are dead, replied Fernando Pessoa, you know everything, that's one of the advantages.*

The quietly stated descriptions of Lisbon tingle with atmosphere. The historical moment – as Europe falls to fascism, and, just over the border, the Spanish Civil War erupts – is vividly evoked in the gossip and news (and fears) of the Lisboners. But Reis himself remains musingly detached, even in his tender, awkward affairs with the chambermaid Lydia and the middle-class Marcendo he cannot fully connect. *The Year of the Death of Ricardo Reis* is one of the most beautifully challenging novels about our tenuous sense of self, the uncertainties of love and the necessity of letting go.

Recommended translation
1992, Giovanni Ponteiro, Vintage (UK) and Harvest Books (US)

Where to go next
The Gospel According to Jesus Christ, 1991, José Saramago
Saramago's daring version of the New Testament story features an all-too-human Jesus distressed to find a very Old Testament God forcing an unwelcome destiny on him.

Barchester Towers

1857, ANTHONY TROLLOPE, ENGLISH

The decline of Trollope's reputation (until recently) seems not just misguided but positively masochistic, for he is without doubt one of the great entertainers in the English language. Less vivid than Dickens, less serious than Eliot, less sensational than Collins, he is absolutely his own master, patient, rich and generous, and one of the few novelists who can be enjoyably read to excess.

Barchester Towers, his most popular novel, is the second instalment of the six-novel "Chronicles of Barsetshire" – over 3,500 pages all told – devoted to the domestic and public lives of the Barsetshire citizens.

> There is, perhaps, no greater hardship at present inflicted on mankind in civilised and free countries, than the necessity of listening to sermons.

The key issues of *Barchester Towers* go to the heart of provincial Victorian life. Who will triumph in the struggle to dominate the new Bishop of Barchester: his terrifying wife, Mrs Proudie, or his oily

The Chronicles of Bartsetshire and The Pallisers

Anthony Trollope (1815–82) wrote just over forty novels in just under forty years, a rate of production sustained – as he revealed in his autobiography – by working a systematic three hours per day starting at 5am. Though the revelation did little for his posthumous reputation, today he is seen as one of the greatest chroniclers of mid-Victorian society, most effectively in his two great sequences of novels, "The Chronicles of Barsetshire" and "The Pallisers". The former focuses on the intertwining daily lives of the citizens of Barsetshire, in particular those employed by or connected to the great cathedral town of Barchester. The latter concentrates on the corridors of power, showing (through one political dynasty) how reputations are won and lost in the world of British politics. Each of the six novels in both sequences can be read on its own, and in "The Chronicles of Barsetshire" there is a surprising variety of tone – from the sharp comedy of *Barchester Towers* to the epic tragedy of *The Last Chronicle of Barset*.

The Chronicles of Barsetshire
- *The Warden* (1855)
- *Barchester Towers* (1857)
- *Doctor Thorne* (1858)
- *Framley Parsonage* (1861)
- *The Small House at Allington* (1864)
- *The Last Chronicle of Barset* (1867)

The Palliser novels
- *Can You Forgive Her?* (1864)
- *Phineas Finn* (1869)
- *The Eustace Diamonds* (1873)
- *Phineas Redux* (1874)
- *The Prime Minister* (1876)
- *The Duke's Children* (1879)

private chaplain, Mr Slope? Which of three rival suitors will marry the saintly Mr Harding's widowed daughter Eleanor? Will brazen

Mrs Lookaloft gain admittance to the tables reserved for the better class of guest at Miss Thorne's *fête champêtre*?

OXFORD WORLD'S CLASSICS

ANTHONY TROLLOPE
BARCHESTER TOWERS

Oxford World's Classics

Trollope's bluff frankness is disarming, his gently trundling prose lulling, but he is slyly alert to both the ironic comedy and moral dimensions of his narrative, and though he repeatedly declares his refusal to tease his readers, his story is an artful sequence of gripping dilemmas and resolutions. His characters, it is true, may be drawn from stock types, such as deans, Oxford dons and rural vicars, but they are beautifully drawn and never predictable – and his completely convincing creation of the sensual cripple Signora Neroni, around whose magnetic charm much of the plot revolves, demonstrates his surprising mastery of the exotic as well as the domestic. Relaxed, but never superfluous, Trollope is the great chronicler of mid-Victorian English life.

Where to go next
The Way We Live Now, 1875, Anthony Trollope
The exception in Trollope's output, a scathing satire on the greed and materialism of mid-Victorian England, centred on the dubious activities of the ruthlessly ambitious and corrupt financier Augustus Melmotte.

A Sportsman's Notebook
1852, IVAN TURGENEV, RUSSIAN

On the point of giving up literature, Turgenev abandoned his apprentice poems and wrote from the heart about what he knew best: the experiences of the huntsman roaming the countryside with a dog and a friend, following the game, watching the sky for changes in the weather, chatting with strangers. The result – an impressionistic series of moods, scenes and encounters – is one of the most movingly human of all books about ordinary rural life in nineteenth-century Russia.

Lyrical descriptions of the natural world are grounded in reality: Turgenev knew it intimately: the order in which birds stop singing at night, the scent of wormwood in a poplar wood, the sounds a birch copse makes in the breeze. He also knew the characters living in the villages, landlords and peasants alike: the furtive survivor Styopushka, subsisting on cabbage stalks; the Miller's ailing wife, disappointed in love; the vagabond hunter Ermolai; village boys telling folk stories of goblins round a camp-fire. To Turgenev the huntsman they spilled out their life stories, tales of love, despair, suffering, innocence. His master-stroke was to put it all down free of plot, moral and overarching structure, to create a work of fiction which conveys a spaciousness impossible in plot-driven novels: a sense of time passing, and, in the characters' chatter, all the unexpectedness and poignancy of ordinary life.

> *Take a summer morning – a morning in July. Who but a sportsman knows the joy of wandering through the brakes at sunrise?*

Recommended translation
1950, Charles and Natasha Hepburn, Everyman Library Classics

Where to go next
Rudin, 1856, Ivan Turgenev
Turgenev's first novel features one of his most distinctive "superfluous men", Rudin, a seductive character full of eloquent talk about revolution, who will be put to the test in France in 1848.

Incredible
worlds

9

N ovelists have always been attracted to the unknown, drawn to the challenge of imagining the unimaginable. What will the future be like? How did our remote ancestors live in a time before history? Does anyone else inhabit the universes of outer space? What worlds lie within ourselves, in our dreams, our fantasies?

Many writers have relished the challenge of creating strange new worlds of beauty and moral dilemma. Stimulated by science and technology, both real and imagined, science-fiction authors have produced convincing new societies here on earth (as in in Ray Bradbury's *Fahrenheit 451* or Aldous Huxley's *Brave New World*), as well as exhilaratingly different worlds in the far reaches of the universe, such as the planet Gethen in Ursula Le Guin's extraordinary *The Left Hand of Darkness*.

The idea of other worlds allows novelists not only to imagine but to argue and debate. Fantasy holds a distorting but revealing mirror up to our present lives. From *Gulliver's Travels* on, novelists have created places where they can question and sometimes savage prevailing beliefs. Orwell's *Nineteen Eighty-Four*, for example, was inspired by the horrific political regimes of the first half of the twentieth century, while in Atwood's *The Handmaid's Tale* sexual and moral orthodoxies are pushed to logical and disturbing conclusions. Perhaps strangest of all are those rare imaginary places in which private wishes, fears and anxieties are transmuted into the fantastical, as in Lewis Carroll's *Alice in Wonderland* and *Through the Looking Glass*. With all these incredible worlds, novelists have startled and stimulated our own imaginations.

The Handmaid's Tale

1985, MARGARET ATWOOD, CANADIAN

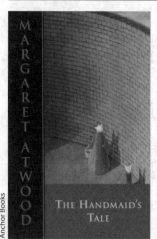

Anchor Books

Atwood's sensual intelligence is matched by her steely narrative gifts. *The Handmaid's Tale*, in which her talents as both poet and novelist come together, is a weirdly beautiful description of an enslaved woman's life in a puritan dystopia ruled by men, a novel full of extraordinary scenes and inflammatory discussion points.

Handmaids, Guardians, Angels, Ecowives, Marthas and Commanders are designated roles in the Republic of Gilead, a Bible-oriented North American State established in reaction to late twentieth-century sexual permissiveness. Offred ("of Fred") is a handmaid, a woman capable of bearing children in a period of drastically plummeting birth rates: once a month, she services her Commander in the hope of conceiving a child which can be claimed by the Commander's wife. Offred's own husband and daughter are forbidden subjects of the past. But even in an age of absolute submissiveness, underground protest exists, however riskily.

Offred's account of her repressed life, surviving on cassettes discovered in a safe house two centuries later (jauntily discussed by an English historian in a brief afterword), is – very appropriately – a deadpan narrative full of seething images. Lyrical outbursts and grim punchlines punctuate the tale of her deprivation, mental as much as physical. The tension of the story – what has happened to Offred's family, what will happen to her if she rebels? – is terrific. Critics may say that the anger of its feminism dates it, but ultimately it remains an electrifyingly emotional novel about the necessity of the emotions.

> *'I am thirty three years old. I have brown hair. I stand five seven without shoes. I have trouble remembering what I used to look like. I have viable ovaries. I have one more chance.'*

Where to go next
Oryx and Crake, 2003, Margaret Atwood
Atwood's second venture into what she calls "speculative fiction" imagines a not-too-distant world where humans are virtually extinct, replaced by various transgenetic creatures including the humanoid Crakers.

Fahrenheit 451

1953, RAY BRADBURY, AMERICAN

Less intellectual than *We*, less literary than *Brave New World*, less political than *Nineteen Eighty-Four*, *Fahrenheit 451* is nevertheless the most gripping and urgent of the twentieth-century dystopias. Written with a pulp-fiction brio, at once hard-boiled and poetic, it is

Flamingo

a flat-out compulsive tale of one man's rebellion in a technocratic future.

Guy Montag is a fireman, and his job is to set things on fire, specifically books, which are banned. (451 degrees Fahrenheit is the temperature at which paper catches fire.) It is a job Montag enjoys until one night he meets a strange seventeen-year-old girl who sees the world in a very different way, provoking in him feelings of uncertainty which will rapidly lead to a deadly confrontation with the authorities.

The future here is uneasily familiar. Blank-faced people walk the streets wearing "thimble radios" in their ears or sit at home watching non-stop personalized entertainment and instant sound-bite news on their wall-surround TVs, numb to the bombers flying overhead on their way to a remote war. The few who dare to be different are instantly detected by state surveillance in the form of the Fire Department's "Mechanical Hound", a computerized tracker armed with a lethal hypodermic.

It was a pleasure to burn. It was a special pleasure to see things eaten, to see things blackened and changed.

The State's real quarry, however, is ideas – in the form of books – and *Fahrenheit 451* is an angry vision of a world in which they are fragile. It is a theme also developed by other writers, but none matches Bradbury's jumpy, spare style or freewheeling cinematic action.

Where to go next
The Martian Chronicles, 1950, Ray Bradbury
A gripping collection of twenty-seven, loosely connected stories describing

repeated attempts by humans to colonize Mars in the face of impending catastrophe on Earth.

Screen adaptation
Fahrenheit 451, 1966, dir. François Truffaut

Truffaut's low-key adaptation, set in a future markedly like the present, is pretty faithful to the original (although there's no "Mechanical Hound"). Oskar Werner is convincing as the fireman who sees the error of his work, Julie Christie less so as both his wife and his girlfriend Clarisse. Sadly, the film seems even more prescient now than when it was made.

The Master and Margarita

1938, MIKHAIL BULGAKOV, RUSSIAN

By the late 1930s, Bulgakov was a broken man, ill and depressed, his work prohibited by the State Censor, his request to emigrate refused via a personal phone call from Stalin. His response was to write a joyful romp of black magic which triumphantly transformed his world. *The Master and Margarita* brings together two distinct but interrelated stories: a dapper fantasy of Satan at play in Soviet Moscow and a strikingly original remake of the last hours of Christ's life.

Just then the sultry air coagulated and wove itself into the shape of a man. On his small head was a jockey cap and he wore a short check bum-freezer made of air.

One warm spring day, in a leafy square in Moscow, a foreign professor courteously introduces himself to two prominent members of the official literary society MASSOLIT. Within moments one of them has been decapitated. Over the next two days, as a result of the antics of the professor and his associates (an emaciated giant clown, a red-headed fanged dwarf, a naked woman with a livid scar and a vodka-tippling black cat), Moscow's literary and theatrical circles will be devastated. Only "the Master", author of a novel about Christ, and his lover Margarita, escape – strangely stimulated by their contact with evil.

Bulgakov's cinematic style, rapidly cutting from scene to scene, gives his plot terrific momentum; his sense of fun and knack for gags makes it deliciously funny. But it is satisfyingly serious too. The dizzying "magic-realist" caper, in which people disappear or end up in asylums, is a heartbreakingly appropriate response to Stalinist brutalities. And, in the moving, quieter scenes involving Christ and Pilate, the novel exposes and confronts hidden universal truths of cowardice and shame.

Recommended translation
1967, Michael Glenny, Vintage Classics

Where to go next
The Heart of a Dog, 1925, Mikhail Bulgakov
A farcical fantasy with strong satirical overtones, in which a Soviet scientist implants human testicles into a stray dog, whose increasingly human behaviour proves problematic.

Erewhon

1872, SAMUEL BUTLER, ENGLISH

Barely a novel, with no plot to speak of, little interest in character and the most rudimentary prose style, *Erewhon* is nevertheless the best Victorian dystopia by the greatest English misfit of the age, a wonderfully deft exercise in controlled rage.

Seeking his fortune in the British colonies (as Butler himself did), Butler's hero strikes out for remoter regions, where he hopes

I could not help speculating upon what might lie farther up the river and behind the second range.

to find virgin land fit for commercial exploitation. Instead, he stumbles across the Erewhonians, an unknown people whose culture seems, in almost every respect, the opposite of his own. Erewhonians abhor illness and ill-fortune, and punish sufferers with imprisonment. Criminals, on the other hand, are sympathetically regarded. Professors at the Colleges of Unreason teach hypothetics, the ideally useless art of the highly unlikely. And, although they are sceptical of an afterlife, they firmly believe in pre-existence, considering birth a crime for which newborn babies are wholly responsible and liable to punishment by their parents.

Readers wanting the excitement of narrative should look elsewhere. The model of Butler's satire is not the novel, but the travelogue and anthropological study: an account of his hero's initial journey to Erewhon

is followed by a series of essay-like chapters on the culture and customs of its people. Here, Butler's skills find their truest expression. Patient, straight-faced, detailed critiques of the Erewhonians' way of life are as inventive and unsettling as Borges's later fables of impossible peoples. In them, Butler holds up a distorting mirror to the Victorian world, in which his contemporaries must see themselves as they really are: hypocritical, sanctimonious and criminally self-assured.

Where to go next
The Way of All Flesh, 1903, Samuel Butler
A young man is forced to become a clergyman by his tyrannical father. This semi-autobiographical work (published posthumously two decades after it was written) is one of the most celebrated fictional savagings of Victorian pieties and hypocrisies.

Invisible Cities

1972, ITALO CALVINO, ITALIAN

Of all Calvino's graceful and suggestive fictions, *Invisible Cities* is perhaps his most absorbing and entertaining: an intellectually playful meditation on the secret meanings of cities.

His scheme is simple: the well-travelled Marco Polo attempts to satisfy the Kublai Khan's curiosity about his far-flung empire by describing to him fifty-five of its cities. Each description is brief, often less than a page, but enigmatic, not only making visible what the Khan has never seen, but giving expression to the special (invisible) qualities that give the cities their particularity. In Octavia, the "spider-web city" strung out on cables above a chasm, its inhabitants paradoxically enjoy a life of certainty, knowing that the cables are bound to break one day. Sophronia, like most cities, can be divided into a temporary and a permanent part – but here it is the fairground that remains all year round, while the town hall, bank and factories are regularly packed up and moved out on lorries.

> *Cities, like dreams, are made of desires and fears, even if the thread of their discourse is secret, their rules are absurd, their perspectives deceitful, and everything conceals something else.*

Polo speaks in metaphors and riddles, but his descriptions are simple and precise, conjuring up places and moods with equal brilliance. Each city commentary is carefully positioned in an overarching framework of dizzying complexity: eleven thematic categories ("Cities and Memory", "Cities and Desire", etc) recurring in nine chapters, each framed by conversations between Polo and the Khan on the nature of storytelling and knowledge. Such a generous and ingenious arrangement – quintessentially "postmodern" – is susceptible to multiple uses. Read it from start to finish, or by theme, or treat it like a book of poems, dipping in at random, and discovering your own connections.

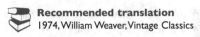

Recommended translation
1974, William Weaver, Vintage Classics

Where to go next
Our Ancestors, 1951–59, Italo Calvino
An eighteenth-century aristocrat who lives in the treetops, a knight with
no body inside his armour, a viscount cloven in two by a Saracen's sword
– the heroes of Calvino's playful trilogy marked the return of the fabulous to
European fiction after the war.

Alice's Adventures in Wonderland *and* Through the Looking-Glass

1865 AND 1872, LEWIS CARROLL, ENGLISH

Known more often through spin-offs and merchandise, Carroll's
twinned masterpieces are not to be missed. Together, they form a
surreal adventure of the mind in which the exhilarating daftness of
the fantasy is supported by brilliantly concrete detail and enriched
by the eerie suspicion that it all has a deeper meaning.

The origin of the stories is well known: Charles Lutwidge
Dodgson, a thirty-year-old mathematical lecturer at Christ Church
College, Oxford, took the three daughters
of Dean Liddell (including Alice Liddell) on
a picnic up the Thames to Godstow, where,
to keep the children entertained, he extem-
porized a bizarre tale of what happened to
Alice when she fell down a rabbit hole.

*'I don't want to go
among mad people,'
Alice remarked.
'Oh, you can't help
that,' said the Cat:
'we're all mad here.'*

The fizzy mix of nonsense and high seri-
ousness is infectious: profound questions are tossed into the air and
juggled with. "Who am I?", asks Alice, after she has shrunk and
grown several times. "I'm sure I can't be Mabel." She is not the only
character to undergo radical change: a cat disappears leaving only
its grin, and a baby turns into a pig ("it would have made a dread-

LEWIS CARROLL
*Alice's Adventures in Wonderland
and Through the Looking-Glass*

fully ugly child, but it makes rather a handsome pig, I think"). Absurdity has its own logic, and Carroll is always showing us the magical in the ordinary, and vice versa: what talking animals chiefly do is bicker. Life is a game (like chess, cards, croquet or any of the other games that appear thoughout the books), and it has rules – though the rules are bizarre.

The first book is sharp, bristly and funny, the second is slower and more contemplative, but both contain great characters and adventures. The Mad Hatter's Tea Party, the Queen of Heart's game of croquet and the Lobster Quadrille of the first part, and, in the second, the slaying of the Jabberwocky and the encounter with Tweedledum and Tweedledee – all now part of our culture – are newly dazzling to read in Carroll's great original.

Where to go next
Phantastes, 1872, George MacDonald
MacDonald's fantasies are more obviously moral and less surreal than those of his friend Carroll. *Phantastes* is one of the best, the tale of Anodos a young man who undergoes a journey of self-discovery after stumbling into Fairy Land.

Screen adaptation
Alice in Wonderland, 1966, dir. Jonathan Miller
This TV version is a dark and very adult reading of the book. Miller eschews animal cuteness, locating the fantasy in a claustrophobic Victorian world. Alice is an awkward, adolescent outsider confronting the various eccentric and officious characters who cross her path (played by a roll-call of English character actors). Ravi Shankar's beguiling music adds to the dreamlike mood.

The Inheritors

1955, WILLIAM GOLDING, ENGLISH

Golding's first novel, *The Lord of the Flies*, is a haunting original, but his second (his own personal favourite) is an even more astonishing leap of the imagination: the bleak, poetic dramatization of a tragic encounter between the last Neanderthals and the first humans – the inheritors.

The action is swift and simple. A group of Neanderthals returns to its summer quarters, a cave in a cliff above a river, expecting to continue the old routines of family life: gathering eggs and shoots from the plain, defending the cave from marauding hyenas, bringing up children. But this year will be different. Mal, the elder, is dying on the packed earth by the fire. Down by the river Ha, his heir, disappears. And lingering in the bushes is the unfamiliar scent of another sort of creature that follows and watches them and has the power to cross the water.

Golding's Neanderthals are powerfully plausible: he gets

> Her hair bristled and her teeth showed. 'There is a smell on the cliff. Two. Ha and another. Not Lok. Not Fa. Not Liku. Not Mal. Not her. Not Nil. There is another smell of a nobody.'

inside their heads, seeing the world through their eyes, describing their fresh and oblique visions of elemental things, capturing their tentative communication of crude utterances and gestures, their superstitious beliefs (in the wakefulness of fire or the evil of slaughter) and the vivid spasms of their imagination as they try to cope with disaster. Above all, he gives them their own personalities: Fa the sensible female, Liku the trusting child, Lok the clown. As a result, their confusion is all the more terrifying, and the end of the Neanderthals seems not so much an archaeological fact as an intimate and involving tragedy, a family being wiped out.

📖 **Where to go next**
Lord of the Flies, 1954, William Golding
Golding's first and most celebrated novel is about a group of young boys, ship-wrecked on an island, who rapidly regress into savagery.

Brave New World

1932, ALDOUS HUXLEY, ENGLISH

Harper Perennial

In the monstrous yet reasonable future of Huxley's famous dystopia, everything is carefully arranged to promote contentment. Genetic engineering produces useful humans of every class from the intelligent Alphas, who occupy the elite management positions, to the moronic Gammas used for manual labour. Hypnopaedia (subliminal messaging) conditions them all to accept their functions without question; any possible stress is instantly relieved by a visit to the feelies or a dose of the wonder drug *soma*. Sexual promiscuity is the rigidly observed orthodoxy. Emotional attachments – disgusting abnormalities – are outlawed.

But in the year A.F. 632 (the number of years since the introduction of the Model T Ford), a notoriously antisocial Alpha-Plus, Bernard Marx, begins to entertain perverse thoughts of dissatisfaction.

Read one way, *Brave New World* is a wonderfully witty comedy of sexual manners: part of the fun is seeing how Huxley brilliantly transposed the vapid mannerisms of the Jazz Age to a science-fiction setting. From another angle, the book delivers a powerful statement

Good place, bad place

The modern tradition of Utopia (literally "no-place", but by implication "perfect-place") began with Sir Thomas More's *Utopia* (1516). Unlike descriptions of paradises of ancient religious writings, his short prose work put the emphasis on the social and political perfectability of life. Translated from the original Latin, it rapidly became a European best-seller. But dystopias ("bad-places") have been even more eagerly seized on by the reading public. Satirical, foreboding and sometimes lurid, dystopian fictions have issued warnings about the future, exposed the fallibility of the best-laid plans and focused on the irredeemable imperfections of human nature. Swift's *Gulliver's Travels* (1726), Samuel Butler's *Erewhon* (1872) and H.G. Wells's *The Time Machine* (1895) are outstanding examples of the form. But it was during the twentieth century, an age of mechanized war, political tyranny and headlong technological advance that dystopias tapped into widespread feelings of anxiety. Zamyatin's *We* (1920–21) and Huxley's *Brave New World* (1932) both describe troubling hi-tech experiments with society in the distant future, while Orwell's *Nineteen Eighty-Four* (1949) presents an all-powerful police state much closer at hand. More recently, fiction has imagined what life might be like after a nuclear war. Works as different as Russell Hoban's *Riddley Walker* (1980) and the comic strip *Judge Dredd* have fed an appetite for post-nuclear possibilities.

about the impact of technology. Either way, Huxley threw a highly original light on the novelist's traditional themes of human relations and needs, and at the heart of his book are debates (always intellectual, often quite formal) about emotions, spirituality, sexuality and psychology.

'That's the price we have to pay for stability. You've got to choose between happiness and what people call high art. We've sacrificed the high art. We have the feelies and the scent organ instead.'

Huxley insisted that in certain conditions contentment is the biggest problem we face. The price of comfort is the abolishment of the freedom to be unhappy. Who would be so stupid as to want to be unhappy? Why then does a world theoretically without unhappiness prove so traumatically inhuman?

📖 **Where to go next**
Riddley Walker, 1980, Russell Hoban
Funny and monstrous, and written in a rich, rude slang, Hoban's masterpiece is a post-nuclear novel about a people blown back into a new Middle Ages.

The Left Hand of Darkness

1969, URSULA K. LE GUIN, AMERICAN

Incredible worlds are rarely so beautifully imagined or so movingly strange as the planet Gethen. Its winter-locked topographies are exactly visualized, its dour cities and generous customs richly detailed. But Gethen's most astonishing feature is its people. Unlike humans of other known planets, Gethenians have the capacity to change gender.

If *The Left Hand of Darkness* is a novel of ideas, it is also a fast-moving, atmospheric political thriller. Genly Ai, the human envoy despatched to Gethen on a mission of alliance, finds himself caught up in intrigue and espionage at the court of King Argaven of Karhide. With the help of the disgraced Lord Estraven, he flees to the neighbouring domain of Orgoreyn, only to discover himself the pawn of opposing factions, and forced to flee a second time – across 800 miles of icy wilderness.

> *They are not neuters. They are potentials, or integrals. The Karhider I am with is not a man, but a manwoman.*

Le Guin's exciting intelligence – never flashy – animates the whole novel: ramifications of ambisexuality (Gethenians are sexually active once a month, as either males or females, and can be both mothers and fathers) are brilliantly projected through the whole psychology and culture of the planet, paradoxical and touching. More moving still is the developing drama of the relationship between Ai and Estraven, which catches the themes of duality and unity, treachery and loyalty, but never overstates them in the major setpiece of the novel: a desperate journey across a wasteland of glaciers and volcanoes, which ends with both the triumph and the vulnerability of their friendship.

📖 **Where to go next**
The Dispossessed, 1974, Ursula Le Guin
Another novel in the "Hainish Cycle" and set in the same fictional universe as *The Left Hand of Darknesss*, Le Guin's story explores an anarchist society in which possession is prohibited.

Nineteen Eighty-Four

1949, GEORGE ORWELL, ENGLISH

Nineteen Eighty-Four is the great über-myth of a dystopian future, the totalitarian nightmare Orwell dreamed on our behalf. Its terrors – Big Brother, Room 101, the Thought Police and Doublethink – have become common cultural jargon, but the novel remains a uniquely powerful experience, an uncanny imagining of the ultimate police state.

In fact, of all the twentieth-century dystopias, *Nineteen Eighty-Four* is the most solidly imagined, partly because Orwell, an astute political commentator, had the example of Stalin's USSR in mind. His functional plot and invisibly plain prose merely prevent distraction from the world he created, a world at once drab and horrific. "Victory Mansions", where dissatisfied citizen Winston Smith sleeps with the smell of "boiled cabbage and old rag mats" in his nose, is of a piece with the torture chambers of the "Ministry of Love". Here, after his briefly liberating sexual idyll with fellow rebel Julia, agony will teach Smith to love Big Brother.

> 'Does Big Brother exist?'
> 'Of course he exists. The Party exists. Big Brother is the embodiment of the Party.'
> 'Does he exist in the same way as I exist?'
> 'You do not exist.'

Orwell the journalist is as much in evidence as Orwell the novelist: intelligent, purposeful and more than a little grim. The militaristic politics of his nightmare society (calmly analysed, midway through the novel, in a forbidden book by public enemy Emmanuel Goldstein) are both plausible and coherent. Absolute repression ensures absolute obedience. Children betray their parents. Slogans of the state – WAR IS PEACE, FREEDOM IS SLAVERY, IGNORANCE IS STRENGTH – have an authentically eerie logic. But, crucially, the novel also contains scenes that give this world its sense of broken humanity: Winston's memories of his mother or his final betrayal of Julia. The combination locks the story in the mind as resonantly as a folk tale.

Where to go next
The Man in the High Castle, 1962, Philip K. Dick
An interesting parallel to *Nineteen Eighty-Four*. Dick imagines the US occupied and divided by the Japanese and the Nazis, following the defeat of the Allies after World War II.

Screen adaptation
Nineteen Eighty-Four, 1984, dir. Michael Radford
Filmed mostly in London, the washed-out cinematography successfully evokes the dingy austerity of post World War II Britain where a suitably crumpled John Hurt as Winston Smith struggles to get by. The interrogation scenes in the Ministry of Love are disturbingly convincing, thanks to Richard Burton's intense but unusually restrained performance as O'Brien.

Gulliver's Travels

1726, JONATHAN SWIFT, IRISH

Expurgated editions for children have made *Gulliver's Travels* one of the world's most famous − and famously playful − classics, but the real thing is much more formidable: a clever, angry novel of human failure. Swift was the first of the Anglophone satirists to perfect the straight-face technique, and in his masterpiece he uses it to amuse, shock and horrify. In the manner of eighteenth-century travellers, castaway mariner Lemuel Gulliver's autobiographical style is sober to a fault, but what he writes about is nothing so ordinary as hostile natives, wild animals or cannibals. The peoples he encountered on his calamitous voyages are the six-inch-tall Lilliputians, the sixty-foot-tall Brobdingnagians, the residents of

> *I could perhaps like others have astonished thee with strange improbable Tales; but I rather chose to relate plain Matter of Fact in the simplest Manner and Style.*

the floating airborne island of Laputa, and the Houyhnhnms − a race of horses infinitely more civilized than humans.

Gulliver's Travels is a novel of big shocking ideas and small shocking details. From the first, Gulliver displays scrupulous, almost fussy, concern with detail, even giving the exact latitude and longitude of the places he visits, a technique he extends to their extraordinary inhabitants. Everything is made irresistible by brilliant touches: a Lilliputian soldier inadvertently awakening Gulliver by exploring his nostril with his pikestaff, or Gulliver in Brobdingnag warding off wasps "as large as partridges". Vivid details like these give Swift's bizarre ideas startling clarity − and disturbing resonance. In the land of the Houyhnhnms, a reversal of roles shows humans at their most bestial, and a novel which began by describing outlandish creatures ends by making humans outlandish. Not just outlandish. A sense of disgust (and, actually, misogyny) is evident from the beginning;

finally, Gulliver is so traumatized by humanity that his own family seems repulsive. *Gulliver's Travels* is not necessarily a novel to warm to, but it is one to marvel at and be chastened by.

📖 **Where to go next**
A Modest Proposal, 1729, Jonathan Swift
Swift's pamphlet, suggesting what could be done with the unwanted children of the poor, is one of the most deft and incisive satires ever written.

The Lord of the Rings
1954–55, J.R.R. TOLKIEN, ENGLISH

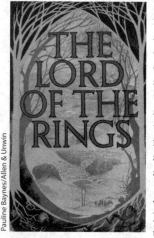

Pauline Baynes/Allen & Unwin

Ignore both derogatory academics and idolizing wargamers. *The Lord of the Rings* trilogy (comprising *The Fellowship of the Ring*, *The Two Towers*, *The Return of the King*), is a grand original and a superbly exciting adventure epic for a troubled century. The story possesses all the flair and weight of a myth from the dawn of humanity, when people mixed with now-vanished races, an age of heroes and monsters locked in a conflict of Good versus Evil.

The vast fictional superstructure which Tolkien created to encompass Middle-Earth – with peoples, dynasties, events, customs, folklore, maps and languages, all worked out in detail – invests his story with the epic weight of history. But the story itself is brilliantly dynamic and absorbing. Modestly ranged against the overwhelming forces of the Dark Lord Sauron are four young hobbits, two men, an elf, a dwarf and an elderly wizard named Gandalf, whose task is to keep a magic ring from falling into the Dark Lord's hands. In the course of their hazardous journey from the green and pleasant Shire to the fiery wastes of Mordor, they will be pursued by Black Riders, ambushed by Orcs, confronted with a Balrog and captured by Uruk-hai. Their fellowship will break, their strength will fail, they will be tempted by evil and fall. But, as general war gathers, the fate of Middle-Earth depends on their endurance.

One ring to rule them all,
One ring to bind them,
One ring to bring them all and
in the darkness bind them.

Leisurely at times, spacious even, and sensitive to the rhythms of journeys through different topographies, the story is never less than intensely suspenseful. Intimate dramas, such as Frodo and Sam's entrapment in Shelob's lair, are as powerful as the spectacular battles with their massed hordes of participants. Though the action is often large-scale, the novel's ultimate focus is on the private trials of endurance, loyalty and resistance to evil. For all its pageantry and scope, *The Lord of the Rings* is a novel in which evil and heroism thrillingly assume individual shape.

Where to go next
The Hobbit, 1937, J.R.R. Tolkien
The kindly Bilbo Baggins journeys to the Lonely Mountain in order to help thirteen dwarves regain their land and treasure from the dragon Smaug. Though geared to a younger audience, *The Hobbit* is the essential companion to *The Lord of the Rings*.

Screen adaptation
The Lord of the Rings, 2001–03, dir. Peter Jackson
All the stops are pulled out in Peter Jackson's assault on Tolkien's trilogy, from the stunning New Zealand scenery, through the CGI animation creatures to the endearingly quirky performance from Ian McKellen as Gandalf. There are moments when the whole thing seems to be just one damn battle scene after another, but the combination of the epic and the apocalyptic is always impressive.

The Time Machine

1895, H.G. WELLS, ENGLISH

If Wells's lucid, compressed fables of strange science remain sharply exciting after a century of accelerating technological advance, it is because no one has bettered his uncanny blend of action and idea. *The Island of Doctor Moreau*, *The Invisible Man*, *The War of the Worlds* and the first of these "scientific romances", *The Time Machine*, are all horrifyingly plausible dramas of impossible scenarios.

Pursuing the hypothesis that it ought to be possible to move along the fourth dimension of time as readily as the other three of space, an English scientist builds a machine to do so, and travels forward to the year 802701. The Thames Valley has become a idyllic garden inhabited by pretty, childish people, the Eloi, who do no work and appear to have no cares. Only when he discovers another kind of human living underground, the Morlocks, does the Time Traveller begin to understand the horrors of the Eloi's existence.

A gust of air whirled round me as I opened the door, and from within came the sound of broken glass falling on the floor. The Time Traveller was not there.

The clarity of Wells's style gives his ideas a disturbing sharp edge but he is also an expert storyteller and bold manipulator of narrative moods and rhythms. The masterstroke of making the Time Traveller a socially conventional Victorian gentleman makes the bizarre future stranger and more real – his shocking appearance among his dinner guests, shoeless, dishevelled and wounded, takes us instantly into the mystery. No less effective are the culminating scenes of an infinitely more distant humanless future, eerie and desolate. Wells is the master of thrilling disorientation.

Where to go next
The Island of Doctor Moreau, 1896, H.G. Wells.
Perhaps the most terrifying of Wells's scientific romances, the story takes the

reader to a Pacific island, where the wayward vivisector Dr Moreau has been "humanizing animals".

Screen adaptation
The Time Machine, 1960, dir. George Pal
While the 2002 version, directed by the author's grandson, dazzled with its special effects, the less sophisticated 1960 film has rather more sense of purpose (both films largely ignore Wells's social critique). Rod Taylor is all rugged Hollywood charm as the Time Traveller, while the pioneering use of time-lapse photography and the blue-skinned hairy Morlocks lend the whole thing a cheesy period charm.

We

1924, YEVGENY ZAMYATIN, RUSSIAN

The first great dystopian fiction of the twentieth century, written in direct response to Soviet totalitarianism by a man eventually exiled by Stalin, is – against all the odds – a delight. Closely related to both *Brave New World* and *Nineteen Eighty-Four* in its depiction of a technocratic one-party regime of the future (the twenty-sixth century AD), it is broader and freer than either, with a playful, fantasizing spirit all its own. Crime mystery, psychological thriller, conspiracy adventure and sci-fi disaster novel, with flashes of *Alice in Wonderland* and *The Unbearable Lightness of Being*, it contains scenes of jumpy comedy, a streak of weird lyricism, topsy-turvy mathematics and tremendous sex.

The citizens of OneState live in a perfectly regimented society cut off from the wild, natural world by walls of glass. Emotional needs are known only to them from histories of the "ancient days"; their own lives, robotically hygienic, mathematically logical, are fused in the communal life of the state. They have no names, only identifying numbers. There are no individuals, only "we".

D-503 is the chief engineer of the INTEGRAL spaceship, which will carry records of OneState's philosophy into space. D-503 himself has been asked to contribute a diary praising the state – but after he becomes involved in a disorientating relationship with the fascinating but subversive I-330, who he meets in a museum of the past, he finds himself writing a very different sort of story.

When the velocity of an aero is reduced to 0, it is not in motion; when a man's freedom is reduced to zero, he commits no crimes. That's clear. The only means to rid man of crime is to rid him of freedom.

The chapter headings – "Frozen Waves", "Everything Tends to Perfection", "I Am a Microbe" – give a flavour of the author's style and imagination. His favourite metaphors of mirrors, glass and wings create both glittering surfaces and weird depths; the breathless and broken sentences of his prose lend the narrative speed and uncertainty. It is always difficult to predict where the story is going to lead: the twin narratives of conspiracy and sexual obsession accelerate towards a totally unexpected ending.

Recommended translation
1993, Clarence Brown, Penguin Books

Where to go next
Solaris, 1961, Stanislaw Lem
A space mission from Earth, attempting to investigate the mysterious planet Solaris, is thwarted when the guilty thoughts of captain and crew take on physical form. The inability of humans to comprehend alien cultures was a perennial theme of Lem's fiction.

Horror and mystery

10

To be teased, tormented, bamboozled or terrified out of your skin are, and have always been, among the most delicious pleasures offered by fiction. In the classic tradition, many different genres – Gothic novels, tales of the supernatural, ghost stories and others – have delivered the same electrifying results of horror and mystery. In all of them, atmosphere is crucial, so too is a gripping plot, and it helps to have a charismatic villain, a supernatural agent of darkness or, better yet, the Devil himself.

The taste for horror was particularly strong in Britain, where the Gothic novel – which takes its name from the gloomy medieval settings which feature to such atmospheric effect – was all the rage in the late eighteenth and early nineteenth centuries. Walpole's *The Castle of Otranto* started it all off, but it was Ann Radcliffe who really established the genre with such novels as *The Mysteries of Udolpho* and *The Italian* in which the bloodcurdling and the romantic are freely mixed.

Horror and mystery fiction took a more psychological turn at the end of the nineteenth century, when writers such as Robert Louis

Stevenson and Oscar Wilde explored the darker side of human nature in terms of a diseased personality. At the same time, writers such as Bram Stoker and Henry James continued to evoke a supernatural world of evil, while the period also saw another strand of mystery fiction – the detective story – reach its classic form with the most celebrated of super-sleuths, Sherlock Holmes.

The Man Who Was Thursday

1907, G.K. CHESTERTON, ENGLISH

Penguin

Before the detective novel became fixated on violent crime, this is what it could produce – an action-packed investigation of ideas, full of twists and revelations.

It begins with an artistic disagreement at a garden party in the elegant London suburb of Saffron Park. The minor poet Lucian Gregory, who loves to shock people with his enthusiasm for Anarchism, is accused by another minor poet, Gabriel Syme, of frivolity. As a result, Gregory reveals himself to be a perfectly serious member of a heavily armed anarchist circle. And as a result of that, Syme reveals himself to be a police detective hunting anarchists. This is only the first of a sequence of astonishing and witty reversals. Elected as "Thursday" on the "Council of Seven Days", Syme infiltrates the foremost European anarchists' group, preparing to pit his wits against its shadowy leader, "Sunday", a man of colossal evil.

Chesterton's paradoxical style (fast, theatrical, witty) is matched by his love of paradoxical, not to say impossible, notions, to which he gives wild and comic expression. Proposing that the greatest danger to Edwardian stability is not bombs but ideas, he sets up a headlong plot of secrecy, pursuit and unexpected disclosures which doubles as a philosophical quest for truth and – ultimately – the meaning of God.

> 'You are not asleep, I assure you,' said Gregory. 'You are, on the contrary, close to the most actual and rousing moment of your existence.'

Part detective novel, part bizarre costume drama of the intellect, it is slick, funny and satisfyingly perplexing.

Where to go next
The Innocence of Father Brown, 1911, G.K. Chesterton
Twelve detective stories with a metaphysical slant as an unassuming Catholic priest investigates some outlandish cases. Father Brown is a "contemporary" of Sherlock Holmes but his method is more about psychology than logic.

The Hound of the Baskervilles

1902, ARTHUR CONAN DOYLE, ENGLISH

Sherlock Holmes and Dr Watson have claim to be the most famous couple in fiction, their eccentric domesticity at 221B Upper Baker Street as entertaining as their crime-solving adventures. Conan Doyle's masterstroke was to allow the unimaginative Watson to narrate them, deepening their mystery and emphasizing the brilliance of his friend's deductive powers. Many of the most ingenious adventures are in the form of short stories. Of the four novels, *The Hound of the Baskervilles* remains the most consistently thrilling.

There can surely be no connection between the death of Sir Charles in the grounds of Baskerville Hall and the old family legend of the curse of the hound. But what was Sir Charles running from when his heart gave out? Was it something he had seen on the moor? And what is Holmes to make of the footprints found nearby – the footprints of a gigantic dog?

The London of Sherlock Holmes, with its fogs and cabs and clubs, is one of the great cities of imaginative literature; it is a mark of Doyle's bold confidence, then, that he abandons it, after a swift series of cryptic warnings and puzzling thefts in the metropolis, for an even more atmospheric Dartmoor with its prehistoric remains, brooding vistas and local superstitions. Even bolder is the decision for the doughty but unperceptive Watson to go there alone, entrusted with the mission of protecting Baskerville Hall's new owner, Sir Henry, and making sense of the enigmatic locals.

A terrible scream – a prolonged yell of horror and anguish burst out of the silence of the moor. 'The hound!' cried Holmes. 'Come, Watson, come! Great Heavens, if we are too late!'

This sort of boldness and variety is characteristic of the novel as a whole, keeping the reader entertained with sudden new plot lines, fresh mysteries and almost giddily brilliant little touches – the inexplicable theft of a shoe or the sound of a woman crying in the night – all put together with a dash of humour. Half-comic, in fact, is Holmes's insouciant ability to be several steps ahead of everyone else, though his uncanny intelligence is only part of his appeal. A maverick who delights in straying onto the wrong side of the law, he makes a profound claim on our sympathies and interest as an eccentric, untamed amateur in an increasingly official world.

Where to go next
The Adventures of Sherlock Holmes, 1892, Arthur Conan Doyle
In the first twelve tales of the amateur detective, written for *The Strand* magazine, Doyle establishes all the essential Holmesian trademarks.

Screen adaptation
The Hound of the Baskervilles, 1959, dir. Terence Fisher
The Hammer horror treatment offers lurid Technicolor, the formidable Christopher Lee as Sir Henry Baskerville and a hound that glows in the dark. There are some small deviations from the novel, but Peter Cushing and André Morrell make a highly convincing Holmes and Watson, though Cushing fails to convey the character's eccentricity quite as well as Basil Rathbone did in the 1939 Hollywood version.

The complete Sherlock Holmes

The great detective first appeared in *Beeton's Christmas Annual* for 1887 in the novel *A Study in Scarlet*. The short stories were written for *The Strand Magazine*, where the illustrations by Sidney Paget helped establish the definitive image of the aquiline, pipe-smoking sleuth. Conan Doyle attempted to kill the character off as early as 1893, in *The Adventure of the Final Problem*, by having him fall after a struggle with master criminal Professor Moriarty at the Alpine Reichenbach Falls. Public outcry meant that his creator was forced to resurrect him. There are a total of four Holmes novels and fifty-six short stories, the majority of which are narrated by his trusted companion and confidant, Dr John H. Watson.

- *A Study in Scarlet* (1887) novel
- *The Sign of Four* (1890) novel
- *The Adventures of Sherlock Holmes* (1892) twelve short stories
- *The Memoirs of Sherlock Holmes* (1894) twelve short stories
- *The Hound of the Baskervilles* (1902) novel
- *The Return of Sherlock Holmes* (1904) thirteen short stories
- *The Valley of Fear* (1914) novel
- *His Last Bow* (1917) eight short stories
- *The Case-Book of Sherlock Holmes* (1927) twelve short stories

The Private Memoirs and Confessions of a Justified Sinner

1824, JAMES HOGG, SCOTTISH

The Private Memoirs and Confessions of a Justified Sinner seemed to the author so terrifying, so sickeningly "replete with horrors", that when it was first published he didn't dare put his name to it.

The novel contains two versions of the same story: the editor's version and the sinner's. The sinner, Robert Wringhim, is a youth brought up as a strict Calvinist in late seventeenth-century Scotland. Believing himself predestined for Heaven, he becomes the instru-

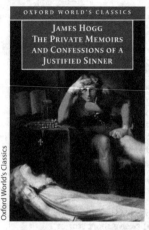

OXFORD WORLD'S CLASSICS

JAMES HOGG
THE PRIVATE MEMOIRS
AND CONFESSIONS OF A
JUSTIFIED SINNER

Oxford World's Classics

ment of God's wrath on earth, all his acts – whatever they are – divinely sanctioned in advance. In a short lifetime of embittered violence, he kills his elder half-brother, his mother and his lover, and, as the officers of the law finally close in on him, disappears into thin air. But who is the mysterious stranger, Gil-Martin, who has been his constant guide?

The answer is contained in the second narrative, the autobiographical account of the sinner himself, a story which distortingly mirrors the first. Other dizzying duplications abound – Wringhim and his half-brother, Scots and English, the body and soul, good and evil – each reflecting and warping the other.

I was a being incomprehensible to myself. Either I had a second self, who transacted business in my likeness, or else my body was at times possessed by a spirit over which it had no control.

At the heart of the confusion is the relationship between Wringhim and Gil-Martin, a gifted man eloquent in his religious arguments, who possesses the sinister ability to change his shape. Is he the Devil, or a figment of Wringhim's diseased mind? For that matter, is the novel a study of evil or psychology? With the authentic power of a nightmare, Hogg's bold but twisted fable seems to reveal and conceal at the same time.

Where to go next

The Fall of the House of Usher and Other Writings, Edgar Allan Poe
Written in the 1830s and 40s, Poe's stories, combine classic gothic horror with psychological depth and an exquisite prose style. They had a huge influence on later writers, not least Arthur Conan Doyle.

The Turn of the Screw

1898, HENRY JAMES, AMERICAN

On first publication there was immediate recognition that James's ghost story was worse than merely frightening. "It is," one reviewer wrote, "the most hopelessly evil story that we have ever read." Written with the usual Jamesian refinement, it brilliantly evokes the comfortable glow of late Victorian England – only to reveal at its heart a stark but inexplicable horror.

Arriving at the spacious and pleasant estate of Bly, the new governess (the story's narrator) is delighted, even astonished, to find the children, Miles and Flora, so charming, so angelic. The sudden death of their old governess, and Miles's recent expulsion from school, are mere puzzles. One golden twilight, however, as she strolls in from the park, she encounters an unknown man staring down at her from the tower of the house, and shortly afterwards finds herself abruptly face to face with him through the dining-room window. His name is Peter Quint, the former valet, a man of notorious depravity. He is no longer of this world, and his silent gaze tells her he has returned for something. Not for her. He has come for the children. And he is not alone.

The apparition had reached the landing. In the cold faint twilight, with a glimmer in the high glass and another on the polish of the oak stair below, we faced each other in our common intensity.

Unlike much of James, *The Turn of the Screw* is short and fast, a compulsive two-hour read from start to finish. Its uniquely disturbing atmosphere (not just frightening but somehow sickening) is partly the result of the new governess's oddly equivocal behaviour. The intensifying drama of the narrative confirms James as a master of suspense. Each unexpected appearance of the silently watching figures shifts everything, revealing a new, more appalling situation, and the horror increases without let-up, through several turns of the screw, to the end.

Where to go next
The Aspern Papers, 1888, Henry James
Comic, tender and suspenseful tale of literary detection and idolatory set in Venice, as an anonymous narrator attempts to track down the letters of a long-dead American poet.

Screen adaptation
The Innocents, 1961, dir. Jack Clayton
A sensitive script by Truman Capote and William Archibald, the enveloping shadows of Freddie Francis's expressionist camerawork, and the intense performances of Deborah Kerr as the governess and Martin Stephens as Miles all contribute to this brilliant and genuinely unnerving adaptation of *The Turn of the Screw*.

The Mysteries of Udolpho

1794, ANN RADCLIFFE, ENGLISH

Penguin

ANN RADCLIFFE
The Mysteries of Udolpho

Ghostly apparitions, fainting maidens, lascivious blackguards and bloodstains on the stairs are all features of classic horror that Ann Radcliffe made her own in this, the earliest best-selling thriller in the English language. Pure sex and violence – though not as we know them.

The plot encompasses kidnapping, extortion, murder and violation, but in the Romantic not the Realistic mode. Sensibility – the cult of feelings – pervades throughout. Will tender-hearted Emily find her way back to her native Gascony, where her sentimental lover Valancourt awaits her, or will she be destroyed at the castle of Udolpho in the Italian Apennines by the black intrigues of the hot-blooded banditto Mantoni?

Don't expect fast action: Radcliffe is a slow and careful plotter, given to leisurely wide-angle panning and infinitely delayed surprises. Don't expect the close-up realism of contemporary thrillers, either. Her music-making peasants have danced straight out of light opera, and the gorgeous scenery (the woods and meadows of Gascony, the wild splendour of the Pyrenees) is lit by the same mellow light as the romantic landscapes of Claude. Her heroine's sweetness and her villain's moustache-twirling dastardliness are the standard props of good and evil. But neither will you find the slick and predictable formulae of genre thrillers today. *The Mysteries of Udolpho* is a pre-thriller thriller, possessing the *naïf* freshness – and awkwardness – of real originality. Though it may have lost its power to horrify, it continues to charm. It also contains one of the most stunning deathbed scenes in fiction, improbably incorporating a heartfelt testimony to the "delirium of Italian love".

> *Emily, bending over the body, gazed, for a moment, with an eager, frenzied eye; but, in the next, the lamp dropped from her hand, and she fell senseless at the foot of the couch.*

 Where to go next
The Italian, 1797, Ann Radcliffe
Though less renowned than *The Mysteries of Udolpho*, many critics have preferred this heady brew of illegitimacy, elopement and persecution among the Italian aristocracy.

Frankenstein

1818, MARY SHELLEY, ENGLISH

During a wet summer in Switzerland, the eighteen-year-old Mary, her lover Shelley and Lord Byron decided to while away the time writing ghost stories. *Frankenstein* – the only story to be completed – was published two years later, and has since, like the monster itself, taken on a life of its own, achieving notoriety far beyond its readers. As a result, the original story comes as something of a surprise: less a horror novel than a sustained adventure in alienation.

At the end of the eighteenth century, an English explorer sailing across the Arctic sea encounters, to his astonishment, an emaciated traveller in a sledge floating on a large fragment of ice. The traveller's name is Dr Frankenstein, and he is in pursuit, he tells the incredulous Englishman, of a monster of his own creation.

By the glimmer of the half-extinguished light, I saw the dull yellow eye of the creature open; it breathed hard, and a convulsive motion agitated its limbs.

The sensational story which follows includes not only the familiar tale of Dr Frankenstein's famous experiment – and his revulsion at the result – but also the Monster's own account of his abandonment and desperate wandering as an outcast. As a writer of Gothic fiction, Shelley's technique seems unsophisticated: long periods of inaction are disrupted by bursts of melodrama, absurd coincidences and improbable occurrences. But the novel is centred not so much in action as in themes – of exile, freedom, guilt, power and nature. In the doomed but inextricable relationship between Dr Frankenstein and his monster, these themes are thrown into dramatic relief, forcing onto the reader the uncomfortable paradox that the unnaturally created monster behaves more naturally than the creator who abandons it, and producing a book which, if not horrific in the genre sense, is profoundly disturbing.

 **Where to go next**
The Golem, 1915, Gustav Meyrinck
A hallucinatory retelling of the medieval Jewish folk tale about a monster made from inanimate material who materializes in the Prague ghetto.

 Screen adaptation
Frankenstein, 1931, dir. James Whale
Although it stands as a classic in its own right, Whale's version of *Frankenstein* is very different from Shelley's original. Gone is the framing device of a polar sea voyage, while the naïve student Frankenstein is replaced by the archetypal mad scientist. It remains moving, however, not least because of Boris Karloff's iconic performance as the inarticulate monster.

The Strange Case of Dr Jekyll and Mr Hyde

1886, ROBERT LOUIS STEVENSON, SCOTTISH

Stevenson was the purest of storytellers, his narratives always natural and daring, but nothing in his sprightly earlier adventures *Treasure Island* and *Kidnapped* anticipates his eerie tale of dual personality, *Dr Jekyll and Mr Hyde*, the original psychological thriller.

His London – like that of Sherlock Holmes – is a city of fogs ("glow of a rich, lurid brown, like the light of some strange conflagration"), muffled crowds and sudden empty corners where the smallest noises are mysterious and menacing – the London also of sober, respectable gentlemen like Utterson the lawyer, Lanyon the physician and the kindly scientist Dr Henry Jekyll. But Jekyll has been behaving oddly, keeping strange hours and disappearing for days on end. Worse, he has rewritten his will, leaving his fortune to a new friend, Edward Hyde, a pale, dwarfish man who inspires all that meet him with disgust.

Penguin

'Gripping ... a dark psychological tale ... sweeps the reader along on a wave of page-turning excitement' Val McDermid, *Guardian*

Like *Frankenstein*, Stevenson's novel taps into the nineteenth-century fear of reckless scientific experimentation, but, like *The Picture of Dorian Gray*, it also expresses horrified fascination with the idea of duality – the personality split between good and evil, respectability and infamy. Though written,

I thus drew steadily nearer to that truth, by whose partial discovery I have been doomed to such a dreadful shipwreck: that man is not truly one, but truly two.

according to Stevenson, as a common "shilling shocker", the tale is a masterpiece of tension, the drily formal style of Utterson and Lanyon, through whom the story is told, contrasting uneasily with its unpredictable action and undercurrents of derangement and bestiality. No more than a novella in length, it can be read in a single sitting, as a superior Gothic tale of unusual drama, intelligence and emotional force.

Where to go next
Treasure Island, 1883, Robert Louis Stevenson
This classic tale of eighteenth-century piracy, in which the boy Jim Hawkins outwits the wily and amoral Long John Silver, has the essential Stevensonian blend of narrative flair and wildness.

Screen adaptation
Dr Jekyll and Mr Hyde, 1931, dir. Rouben Mamoulian
This remains the finest of the many adaptations of Stevenson's novella, with Frederic March giving a remarkable performance as the divided personality. Mamoulian's direction is deliriously inventive in its use of wipes and point-of-view shots, while the transformation scenes are a dizzying combination of sound and vision involving a revolving camera, double and triple exposures and an amplified heartbeat.

Dracula
1897, BRAM STOKER, IRISH

So much cartoonish fun has been had from the Dracula legend that the implacable horror of Bram Stoker's classic version comes as a shock. From the opening description of young English solicitor Jonathan Harker's nocturnal journey through the Transylvanian forests, the story grips like a nightmare. It may be untidy round the edges, but awkwardness is all part of the novel's power: no neat stylishness interrupts the sickening heave of the story's momentum or dilutes the primitive magic of its force; nor can any other Dracula retelling match Stoker's utterly convincing creation of evil in the appalling figure of the Count.

Harker, the vampire hunter Van Helsing and their friends are bland. The Count is exotic, his cruelty and lust exerting a fascination that makes him degradingly desirable. Like his vampire brides who toy voluptuously with Harker in his castle, he reeks of sex, mesmerizing virgins and turning them into addicts of his lust. Against his menace, the knowledge of modern science and the innocence of spotless virtue are equally powerless. To fight evil, Van Helsing must utilize the old magic of crucifixes and wooden stakes, and engage Dracula in an eerie but believable dreamscape of myth and superstition which overlaps, and sometimes obliterates, the real world. Here, in the shadowy territory made of bad dreams, folk belief, lustful fantasies and madmen's ravings, unreality becomes real, and the Undead walk the streets of London, sucking its children's blood. Always one step ahead of Van Helsing and co., we feel their danger. One step behind Dracula, we share their terror. It is one of the truly dark tales, from which there seems no escape.

Penguin

His eyes flamed red with devilish passion, and the white sharp teeth, behind the full lips of the blood-dripping mouth, champed together like those of a wild beast.

📖 Where to go next
In A Glass Darkly, 1872, Sheridan Le Fanu
A collection of five genuinely unnerving tales investigated by Dr Martin Hesselius. They include the much-anthologized "Green Tea" and "Carmilla", a vampire story that influenced Bram Stoker.

🎬 Screen adaptation
Dracula (aka *Horror of Dracula*), 1958, dir. Terence Fisher
The 1931 film of Stoker's classic, starring Bela Lugosi, may be strong on atmosphere but this later version is much more compelling despite playing fast-and-

Literary bloodsuckers

The grisly myth of creatures living on human blood is as old as humanity itself, but modern vampire legends originate in South-Eastern Europe, where they became associated with the terrible deeds of historical figures such as Elizabeth Bathory (1560–1614), who bathed in the blood of virgins and Vlad III, Prince of Wallachia – "the Impaler" – otherwise known as Dracula ("son of the dragon"). Vampires make their first appearance in English literature in Byron's poem "The Giaour" (1813), then in the story *The Vampyre* by Byron's personal physician, John Polidori, who based his dissolute vampiric Lord Ruthven on Byron himself. In 1872, the Dubliner Sheridan Le Fanu pushed the genre further when he published "Carmilla", a story of lesbian vampirism. Sex, as much as cruelty, has been a feature of the vampire legend from the start, and in 1897, Bram Stoker gave the myth its classic fictional form with *Dracula*. Our obsession with the vampire shows no sign of abating, however. Count Dracula features in more movies than any modern fictional character except Sherlock Holmes, and new generations have encountered vampires in contemporary works, most notably in the eight novels that make up Ann Rice's *The Vampire Chronicles*.

loose with the plot. Christopher Lee, complete with fangs and bloodshot eyes, makes the Count both frightening and alluring, while Peter Cushing brings his customary gravitas to the role of Van Helsing.

The Castle of Otranto

1764, HORACE WALPOLE, ENGLISH

The earliest Gothic novel created a sensation in mid-eighteenth-century England when it first appeared, published anonymously and presented as an authentic medieval manuscript, written in "the purest Italian". Only its immediate success persuaded the author to reveal himself the following year as Horace Walpole, son of the English prime minister. Ever since, his name has been associated with the

Gothic tradition of blood-soaked deeds and supernatural revenge.

All the Hammer House of Horror props are here: hidden dungeons, labyrinthine caves, gloomy staircases, lonely shrines and the walking dead. All the hysterics of the stars of the silent screen, with their huge gestures of despair, ecstasy and torment, melodramatize an ingenious plot packed with unexpected twists, sudden reversals, hidden identities, violent passions and dastardly scheming. The effect is wildly operatic. It is the purest Italian after all.

Sensationalism is not the novel's only attraction, however. The portrait of Manfred, false Prince of Otranto, is a wonderfully penetrating study of human psychology at its darkest, encompassing

And the figure, turning slowly round, discovered to Frederick the fleshless jaws and empty sockets of a skeleton.

the fearfulness and bullying of villainy, and the mania and momentum of (human) evil. The plot, ostensibly about inheritance, in fact revolves around love and lack of love. And the feverishly rapid narrative anticipates cinema in cutting abruptly from scene to scene to maximize a sense of drama and suspense.

 Where to go next
The Monk, 1796, Matthew Lewis
Written to titillate as much as to scare, *The Monk* tells of a charismatic and devout Spanish preacher who becomes the slave of his own sexual depravity.

The Picture of Dorian Gray

1891, OSCAR WILDE, IRISH

Wilde's only novel is famous, like his plays, for the wit and immorality of the debonair upper-class characters, but it possesses an eeriness all its own, and is moreover a down-to-earth rattling good read, accelerating with the inescapable logic of a fable towards its grisly conclusion.

The story begins with Wilde's customary elegance and cleverness. Just as his portrait is being finished, Dorian Gray comes under the corrupting influence of the artist's charismatic friend, Lord Henry Wotton. Persuaded that his beauty is better than genius, that pleasure is more important than goodness, Dorian makes an impulsive wish never to grow old – to live, forever young, for new sensations. To his horror, his wish comes true.

Wilde's style is both paradoxical ("the only way to get rid of a temptation is to yield to it") and radical ("it is only shallow people who do not judge by appearances"): Lord Henry Wotton's golden, barbed pronouncements are genuinely witty because they are genuinely thought-provoking. Read one way, the novel is a manifesto for a new style of living. But, read another, it is a tale of corruption with traditionally harsh results. Vanity leads to debauchery; immorality to sin; sin to punishment. The marvellous conversations which seem innocent at the beginning of the novel are dead and empty by the end.

> *'If it were only the other way! If it were I who was to be always young, and the picture that was to grow old! For that – for that – I would give everything!'*

Does the story of a charmed but doomed double life contain autobiographical undertones? Within five years of publication, Wilde was imprisoned for homosexual practices, then a criminal offence; within ten years he was dead. A mainspring of Wilde's wit is his fury at a society which forced him underground.

Where to go next
The Lost Stradivarius, 1895, John Meade Falkner
A ghost story, with a markedly decadent tone, about the corrupting influence of a violin able to conjure up the spirit of a previous, long dead, owner, when a certain melody is played on it.

Screen adaptation
The Picture of Dorian Gray, 1945, dir. Albert Lewin
Slow-paced and almost too respectful to the original, this adaptation nevertheless exudes a genuine sense of perfumed *fin-de-siècle* decadence. The cool and epicene Hurd Hatfield is well cast in the title role – the perfect foil to George Sanders's sardonic Lord Henry Wotton. Hatfield's mask-like face makes the final viewing of the grotesquely transformed painting all the more shocking.

Crime and punishment

Our obsession with wrongdoing is an ancient one, long preceding the modern genre of crime fiction. The appalling drama of the criminal act, the terrible fascination of the villain, the mystery of the investigation, the tension of the chase, the horrifying closure of the punishment – all these have combined many times over the centuries to produce classic narratives of terrific excitement and power.

In no other type of fiction are the stories so relentlessly gripping. Varied they may be, but they have in common the racing plot line, whether it revolves round a mystery (as it does in Mary Braddon's tantalizing *Lady Audley's Secret*) or the more visceral excitement of a man on the run, like William Godwin's Caleb Williams.

Realism is another strong point of the crime novel. To read Defoe's *Moll Flanders* or James Ellroy's *L.A. Quartet* is to find yourself totally immersed in the criminal underworlds of eighteenth-century London and twentieth-century Los Angeles. Not that the crime novel is limited to its immediate locale. The natural territory of the fabulously eccentric *That Awful Mess on Via Merulana* is the dark history of Italy. Ismail Kadare's *Broken April* takes the reader into the nightmarish world of the Albanian blood feud.

Finally, what better way to dramatize the (often ambiguous) struggle between good and evil than a story of crime and its punishment? Here we find some of the greatest characters in fiction: the criminal mastermind Count Fosco (in Wilkie Collins's *The Woman in White*), private investigator Philip Marlowe, and Dostoevsky's guilt-tormented axe-murderer Raskolnikov.

Lady Audley's Secret

1862, MARY ELIZABETH BRADDON, ENGLISH

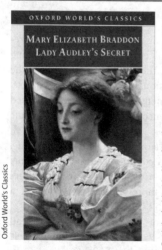

Oxford World's Classics

Like Wilkie Collins, Braddon was a leading writer of "Sensation" novels, popular with a Victorian public avid for crimes, scandals and other stimulations – novels so violent that the Archbishop of York was moved to preach against them, as "one of the abominations of the age". By Victorian standards, Braddon's private life was also irregular: for years she lived with her publisher (caring for five of his children and bearing six of their own) while his wife was confined in a mental institution. Many of these themes – crime, scandal, enigma and insanity – find their way into her best novel, *Lady Audley's Secret*.

The beautiful, sweet-natured Lucy Graham, a penniless governess, catches the eye of Sir Michael Audley, and is soon his wife. Meanwhile, George Talboys returns with a fortune from Australia to reclaim the wife he abandoned three years earlier, and, on a visit to Audley Court, vanishes without trace. His friend Robert, an amiable, idle barrister who would rather not discover any unpleasant truths, is nevertheless compelled to pursue a trail of improbable and increasingly disturbing clues.

> *To call them the weaker sex is to utter a hideous mockery. They are the stronger sex, the noisier, the more persevering, the most self-assertive sex.*

Braddon's style is easy and familiar, almost gossipy in the mid-Victorian self-confident manner, and she prefers melodrama over subtlety: sudden mysteries, bizarre coincidences and chance revelations are deployed in cliff-hanging scenes which succeed each other with cinematic abruptness. Unsettling sometimes, particularly at first, the excitement of the story eventually takes hold and the characters reveal themselves in unexpected ways; the device of the reluctant detective is particularly clever. Most interesting of all is the way the mystery is complicated by other urgent issues – of propriety and duty and, above all, sexual morals. How should society judge and, if necessary, punish a beautiful and self-assertive woman?

Where to go next
East Lynne, 1861, Mrs Henry Wood
A huge best-seller in its day, this melodrama deals severely with the adultery of a married woman, Lady Isobel Vane, who, made destitute by her folly, returns heavily disguised to her family home to take up the position of governess to her own unsuspecting children.

The Naked Lunch

1959, WILLIAM BURROUGHS, AMERICAN

With its pornographic fantasies, sadomasochistic violence and obsessive interest in bodily functions, *The Naked Lunch* is not for everyone. It is – frankly – a thoroughly unpleasant read. But, in the best tradi-tions of the counter-culture, it is powerfully subversive, mordantly funny and impeccably avant-garde.

Burroughs tells us in the introduction that Jack Kerouac thought up the title, reference to the "frozen moment when everyone sees what is on the end of every fork" – horrors usually unseen. Horrors duly follow: alarming stories from the underworld of drug addiction, where "pushers", "buyers" and "junkies" kill themselves and each other for their habits, and lengthy, detailed accounts of their psycho-sexual nightmares: bestiality, torture, killer aliens, sexually motivated hangings and sodomy.

I awoke from the Sickness at the age of forty-five, calm and sane, and in reasonably good health except for a weakened liver and the look of borrowed flesh common to all who survive.

The Naked Lunch can be read as a satire of political repression ("democracy is cancerous") or barbarous legalities (Burroughs claimed it was in part a "tract against capital punishment"), though its tone is disturbingly self-indulgent. More meaningful and entertaining shocks are provided by the Burroughs's style – a bracing mix of fastidious Harvard-educated eloquence and obscene street slang. Indeed, perhaps his true gifts are comic, his fantasies often taking a cartoonish turn, and he is a great mimic too, taking off semi-crazed junkies and stuffy English colonials with equal brilliance. His "cut-up technique", an innovation (borrowed from the Surrealists) whereby existing text is cutup into fragments and then rearranged to create new meanings, gives everything a kaleidoscopic twist. The result creates swirling anti-sequences of random passages – an appropriate medium for a novel about disorientation.

Where to go next
The Soft Machine, 1961, William Burroughs
Even more fragmented and experimental than *The Naked Lunch*, *The Soft Machine* is not for the faint-hearted. Plotless and with a prevailingly paranoiac tone, the novel is compelling – or repellent – according to how you respond to the violent "music" of Burroughs's unique prose-poetry.

Screen adaptation
The Naked Lunch, 1991, dir. David Cronenberg
An attempt to film the unfilmable that largely succeeds because the surreal
musings are given a layer of coherence by adding details from the author's
own life. Peter Weller plays Burroughs's alter ego Bill Lee, a bug exterminator
addicted to his anti-bug powder, who accidentally shoots his wife and is beset
by increasingly bizarre and paranoiac hallucinations (most memorably when his
typewriter turns into a cockroach).

The Big Sleep

1939, RAYMOND CHANDLER, AMERICAN

A racing plot line is the minimum
expectation of a satisfying crime
novel, but *The Big Sleep* delivers much
more: a brilliantly tangible South
Californian scene of mean streets and
millionaire mansions, an electrifyingly
deadpan private eye, and a beautifully
lucid style, both delicate and brutal.

After Sherlock Holmes, Philip
Marlowe may be the most famous
detective in fiction, coolly laconic and
seedily handsome, world-weary and
more than a little cynical, but still
doing his bit for justice. Accepting a
commission to investigate a blackmail
scam involving Carmen, the wayward
daughter of the elderly General Sternwood, he soon finds there is
a lot more going on than meets the eye. Where is Carmen's sister's
bootlegger husband, Rusty Regan? What sort of racket is the black-
mailer, Geiger, really running from his antique bookstore? And why
is casino-owner Eddie Mars always showing up?

The explosive action and droll narration is a winning combination, much imitated – and usually mangled – by lesser writers. But Chandler is an original. Like Conan Doyle, he is capable of creating

> *I climbed over the railing again and kicked the French window in. Neither of the two people in the room paid any attention to the way I came in, although only one of them was dead.*

a complete fictional world: not only does he know how to set a scene, pace a story and bring a character to life – all with the deftest of touches – he has the magical ability to make the reader feel the Californian fog against his face, smell the back stairs of a low-rent office block, or taste the smoke of a cheap cigar blown across a bar. *The Big Sleep* is exciting, funny and suspenseful, and wonderfully generous in its detail.

Where to go next
The Long Goodbye, 1953, Raymond Chandler
Chandler's darkest (and some say his best) novel blurred the boundaries between the crime genre and literary fiction. Marlowe is again the protagonist, but this time rather less able to handle the corruption and duplicity he confronts.

Screen adaptation
The Big Sleep, 1946, dir. Howard Hawks
A crack writing team – including William Faulkner – adapted Chandler's novel to great effect, retaining all the sharp wit while upping the romance between Marlowe and Vivian Sternwood (played by real-life lovers Bogart and Bacall). The result is high on atmosphere and sexual tension but, arguably, sacrifices something of Chandler's cynical vision of a morally rotten Los Angeles.

And Then There Were None

1939, AGATHA CHRISTIE, ENGLISH

The Queen of Crime's most brilliant asset was her ingenuity, the magician's ability to defy belief, and this novel is her most rigorously bewildering. Like Houdini, she had a gift for the impossible, setting formal problems too difficult ever to be solved – then solving them.

Ten characters unknown to each other are invited to a house party on Soldier Island. When they arrive, they discover that their host – the enigmatic U.N. Owen – is perplexingly absent. On the wall of each bedroom is a framed print of an amusing nursery rhyme, beginning "Ten little soldier boys went out to dine/One choked his little self and then there were nine". But, as the butler is serving coffee after dinner, a record suddenly begins to play in the adjourning room, and to their horror, they hear a voice accusing them each in turn of an unpunished crime in their past. Their indignation is matched by their uneasiness when they learn that they are stranded on the island, and uneasiness turns to terror when one of them takes a sip of his whisky and soda and chokes his little self to death.

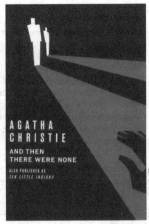

AGATHA CHRISTIE

AND THEN THERE WERE NONE

ALSO PUBLISHED AS TEN LITTLE INDIANS

St Martin's Griffin

> Blore said hoarsely: 'He's a madman! A loony.' The judge coughed. 'That almost certainly. But it hardly affects the issue. Our main preoccupation is this – to save our lives.'

The pace of the novel accelerates electrifyingly as the deaths multiply. But the book is not merely a thriller, nor only a mystery. It crawls with authentic horror. Christie's understanding of psychology is often underrated. Here, she pulls off the extraordinary trick of getting into the heads of ten different characters, and bringing their guilty thoughts to the boil.

Where to go next
The Murder of Roger Ackroyd, 1926, Agatha Christie
Christie's seventh novel is a ground-breaking masterpiece. Belgian sleuth

Hercule Poirot, recently retired to the quiet town of King's Abbot, finds himself involved with the murder of a local wealthy businessman, Roger Ackroyd. Suspicion (typically) falls on almost everyone around him.

Screen adaptation
And Then There Were None, 1945, dir. René Clair
The first of five screen versions of Christie's thriller is still the best, thanks largely to a series of quirky character turns from the likes of Barry Fitzgerald, Walter Huston and Louis Hayward. Black humour prevails as much as – if not more than – suspense, even though Clair adopts the "happy" ending that Christie wrote for the stage version. Not quite Alfred Hitchcock but still pretty good.

The Moonstone

1868, WILKIE COLLINS, ENGLISH

In T.S. Eliot's opinion, "the first and greatest English detective novel", *The Moonstone* is also one of the most purely enjoyable of all English classics.

In 1799, during the conquest of India, an outsized diamond sacred to Hindus – with a curse laid on it by a dying priest – is plundered by a Colonel in the British Army and taken to England. At once three vigilant high-caste Indians make an appearance in London. Fifty year later, bequeathed to the Colonel's niece, the diamond is conveyed to a country house in Yorkshire – where it disappears. Who is to blame, the love-stricken housemaid, the jealous suitor, the pushy philanthropist, or the Indian travelling jugglers who coincidentally appear outside the house?

'Well, Betteredge,' he said, 'how does the atmosphere of mystery and suspicion in which we are all living now agree with you?'

The Moonstone is not simply a thriller (though it definitely thrills). Dickens called it "wild and domestic", and the novel blends elements of the detective story, the "Sensation" three-volume novel (or "triple-decker") and the country-house novel, to provide both

The first detective

Crime has always been a popular subject of literature, but literary detectives – like the real thing – are a much more recent invention.

C. Auguste Dupin is generally acknowledged to be the first. Appearing in three stories by Edgar Allan Poe ("The Murders in the Rue Morgue", 1841; "The Mystery of Marie Roget", 1842; and "The Purloined Letter", 1844), he solved crimes by the method of "ratiocination" – recreating the criminal's train of thought – a mixture of intuition and deduction which would become a standard technique of future literary detectives.

In the 1850s, detectives took minor roles in a number of key novels, including the charismatic Inspector Bucket of the Metropolitan Police, who investigates the death of the lawyer Tulkinghorn in Dickens's *Bleak House* (1853). But it wasn't until the 1860s, helped by the rise of the "sensation novel" (and the increasing numbers of real detectives in major cities), that detectives regularly took centre stage in novels. Female literary detectives made their first appearance too, in Andrew Forrester's *The Female Detective* (1864), though for some time, the most popular literary detective was Émile Gaboriau's Monsieur Lecoq of the Sûreté (*The Lerouge Case* (1866), etc), based on a real thief-turned-detective. Then, in 1868, came the first major full-length detective novel in English, Wilkie Collins's *The Moonstone* (1868), featuring the enigmatic – and fallible – Sergeant Cuff of Scotland Yard. There were still twenty years to go before the appearance of the world's most famous sleuth Sherlock Holmes (see p.289), but the literary detective already had a solid pedigree.

suspenseful excitement and intimate descriptions of the Victorian social world. Using a technique developed in *The Woman in White*, Collins employs a number of different narrators – the faithful butler, the prim evangelist, the outcast scientist, the bluff lawyer and eccentric police detective – who step up one by one, like witnesses in the dock, to carry the story forward. Collins had a passion for the sharp particularities of character, and his exuberantly detailed narrators don't just further the plot, they dramatize it in unexpected ways.

Below the surface of the novel lie a whole range of social issues, but Collins resists the urge to ride his favourite hobbyhorses. Perhaps as a result, *The Moonstone* is not only Collins's fastest narrative, but also his funniest. His unadorned style (so much plainer than that of Dickens) and deadpan comic timing produce – as a sort of added bonus for his readers – frequent moments of pure hilarity.

 Where to go next
No Name, 1862, Wilkie Collins
A novel which combines thrillerish, page-turning qualities with an evangelical interest in social issues – in this case the rights of non-married couples. Two sisters, disinherited after it is revealed that their parents were not married, fight to regain their fortune.

The Woman in White

1859–60, WILKIE COLLINS, ENGLISH

A sensational best-seller on publication (complete with its own range of merchandise including *Woman in White* perfume, cloaks and bonnets), Collins's novel has lost none of its power to entertain. Its superbly intricate plot, full of secrets, deceptions and sickening reversals of fortune, never slackens; and, in Marian Halcombe and Count Fosco, it contains two of the most mesmerizing characters in English fiction.

Late one night on a deserted London road, Walter Hartright encounters a frightened woman dressed in white, who talks – in a distracted, ominous way – of the very place in Cumberland to which Walter is bound as the newly appointed drawing master. Although he doesn't know it yet, she is the key to the mystery about to engulf him. At Limmeridge Hall, Walter is delighted by his two pupils, the delicately feminine Laura Fairlie and her mannish half-sister, Marian Halcombe. But their guardian, Laura's uncle Frederick Fairlie, is an effete hypochondriac, careless of the young women's futures, who does nothing to challenge the advances being made to Laura by the shady nobleman Sir Percival Glyde assisted by the suave and mysterious Italian Count

Fosco. Walter, who has already fallen in love with Laura, watches with horror as Glyde and Fosco close in on their prey. Only when he remembers the woman in white will Walter begin to unravel their secret intentions.

To bring out the natural drama of his highly complex plot, Collins devised an ingenious method of multiple narration, each of the principal protagonists – and quite a few of the minor ones – taking turns to move the narrative on with a variety of statements, diaries and letters. For such a fast-moving story, it engages surprisingly well with social issues of the day, including the proper roles of the sexes and the legal identity of women (incorporating,

Penguin

at one point, a wonderfully bitter outburst against men). Read another way, it tells the old story of good versus evil, at the heart of which is the mortal conflict – and mutual fascination – of Marian Halcombe, the rational and (Collins stresses) distinctly

There, in the middle of the broad, bright high-road, as if it had that moment sprung out of the earth or dropped from the heaven, stood the figure of a solitary Woman dressed from head to foot in white garments.

ugly woman of action, and the exquisitely sinister Count Fosco, with his messianic self-belief and dainty manners – a hypnotically charismatic Napoleonic villain of literally vast proportions.

Where to go next
Armadale, 1866, Wilkie Collins
An almost unbelievably convoluted plot featuring no fewer than five characters called Allan Armadale, murder, adultery, misplaced inheritances, shocking coincidences and bizarre accidents – the sensation novel that out-sensations them all.

Moll Flanders

1722, DANIEL DEFOE, ENGLISH

It is odd that a novel so much about deception should give such a strong impression of honesty, but Moll Flanders's unflinching account of her incest, bigamy and other crimes is one of the great self-revelations in fiction, all the more astonishing for being so artlessly told.

Candid, though not contemplative, steady rather than sensational, Moll is a plain-speaking narrator who, in lifelike fashion, remembers certain particulars "to a tittle", and passes over others without a mention. Like Robinson Crusoe, she is utilitarian rather than imaginative, with a good memory for the value of goods (mainly stolen), the bustle of action (in dimly lit streets, dubious inns and shady boarding houses) and the desperate business (often literally commercial) of relationships.

Was Twelve Year a Whore, five times a Wife (whereof once to her own brother), Twelve Year a Thief, Eight Year a Transported Felon in Virginia, at last grew Rich, liv'd Honest, and died a Penitent.

But necessity, not indulgence, is the keynote of her life. Born in Newgate Prison to a mother soon transported to Virginia, Moll always has to shift for herself. The tangled liaisons and marriages of her early life are motivated by her need for security, and it is poverty that drives her to crime in her later years. The second half of the book is remarkable for the knowledgeable detail it provides about an extraordinary variety of thefts and confidence tricks. At one point she even steals a horse (not knowing what to do with it, she gives it back). Utterly free from self-pity and sentimentality, even after she finds herself back in Newgate sentenced to death, her story retains its awkward purity, a welcome change from confessional novels with predictably unreliable narrators.

📖📖 **Where to go next**
Roxana, or *The Fortunate Mistress*, 1724, Daniel Defoe
Two years on from *Moll Flanders*, Defoe was treading similar ground with the history – written in the first person – of a woman who takes up prostitution, with considerable financial success, after being abandoned by her rakish husband.

Crime and Punishment

1865–66, FYODOR DOSTOEVSKY, RUSSIAN

The greatest of all crime novels is also one of the most original, written inside out, from the point of view of the murderer, the impoverished student Raskolnikov. It lacks nothing in tension or mystery, however: every chapter balances on a knife edge. Will Examining Magistrate Porfiry Petrovich discover the murderer's identity? Will Raskolnikov succumb to the irresistible urge to confess? As the plot races on, other questions become even more urgent: why did Raskolnikov commit the murder – and how must he atone for it?

OXFORD WORLD'S CLASSICS

FYODOR DOSTOEVSKY
CRIME AND PUNISHMENT

Oxford World's Classics

It is a novel of appalling shocks. The crime itself, a double axe murder, is sickeningly realistic: beginning with Raskolnikov daring himself to triumph Napoleon-style over his poverty, and ending with him in a fumbling panic butchering an old moneylender and her sister.

Dostoevsky's descriptive realism finds its most dramatic expression in the Petersburg slums and broken streets crowded with rag-and-bone men, drunken soldiers and prostitutes, where the tubercular poor die in blood-gushing fits in the gutter. The novel is filled with their voices, passionate and argumentative, as they spill out their life stories to anyone who will listen, tales of sickness and desire. In these monologues

> *He pulled the axe out, swung it up with both hands, hardly conscious of what he was doing, and almost mechanically, without putting any force behind it, let the butt-end fall on her head.*

and conversations the plots multiply. Raskolnikov argues violently with his sister's fiancé, Luzhin, who in turn tries to incriminate the young prostitute Sonia, befriended by Raskolnikov. The eccentric landowner Svidrigailov arrives in Petersburg to make a wild offer to Raskolnikov's sister. And the tricky investigator Porfiry Petrovich makes a habit of bumping into Raskolnikov to ask him a few innocent-seeming questions.

These dizzyingly psychological interrogations not only spin the plot in unexpected directions, but prompt larger questions about the nature of crime, punishment, society and the weirdness of relations between men and women. And as the novel intensifies towards the end, it breaks through into another dimension altogether: the spiritual one, as Raskolnikov seeks redemption.

Recommended translation
1953, Jessie Coulson, Oxford World's Classics

Where to go next
The Gambler, 1866, Fyodor Dostoevsky
Needing to settle his debts, Dostoevsky took a few weeks off from *Crime and Punishment* to write this short novel set in the gambling houses of "Roulettenburg". Money and sex are its twin themes, and its roller-coaster plot is perfectly appropriate to a novel about gambling (to which Dostoevsky himself was addicted).

The Name of the Rose

1980, UMBERTO ECO, ITALIAN

The medieval world of Eco's imagination is a terrifying place, a living Book of the Apocalypse, where the Devil, a vibrantly literal presence, goes busily among the corrupted, fomenting heresy and sin. Even in a quiet, well-ordered Italian abbey famous for its labyrinthine library, there is unrest. The body of a young illuminator, Adelmo of Otranto, is found below the walls of the Aedificium, the great symbolic building which houses the library. Needing help, the Abbot calls in William of Baskerville, an English Franciscan with a famously sharp if unconventional mind. What William finds is a monastery rife with fierce rivalries, bitter memories and a deadly secret which keeps drawing him back to the library and its hidden collection of forbidden books.

> 'It is a story of theft and vengeance among monks of scant virtue,' I cried dubiously. 'Because of a forbidden book, Adso. A forbidden book!' William replied.

There's no doubting Eco's erudition. His medieval detective story – with playful nods to Sherlock Holmes and Walpole's *The Castle of Otranto* – is a historical adventure of the mind: a luridly lit drama of clashing theological and philosophical ideas, set at a time when a wrong idea might send you to the stake. The humanist William is on dangerous ground, and must meet learning with learning in his frequent disputations with the monks of the abbey. Sometimes, especially in the novel's opening stages, these debates can be wearying; on other occasions – during a spectacularly frightening interrogation by the Papal Inquisitor, for instance – they generate terrific excitement. Towards its ingenious conclusion, as the inexplicable murders multiply and William runs out of time, the narrative accelerates and the book acquires real emotional power too.

Recommended edition
1983, William Weaver, Vintage Classics (UK), Harvest Books (US)

Where to go next
Foucault's Pendulum, 1988, Umberto Eco
Three friends perpetrating a harmless hoax about the Knights Templar find themselves caught up in a real conspiracy by a sinister secret society dedicated to the belief that descendants of the Knights are the true guardians of the Holy Grail.

Screen adaptation
The Name of the Rose, 1986, dir. Jean-Jacques Annaud
This clever adaptation of Eco's metaphysical thriller convincingly suggests the "otherness" of the medieval world while retaining a sense of the original's playful wit. As William of Baskerville, Sean Connery achieves a fine balance between gravitas and humanity – the mellow voice of reason opposing the authoritarian obscurantism of F. Murray Abraham's Inquisitor.

The L.A. Quartet

The Black Dahlia | The Big Nowhere |

L.A. Confidential | White Jazz

1987–92, JAMES ELLROY, AMERICAN

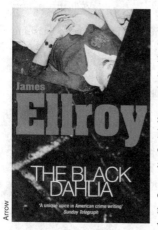

Arrow

Four ferocious, lurid novels of psycho-sexual murder and corruption together form one of the artistic high points in crime fiction – a hugely powerful and inventive narrative which brings to life the glamour and violence of 1950s Los Angeles, where crazy mobsters, crooked politicians, hopped-up hookers, hoodlums, snitches and out-of-control policemen fight for power and survival.

The crimes are horrific: women cut in half and drained of blood, men castrated by perverts wearing wolverine teeth. The investigations are even worse, with out-of-control policemen hellbent on bloody revenge. In Ellroy's novels, it always gets personal. His métier may be sex and violence, but his true subjects are love and pain. All his characters struggle with their demons. For sex-crime-obsessed Lt.

Bucky Bleichert, Howard-Hughes-bagman "Buzz" Meeks, uptight wonder-kid Chief Inspector Ed Exley, musclebound Bud White and Veronica-Lake-lookalike Lynn Bracken, the motto (the last line of the final book) is the same: "love me fierce in danger".

Journalistic nitroglycerine – scorching, scalding, burning hot revelations, the confessions of a crooked Los Angeles policeman on the run from the mob, the cops and his own violent past.

The four self-contained stories are united by these reappearing characters, the Los Angeles scene and Ellroy's radical style of delivery: a discordant amalgam of street slang and tabloid headlines – staccato bulletins from the killing fields. The action is similarly remorseless, skidding abruptly from riot to shake-down, from savage beating to sweaty sex. But though each of the novels focuses on a different crime (the torture of a young woman who the press christen the "Black Dahlia" or, in *L.A. Confidential*, a mass slaying at the Nite Owl coffeeshop), the wider subject is the institutionalized corruption of police and politicians. Most impressive of all, however, is Ellroy's dramatization of private obsessions: brutalized men ostensibly committing or solving crimes, but really seeking redemption through booze, money and violence.

Where to go next
American Tabloid, 1995, James Ellroy
The first novel in Ellroy's ongoing "Underworld USA" trilogy, *American Tabloid* is a high-octane mix of fictional and real-life characters and events, covering the period from 1958 to the eve of President Kennedy's assassination.

Screen adaptation
L.A. Confidential, 1997, dir. Curtis Hanson
Curtis Hanson's masterly version of the third instalment of the L.A. Quartet is unquestionably the best screen adaptation of an Ellroy novel so far. Excising several back stories and a host of minor characters, the film takes a cold, hard look at the sleaze and corruption of 50s L.A., evoking all the glitter and allure of the period without ever sliding into nostalgia.

That Awful Mess on Via Merulana

1957, CARLO EMILIO GADDA, ITALIAN

A bloody murder mystery, *That Awful Mess on Via Merulana* is a crime novel utterly unconfined by the genre. Mocking, allusive, pensive and cryptic, it is as verbally inventive as *Ulysses*, as ruminative as *In Search of Lost Time* (other Modernist classics to which it is often compared) but darker and more satirical than either.

Rome, March 1927. In the "palace of gold" at 219 Via Merulana, two crimes are committed: first, the Contessa Menegazzi is robbed at gunpoint of all her jewellery; then, a few days later, her neighbour Signora Liliana Balducci is found butchered in her dining room, her head half cut off. So begins the nightmare for Officer Francesco Ingravallo – a secret admirer of

> The world of the so-called verities, he philosophized, is merely a tissue of fairy tales: and sad dreams.
> So that only the mist of dreams and fairy tales can have the name of truth.

Signora Liliana. His investigations will take him into the darkest recesses of Mussolini's Rome, its brothels and sweatshops, and – in Ingravallo's imagination at least – other places and different eras of history, as the significance of the crimes deepens.

Mystification is common to crime novels, but Gadda – one of the bounciest, most unpredictable of writers – is more than usually dislocating; his sudden digressions swoop away from the plot to passionately evoke his beloved Rome or excoriate the fascists, in particular Mussolini ("the Turd").

Don't expect a fast, snappy read. Slow, sometimes hard to follow, *That Awful Mess* is rich and meandering, continually wrong-footing the reader, just as the crimes wrong-foot Ingravallo. Indeed, at the novel's conclusion, the detective's investigations are incomplete. The focus of the novel is elsewhere, on more urgent themes: the murderous sleaze of Mussolini's politics, History, Rome, and good and evil.

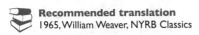

Recommended translation
1965, William Weaver, NYRB Classics

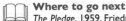

Where to go next
The Pledge, 1959, Friedrich Durrenmatt
Another very European literary crime novel (this one set in Switzerland), *The Pledge* is an engrossingly existential tale of a maverick detective obsessed with the notion that the wrong man has been found guilty of a child's murder.

Caleb Williams *or* Things as They Are

1794, WILLIAM GODWIN, ENGLISH

WILLIAM GODWIN
Caleb Williams

Penguin

Recently orphaned, the eighteen-year-old Caleb Williams is grateful to be taken into service by the nobleman Falkland, who is in need of a secretary. But Falkland turns out to be an unnerving employer, a man of high ideals given to unaccountable fits of violent melancholy. Worse is to come. Falkland has a guilty secret which his devoted servant feels compelled to investigate. When the truth is finally revealed, Williams becomes a victim of his master's persecution. Imprisoned on a trumped-up charge, he escapes only to be hunted across England. After falling in with a gang of robbers, he fetches up in London's East End where, disguised as a Jew, he earns an anonymous living as a writer. All this time, Falkland's "blood-hunters" – in particular the demonic Gines – are closing in on him.

Given that Godwin was one of the leading English radicals of his day (his breathtakingly subversive *Enquiry Concerning Political Justice*

called for no less than the overhaul of the entire English establishment), it is no surprise that his novel highlights themes of tyr-

My life has for sev-
eral years been a
theatre of calamity

anny and injustice. Like *Frankenstein* (written
by Godwin's daughter, Mary Shelley), *Caleb*
Williams can be read for its vigorous – sometimes relentless – social and political criticism.

Often didactic and written in a high-flown and melodramatic style,
the novel takes off after Caleb's imprisonment, when the thrillerish
action gathers momentum to a highly dramatic and largely unexpected denouement.

Where to go next
Memoirs of Emma Courtney, 1796, Mary Hays
Mary Hays was part of the radical circle of Godwin and his wife Mary
Wollstonecraft. Her epistolary novel, *Emma Courtney*, created a stir because of
its intimate revelations and apparent espousal of free love.

The Scarlet Letter
1850, NATHANIEL HAWTHORNE, AMERICAN

Hawthorne's masterpiece is a brooding, ambiguous book – an
account of a woman's challenge to patriarchal authority, or an
exploration of American Puritanism, or the triumph of a literary
credo, depending on your starting point. But it is also a mesmerizing, harrowing dramatization of the darker passions of guilt, hatred
and despair, and can be read, like a folk tale, for the sheer thrill of a
troubling story bewitchingly told.

In 1642 the scholar William Prynne arrives in Puritan Boston to
find his young wife Hester (whom he had sent on from England
ahead of him) condemned for adultery and displayed at the town
scaffold with a baby in her arms and the scarlet letter "A" pinned to
her breast. Who is the father? Assuming a new identity (of which
only Hester is aware), Prynne devotes his irresistible mental powers

to a vindictive search, which will end on the same spot, seven years later, in a cathartic scene both revelatory and destructive.

Hawthorne's rich, complicated sentences, now stately, now passionately swift, are sensitive to both the Puritans' self-controlled seriousness and their inward volatility. His perplexing motifs – the free, wild forest, Hester's innocently savage child Pearl, the beautifully embroidered letter "A" itself – are as hard to interpret as the crime and punishment at the heart of the story. Is Hester a martyr or fallen woman? Does her husband's quest for vengeance spring from love or hatred? In a passage from the book's long preface, the author muses on the way moonlight strangely illuminates the furniture in his house – as if in "neutral territory, somewhere between the real world and fairy-land, where the Actual and the Imaginary may meet". The same delicate and restless ambiguity is achieved in his novel, its great opposing themes – godliness and witchcraft, darkness and light, truth and lies, love and hatred, secrets and disclosures – seeming to flicker disturbingly from one state to the other as the story progresses to its bitter finale.

> *She will be a living sermon against sin, until the ignominious letter be engraved upon her tombstone.*

Where to go next
Mosses from an Old Manse, 1854, Nathaniel Hawthorne
Hawthorne's other novels tend to disappoint but his highly wrought short stories, with their themes of obsession, guilt and the supernatural, rival those of Poe for both intensity and weirdness.

Broken April

1982, ISMAIL KADARE, ALBANIAN

A tale of blood feuds in Albania between the wars, *Broken April* is at once barbarically realistic and eerily mythical: documentary history in the form of a folk tale.

Kanun, the code of customary law which governs life on the desolate High Plateau, enshrines the terrifying etiquette of the blood feud, a compulsory ritual of murder and revenge passed down through the generations. Compelled to kill Zef Kryeqyqe, who has killed his brother, Gjorg Berisha forfeits his own life in turn. According to the *Kanun*, he is allowed a truce of thirty days – lasting until the middle of April – before the Kryeqyqes can kill him. In the time left to him, he decides to go on a journey, a pointless "wandering" from inn to inn along the bleak and empty roads; and at one of these inns, he exchanges glances with a young woman, a stranger to the district.

'In no other country in the world can one see people on the road who bear the mark of death, like trees marked for felling.'

The High Plateau is a domain of doomed quests; life is primitive. According to the writer Bessian, who is honeymooning there, it is a place "half-real, half-imaginary" – the land of the dead, where people like Gjorg, whose lives are forfeit, aimlessly roam the roads or immure themselves in towers of refuge. Systematic oppression is an understandable theme for a writer living under a Communist regime, as Kadare was when he wrote this novel in 1978, but the real power of the novel is less political than universal. Kadare finds a haunting form for human relationships agonizingly constrained, played out in a zone of uncertain fate, where people seem always on the point of sudden change, and death waits.

Recommended translation
1990, John Hodgson, Vintage (UK), New Amsterdam Books (US)

Where to go next
The General of the Dead Army, 1963, Ismail Kadare
Kadare's other recognized masterpiece. An Italian general returns to Albania after World War II, to search for the bodies of Italian soldiers killed there in action.

The Trial

1925, FRANZ KAFKA, CZECH

Dead from tuberculosis at forty-one, Kafka left instructions that all his unpublished writings should be destroyed. His wishes were ignored, and *The Trial* was the first of his fictions to make him famous after his death. If "Kafkaesque" has become a jaded term referring loosely to the senseless but inescapable machinations of a faceless bureaucracy, *The Trial* has lost nothing of its twisted originality: an expressionist *tour de force*, eerie, enigmatic, and disturbingly funny.

"Someone must have been telling lies about Joseph K., for without having done anything wrong he was arrested one fine morning." The whole novel proceeds, with surreal logic, from this initial premise, recording the attempts of junior bank manager K to cope with an inexplicable criminal case brought against him.

The central accusation is never explained – and never challenged. In this, Joseph K's behaviour is as bizarre as that of the "Examining Magistrate", the "Advocate", or any of the other semi-abstract figures who persecute him. His constant, wiggling attempts to clear up misunderstandings remain futile, for he dwells on the wrong misunderstandings, and the larger case against him moves forward.

Like a malevolent species of children's literature, *The Trial* records the terrified helplessness of a childlike character in an unfathomable adult world, where danger and sex lurk in every situation. K's shadowy encounters with a sequence of depraved, deformed girls,

> '*I am not guilty,' said K.; 'it's a misunderstanding. And if it comes to that, how can any man be guilty?' 'That is true,' said the priest, 'but that's how all guilty men*

alternately seductive and hostile, and other magnificently unsettling scenes, such as K's discovery of the "Whipper" in the lumber room of his bank or the savage denouement in a quarry at the edge of town, show Kafka to be a great set-piece specialist. Though left incomplete at his death, all the elements are in place – including inappropriately hilarious dialogue and bizarre imagery – to create the most suffocatingly disturbing nightmare in literature.

 Recommended translation
1935, Willa and Edwin Muir, Everyman's Library

 Where to go next
The Castle, 1926, Franz Kafka
Kafka's other unquestionably great novel, also concerning a character called "K", a land-surveyor who is summoned to a castle but finds himself continuously prevented from keeping his appointment by the very officials responsible for the summons.

 Screen adaptation
The Trial, 1963, dir. Orson Welles
One of the less feted of Welles's films is, nevertheless, a colossal achievement. Filmed with the meagrest of funds, in Paris and Zagreb, Welles plunders the conventions of *film noir* and horror to create a genuinely nightmarish experience. Antony Perkins plays the hapless protagonist caught up in shadowy world in which justice seems an infinitely flexible concept.

Darkness at Noon

1940, ARTHUR KOESTLER, HUNGARIAN

Koestler was one of those "new" writers of the mid-twentieth century, part-novelist, part-journalist, who were always dashing from one hot spot to another, sending back vivid despatches from the war zone. One of his great strengths was his ability to convey the immediacy and authenticity of his subjects; another was his grasp of big ideas, the sweeping political currents of history. Both these strengths are present in this, his best-known book, which fictionally recreates the experiences of the victims of the Moscow Show Trials, many of whom had been personally known to Koestler.

Arrested in the middle of the night, ex-Commissar of the People, Rubashov, knows immediately what is in store for him. In his time, he has sent others to the same fate; now it is his turn. In prison, his interrogators begin to work on him, first Ivanov, ironically one of the ex-colleagues he had earlier betrayed, then Gletkin, an example of the new generation of mechanically efficient interrogators, who believes the extortion of a confession to be simply a matter of breaking a man's constitution.

> *I have thought and acted as I had to; I destroyed people whom I was fond of, and gave power to others I did not like. History put me where I stood.*

In fact, the horror of the book comes not from descriptions of physical beatings, but from the grim logic of a regime requiring sacrifice in the name of History. Koestler's handling of the debates between Rubashov and his interrogators is a *tour de force*, never dull, always taut and dramatic. Ultimately, Rubashov is imprisoned, and condemned, by ideas – the mind in its skull as lonely and terrified as the prisoner in his cell. The effect is heightened by Koestler's brilliant evocation of the prison itself: Rubashov's stark cell with its Judas-hole and can of faeces in the corner; the hopeless messages tapped out between prisoners; and the eerie drumming of hands on doors, which tells the prisoners when the execution guards are approaching.

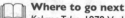 **Where to go next**
Kolyma Tales, 1978, Varlam Shalamov
Kolyma Tales is an equally searing indictment of the horrors of the Soviet system. Shalamov spent many years in a Siberian labour camp, and these stories recount the everyday cruelties and humiliations in a way that is all the more effective for its cool objectivity.

Dirty Snow

1948, GEORGES SIMENON, BELGIAN

Written in a brutal style, and dark beyond *noir*, *Dirty Snow* is a horrifyingly intimate account of squalor and violence, the tale of a juvenile delinquent discovering himself through robbery, murder and rape.

For Frank, who was nineteen, to kill his first man was another loss of virginity hardly any more disturbing than the first.

One winter during wartime, in a country under occupation, the black market is booming: the bars are full of shady characters drinking champagne with foreign officers, while the rest try to keep themselves warm in their unheated tenements. Young Frank Friedmaier, a petty thief living in his mother's brothel, is comfortable enough – he has flash

The best of Maigret

Commissaire Maigret is Simenon's most celebrated creation and one of the most famous of all literary detectives. A heavily built and somewhat irascible character, he relies as much on intuition as on the accumulation of evidence, chewing on his trademark pipe as he ponders the motivation of the criminals he is pursuing. Dedicated to his work, he lives with his wife (usually referred to as simply Madame Maigret) in a Paris apartment on the Boulevard Richard-Lenoir. The detective's first appearance was in 1931 (in *The Case of Peter the Lett*), his last in 1972 (in *Maigret and Monsieur Charles*). Between these dates Simenon produced a further seventy-three Maigret novels and twenty-eight stories. The following are ten of the very best novels available in English.

- *Lock 14* (Le Charretier de "la Providence"), 1931
- *The Yellow Dog* (Le Chien jaune), 1931
- *Maigret at the Crossroads* (La Nuit du Carrefour), 1931
- *The Bar on the Seine* (La Guinguette à deux sous), 1932
- *The Madman of Bergerac* (Le Fou de Bergerac), 1932
- *The Hotel Majestic* (Les Caves du Majestic), 1942
- *My Friend Maigret* (Mon ami Maigret), 1949
- *Maigret and the Young Girl* (Maigret et la jeune morte), 1954
- *Maigret in Court* (Maigret aux assises), 1960
- *Maigret and the Ghost* (Maigret et le fantôme), 1964

clothes, all the food he can eat, and privileges with his mother's girls – but he wants more. He wants to make his mark. His casual murder of a member of the Occupation Police sets up an unexpectedly self-destructive momentum of crime and abuse, leading him to a final trial of agonizing endurance and stark self-knowledge.

Simenon's style is extremely laconic, he famously limited his vocabulary to 2,000 words. It is also razor-sharp, with short, stabbing descriptions of brothels, nightclubs and movie theatres and snatches of banal conversation full of awkward silences. Characters are created out of one or two snagging details, like the rapist Kromer, with his "thick, coarse skin, like an orange's", or the prostitute Bertha, rubbing the marks of the sheets off her body as she talks to herself. But for all the emphatic objectivity of his language, the book's great power is interior: inside the mind of Frank, the teenage killer, whose arrogance, self-disgust, sudden rages and circling obsessions are all utterly convincing.

Recommended translation
1951, Marc Romano and Louise Varese, NYRB Classics

Where to go next
The Man Who Watched the Trains Go By, 1946, Georges Simenon
Though Simenon's novels featuring the detective Maigret are more famous, his "psychological" novels are brilliantly powerful. In this one, a solidly middle-class man who loses his savings when the company he works for collapses becomes a criminal psychopath playing a murderous game of cat and mouse with the police.

Comedy and satire

The uses of comedy are many, but the varied novels chosen here have one thing in common. Zany, uproarious, gentle, profound, bewildering or just plain wicked, they all provoke laughter.

Of course, the reader may be crying at the same time. Some of the greatest comic novels are tragic too. In his painfully hilarious *A Handful of Dust*, Evelyn Waugh plots the utter destruction of a perfectly well-meaning man; Graham Greene's Cold War comedy *Our Man in Havana* features murder, torture and deceit. In the hands of a great writer, comedy deepens the pain.

It also sharpens anger. The great satirists – Gogol from Russia, Galdós from Spain, Smollett and Peacock from England – are bitingly funny in ridiculing social pretension and exposing political corruption. Comedy gives them licence to let rip. And letting rip is the speciality of those wayward geniuses like Lawrence Sterne and Flann O'Brien, whose topsy-turvy entertainments give such dizzying original perspectives on the world.

This is not to say that comedy doesn't have its gentler side too. The irresistible *Pickwick Papers* captures the sheer fun of life, and furthermore offers one of those touching friendships (between Mr Pickwick and Sam Weller) that so frequently occur in comic fiction. Indeed, the great comic characters are among the immortals: Wodehouse's Psmith, Svevo's Zeno and Roth's Portnoy will give pleasure as long as fiction is read.

Illywhacker

1985, PETER CAREY, AUSTRALIAN

Peter Carey, like his novel's hero Herbert Badgery, has the gift of the gab. Badgery is a fake, but Peter Carey is the real thing, and *Illywhacker* (Australian for a con man) is a gleeful farrago of untruths which narrates a series of picaresque adventures, tells an extraordinary family saga and, in the process, invents Australia.

The 139-year-old Badgery killed his father back in 1896 (he says) and was brought up by a Chinaman who taught him how to disappear. But it is his charm and his lies that have carried him in such lively fashion through life as an unpredictable aviator, unorthodox car salesman, frankly terrible stage performer, confidence trickster extraordinaire, and honest lover of unpredictable women.

> I knew, that day, that God is a glutton for grief, love, regret, sadness, joy too, everything, remorse, guilt – it is all steak and eggs to him. But what am I saying? There is no God. There is only me, Herbert Badgery.

Carey is a spellbinding narrator of tall tales, a master of the opening hook, the brilliant digression, the teasing delay and the marvellous payoff. There are some heart-stopping scenes with snakes and goannas, and a charming if extremely risky act of love on the roof of a house. But *Illywhacker* is as much about inner stories as outer ones. Like the men, the strong-minded female characters are fantasists, pursuing their own dreams of love and freedom – Phoebe McGrath, heavily pregnant with Badgery's child, wanting only to fly planes and write (awful) poems, or Leah Goldstein, wife to a Marxist intellectual, Badgery's lover, on stage performing the emu dance. Both comedy and tragedy result. Not the least of Carey's achievements is that such a funny book also contains scenes of devastating sadness. For a country founded on the lie that it was no one's land before white men arrived, it feels like a national history.

Where to go to next
Oscar and Lucinda, 1988, Peter Carey
Oscar and Lucinda tells the story of a love affair in the 1860s between an Oxford seminarian addicted to gambling and a Sydney heiress obsessed with glass. Full of tremendous scenes and brilliant writing, it is an unfailingly entertaining enquiry into both Australian history and human nature.

The Pickwick Papers

1837, CHARLES DICKENS, ENGLISH

The unique early Dickens style, in all its breadth and breezy humour, is at its zestful best in the often overlooked *Pickwick Papers*. Dickens's later novels may be more socially engaged and more brilliantly plotted, but none captures the glorious novelty of life like *Pickwick*. A sort of inspired reportage, it animates the ordinary Victorian world – of London streets and village greens, inn-yards and turnpikes – and populates it with a dizzyingly varied cast of characters, from gentlemen to boot-blacks, and matriarchs to serving-maids. At its heart, kindly and curious, is Moses Pickwick, a gentleman of means devoted to the quainter minutiae of life, which he and his irrepressible cockney

> 'I shall never regret having devoted the greater part of two years to mixing with different varieties and shades of human character, frivolous as my pursuit of novelty may have appeared to many.'

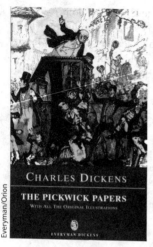

servant Sam Weller tour the south of England to find. Out of the inevitable adventures and incidents, two main plot lines emerge: Pickwick's mission to expose the scoundrel Jingle, and his attempts to clear his own name in the lawsuit brought against him for false promises of matrimony.

Good-naturedness gives the book a friendly glow. Though sometimes sentimental (and frequently facetious), Dickens is never slack or trite. His comic observations have real fizz, his dialogue is colourful and sharp, and the famous scenes – Christmas at Dingley Dell, the cricket match with All-Muggleton, the election at Eatanswill – are uproariously entertaining. It all might seem too effervescent if the novel didn't also have a sombre side: Pickwick's persecution by unscrupulous lawyers taking him from his parties and dinners and leading him eventually to the Fleet debtors' prison, to rub shoulders with life's losers. So the lights of good humour are balanced by the "dark shadows on the earth", and Pickwick's relationship with Sam Weller, already touching, develops into one of the great servant-master relationships in literature.

Where to go next
Bleak House, 1853, Charles Dickens
One of Dickens's mature masterpieces, centred around the interminable lawsuit of Jarndyce versus Jarndyce and featuring a splendid array of characters – from the sinister lawyer Tulkinghorn to the first detective in English fiction, Mr Bucket.

That Bringas Woman

1884, BENITO PÉREZ GALDÓS, SPANISH

It is a pity that Galdós is not better known in the English-speaking world. Less intense than Balzac, less theatrical than Dickens, he is as shrewd and observant as either, with natural gifts of comedy. His masterpiece is the massive *Fortunata and Jacinta*, but *That Bringas Woman* is perhaps a better place to start, a short, intelligently mocking tale of trivial obsessions among the genteel snobs of Madrid, beautifully plotted, vividly detailed and, in the end, deeply resonant.

Rosalía Bringas's passion for clothes leads her into debt, a fact she has to hide from her penny-pinching husband, an official at the Royal Palace. Debt leads to borrowing, first from friends, then from loan sharks. Secrecy leads to intrigue, helplessness to desperation, until eventually, to redeem the worsening situation, Rosalía is forced to choose between calamitous humiliations. In doing so, she discovers hidden truths about Spain, her family, her friends and herself.

The chatty, knowing tone is established at once by the narrator, himself a bit player in the story. The characters, solidly distinct but never overdone, are drawn from life, and are revealed primarily through their relationships: the smooth but insubstantial politician Manuel del Pez, obsessively anxious Francisco Bringas and Rosalía herself

> This place is a sort of ongoing carnival, where the poor dress as rich people. It's sham, ma'am, pure sham; there are families who survive all year on nothing but potato omelettes just so they can dress well and go to the theatre.

(who fluctuates wildly between abject self-accusation and aggressive preening), combine brilliantly in a shifting dynamic of mutual support and antagonism. Individual scenes – including a toe-curling showdown between the desperate Rosalía and an affluent but disreputable relation – are short, exact and often hilarious. Artfully set against the events of the 1868 Revolution, they also, with polite severity, hold up a mirror to Spanish public life.

Recommended translation
1996, Catherine Jagoe, Everyman Classics

Where to go next
Fortunata and Jacinta, 1887, Benito Pérez Galdós
Set in Madrid, this sprawling, panoramic masterpiece focuses on the relation-ship – across the class divide – between two women both in love with the charming, pampered and self-indulgent Juanito.

The Polyglots

1925, WILLIAM GERHARDIE, ENGLISH

The comic laureate of anxiety, William Gerhardie has been almost lost to sight, but no other English writer of the 1920s – not even

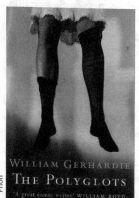

Evelyn Waugh, who venerated him – was funnier or more penetrating, and no one produced anything quite like Gerhardie's droll but tender celebra-tions of human foibles.

Polyglots, those people who speak many languages but seem at home in none, are his natural subject. His story is set in Russia during the civil war that followed the Revolution of 1917. The narrator, Georges Diabologh (born in Japan, brought up in Russia, educated in England) returns to Vladivostok as a British military attaché, where he encounters his polyglottal extended family: English Aunt Berthe, Belgian Uncle Emmanuel, Uncle Lucy (officially denationalized by the Revolution), and his many (mostly Russian) cousins – a chaotic collection of eccentrics. But most of all he encounters the alluring Sylvia-Ninon, a law unto herself.

All are in exile, their lives ruined by bankruptcy, breakdowns and death. Yet the novel is wonderfully funny. Gerhardie resembles a comic Kafka (producing mind-boggling descriptions of the utterly incompetent War Office) or a Chekhov who can't resist sending himself up. A scene in an expensive restaurant to which Diabologh rashly takes Sylvia-Ninon is hilarious. A scene in which Uncle Emmanuel weeps inarticulately for his lost son is agonizing. The miracle of *The Polyglots* is not only that two such scenes can appear in the same book, but that they can seem to complement each other perfectly.

> *I am a serious young man, an intellectual. I am so constituted that at these moments when it would seem most proper to expand, to drink life purple, to invoke brass trumpets, I suddenly lose heart.*

Where to go next
Futility, 1922, William Gerhardie
The novel that first made Gerhardie's name has an almost identical backdrop to *The Polyglots*. Less funny than the earlier novel, it is more atmospheric, with the author paying obvious homage to Chekhov by centring the narrative around three beautiful sisters.

Cold Comfort Farm

1932, STELLA GIBBONS, ENGLISH

Like the Christmas panto or Monty Python, *Cold Comfort Farm* has become an English institution. Beginning as a hilarious send-up of the excessively earthy fiction of rural life by such writers as D.H. Lawrence and Mary Webb, it rapidly developed into a finely created comic world of its own, with uniquely bizarre characters, sparklingly funny scenes and an arch prose style bristling with quotable phrases.

Planning to live off her relatives, the recently orphaned but self-assured Flora Poste invites herself to the ancestral farm of her cousins, the Starkadders of Howling, Sussex. On arrival, she sees at once

STELLA GIBBONS
Cold Comfort Farm

that the prospects for a tidy-minded, metropolitan person like herself are not good. Sin-obsessed Amos thinks only of his preaching at the Church of the Quivering Brethren; Urk divides his time between the fey Elfine and his beloved water-voles; sex-god Seth enjoys himself "mollocking" down in the village; while Great Aunt Ada, who saw "something nasty in the woodshed", hasn't left her room for twenty years. Undeterred, Flora determines to take them all in hand.

Part of the fun lies in the knowing manipulation of the clash between opposites – city and country, old and new, flippant and superstitious. The twisting plot embroils all the characters, as Flora ("Miss Interference") bossily reforms everyone, deftly ridding them of their unsavoury obsessions and ridiculous dreams and giving them what – though they didn't know it – they really wanted all along. But the novel wouldn't be half such fun if Gibbons didn't

'The cows are barren and the sows are farren and the King's Evil and the Queen's Bane and the Prince's Heritage ravages our crops. 'Cos why? 'Cos there's a curse on us, Robert Poste's child.'

have perfect pitch for zanily rustic dialogue and a pitiless genius for comic timing. Wickedly alert and ironic, the novel succeeds by virtue of sheer fun.

Where to go next
Precious Bane, 1924, Mary Webb
Though this dark tale of farming folk is thought to be one of the main targets of Gibbons's mockery, it is actually a powerful and deeply moving story in its own right.

Screen adaptation
Cold Comfort Farm, 1995, dir. John Schlesinger
Made for BBC TV but released as a feature in the US, this rollicking version
occasionally coarsens the subtlety of Gibbons's humour. An ensemble piece
in which the actors appear to be competing for the most outrageous accent
(with Ian McKellen taking the prize as the Bible-bashing Amos), it's all held
together by Kate Beckinsale's appropriately controlled Flora Poste.

Dead Souls

1842, NIKOLAY GOGOL, RUSSIAN

Gogol is a raw and primitive master, one of those unnerving writers
capable of transforming life into fiction without benefit of the usual
filters of reflection, style and order. *Dead Souls*, his masterpiece, is a
brilliantly comic adventure distorted by anarchic digressions, gloriously
unnecessary detail and obsessive soliloquizing on the theme of "poor,
disordered" Russia. If it all seems unsustainable, it's because it was.
After completing the first part, Gogol collapsed under the twin pressures of literary ambition and religious
mania. He burned Part Two at least
twice, and what remains of it is more
or less a recantation of all the things
that makes Part One so extraordinary.

The adventure of Part One revolves
around the figure of Chichikov, a
smooth-talking swindler with a bizarre

*Chichikov's purchases
became the talk of the
town. Rumours, surmises
and opinions as to the
profitability of purchasing
peasants for resettlement
were the order of the day.*

plan to get rich quick. In the nineteenth century, Russian landowners
owned serfs (or "souls"), who were registered at periodic censuses.
When serfs died they remained registered until the following census,
and landowners continued to pay tax on them. Chichikov's idea was
simple: buy these dead but administratively extant souls at a fraction
of the cost of living ones, and raise a large mortgage on the strength
of his apparently impressive holdings of serfs.

But in Gogol's anarchic world, Chichikov's crazy scheme meets with equally crazy responses from the people he tries to do business with. A doubtful widow begins to believe that her dead serfs may be useful after all. A stubborn landowner demands top prices because his dead serfs were such good workers when alive. A compulsive gambler wants to stake all his dead serfs on a game of chess. Each new encounter is hilariously frustrating, and time after time Chichikov climbs back in his carriage to try his luck elsewhere. The carriage travelling across the vast Russian landscape becomes a poignant motif, hinting at vast failures and ambitions, and ending with the weird image of Russia itself as a carriage, wheels furiously spinning, going nowhere.

 Recommended translation
2004, Robert A. Maguire, Penguin Classics

 Where to go next
Collected Tales, Nikolay Gogol
The fine, recent translation by Richard Pevear and Larissa Volokhonsky contains both Gogol's early folk-style tales and his later more famous fantastical stories, such as "The Nose" and "The Overcoat".

Our Man in Havana
1958, GRAHAM GREENE, ENGLISH

Seedy, pessimistic novels of guilt and failure such as *The Power and the Glory* or *The Heart of the Matter* may have made his reputation, but Greene was also a natural, sprightly writer of what he called "entertainments", the funniest of which is *Our Man in Havana*, an outrageous, tense comedy of the British Secret Service during the Cold War. Like many of Greene's novels, it begins with a simple, striking premise: what would happen if a perfectly ordinary man – a vacuum-cleaner salesman, for instance – were recruited by the Secret Service?

At the height of the Cold War, the British Government is desperate to establish a local agent in Cuba – expense no object. Mr

340

Wormold's vacuum-cleaner franchise is not doing well; he could do with the money. But how is he, a humble shopkeeper, to hire sub-agents, obtain information, send reports? As his philosophizing alcoholic friend, Dr Hasselbacher, says, "all you need is a little imagination".

Graham Greene
Our Man in Havana
With an introduction by Christopher Hitchens

Vintage

The novel is a master-class in plot, suspenseful and romping, drawing in a dozen (expertly drawn) characters to play their parts: Carter, the bluff, uptight agent working for the other side; Police Chief Captain Segura, the "Red Vulture", who carries a cigarette case made of human skin; and Wormold himself, one of life's innocents, who learns the habit of inventing, and reinvents himself in the process.

The usual Greene themes are here – doubt and belief, the betrayal of romance – but they are lightly done. More serious, and chilling, are the violent consequences of clandestine politics, which Greene carefully exposes: Hasselbacher needlessly murdered in his favourite bar, Captain Segura politely explaining the etiquette of torture.

> *He wondered how one recruited an agent. It was difficult for him to remember exactly how Hawthorne had recruited him – except that the whole affair had begun in a lavatory, but surely that was not an essential feature.*

But the light touch prevails, absurdity triumphs, and Greene proves himself to be one of the great comic novelists.

Where to go next
The Power and the Glory, 1940, Graham Greene
Famous story of a whisky priest on the run in communist Mexico during the

persecution of the Church, written, Greene said, to a thesis: that a woefully inadequate man could triumphantly fulfil his sacred office.

 Screen adaptation
Our Man in Havana, 1959, dir. Carol Reed
Filmed in Cuba just after Castro seized power, this is a highly enjoyable adaptation of Greene's espionage spoof, despite the fact that the blackness of the humour is diluted and not all the casting works. Alec Guinness does well as the unassuming Wormold but is upstaged by the suavely camp Noel Coward as Hawthorne and the larger-than-life Ernie Kovacs as Captain Segura.

At Swim-Two-Birds

1939, FLANN O'BRIEN, IRISH

At Swim-Two-Birds was first published on the eve of World War II. It sold badly, all stock was destroyed in an air raid on Dublin, and it remained forgotten until a speculative reissue in 1960 suddenly established it as a masterpiece. To label it an "experimental" novel would be true but unjust. To shelve it under "humour" would be to sell it short. It belongs in a genre of its own, idiosyncratic, ribald, learned, and very, very funny.

One beginning and one ending for a book was a thing I did not agree with. A good book may have three openings entirely dissimilar and inter-related only in the prescience of the author, or for that matter one hundred times as many endings.

In between prolonged periods in bed and the pub, a student in Dublin is fecklessly trying to write a novel. His novel is about a novel-writing publican who compels his characters to live with him in the Red Lion Hotel. These characters include: John Furriskey, a man born at the age of twenty-five "with a memory but without a personal experience to account for it"; the Pooka MacPhellimey, "a member of the devil class"; the giant Finn MacCool; the insane bird-king Sweeny; the cow-punchers of old Dublin, Shorty Andrews and Slug Willard; Jem Casey, the "Poet of the Pick"; and assorted others.

The result is inspired madness, held together by sustained invention, buoyancy of spirit and, above all, O'Brien's rarefied comic style. Crazy parodies of Irish legends mix happily with beautiful evocations (rainy streets, seedy pubs, golden talk) of 1930s Dublin. There is more than a hint of despair below the brilliant surface (and violence keeps breaking out), but the overall effect is joyous, and the Pooka MacPhellimey is, quite simply, the most delightfully courteous incarnation of evil in all literature.

Penguin

📖 **Where to go next**
The Third Policeman, 1968, Flann O'Brien
More comic genius in a tale about policemen turning into their bicycles (they ride them so often), and a killing in which the murderer is haunted not only by his victim but by his own soul, whom he calls "Joe". It was published some thirty years after it was written.

Nightmare Abbey

1818, THOMAS LOVE PEACOCK, ENGLISH

Like P.G. Wodehouse, Peacock wrote a pure and fantastic form of satire, creating his own sealed societies of absurdity in which the dominant ideas of his day received their most ridiculous expression. Though he was the wielder of an exact and punishing style, he had the irreverent sympathy of all great humorists, and his novels – of which *Nightmare Abbey* is the best – are both scrupulous records of contemporary debate and master-classes in deadpan comedy.

Close associate of many of the English Romantics, Peacock took the opportunity in *Nightmare Abbey* to satirize his poetical friends: Shelley (who appreciated the joke) is Scythrop, a dreamer of "deep schemes for a thorough repair of the crazy fabric of human nature", caught between two women; Lord Byron becomes Mr Cypress, a poet who, having quarrelled with his wife, finds it necessary to leave the country; and Coleridge is Mr Flosky, a transcendentalist utterly opposed to plain speaking. The action takes place simultaneously on two planes: the intellectual (via highly mannered dinner-table debates) and the realistic (slapstick farce), and the distinctive power and charm of the novel comes from their illuminating juxtaposition. Against expectations, the sublime Gothic abbey, with its hidden chambers and ruined towers, is the setting for the most irritatingly humdrum scenes of domestic life, and the most decisive characters prove to be not the loquacious men, but two feisty women: intellectual Celinda, on the run from her father, and manipulative Marionetta.

> 'It is the fashion to be unhappy. The art of being miserable for misery's sake has been brought to great perfection in our days.'

 Where to go next
Northanger Abbey, 1817, Jane Austen
Written almost twenty years before its publication, this is a hugely enjoyable romantic satire on the Gothic novel and the perils of taking what you read too seriously.

Exercises in Style

1947, RAYMOND QUENEAU, FRANCE

So odd is this book that its first critics saw it as an attempt to "demolish literature". Queneau – poet, novelist, philosopher and mathematician – responded by humbly claiming he had only intended it to act as a literary "rust-remover".

The premise is simple: a brief and unimportant incident on a bus in Paris is described in ninety-nine different ways. In a sense, this is a novel with three characters and ninety-nine different narrators. Its inspiration is Bach's *The Art of Fugue*, in which a slight theme gives rise to almost endless variations. Like that piece of music, *Exercises in Style* displays ingenuity, wit, fascination and joyousness in its exploration of the different ways of describing something. It is also a great work of comedy. The pieces are always sharp, mostly light and witty, and never overdone. Many, like "Opera English" (a Gilbert and Sullivan rip-off), "Blurb", "Cockney", "Tactile", "Hesitation" and "Official Letter" are quite simply laugh-out-loud funny.

New Directions

Rhyming Slang: I see a chap in the bus with a huge bushel and peck and a ridiculous titfer on his loaf

Abusive: The most bastardly of these bastards was a pustulous creature with a ridiculously long windpipe

Despite Queneau's lightness of touch, the book has its obvious technical side, showing an interest in rhetorical forms ("Apostrophe", "Reported Speech", "Cross-Examination"), hard-core linguistic techniques ("Apheresis", "Apocope", "Syncope") and even mathematical game-playing ("Permutations by Groups of 2, 3, 4 and 5 Letters"). Above all, Queneau is interested in language as it is spoken, the ways in which speech frees language from conventions of style, spelling and vocabulary. If only those lessons could be learned by writers, he says, language would soar away like a butterfly from its historical cocoon.

Recommended translation
1958, Barbara Wright, John Calder (UK), New Directions (US)

Where to go next
Zazie in the Metro, 1959, Raymond Queneau
Another linguistic *tour de force* about the adventures of a foul-mouthed country girl on a visit to her Uncle Gabriel (a female impersonator) in Paris.

Portnoy's Complaint

1969, PHILIP ROTH, AMERICAN

A taboo-exploding book about "whacking off", *Portnoy's Complaint* is also a ragingly heartfelt description of Jewish life in America and a jaw-droppingly vivid exposé of the secret lives of respectable teenage boys everywhere. It is, furthermore, very, very funny.

On his analyst's couch, 33-year-old Alexander Portnoy pours out his sexual angst. The brilliant, cosseted child of a hyper-protective Jewish family (and now Assistant Commissioner for The City of New York Commission on Human Opportunity), he has graduated from

Doctor Spielvogel, this is my life, my only life, and I'm living it in the middle of a Jewish joke! I am the son in the Jewish joke – only it ain't no joke!

masturbation to perversion and finally to impotence, his whole life a sexual tragi-comedy. But his outpouring of childhood and adult memories reveal many subjects apart from the obvious one: his overwhelming mother with her ceaseless advice about peeing, hamburgers and *goyische* girls; his permanently constipated father overworked by the "Firm of Worry, Fear and Frustration"; his lover The Monkey; Jewishness; baseball; adolescence; and the bewildering meanings of lust.

One of the book's glories is the Rothian voice: insistent, baffled, outraged, despairing and insanely funny. Another is Roth's sheer rebelliousness: this is a book which defiantly, even joyously, takes up subjects avoided by other writers, and juggles with them. His let-it-all-hang-out analysis of great, big subjects (like The Jewish Momma) and furtive, little subjects (like the sexual uses of raw liver) provide constant astonishment. Finally, in a book which concludes with a protracted scream followed by a "punchline", Roth's comedy is always close to seriousness, his jokes springing double-edged from the agonies of dissatisfaction.

 **Where to go next**
The Counterlife, 1986, Philip Roth
A dizzying exploration of the boundaries of fiction and fact, featuring Roth's alter ego and greatest fictional hero, Nathan Zuckerman. Jumping between America, England and Israel, the novel takes in – among other subjects – the nature of Judaism, family life, and facing up to one's own mortality.

The Expedition of Humphrey Clinker

1771, TOBIAS SMOLLETT, ENGLISH

For anyone who wants to know what life was like in the eighteenth century, here it is: a blazingly vivid and varied fictional travelogue of Georgian Britain, from the corrupt luxury of Bath to the bracing simplicity of the Highlands and back again.

We should sometimes increase the motion of the machine, to unclog the wheels of life; and now and then take a plunge among the waves of excess, in order to case-harden the constitution.

The tour is undertaken by Matthew Bramble, a cynical but kindly gentleman of Monmouthshire. With him goes a retinue of relatives and servants: his manhunting spinster sister Tabitha, his sentimental niece Liddy, his facetious nephew Jery and gossipy servant Win Jenkins. Each of them writes home to tell the news of their travels, contributing to an overlapping correspondence that builds into a gazetteer of places and people written in every possible tone from sharp sarcasm to uplifting enthusiasm.

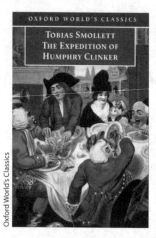

Plot continuity is half-heartedly provided by an intermittent love affair of Liddy's and the changing fortunes of a servant picked up en route, the foolish but saintly Humphrey Clinker. But the novel's real power is descriptive. Smollett anatomizes the places visited by his characters (London, for instance, where "all is tumult and hurry", or Durham, "a confusing heap of stones") and provides exact and hilarious descriptions of the people living there (the "insipid animals" of Bath or Yorkshiremen with their famous "arrogant civility"). Along the way he finds time to rage against a hundred different evils of the day, many strangely contemporary, such as factory farming and the dangerous freedom of the press ("a national evil"). Smollett's last and best novel is a vibrantly smart and opinionated record of an age.

Where to go next
The Adventures of Roderick Random, 1748, Tobias Smollett
Energetic if cartoonish satire of eighteenth-century England, in which the apparently unheroic Roderick Random battles to survive a succession of calamities.

The Life and Opinions of Tristram Shandy

1760, LAURENCE STERNE, IRISH

There are few novels so bizarre as *Tristram Shandy*, a book of neverending digressions, in which the Preface appears near the middle (about the same time as the birth of the narrator) and the death of one of the central characters (marked by two totally black pages) at the very beginning. Several (short) sections are in Latin, others are apparently censored, one whole chapter is advertised as missing, and several more belong, according to the author, to other books. The reader is addressed sometimes as "gentle reader", more frequently as "madam", and is often given peremptory instructions: "Shut the door!" or "Don't answer me rashly!" The reader's inevitable question – "What's the point?" – is anticipated and answered by Sterne himself: the point is to inspire "the more convulsive elevation and depression of the diaphragm". In other words, laughter.

Digressions, incontestably, are the sunshine – they are the life, the soul of reading – take them out of this book for instance – you might as well take the book along with them.

Tristram Shandy, the narrator and nominally the hero of the novel, features remarkably little; his recollections focus mainly on a circle of relatives and friends, including his philosophical father, the waggish Parson Yorick (a self-portrait of Sterne), Uncle Toby, the injured veteran of the Siege of Namur, his admirer the Widow Wadam and his faithful companion, the prolix Corporal Trim. But their misadventures are continuously interrupted by Shandy's digressions and shaggy-dog stories: something more interesting is always popping into his mind, new topics are excitedly introduced, dropped and picked up again, thirty or forty pages later, subtly altered. Over everything hovers the problem of death, and the whole virtuoso performance is peppered with dizzying jokes about weighty issues, such as time or "reality", and great disputations about trivial matters. What could be more human?

Where to go next
A Sentimental Journey Through France and Italy, 1768, Laurence Sterne
Revealingly autobiographical and largely plotless, *A Sentimental Journey* is narrated by the engaging Parson Yorick who recounts his adventures and encounters with assorted travellers in the form of a rambling travelogue.

Screen adaptation
A Cock and Bull Story, 1995, dir. Michael Winterbottom
Classic fiction's most unclassifiable work gets a suitably oblique approach from

Winterbottom who mirrors Sterne's self-reflexive text by having his principal actors (Rob Brydon and Steve Coogan) discuss their roles before exploring the whole process of filmmaking. Not so much an adaptation as a free-flowing improvisation inspired by the original.

Zeno's Conscience

1923, ITALO SVEVO, ITALIAN

Penguin

Zeno's Conscience (also translated as *The Confessions of Zeno*) is the fictional memoir of a compulsive smoker, whose psychoanalyst has recommended autobiography as therapy. His autobiography, however, reveals a character compulsive in different ways – compulsively funny, eccentric, curious, poetic, conceited and anxious – whose adventures throw everyday life into a hilarious new light.

Each main chapter of the memoir focuses on a key area of Zeno's life: the relationship with his father, his marriage, his mistress, and his business career. But such an unremarkable list of topics in no way prepares the reader for Zeno's unique perspective. Like the hero of Proust's novels, Zeno sees below the surface of things, finding unexpected meanings in the simplest gestures or conversations. Unfortunately, they often only deepen his confusion. His analysis is seldom practical, and his intuition only strengthens his quirks, which run firmly counter to plain common sense. His memoir is a great testament to the comic craziness of normal mental life.

One of the pleasures of the book is its aphorisms. Life, Zeno avers, is neither beautiful nor ugly, but "original". Female beauty "stimulates feelings that are totally unrelated to it". His other great preoccupations – fear of dying, hypochondria, love, children and parents, time and loss – are all enlivened by unexpected, off-the-cuff insights which seem to baffle and delight Zeno as much as the reader. Luckily, consolation is a key theme of the book. Finally, Zeno is a poet of happiness. Out of his mishaps and fantasies comes a feeling that life is full of "sweetness".

> *To tell the truth, I believe that, with his help, in studying my consciousness, I have introduced some new sicknesses into it.*

 Recommended translation
2001, William Weaver, Penguin Classics

Where to go next
A Perfect Hoax, 1929, Italo Svevo
A sparkling novella, newly translated by J.G. Nichols, about a failed writer hoodwinked into believing that he is about to hit the big time. Partly based on Svevo's own late success, *A Perfect Hoax* is a wittily ironic cautionary tale.

Candide, *or* Optimism

1759, VOLTAIRE, FRENCH

A satire on human cruelty, a picaresque series of bizarre adventures, a *bildungsroman* (see p.140) in which the put-upon hero attains maturity, and a star-crossed romance, *Candide* is one of the hardest-hitting and funniest books ever written. Published simultaneously in five countries, it was an immediate sensation, and has remained a literary touchstone for anyone wanting to be entertained, instructed or outraged.

Banished from his home for an indiscretion with his benefactor's daughter, Cunégonde, Candide is hurled into a series of hair-raising adventures with only the advice of his former tutor, Dr Pangloss, to sustain him. This advice, that "everything in this world is for the best", is difficult to accept when, in astonishingly rapid succession, Candide witnesses brutality, theft, slaughter, *auto-da-fé*, rape, murder, torture and slavery.

For all its anger, *Candide* is an extraordinarily funny book. Partly, the exhilaration comes from the tumbling speed of events: whole novels seem condensed into single chapters, complete with topsy-turvy action, fable-like morals, and sudden leaps into the next wild escapade. Partly, the effect is the result of Voltaire's wit, at once sly, devastating and surreal. When Cunégonde complains that no one has suffered as she has, an old woman with only one buttock replies calmly, "If I were to show you my bottom you would not speak as you do." In *Candide*, there is nearly always something worse that can happen. Though Candide acquires other advisers in addition to Dr Pangloss, who offer alternative ways of interpreting experience (religiously, cynically, pessimistically and stoically), in the end he must develop his own more humble, but more practical, means of coping with the outrageous awfulness of life.

> 'What's Optimism?', asked Cacambo. 'I'm afraid to say,' said Candide, 'that it's a mania for insisting that all is well when things are going badly.'

 Recommended translation
1990, Roger Pearson, Oxford World's Classics

Where to go next
Jacques the Fatalist, 1796, Denis Diderot
A witty, philosophical romp, partly inspired by *Tristram Shandy*, which explores the notion of free will through a series of tales mostly narrated by the easy-going Jacques, as he travels with his master to nowhere in particular.

A Handful of Dust

1934, EVELYN WAUGH, ENGLISH

With its plot of pure tragedy, and delivery of wicked hilarity, Waugh's first masterpiece is a rarity: a mercilessly funny comedy of despair. Few novelists have Waugh's gifts of mimicry, surreal invention or anger, and here everything is beautifully but horribly in balance.

Penguin

At the beginning of the novel, Tony Last is celebrated by his friends as the luckiest man they know, living securely in his ancestral Hetton Hall with his beloved son, John Andrew, and his devoted wife, Brenda. By the end of the novel, having lost everything, he will find himself utterly destitute in an exile as remote from Hetton Hall as it is possible to imagine.

Brenda is bored in her country house. The idle and penniless John Beaver is bored in London. Jock Grant-Menzies can see trouble brewing, but he's too anxious about his maiden speech (on pigs) in the House of Commons to have a word with his friend Tony. Waugh's ability to capture the manners

> 'I shall go on saying that I think you're making a ridiculous mistake.' 'It's just that you don't like Mr Beaver.' 'It isn't only that. I think it's hard cheese on Tony.'

of the English upper classes are nowhere so wonderfully sharp or pertinent. His characters' broken bits of conversation, jumbled with well-worn niceties, fashionable jargon and bizarre inconsequences, are brilliantly inarticulate: sometimes funny, sometimes desperate, often both at once. Individually, his scenes are comic, if frequently painful, marvels of drama (a game of Animal Snap after a disastrous fox hunt, an excruciating house party, a drunken visit to a club of ill-repute); collectively, they form a precisely proportionate narrative, in which Tony Last's progressive dereliction is made heartlessly inevitable. And, throughout, Waugh's carefully brutish imagery and glittering symbolism amplify his engagement with contemporary moral chaos.

 Where to go next
Scoop, 1938, Evelyn Waugh
A hilarious satire on the world of newspapers, in which the feckless and ill-equipped William Boot fails to make it as a war correspondent in Abyssinia.

 Screen adaptation
A Handful of Dust, 1987, dir. Charles Sturridge
Despite an almost perfect cast (in which Kristin Scott-Thomas and James Wilby shine as Brenda and Tony), this handsomely filmed adaptation lacks the satirical viciousness of Waugh's novel, preferring to emphasize the story's tragedy at the expense of the moral vacuity that caused it.

Psmith in the City

1910, P.G. WODEHOUSE, ENGLISH

P.G. Wodehouse, creator of airy fantasies in which sublimely ridiculous characters engage in lunatic farce, is the great connoisseur of the ludicrous. There are around a hundred of his novels to choose from, all written in the distinctive Wodehousian manner. *Psmith in the City* is one of his earliest, the first in a four-novel sequence featuring two characters, Mike and Psmith.

Mike is in the tradition of English schoolboy heroes, sporty, decent and inarticulate, and the improbably, even monstrously, debonair Psmith is his friend and protector. When his father's financial ruin compels Mike to pass up the chance to spend three years playing

Wodehouse's world

P.G. Wodehouse said, "I believe there are two ways of writing novels. One is mine, making a sort of musical comedy without the music and ignoring real life altogether; the other is going right deep down into life and not caring a damn." With his method, he created some of the most glorious comic characters in fiction, many of whom recur from novel to novel. By far the most celebrated are the catastrophe-prone Bertie Wooster and his unflappable valet Jeeves who appear in a dozen or so novels. Almost as popular is the Blandings series, presided over by the somewhat absent-minded Lord Emsworth whose greatest enthusiasm in life is reserved for his majestic prize sow, the Empress of Blandings.

Six of the best Jeeves & Wooster
- *The Inimitable Jeeves* (1923)
- *Very Good, Jeeves* (1930)
- *Right Ho, Jeeves* (1934)
- *The Code of the Woosters* (1937)
- *Joy in the Morning* (1947)
- *The Mating Season* (1949)

Five great Blandings Castle novels
- *Something Fresh* (1915)
- *Heavy Weather* (1933)
- *Uncle Fred in the Springtime* (1939)
- *Pigs Have Wings* (1952)
- *Summer Lightning* (1954)

The best of Psmith
- *Psmith in the City* (1910)
- *Psmith Journalist* (1915)
- *Leave it to Psmith* (1923)
- *Mike and Psmith* (1953)

cricket at the 'varsity and join the New Asiatic Bank instead, he finds to his surprise that Psmith is his companion in the Postage Department, having insouciantly succumbed to his own father's whim. "'Commerce,' said Psmith, as he drew off his lavender gloves, 'has claimed me for her own.'" In the adventures which follow, Psmith is revealed to be not only a wonderful entertainer (he likes to pass himself off as a taciturn Socialist), but a schemer of deadly effectiveness.

'Between ourselves,' confided Psmith, 'I'm dashed if I know what's going to happen to me. I am the thingummy of what's-its-name.' 'You look it,' said Mike, brushing his hair.

The fictional world of *Psmith in the City* is institutional, a male world of school, bank, gentleman's club and the MCC, institutions which are either mocked or revered, and sometimes both at once. It is hard, in fact, to pinpoint the Wodehousian attitude. The wild farce of individual scenes and his surreal prose style, at once slangy and ostentatious, create a sort of narrative delirium utterly at odds with his neatly constructed plots. But in a sense we are not dealing with the real world. Although, with their schoolboy stories and eccentric characters, the Englishness of Wodehouse's novels is not in doubt, what he essentially created was not so much an outdated late-Edwardian England as a fluent fantasy all his own.

Where to go next
The Code of the Woosters, 1938, P.G. Wodehouse
One of the best of the novels featuring upper-class twit Bertie Wooster and his steadfast manservant Jeeves, in which the two get the better of the unspeakable politician Roderick Spode.

Index

L

M

Rough Guides presents...

"Achieves the perfect balance between learned recommendation and needless trivia" *Uncut Magazine* reviewing Cult Movies

Rough Guide Film & TV titles include:
American Independent Film • British Cult Comedy • Chick Flicks
Comedy Movies • Cult Movies • Film • Film Musicals • Film Noir
Gangster Movies • Horror Movies • Sci-Fi Movies • Westerns

D: Rough Guide
DIRECTIONS for
short breaks

Available from all good bookstores

For more information go to www.roughguides.com

ROUGH GUIDES

ROUGH GUIDES Complete Listing

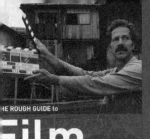

PENGUIN CLASSICS

THE BEST BOOKS EVER WRITTEN

So what makes a Penguin Classic a classic? Simple.

It has to be 'one of the best books ever written'. And that doesn't mean ladies with parasols strolling through Victorian gardens admiring the roses.

It means the most shocking sex scenes and the most gratuitous violence.

It means love – at its most enthralling and its most heartbreaking.

It means the most complex criminal minds, the cheekiest minxes and the most inspiring heroes ever committed to paper.

The best books ever written

PENGUIN CLASSICS

SINCE 1946